OTHER BOOKS BY BARRY MATHIAS

THE ANCIENT BLOODLINES TRILOGY

BOOK ONE
THE POWER IN THE DARK

BOOK TWO
SHADOW OF THE SWORDS

BOOK THREE
KEEPER OF THE GRAIL

CELTIC DREAMS OF GLORY

EBB TIDE
COLLECTION OF POETRY

WOLF HOWL
A COLLECTION OF SHORT STORIES

Copyright © 2018, Barry Mathias. All rights reserved.

Without limiting the rights under copyright reserved above, no part of this publication may be reproduced, stored in or introduced into a retrieval system, or transmitted, in any form or by any means (electronic, mechanical, photocopying, recording or otherwise), without the prior written permission of both the copyright owner and the publisher of this book.

Disclaimer—This is a work of fiction. Names, characters, places and events are the product of the author's imagination or are used fictitiously. Any resemblance to actual persons living or dead, events or locales is entirely coincidental.

Agio
PUBLISHING HOUSE
Canada V0R 1X4

For information and bulk orders, please go to
www.agiopublishing.com
Visit this book's website at www.barrymathias.net

ISBN 978-1-927755-73-0 (paperback)
ISBN 978-1-927755-74-7 (ebook)

Cataloguing information available from Library and Archives Canada.

10 9 8 7 6 5 4 3 2 1

In the Ashes of a Dream

SEQUEL TO *Celtic Dreams of Glory*

BARRY MATHIAS

Agio
PUBLISHING HOUSE

LIST OF CHARACTERS

Harold Godwinson:	Saxon Earl of Wessex who becomes King Harold of England
Bowdyn:	messenger
Lady Angharad:	wife to Lord Gwriad ap Griffith
Lady Teifryn:	wife to Lord Dafydd ap Griffith
Tegwen:	baby daughter to Lady Teifryn
Alys:	wet nurse to Tegwen
Gruffydd ap Llywelyn:	former King of all Wales
Hywel and Rhodri:	young soldiers
Lord Edwin ap Tewdwr:	Welsh general and cousin to Prince Anarwd of Morgannwg
Sir Maelgwn:	Welsh general, friend of Lord Edwin
Lord Dafydd ap Griffith:	former Personal Secretary to King Gruffydd ap Llywelyn
Lord Gwriad ap Griffith:	former General of the Central Army, older brother of Lord Dafydd
Lidmann:	ambitious courtier to Earl Harold
Duke William of Normandy:	'The Bastard', claimant to Crown of England
Father Williams:	priest for Llanduduch
Merfyn:	Gwriad's master of hounds
Jon:	scullery boy who rises to become Gwriad's squire
Iago:	injured soldier
Lieu and Gavin:	older soldiers

Owen and Davis:	young soldiers
Megan:	cook in charge of the castle's kitchen
Penn:	sergeant, senior soldier in the castle
King Edward the Confessor:	King of England, extremely religious
Mistress Lewis:	aged spinster with whom Jon once lived
Dai	father to Jon
Prince Bleddyn ap Cynfya:	ruler of Powys
Queen Ealdgyth:	widowed wife of King Gruffydd, recent wife of Earl
Harold Meredith:	cavalry soldier with Sir Maelgwn
Deryn and Rhiannon:	peasants living in Llanduduch
Megan:	girl from the village, friend of Jon
Lord Gyrth:	second youngest brother to Harold
Lord Leofwine:	Harold's youngest brother and his favourite
Lord Tostig:	next brother to Harold and competitor for the throne
Mrs. Reece:	Father Williams' housekeeper
Derryth:	Wise Woman from Llanduduch
Ceri:	mother who abandoned Jon
Elditha Swannuck:	mistress and handfast wife to Harold
Waelfwulf:	Saxon officer
Alan 'the Onion':	Welsh soldier
Hildering:	Saxon officer
Huw:	pig farmer in village of Gelligaer
Iago:	old soldier in Gelligaer
Vernon:	blacksmith in Gelligaer
Prince Anarwd:	ruler of Morgannwg
Merydyth and Roy:	Welsh soldiers
Egbert:	Saxon cavalry officer

Emrys:	Welsh cavalry officer
King Hardrada:	King of Norway and ally of Tostig
Davis:	Llanduduch fisherman
Abbot James:	acquaintance of Dafydd
Geraint:	Welsh monk
Father Luke:	one of Dafydd's correspondents
Father Alexander:	abbot of the Monastery of Saint Peters
Brother Paul:	deaf-mute monk
Brothers Adam and James:	monks at Saint Peters
Lord Aethelstan:	security officer at the Palace
Earls Morcar and Edwin:	younger brothers of King Harold
Sister Ceri:	Prioress of small Priory in Morgannwg
Sister Elen:	new nun initiate
Sisters Megan, Joan, Neta:	senior nuns
Isaac Goldman:	London moneylender and dealer in gold and silver
Bishop of Morgannwg:	has authority over the Priory
Angwen:	formerly Elen
Garyth:	village drummer and blacksmith
Bethan:	Welsh weaver
Gwenllian:	Bethan's daughter
Pierre:	courtier to Duke William
Ord:	stable boy
Captain Morgan:	ship's master, trading between Chichester and Caerdydd

WELSH PATRONYMIC NAMING

In early times, the Welsh family name changed through the male line with each generation. A son was given a first name and linked to his father. Hence *Gruffydd ap Llywelyn* was *Gruffydd son of Llywelyn*, and his son *Cydweli* became *Cydweli ap Gruffydd*. The word *ap* is a contraction of the Welsh word *mab*, which means *son*. Occasionally, some women were given their full family name: *Angharad* might be known as *Angharad ferch Cadell ap Bleddyn*, or *Angharad daughter of Cadell son of Bleddyn*.

Over the years, and for reasons including outside pressures, the Welsh took on continuing family names such as Jenkins, Jones, etc.

In this novel, the women are known generally by their first name and sometimes, as with *Teifryn of Ynys Mon*, it is her birthplace that defines her.

I have used the traditional patronymic naming for people of rank, and a first name only for peasants and slaves. In some cases, characters have two names, such as *Prince Rhodri ap Williams*, when introduced for the first time

ANCIENT WELSH PLACE NAMES USED IN THIS STORY WITH MODERN NAMES WHERE APPROPRIATE

ABERTEIFI:	now known as Cardigan
CAERDYDD:	Cardiff, now capital of Wales
CAERNARFON:	Caernarvon. Port opposite island of Ynys Mons
CEREDIGION:	kingdom in mid-west Wales, including the village of Aberteifi
CONWY:	Conway, port off north-west Wales
DEHEUBARTH:	ancient name for region of south-west Wales
GELLIGAER:	village in northern Morgannwg
GWENT:	important kingdom in south-east Wales, adjoining Morgannwg
GWYNETH:	the most important of the Welsh kingdoms, situated in the north-west, including modern Snowdonia
LLANDUDUCH:	St. Dogmaels. Village on the Teifi River
MORGANNWG:	kingdom in south Wales
OFFA'S DYKE:	ancient earth barrier constructed by Offa, Saxon King of Mercia, approximately 770-790 AD. Stretched from estuary of River Dee in the north to River Wye in the south. Separated Wales from Saxon lands.
POWYS:	powerful kingdom, second to Gwyneth in mid-eastern Wales
RHYD-Y-GROES:	site of famous battle near the border with Saxon England
YNYS MON:	Anglesey. Large island off north-west Wales. Ancient Druid centre. Teifryn's birth place.

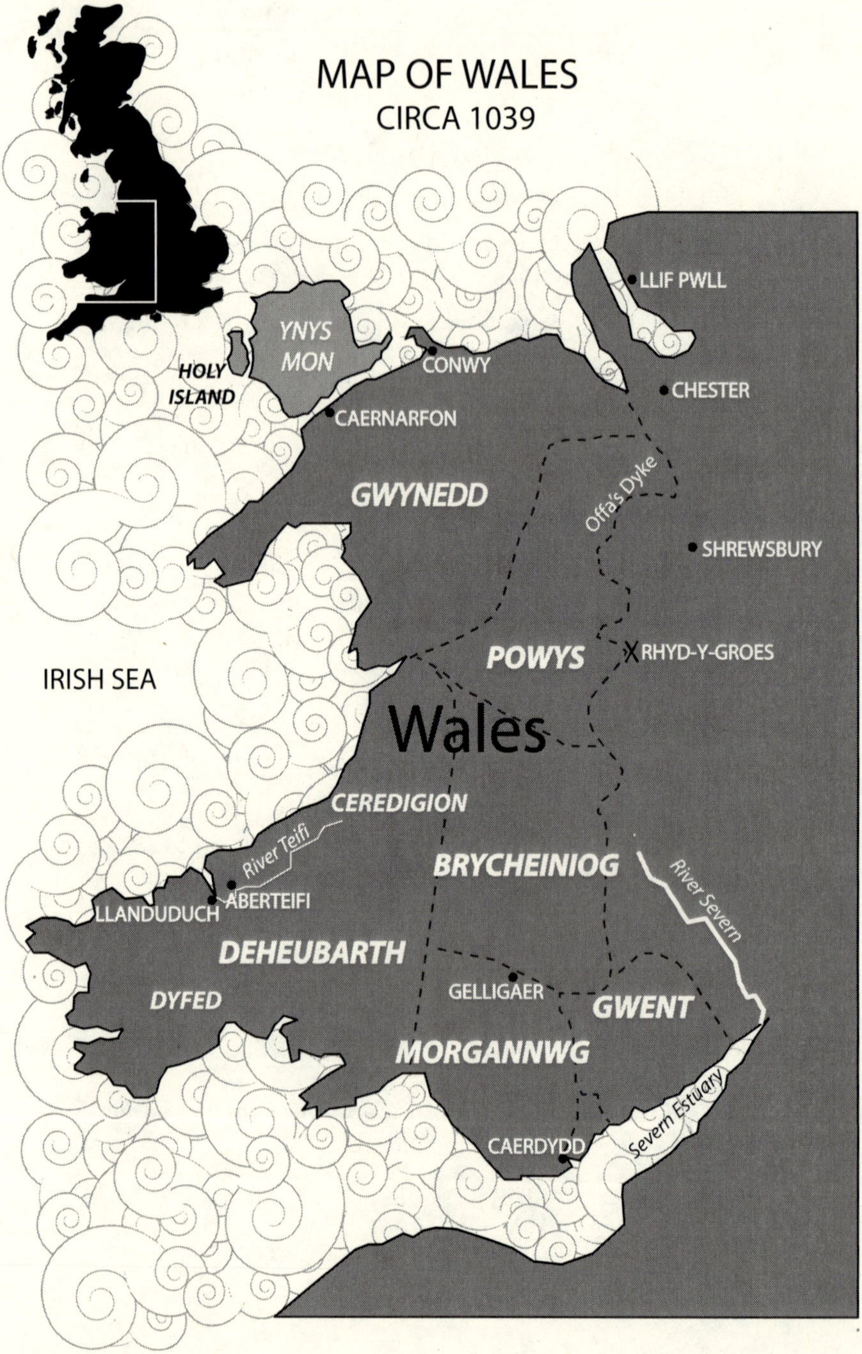
MAP OF WALES
CIRCA 1039
YNYS MON
HOLY ISLAND
CONWY
CAERNARFON
LLIF PWLL
CHESTER
GWYNEDD
Offa's Dyke
SHREWSBURY
POWYS
RHYD-Y-GROES
IRISH SEA
Wales
CEREDIGION
River Teifi
BRYCHEINIOG
River Severn
ABERTEIFI
LLANDUDUCH
DEHEUBARTH
DYFED
GELLIGAER
GWENT
MORGANNWG
Severn Estuary
CAERDYDD

PROLOGUE

"My Lord?" the servant stood hesitantly in the doorway of the great hall. "My Lord?"

There was no reaction from the tall, flaxen–haired man who sat like a statue in front of the remains of a log fire. His eyes gazed unseeing into the red embers, while his mind roamed obsessively over the occurrences of the past week. He had won a victory, but it felt like a defeat.

Acting against all conventional military strategy, he had launched a winter attack on the northern palace of Gruffydd ap Llywelyn, the Welsh King. For seven years, this Gruffydd, the only king ever to unite all of Wales, had made increasingly more serious attacks on the Saxon towns along the border. As a result, Harold, the Saxon Earl of Wessex, had been under pressure from the ailing King Edward the Confessor to act. Harold's ambition was to be the next king of England; and to maintain his power over Edward, he had been forced to risk everything.

In spite of February storms, bitter cold, and knee-deep snow, he had led his cavalry and other army divisions in a lightning invasion from the east, while a strong force of his foot soldiers had been transported by galleys and fishing boats to the beaches north of Gruffydd's palace.

Harold had succeeded in defeating elements of Gruffydd's northern army and burning his palace to the ground. But the Saxons also had suffered heavy losses: his cavalry had been badly mauled, and the bulk of his army had either drowned or been slaughtered by Gruffydd's cavalry. Despite winning the last battle, Harold had failed to kill or capture the Welsh king, who had escaped to rally his men. In the ensuing stalemate, the Saxons had been forced by the weather and lack of supplies into an ignominious retreat back across the border. In spring it was expected Gruffydd would, once again, be harrying the border towns and would be seeking revenge for the loss of his palace. His southern armies were intact, and his powerful northern fleet would continue to dominate the Irish Sea.

Harold had gambled everything. Now, he would be forced into penury to pay for his failed campaign as King Edward had vowed he would not pay for a defeat. The local lords who had supported him were dead, and his ambitious plans to become the next king were in tatters. He had no future.

"My Lord?" the servant moved cautiously into the hall, leaving the door ajar for a quick exit. Since his return, Earl Harold had been unapproachable: eating little, drinking jugs of ale and speaking to no one. "My Lord, there's a message from Wales."

After a long pause, Harold Godwinson, the second most powerful man in England, turned to face the terrified servant. "I said no messages!" he roared. He staggered to his feet, kicking over his three-legged stool, his huge hands bunched into fists. He towered over the emaciated peasant, Harold's size made greater by his armour, which he had yet to discard.

"My Lord!" the servant wailed, forcing himself not to turn and run. "The King of Wales is dead!"

Harold stared; his tensed arms fell to his sides. "What?" he whispered dangerously. "What did you say?"

"My Lord, King Gruffydd has been murdered by his own men!" The servant relaxed his shoulders, cleared his throat and continued. "He was murdered while crossing the mountains on his way to the west coast."

"By his own men?" It seemed too good to be true.

"And his northern fleet has been destroyed."

"By all the Gods! By whom?" It was like a dream come true.

"One of your galleys survived the crossing and ended up in the bay at Conway. It was where all the Welsh fleet was riding out the storm. Their ships were burnt at anchor."

"Burnt at anchor?" Harold repeated, as though unable to grasp the meaning. He rubbed his face vigorously. "Are these reports true? Is Gruffydd really dead?"

IN THE ASHES OF A DREAM

"Yes, my Lord. Reports have been coming in for the past few hours."

Harold's face darkened. "Why wasn't I told sooner?"

The servant took an involuntary step backwards. "Nobody dared to tell you, my Lord." He licked his dry lips. "You'd threatened death to anyone who disturbed you."

There was a long silence as Harold regained his composure. He sat down on his stool, and breathed out loudly. "What's your name?"

"Bowdyn, my Lord."

"Bowdyn! How appropriate." Harold's face creased into a rare smile. "How long have you been in my household?"

"Only a short while, my Lord. I was hired after you left to fight the Welsh." He paused, uncertain how much to say. "That was why I was chosen to bring you the news, my Lord."

Harold nodded. He felt the shackles of defeat fall away, and with them the dark cloud that had enveloped him. It was a long time since he had had anything to celebrate, and in a moment of generosity he turned towards the impoverished man in his tattered rags. "My former servant, Brandon, has vanished, so I'm appointing you as my personal servant, Bowdyn."

"Oh!" Bowdyn gasped. "Thank you, my Lord. Thank you." Moments before he had believed he was a dead man; now, his life had improved beyond his wildest hopes.

"Can you use a sword?"

"I have some training, my Lord." He could not stop himself from grinning.

"Good." Harold smiled back. He could imagine the upset this would cause in his rigid household. "Tell the steward to give you some food, and clothes fit for an Earl's personal servant. Report back to me when he's done so."

The servant bowed his way out of the room, as Harold, lost in thought, began to methodically rebuild the fire.

CHAPTER ONE

(WEST WALES MAY 1064)

An attractive, buxom woman sat in the courtyard of a small stone castle, one of the few of this type of construction in Wales. She was enjoying the May sun and spinning wool with accomplished hands. In front of the open gates, two young soldiers kept up a pretence of being on guard, while secretly watching some local girls who were washing clothes at the edge of the opposite bank of the Teifi River. It had been a hard winter, a wet spring and finally warm dry days had arrived with their promise of easier times and full bellies.

The woman sat back, closed her eyes and turned her face up to the welcome sun. Around the courtyard she could hear the excited chirping of small birds and in the background the deep roar of the river, like a barely confined monster. The castle was unusually quiet as, apart from the two young soldiers, all the menfolk were away; she realized that she was enjoying a rare moment of contentment.

"Angharad, have you seen Dafydd?" A slim, pretty woman emerged from the main hall. She was nursing a baby and carried with her an aura of maternal good health.

"He's gone off to Llanduduch. He wants to talk to old Father Williams. The priest has long wanted the young men of his village to get some military training, so they can defend their homes against the Picts. Your husband thinks it's a good idea."

Teifryn smiled. "Now that he's no longer secretary to a king, he seems to be looking for something to get his teeth into. He loves nothing better than writing reports and reading dusty religious records." She laughed. "That is, if the Archbishop will loan them to him."

"Both of our husbands are finding it hard to settle down to being mere nobles after their years of responsibility at the centre of Welsh life." Angharad stood up and made faces at the baby, who chuckled happily. "I think it would be a good idea to arm the fishermen and give them some military training. Not only would they be able to defend their homes from the Picts, but they would also provide a first line of defence for us here at Aberteifi, and for the farms up river."

"It makes one wonder why it's not been done before," Teifryn said.

"Oh, that's an easy one to answer," Angharad glanced towards the two young guards who were waving down at the girls by the river. "My late father-in-law, Lord Gomer ap Griffith, was very tight with his money. He did not want to have to pay for their training or their weapons. Also, he was afraid that if he made soldiers of them, they would leave the village and seek employment elsewhere. All that money wasted!"

"But he died some years ago," Teifryn said. "Why hasn't Gwriad made it happen?"

Angharad shook her long black hair, which she wore loose and heavy past her shoulders. "He was too busy. As General of the Central Army, he was always focused on the Saxon enemy on our eastern border. He let the northern fleet deal with the Pictish raiders." Her smile slowly faded. "That is, when we had a northern fleet."

"Did Gwriad go with Dafydd today?"

"Ha!" Angharad exploded in mock derision. "Can you imagine Gwriad attending a meeting, when he could be outside killing something?" She paused reflectively, then added happily, "I suppose that's what makes him such a vigorous lover!"

Teifryn giggled. There had been a time when she would have been embarrassed by her friend's outrageous sexual remarks, but motherhood and a close friendship with Angharad had broadened her experience. "It seems odd that Dafydd would take on the role

IN THE ASHES OF A DREAM

of arranging for the fishermen to be trained as soldiers. That's more in Gwriad's line."

"I dare say Gwriad has already discussed it with his brother. I know my husband has set his mind on catching some large animal so we can all celebrate the end of the bad weather. He thinks if we have a feast and invite all those who work for us to some free food and drink, it will restore everyone's spirits."

"We need music and dancing too," Teifryn said. "I know the younger ones will be delighted to have a chance of getting together." She nodded towards the two guards who were acting the fool to the delight of their female audience.

"Hywel! Rhodri!" Angharad yelled. "You're supposed to be guards, not clowns!" She walked over to the gates and stared down at the girls. As soon as they saw her, there was an immediate concentration on their work. She turned to look at the two red-faced youths who were standing rigidly to attention. They wore brown uniforms, round pot helmets with cheek guards, and each held a spear and carried a short sword. "You look like guards to me," she said mischievously. "What do guards do, Hywel?"

"Guard the castle, m'Lady."

"So, what's your main duty, Rhodri?"

"To stand to attention, m'Lady?" He realized this was not the answer. "And look tough, m'Lady?"

"No, you clown," she punched him gently on his shoulder. "Your job is to watch the road and the river and raise the alarm if you see anyone you don't recognize."

"Yes, m'Lady," they chanted together. Both looked suitably embarrassed.

"Are you the only ones on duty?"

"Yes, m'Lady," Hywel replied. "The three older men went with Lord Dafydd to Llanduduch, and the remaining ten soldiers went hunting with Lord Gwriad."

"Even the two stable lads and the scullery boy were allowed to go," Rhodri added resentfully.

"Well, I'm glad you two were chosen to guard me and Lady Teifryn." She tried to keep a straight face. "You can forget standing to attention, just keep your eyes on the road and the river. Close the gates and raise the alarm if you see any strangers. Understood?"

"Yes, m'Lady." Each relaxed and took up a position that would allow them to see the approaches to the castle.

She glanced down at the river, where the young girls were staggering away with their heavy baskets of washing. "You'll have no distractions from now on." A worried look crossed Rhodri's face: he was uncertain what a distraction was.

Teifryn joined Angharad, who was gently rocking her sleeping baby. They sat on a low wall overlooking the river that raged sixty feet below them, swollen by the continuous spring rains. Further downriver, they could see the stone bridge that connected their small settlement of Aberteifi·on the northern bank, with the twisting path that ran along the southern bank towards the fishing village of Llanduduch and the mouth of the river. Coming over the bridge from the south, the path divided: the left branch sloped up to the village of Aberteifi, the other led steeply up to the castle.

"If the Pictish galleys decided to venture up river, we wouldn't see them until they came around the bend, over there." Angharad pointed along the forested banks of the Teifi, where the river broadened before disappearing towards the west, barely half a mile away. "It's the same with the bridge, we can only see a short distance beyond. If we were attacked by an enemy on horseback, they'd be across the bridge very quickly." She glanced back to where the two youths were taking their duties more seriously. "That's why I gave them a short lesson. I realize how vulnerable we are when Gwriad's away with our small collection of real soldiers."

"But, there's no chance of the Saxons getting here, is there?"

"I don't think so," Angharad said hesitantly. "But everything has changed since the death of King Gruffydd. The northern army has disintegrated, and Gwynedd has, once again, chosen its own king. Powys is no longer a part of an integrated Wales, and I hear that the southern army under Prince Anarwd is much reduced and Gwent is under constant threat. When a strong king ruled Wales, the Saxons suffered. Now, they want to get their own back on us."

"Why doesn't Gwriad raise the Central Army again? He was a popular general."

IN THE ASHES OF A DREAM

"There's nothing he would like to do more," Angharad agreed. "But there's no money. He had to disband the Central Army to allow the men to get back to their farms. An army has to be paid or have the chance of getting rich through looting and pillaging."

"It's been a tough time," Teifryn agreed.

"Indeed. With the king dead and the palace burned to the ground, the central organization has collapsed. Ambitious tribal chiefs have appointed themselves kings and princes and fight each other for power. All the money from the Irish trade stopped with the destruction of the Northern Fleet, and we are vulnerable once again to Pictish attacks."

"I know. I've tried to talk to Dafydd about it," Teifryn murmured. She looked pensively down the river. "He doesn't want to worry me, in case it somehow affects the baby." As though on cue, Tegwen opened her eyes and, recognizing her aunt, began to gurgle happily.

"No one's going to hurt you, my little love." Angharad leaned forward, and Tegwen held out her plump arms for a cuddle. "There's such a beautiful baby, you are." She leaned forward, and lifted Tegwen up in the air. The baby shrieked with pleasure.

Teifryn smiled, but there was sadness in her eyes. She knew Angharad loved children and would make a good mother; it seemed unfair that life had cheated her out of motherhood. She had talked to Dafydd about it. He agreed that Gwriad had claimed to have seduced dozens of women before he met Angharad; as far as Dafydd knew, none of the women had become pregnant. When Teifryn first met Angharad, the older woman had also boasted of numerous lovers. Perhaps, she and Gwriad were both infertile? She pondered the idea. Or perhaps, they were both inveterate liars? She was unable to restrain a giggle.

Angharad looked up. "What's so funny?"

"I was thinking what different brothers we're married to."

"Yes, it's hard to believe they're brothers when you look at them: Dafydd, with his red hair and his tall, lean body, and Gwriad with his black hair and his short, stocky physique. People have often wondered what their father, the great General Cydweli ap Griffith, got up to!"

"Dafydd's green eyes are so unlike Gwriad's deep blue," Teifryn agreed. "And then their personalities!"

"Indeed! My Gwriad loves fighting, hunting and training soldiers. He hates sitting down to meetings, and he never reads or writes anything unless he's forced to." She handed the baby back to Teifryn.

"My Dafydd would read all day, given the chance. Although he avoids hunting, he's not afraid to stand up for himself. Gwriad told me that when the Picts attacked Llanduduch eleven years ago, Dafydd killed a number of them himself." She laughed, "I think he even impressed his brother."

"What interests me is that they rarely argue," Angharad said. "When I first married Gwriad he would tease Dafydd unmercifully about his lack of experience with girls. Yet, Dafydd always took it in good part. Then, when he met you, he began to stand up for himself, and since he married you the two brothers have never had a disagreement."

"Just like you and me," Teifryn said. "You even share my baby." She gazed down at the child who had drifted off to sleep.

"Like all good aunts should do," Angharad jested. She turned away quickly to stare at the bridge.

"Alys!" Teifryn called to a powerful young woman who had appeared in the courtyard. Alys walked past the admiring young guards without giving them a glance. "Tegwen's been fed, I think she'll sleep for a while."

"Yes, m'Lady." Alys curtsied, and carefully took the child. She nodded courteously to Angharad. All three women gazed lovingly at Tegwen, each lost momentarily in their own thoughts.

"Riders, m'Lady! Riders!" Hywel's sudden yell took them all by surprise.

Approaching the bridge from the southern side was a group of horsemen riding fast. They wore leather body armour, helmets and some carried spears and small shields.

"They're not our men!" wailed Rhodri. "They're strangers!"

"Inside! Quickly!" Angharad grabbed Teifryn's arm and with Alys cradling the baby, they ran the short distance into the castle.

Once inside, Angharad helped the guards close the heavy gates,

IN THE ASHES OF A DREAM

while Teifryn and Alys ran towards the main hall. "Get inside and bar the door!" she yelled at Alys, who had returned Tegwen to her mother. "Don't open it unless I tell you!"

While the guards bolted the gates, Angharad raced up a flight of stone stairs to the narrow parapet that overlooked the entrance and watched with rising anxiety as the horsemen galloped up the causeway towards the castle. "Hywel! Rhodri!" she bellowed. They charged up the steps, clutching their spears; they were close to panic.

"Now listen," she ordered. "Stand on both sides of me, look tough and don't say anything."

The first riders had reached the area where moments before the women had been standing. They milled about before the gates staring up at Angharad. It was a confined space, room for only about a dozen of the riders, and the rest came to a halt on the causeway.

"Open up!" the leader yelled in Welsh. Unlike the others, he was wearing a bright mail shirt, a distinctive helmet and was carrying a long sword on his left side. He was a broad-chested man with a full beard, and he had an air of authority. His horse was larger than the others, but all of the animals showed signs of having been ridden hard. None of the men was brandishing weapons, and they did not appear to expect any opposition.

"Who are you?" Angharad yelled back. "What do you want?"

"I must see General Gwriad ap Griffith. Immediately! Open up!"

"Who are you?" she persisted.

"Tell your master Lord Edwin ap Tewdwr, cousin to Prince Anarwd of Morgannwg, is here to see him. Now open up these bloody gates before I have you all flogged!"

Angharad went red with anger, suddenly conscious of her simple clothes. "I am Angharad, Lady of the Castle," she said, her rich voice carried clearly in the quiet air, "and my Lord is away on business. If there's any flogging to be done, it will not be done by you."

Lord Edwin blew out his cheeks and slowly removed his helmet. His black hair was sticky with sweat, and his horse tossed its head impatiently from side to side. "I apologize, my Lady." He forced a tired smile. "We have travelled fast across difficult country, and time is of the essence." He dismounted, and slowly stretched his back. "However, with General Gwriad away, there is no longer any need to hurry." He bowed in an extravagant manner. "Our horses need attention, and we," he waved his left arm at the assembled horsemen, "would be grateful for your hospitality."

Angharad smiled, and turned to Rhodri. "Do they look like Saxons to you?"

"No, m'Lady," Rhodri looked confused. "They're Welsh."

"Then, for goodness sake open up the gates and let them in!"

. . .

DAFYDD HAD ALWAYS LIKED LLANDUDUCH. It was an attractive fishing village set on a steep hill on the south bank of the river Teifi, two miles from the sea, and overlooking one of the few safe moorings on the river. It was a meagre collection of stone and wood hovels with slate or rush roofs that perched defiantly, without any sense of order, on the few flat surfaces along the hillside. Most were single room abodes with a fire pit in the middle of the floor, a raised sleeping area, a wooden door and sometimes a window. The largest homes were also the oldest, and were built on either side of the commons, near the steep path down to the river.

Since the last attack by the Picts eleven years ago, Gwriad, their new Lord, had shown the villagers how to build a sturdy wooden stockade at the top of the narrow path from the river. Its purpose was to prevent attackers from storming off their boats and straight into the village. Everyone coming up the final stretch was forced to turn to the right, and again to the left, to get round the ten-foot stockade.

"It's too expensive to build a gated wall around a fishing village," Gwriad had explained to the villagers, "but this way you can build something that will give you an advantage by slowing the attackers down and funnelling them into a narrow opening." It had taken them weeks to build, but its completion had created a pride among the villagers, and the fear of the Picts had lessened. When conditions might favour an attack from the sea, the young men

IN THE ASHES OF A DREAM

took it in turns for lookout duty. At other times they relied on dogs and geese to give a warning.

Dafydd arrived unexpectedly at the village, and stopped by the small church where he hoped to find the elderly priest, Father Williams. The stone church had been built on a high flat promontory, with a spectacular view of the village and the river valley. It had a low, square bell tower, whose single bell called the villagers to service, announced the end of the working day and warned of danger. Close by was what Father Williams liked to call his priest's cell: a sizeable building with more comforts than any other in the area.

Father Williams was in his sixth decade, and had become a rotund man with a liking for venison and good wine – although he had never been known to refuse beer if it were offered. He was no longer the agile man who had defied the Picts eleven years ago, but his mind was as sharp as ever, and he was a great friend of Lord Dafydd. As the youngest son of a noble family, the priest had quickly understood that his chances of gaining an inheritance were slim, and as he enjoyed the education that his brothers despised, he had joined the Church. He found to his surprise that he had been able to embrace the spiritual world with some sincerity, and had no bother in ignoring the Bible's teachings concerning poverty and hardship. Furthermore, he had proved to be a popular priest, with a relaxed approach to minor indiscretions, especially the hunting of the Lord's venison.

"My Lord Dafydd!" he exclaimed happily, as he emerged from his house. "If I had known you were coming I would have arranged a celebratory meal."

Dafydd embraced him. "Just a glass of your fine wine will do, my friend." He turned to the three riders who accompanied him. "Go down to the village and see if you can get a drink."

The three soldiers nodded their agreement, and with broad grins slowly descended the steep track to the village.

Dafydd led his horse to a small grassy enclosure, where the priest sometimes kept a sheep. "No animal this year?"

"I'm getting a bit old for that nonsense," the priest shook his cropped head. "I'm happy if anyone wants to graze their own animal here, but I always felt sad when it was time to slaughter the creature: by then, I had become friends with it." He laughed, "Anyway, the village always got most of the meat." He stared out at the distant sea. "Also, these last months have been so good for fishing that nobody has bothered to fatten-up a sheep." His bright eyes missed nothing. "How are you coping at Aberteifi, my Lord? Big changes indeed?"

"That's partly why I've come to see you."

"We'll discuss it over some wine, shall we?"

"That will do well." Dafydd beamed with pleasure as he followed the rotund figure through the solid oak doorway, and into a cosy room. A log fire glowed in a stone fireplace, and a single framed window lit the room with sunlight. The priest indicated a large chair by the window, and sat on a polished bench next to a small table and opposite Dafydd.

"Well, my Lord, what brings you to my poor abode?" he said as he poured two mugs of wine from a jug.

"I would hardly call this a poor abode," Dafydd laughed. "But I need you to keep reminding me of the way we lived under Gruffydd." They raised their cups to each other.

"He was a good king," the priest agreed, and sipped his wine.

"He had his faults," Dafydd murmured, admiring the view of the river valley. "But he was the only man capable of holding this warring country together. Since his death, the country is breaking apart. Gwyneth and Mons have appointed their own kings." He paused, unwilling to mention the name of Cynan ap Iago, who had murdered King Gruffydd after his defeat by the Saxon Earl Harold. He stared into his wine. "I hear that Powys has declared itself independent."

"I hear some of this from the wandering friars," the priest agreed, "but the Bishop is ever optimistic. He says that the Saxons are Christians, and that we should be able to negotiate with them now the King is dead." He refilled both mugs. "I think he believes he can assume more power now that King Gruffydd is no longer lording it over him. He imagines a holy realm where the Welsh and the Saxons will live in harmony under the rule of the Church."

"Really?" Dafydd almost choked. "Doesn't he realize that the

IN THE ASHES OF A DREAM

Saxons are land-hungry, and see us as their enemy, no matter what God we worship?"

"The Bishop is a holy man," the priest spoke judiciously. "He's also a very ambitious man."

"Have you thought how this will affect us?" Dafydd asked.

"I have indeed. The one thing I like most about being the local priest in a small village like Llanduduch is that I have plenty of time to think." He passed over a bowl of dried fish pieces and a platter of fresh baked bread. He paused while he cut thick wedges. "We're at a crossroads. If we do nothing, we will suffer. The Saxons will find our weaknesses, and bit by bit will overrun our country. If we try to reform ourselves as a whole country, as we were under Gruffydd, we will fail: the northern areas will not give up their newfound power, unless they become the masters."

Dafydd nodded. "It's the old problem: the Welsh are really two nations: the north and the south. Each is envious and distrustful of the other. Somehow, Gruffydd managed to embrace the whole country, and for a mere seven years we had national peace and prosperity." He savoured his wine. "But even then, Gruffydd favoured his northern friends over the southern nobility."

"You and your brother did more to hold this nation together than either of you is prepared to admit." The priest chewed reflectively. "I was glad when you and Lord Gwriad returned to live here. I feel much more secure now. We all do." He waved a hand towards the village. "Building that stockade was a good move: it makes them feel safer from pirates. But soon we could be facing danger from beyond the mountains. Then what do we do?"

Dafydd nodded grimly. "I think a small start might be to give some military training to the young men of this village, and encourage some of the hill farmers to take part. I know a few were enrolled in Gwriad's Central Army, but since the demobilization, the structure has disappeared."

"The ones who fought with Lord Gwriad are the ones who are the keenest to do sentry duty at the stockade, but they are essentially fishermen, and most have a family to feed." The priest cut more bread and refilled their mugs. "If Gwriad were to make them sergeants, and pay them a small amount each year, I am sure they would persuade the others to take part," he paused. "Of course, they'll need weapons."

"That can be arranged," Dafydd mused. "We have two blacksmiths in the Aberteifi village. Gwriad can provide the iron; he has his contacts." He stood up and stretched. "That would be a start. If we could persuade every village to provide its own defence force, we could muster an army if we were threatened. Every man with some training is worth a dozen heroic untrained farmers and fishermen." He emptied his mug, wiped his mouth and with renewed energy strode for the door. "Are the men in from fishing?"

Father Williams glanced regretfully at the unfinished wine jug, and with a hint of reluctance rose slowly to his feet. "Yes, it's high tide. They were out early this morning. I imagine they're back and entertaining your soldiers."

"Well then," Dafydd said enthusiastically, "with your help, we'll choose the sergeants."

CHAPTER TWO

The hunters spread out in a long line, weaving their way slowly through the forest of ancient elms, alders and oaks; their horses trod carefully over the twisted roots and avoided the thick ferns and brambles in the clearings. It was midday, yet still cool in the verdant shade. The bright sun illuminated patches of open ground where the thick canopy of the forest allowed, and small streams were still percolating through the soil after the recent rains. Ahead of the riders, the hounds were suddenly baying, and there was no doubt they were following the scent of a large creature.

"Do ye think they've found a bear, m'Lord?" Merfyn asked anxiously. He was normally in charge of the stables, but had been appointed as Lord Gwriad's master of the hounds, and was not confident in his newly acquired role.

"I think it's more likely to be a deer," Gwriad said, and he blew a long note on his horn.

They had been hunting all morning for something, anything, to provide the basis for a feast. In Gwriad's mind he would be happy to capture a deer, a bear, or even a wild boar, although the last was most unlikely. He had never come across a wild boar in all his days of hunting, and it was widely believed that the animals had been killed off, or had retreated to the mountains. However, bears were a possibility: they moved around the country finding mountain dens during winter and in the spring raided the lower lands in their search for roots, small creatures and easy food, especially salmon and berries. A bear would be a challenge.

A roar went up from the hunters, as a fine stag broke cover and raced away across some cleared ground, pursued by the pack. "So much for your dangerous bear!" Gwriad yelled as he spurred his horse into a gallop.

The stag was in peak condition and quickly distanced itself from the excited pack. Behind, the riders became separated from each other, as their varied abilities and experience of riding began to tell. For the majority, it was a rare event for them to ride a horse, though for Gwriad and a handful of others it was a regular part of their lives.

The scullery boy, Jon, whom Rhodri had complained about, was the least able. Only on rare occasions had he been allowed to sit on a horse, and then only within the confines of the stables. He boasted he was sixteen, although others thought him younger. Gwriad had allowed him to work in the kitchen after Jon's father, his only relative, had died of food poisoning while serving with the Central Army. Jon was always cheerful, in spite of his abject poverty, and was keen to seize any opportunity to better himself or expand his knowledge of life. He considered horses to be god-like, and was amazed when Lord Gwriad had offered him a chance to ride.

"Remember," Gwriad had warned him, "I have given you the quietest animal in the stables, and I don't want you to kill yourself, or this horse, trying to prove you can do more than just sit in the saddle."

Jon had concentrated on staying upright, watching carefully how the other riders behaved and, thanks to the docile nature of the animal, had avoided falling off. He had barely kept up with the rest of the hunters when they moved from a quiet walk to a swaying trot; thankfully, his horse had no intention of exerting itself and was content to be at the back of the group.

In the courtyard Jon had been given a rusty sword, of which he was immensely proud, but he had not been allowed a spear or a shield. "Keep both hands on the reins, and if ye starts to slip off, use one hand to hold onto the saddle," one of the soldiers had advised. "If ye falls off, ye'll be cleaning the jakes."

But he had remained in the saddle, and when the others broke into a mad gallop, Jon urged the horse on with delighted abandon. But, it refused to go faster than a trot, and he was soon well behind the rest of the riders, and suffering from cuts and grazes from low-hanging branches.

He became anxious when the baying of the hounds and the yelling of the riders began to fade, and was unsure if he was going the same way as the others. The forest seemed suddenly unfriendly, as though the trees and bushes were actively against him. His joy and excitement of being part of the hunt was replaced with an uncomfortable feeling that he was lost, and that something awful was likely to happen. He realized how little he knew of the forest even though it was so close to the castle. Apart from a few, short, fishing sorties along the river, this was his first experience of being alone and away from the village.

Jon's mother had run off with another man when he was a baby. This was the only information his drunken father, Dai, had ever given him. Although a fisherman, Dai had spent much of his time serving as a soldier to the previous lord, Gwriad's uncle, Lord Gomer ap Griffith. As a result, an elderly spinster who kept home for Dai had raised Jon. She knew nothing about children and did not want to learn; she had demanded he be quiet when he was a baby, and had treated him as a slave as he grew up. His father had rarely shown any interest in his son, and when Dai died, the hovel was sold. The aged spinster moved in with another old woman, forcing Jon out to seek shelter on his own. He could not believe his good fortune when, two months ago, Lord Gwriad had said he could work in the castle's kitchen. Although Jon learned quickly when he was given the chance, he was constantly bullied by the other servants over his lack of basic skills. His maxim became: "*Now*, I know how to do it."

The aged horse slowed down to a walk, and Jon became acutely aware of the noises of the forest: the slight movement of leaves and bushes in the light breeze, the distant gurgle of running water and the worrying snap of a branch. He looked anxiously about, certain he was being watched, and urged the reluctant horse into a short burst of speed, ducking his head to avoid the branches, and leaving the creature to choose its own path.

Without warning, the horse stopped abruptly. Jon was thrown over its head and landed heavily on the damp ground, winded and disorientated. From his right he saw a blur of movement as a large creature rushed past him and attacked the horse. He sat up, gasping for breath, and was horrified to see a massive boar, with vicious tusks, tearing out the belly of the screaming horse, and forcing the struggling animal down on its side. It was an image beyond his worst nightmares: a huge, blood splashed creature that grunted and gurgled and moved in sickening bursts of violent rage as it dragged out the hot innards of its dying victim.

Cautiously, Jon stood up, supporting himself against a tree and stared in horror as the incensed boar, its red eyes full of hatred, turned to face him. He backed into the solid bark of a large tree and, glancing up, realized it had low branches. With a reaction based on panic, he jumped for a stout branch above his head and, with unusual dexterity, managed to pull himself out of range of the deadly tusks of the blood-crazed boar.

Slowly, he eased himself into a standing position by holding on to the branch above, and gradually took control of his rapid breathing and the frantic pounding of his heart. He did not consider himself brave, having never before been in any dangerous situation, but neither was he a coward: his loveless life had proved him to be a survivor.

"Ye'd better watch it," he muttered to the panting creature five feet below. It eyed him malevolently with its bright, narrow eyes, and scuffed the damp ground with its cloven hoofs. "I got a sword see," he giggled nervously. "I could cut you up, I could." He trembled as he began to react to the shock of the event, and almost lost his balance.

The huge boar seemed unconcerned with the horse now it was dead, and began to dig up mushrooms, occasionally stopping to glare up at Jon.

"I'm not afraid of you!" Jon called down. The boar ignored him. Jon slowly regained his composure, and listened for any sounds of the other hunters, but the forest was silent except for the growling, slobbering sounds beneath him. He began to shout for help as loudly as he could, but there was no answering call. The boar had begun to dig up a patch of clear ground, snuffling in the loose earth; it interrupted its meal to make a half-hearted charge at the tree but, realizing there was nothing to attack, returned to its feasting.

Jon looked around and considered his position. It would get dark in a while, and even if he did manage to leave the tree without the boar noticing, he did not fancy his chances of finding his way safely back to the castle. Either he had to act now, or be prepared to sit in the tree for a long time until he was rescued. He frowned. Perhaps they wouldn't come looking for him; maybe he wasn't that important. "They'll surely want their horse back," he muttered. "Unless they think I stole it."

The fact that people might think badly of him, especially Lord Gwriad, was more important to him than his safety. "I 'ave to do something," he whispered to himself. "I can't stay up here forever."

He began to move slowly round the tree, moving carefully from one branch to the next, until he was behind the trunk, and could no longer be seen by the boar. Very carefully, he peeped round, and was relieved to see the boar was completely focused on its meal of worms and small insects. With infinite care he lowered himself to the damp forest floor, and moved off silently into the gloom, following what appeared to be a little used path. He kept glancing back, but there was no sign of the boar. After he had covered what he considered to be a safe distance he began to run, following animal tracks, dodging around trees and passing large stones and boggy areas.

Jon was hot and beginning to tire by the time he reached a fast-flowing stream lined by large willows. He stopped and listened intently but, hearing no sound of pursuit, he waded into the shallow waters and dunked his head into the cold stream. Cupping his hands, he drank deeply, and with a native wit he did not know he possessed, he waded downstream to prevent the boar from picking up his scent.

After a while, he climbed up the opposite bank, and began to walk as fast as he could along the bank, constantly looking behind, following the direction of the water. Eventually, he reasoned, it would either flow into the river or directly into the sea, and then he would know where he was.

At times, he found himself in low, narrow hollows, with tall trees shutting out the light, as the stream weaved its way through the difficult terrain. He was near to exhaustion: his feet ached and his stomach reminded him that he had not eaten since a rushed breakfast of milk and stale bread at first light. He became careless, catching his arms and face on unseen branches, and stumbling as he tripped over an unending network of roots. He stopped to rub his scratched arms, and was immediately aware of a different sound: no longer the gentle murmur of the rushing stream, but ahead was the deep, sullen roar of the swollen river.

"Oh, thank God," he muttered. He staggered on, forcing his way through a thick wall of smaller trees and dense bushes, and finding himself on the southern bank of the River Teifi, with the stream emptying itself on his right. Over time, erosion had caused a small muddy beach to be formed on either side of the stream's mouth. A wide path crossed the stream and he guessed the village of Llanduduch was somewhere to his left, and the way back to the castle at Aberteifi was upriver.

"Thank God," he repeated as he collapsed on the dry path, "Thank God." He would have been hard put to explain which God he meant. His father and the old woman had always avoided Father Williams and his stone church, preferring to pay lip service to those who followed the old ways. The old woman would disappear at certain times of the year, and had always refused to explain anything to him, other than to condemn the "bloodsucking priests", sentiments his father had echoed. Jon had never been inside a church, and whatever understanding he had about spiritual matters was gained from snippets of overheard village gossip and listening to the older men at the castle.

He knelt down by the side of the stream and gently washed his scraped face, hands and arms. He drank some more water, and then lay on his back on the dry sand, stretching out his aching limbs. "Just a short rest," he murmured. The sun relaxed him, and in moments he was asleep.

• • •

LORD GWRIAD LED HIS MEN at a canter along the wide river path that led back to his castle. At the back of the group two soldiers shared a mount, and led a reluctant horse that carried a large, gutted stag. The hounds had been fed on the entrails, and would return later with Merfyn and the stable boys.

They had been hunting since early morning and Gwriad was anxious to get back. "If we don't hurry, we won't be eating venison until tomorrow," he urged. He was an impetuous man, given to wild enthusiasms and possessing seemingly endless energy.

He rounded a bend in the path, the dangerous river on his left, when he suddenly brought his warhorse to a dramatic stop, causing chaos among the following riders as they tried to avoid their Lord's horse. Two animals collided, one falling heavily on the dry earth and trapping its rider's right leg. For a brief moment, there was yelling, cursing and screams of pain as the men fought to regain control of their mounts.

Oblivious to the uproar, Gwriad jumped off his horse, and ran the few feet towards an unconscious boy, whom he had only narrowly avoided trampling. He was aware that if he had failed to notice the body, his destrier and the following horses with their iron shoes would have dismembered the boy.

Amid the uproar, Jon awoke with a start. He sprang to his feet, his dulled mind trying to comprehend the situation: there were panting, agitated horses everywhere, their eyes wide with terror, their riders fighting to control them. One was screaming as it tried to get back on its feet, and below it a man was sobbing and swearing as he tried to extract his broken leg from beneath the crazed animal.

As Jon stood up, he found himself staring at the angry face of Lord Gwriad, and behind him a sea of hostility.

"Bloody Hell, it's only that dimwit Jon!" a soldier at the front called back to the others, many of whom had dismounted and were intent on helping their friend. The fallen horse tried to stand, but it was clear that it was badly injured.

"Well?" Gwriad snarled at the horrified boy. "What are you doing here?" He looked around. "And where's my horse?"

"I were attacked by a wild boar, m'Lord," Jon stuttered.

"Fell off his bloody horse more like," one called out. The nearest soldiers let out a roar of derision.

Gwriad rounded on his men. "Enough!" he bellowed. He quickly assessed the situation. "Get a splint on Iago's leg, and put that poor animal out of its misery." He returned his gaze on Jon. "Tell me, slowly now. What happened?"

Jon took a deep breath; he was shaking with fear and desperate that his Lord would believe him. "I got separated, m'Lord. I'm sorry. Everyone galloped off, my horse wouldn't keep up, an' I got lost. Then, this huge boar attacked, and I were thrown off the horse. It attacked the poor old horse. It tore out its guts. It were awful, m'Lord." He was unable to continue as a fit of sobbing and hiccupping consumed him.

Gwriad returned to his horse, and handed the terrified boy a leather water bottle. "Drink this," he said quietly. "There is nothing to fear."

Jon took a long drink and after breathing deeply, managed to get himself under control.

"Do you think you can remember how to find the place where you were attacked?" Gwriad spoke quietly, but his eyes flashed with excitement.

Jon fought back the panic, which threatened to overwhelm him again. "I think so, m'Lord." His mind cleared. "'Tis up this stream 'til you come to some big trees. Their branches hang in the water," he added quickly. "Then follow a small path on that side," he pointed. "It were in a clearing. It were very strange, m'Lord, after killing the horse it began eating worms and mushrooms."

"Well done, Jon, that makes sense." He turned back to his men, who had all dismounted. The injured horse was quickly slaughtered, and Iago was soon having his leg splinted. Many of the men were experienced soldiers, used to dealing with death and wounded friends. The injured man had passed out, and his face seemed drained of blood.

"I wouldn't want to be Jon when Iago gets back on his feet," one soldier muttered as they lifted the now unconscious man onto the horse of a large, flaxen-haired youth.

"My uncle could take 'im out to sea and dump 'im," the youth jested, giving Jon an angry look.

"Lleu and Gavin, take Iago back to the castle," Gwriad ordered, nodding at two of the older men. "You, Owen," he pointed to the flaxen-haired youth, "wait here until Mervyn and the stable boys arrive." The young soldier scowled. Gwriad advanced menacingly towards him, and Owen backed away, quickly bobbing a short bow. "Take off the saddle and reins, and have the beast gutted when they arrive! I want the carcass taken back for the dogs and the poor in the village. Understand me?"

"Yes, m'Lord." Owen looked away.

Gwriad quickly mounted his horse. "The rest of you follow me." He looked down on Jon. "You lead the way, Jon. Hurry now!"

Knowing he had to prove himself, Jon led the way upstream, moving as fast as he could against the swift current. At times, when either border was passable, he jogged along the bank, while the riders followed, keeping to the stream which never exceeded knee depth. He was soon hot and sweating, but determined to keep up a fast pace. It was not only his Lord he had to convince, but also the seasoned soldiers. His life in the castle would be a misery if he failed to prove his story.

Jon stopped when he came to the big willows. "Down this path, m'Lord," he panted, pointing to the animal track down which he had previously escaped.

"How far?" Gwriad demanded, his voice loud with excitement.

"'Tis only a short way on your horse, m'Lord." Jon was not experienced at giving directions.

Gwriad nodded impatiently. "Lead the way." He turned to the rest of his men. "Draw your weapons and keep silent in the forest!"

Once they were away from the sound of the stream, the forest seemed unnaturally quiet. Jon hurried on down the narrow path, trying to recall the particular shapes of trees, and odd stones. Behind him Gwriad followed, his sword drawn and his body tensed with anticipation. The soldiers rode silently in a long file, hemmed in by the trees and bushes, each clutching a sword or a spear. Most had never seen a wild boar, and some were still unconvinced that such an experience could have happened to a mere kitchen boy.

Jon stopped. He was certain he could hear a noise up ahead. He raised his hand and Gwriad stopped.

"I think it's just ahead m'Lord," he whispered.

"Get out of the way of the horses," Gwriad hissed. He turned in his saddle and raised his sword. The nearest horsemen raised their weapons in response. With a lusty shout, Gwriad urged his horse forward, ignoring the low branches and the uneven ground.

Jon watched from behind the safety of a large tree, as the single file of horsemen raced past, desperate to be part of the action. A short distance away there was a cacophony of screams and yells, the terrified cries of horses and the deep, brutal bellow of the giant boar.

As the last horse hurried past, Jon stepped back onto the path, and drew his rusty sword. He was excited and fearful at the same time, but was unable to work out what was happening. He could hear the shouting of the men and the screams of the horses, but he could not picture how the attack on the boar was developing.

Jon was taken completely by surprise when, without warning, the huge boar careered round the narrow path, and headed directly towards him. It was covered in the blood of the old horse and from the injuries the spears had inflicted, and it was in desperate retreat. This was an unusual creature, in that no other animal had ever beaten it: it had defeated lesser boars, defended itself against wolf packs and solitary bears, and felt inviolate. Men had never challenged it before. Now, in a complete reversal of its normal behaviour, it was running for its life. It was bleeding badly and knew it had to find an escape if it was to live.

Jon was horrified. There was no time to hide. The awful creature was bearing down on him, and in a paroxysm of fear, he swung his sword in a wide arc to defend himself. He felt his arm jar as the blade came into contact with solid flesh. The sword was snatched out his hand, and he was propelled backwards into a thick bush.

For a moment the world seemed to become very quiet, then he was aware of the horses, and the yelling of men. He was dragged to his feet, and he heard voices saying: "He's alright! He's alive!"

Jon opened his eyes, and tried to focus as Lord Gwriad dismounted and pummelled his shoulders. "Well done, Jon. You're a hero, boy!" There was a huge cheer and people began to pat him on the back.

IN THE ASHES OF A DREAM

He looked to his left, and there was the huge boar lying dead on the ground a few feet away. He took in a gulp of air and stared unbelieving at the enormous mound of dead flesh.

"Ye cut his throat, boy!" one of the soldiers shouted. "Bloody brilliant!"

The next hours were beyond his wildest dreams — and nightmares. He, Jon, the lowest member of the castle, had become the hero of the hunt. On arriving back at the castle, the tall, bony steward, to whom Jon had never spoken, arranged for him to have new clothes, but not before some other servants had produced a copper tub, and stripped him naked and given him a scrubbing.

He never took his clothes off, and as far as he knew nobody had ever seen him naked. His indignant protestations were ignored, and he was held down in hot water while some of the servants, including the cook, washed him thoroughly.

Megan was a thickset woman with greying hair and a no-nonsense approach, who ruled the kitchen like a dictator. She gave orders, and everyone obeyed, or risked a clout from her strong, calloused hands. Now, she was part of a gang that had stripped him of his clothes and forced him into the bath, and was rubbing parts of him that he considered very private. "For goodness sake, stop wriggling around, boy. If you washed more often, you wouldn't stink like a pig, and I wouldn't have to waste my time cleaning you."

Jon was mortified. It had never occurred to him that he stank, or that others washed regularly.

"We've got to get him out of this kitchen!" she roared. "Typical of our Lord Gwriad that he should order us to do this when we have a feast to prepare!" She turned to Jon, "Get up and dry yourself."

But he refused to stand up until a towel had been passed to him.

"Oh, for crying out loud!" Megan roared. "Do you think I've never seen a naked boy before?" She handed him a towel amid loud guffaws from the other male servants. She glared at them. "At least he's better equipped than most of you wet-nosed idiots!"

The men's laughter ended abruptly, and two of the kitchen drabs cackled loudly in the doorway.

"The steward has ordered that you wear these," a senior soldier named Penn said coldly, pointing to the most amazing clothes Jon had ever seen. Instead of his single, coarse brown tunic, and his foul clout, he was to wear an off-white shirt, a dull blue, thigh-length tunic and a pair of light brown leggings with an undergarment to replace his clout. Others might have seen these as old cast-offs, but for Jon, these were the first real clothes he had ever been given. He had never worn leggings, even in the coldest winter, and he was delighted when Penn gave him a pair of rough sandals.

"I don't know if these'll fit you, but it's the best the steward can find," the soldier said. Although a tough and unemotional man, even Penn was touched by the boy's obvious happiness.

"Come on now, Lord Gwriad and his Lady won't wait forever," Penn said gruffly. He was annoyed with himself for being soft.

"Why did the boar kill the horse and then not eat it?" Jon asked.

Penn glared around the kitchen. "Boars don't eat big creatures usually. They keep to small fish, insects and worms sometimes, but mainly nuts, roots and fruit. I reckon it killed the old horse because it was fleeing the hunt, and the horse was in its way." He looked pleased with himself for having devised this explanation. "I'm off now. I'm invited to the hall, see," he said importantly, and left.

Jon was still drying his hair when the Lady Angharad appeared. All of the servants stood to attention and bowed. Jon was self-consciously standing in the middle of the room next to the copper bath.

"M'Lady?" Megan dropped a curtsy.

Angharad had changed from her casual clothes to a fine red dress decorated with freshwater pearls, an echo of her earlier life. She swept into the large room, and quickly took in the situation.

"Is the meat cooking, Megan?"

"Both venison and pork, m'Lady," Megan said, pointing to the courtyard, where the roasting was taking place. "I was just getting the kitchen organized when Lord Gwriad wanted this boy cleaned up."

"Ah yes! Our boar-slaying hero!" She winked at Megan. "We

IN THE ASHES OF A DREAM

have visitors, Jon, and while Megan and her servants cook, it will be your job to entertain us."

"M'Lady?" Jon gasped. He had no idea what she meant.

"Come this way," she said, placing a hand on his shoulder. He felt himself glowing with embarrassment, as she led him out of the kitchen and across the cluttered courtyard.

There were too many horses for the stables to cope with, and weary horses stood in quiet groups, chewing slowly on scattered hay bales. Everyone was either helping prepare the feast or clustered near the main hall. The courtyard was littered in horse dung.

"Step carefully," Angharad commanded as they made the short journey to the hall, "you don't want to enter the hall with your sandals covered in horse turds."

"How … how will I entertain you, m'Lady?" Jon tried not to stutter. A slight breeze moved his clean, long hair.

"We have some visitors, Jon. A noble, and some knights from Morgannwg." She paused, "You know where that is?"

"No, m'Lady." Another thing he didn't know. "But I'll learn, I promise."

Angharad gave him a playful dig in the arm. "Doesn't matter where they come from, Jon. Just remember this: they have all heard about your bravery in killing such a huge and dangerous creature. They will want to know the whole story, and you will tell them in your own words. Don't worry who they are, just remember that Lord Gwriad and I are very proud of you."

Jon stared at her in amazement. She was the most beautiful woman who had ever spoken to him. His place had been in the kitchen where he worked, ate and slept. It was his job to take out the slops, wash the dirty cooking pots and sweep the floor. He brought in the wood and attended to the fire and carried the water from the well, and any mistake led to his having to clean out the jakes. He was not allowed to touch the food, and whenever possible he stayed very quiet, trying to learn from the conversations of the others.

"How long have you been here at the castle?"

"I come after Easter, m'Lady."

"Well, good then," she smiled. "Just tell them how it happened. Everyone thinks you're a hero. Enjoy it."

They were outside the main hall, where two soldiers were standing to attention. The men bowed quickly and opened the main doors. Angharad swept into the hall with Jon behind her.

Jon had never been allowed to enter the main hall, except to sweep the floors and apply clean rushes. He stared in amazement at the noise and colour, and quickly identified those he knew. Lord Gwriad sat at the centre of the high table wearing a red gown with a gold chain, and on his left an unknown man with a full beard was laughing loudly, and waving his goblet of wine to other men in the hall. There was a spare seat on Lord Gwriad's right, presumably for Lady Angharad, while next to the bearded man was the Lady Teifryn, and another stranger also with a full beard. Next to the empty seat was Lord Dafydd, brother to Lord Gwriad, and old Brother Williams, the priest from Llanduduch.

Jon glanced anxiously around the room. There were two long tables, one on each side of him as he followed Angharad towards the high table. Local landowners and their wives occupied the benches on his left, while on his right Sergeant Penn, who controlled the soldiers in the castle, sat with a host of faces he had never seen before.

A huge fire was burning in the grate, for even in summer this hall was cool, and around the walls flaming torches provided inconstant light, assisted by thick candles on the tables. Around the fire, hunting dogs, overly satiated on the offal of deer and boar, yelped and twitched in their sleep as they relived the hunt.

Servants were rushing around with jugs of beer for the local people and wine for the high table. Fresh loaves of bread had been provided to take the edge off the general hunger, while everyone waited for the meat to arrive.

Lord Gwriad noticed Angharad and stood up, and the forty or more revellers went quiet, hurriedly rising to their feet. "My Lord Edwin!" he said in a booming voice, turning to the man on his left. "I believe you have met my wife, the Lady Angharad?"

Lord Edwin ap Tewdwr stood and raised his goblet. "To the most beautiful Lady in the Hall." There was an explosion of agreement.

IN THE ASHES OF A DREAM

"God help any poor Saxon who attacks this castle when she's in command!" He sat down to much applause.

"Obviously a diplomat," Dafydd muttered to the priest.

"Best to be so, when you want something," the priest answered in his ear.

"Thank you, Lord Edwin," Angharad said as she approached the high table, "I'm delighted your eyesight has improved." There was a roar of laughter, as everyone had heard the story of Lord Edwin's arrival.

"And this is Jon," she announced in her strong voice, "the hero of the hunt! The young man who single-handedly killed the biggest wild boar in recent history!"

Jon bowed awkwardly, unable to prevent his face from glowing with embarrassment. Angharad raised Jon's right arm, and turned him slowly round so that everyone had sight of him. Then she clapped her hands and a servant brought her a cup of wine, which she handed to Jon.

"Have you ever had wine before?"

Jon shook his head. "No, m'Lady. But I know it must be good if you and m'Lord drink it."

The audience greeted this with lively approval. Everyone was on his side.

"Well said, Jon," she clapped her hands. "Now drink up, it will give you courage to speak, though you were certainly not short of courage on the hunt."

Getting started was the worst part, but once the wine began to relax him, and encouraged by Angharad who stayed by his side, Jon told his story. Later he could hardly remember what he said, but at the end the men were banging their fists on the tables, and a huge cheer went up.

"Well done, Jon." Angharad led him back to the main doors where a guard opened one side. "Now go back to the kitchen and get something to eat. Come and see me tomorrow. I have an idea."

Jon bowed. His head was swimming and his stomach was groaning, and he had never been so happy in his whole life.

CHAPTER THREE

"Now we've had a chance to celebrate, let's get down to business," Lord Gwriad said as he led the way into his bedroom. To his left, four chairs had been placed around a small table close to a shuttered window, while at the other side a huge draped bed dominated the space. Apart from one other small table, two stools, and an assortment of wooden chests, the room was Spartan. In a family castle, space was at a premium, and while the men met in one room, their wives occupied Dafydd's and Teifryn's bedroom next door.

Gwriad poured himself some wine and filled the cups of the other three. Opposite him sat Lord Edwin ap Tewdwr with his military adviser Sir Maelgwn ap Owen on his left, and on Gwriad's right was his brother Lord Dafydd ap Griffith.

Dafydd was a renowned scholar, who had been the secretary to the late King Gruffydd ap Llewelyn. He was used to recording all the important decisions made at meetings, and although Gwriad hated meetings, he was grateful for the support of his brother's meticulous recordings.

"So, Edwin, you are the cousin to Prince Anarwd ap Tewdwr?" Gwriad said as he briefly appraised the parchment that Edwin had given him; he passed it on to Dafydd, who read it with a critical eye. "How is it that we've never met?"

Edwin drank deeply, and smiled across at Gwriad, revealing a fine set of teeth, unusual for a fighting man. "When you and King Gruffydd came south, and began to create the southern fleet, I was keeping the Saxons busy on the borders of Brycheiniog and Powys." He pushed back his thick black hair with both hands. "We did well in those days."

IN THE ASHES OF A DREAM

"I arrested a certain young Prince from Brycheiniog, who was threatening to oppose Gruffydd. A friend of yours?"

"Ha!" Edwin guffawed. "That young whelp, the self-styled Prince Eoin? No, he was never a friend of mine or of my cousin Anarwd. He was an ambitious upstart who thought it was all a game. Once he was in prison, I re-established the security on that border. You will have heard of me in dispatches?" he said looking confidently at Dafydd.

"Indeed," Dafydd nodded. "Prince Anarwd speaks well of you." He smiled thinly as he handed the parchment back to Edwin.

Edwin was in good spirits. He had eaten well and drunk more cups of wine than he could remember. "This is my second in command, Sir Maelgwn ap Owen," he slapped Maelgwn on the back. It was clear they were close friends. "He is a general with Anarwd and will answer any questions that I am unable to deal with." Maelgwn was a short, stocky man, with the powerful shoulders of a knight. His blue eyes were alert, and although perhaps the eldest, he moved with the agility of a young man. Only the grey wisps in his hair suggested otherwise.

Gwriad raised his thick eyebrows. "Why are you not with the Prince Anarwd?"

Maelgwn frowned at the suggested insult. "He sent me to speak on his behalf, and in support of his cousin, Edwin," he growled. "Prince Anarwd felt I could achieve more coming to see you...."

"As I have been serving on the northern Brycheiniog border for some months," Edwin interjected, "Maelgwn knows the latest situation."

"Ah. My apologies," Gwriad said, adopting a friendlier tone. "Well, now the introductions are over, let's drink to friendship." He recharged the wine. They all stood and touched cups. "Now, tell us why you're here."

"It's been good to have time to relax and get my thoughts in order," Edwin said. He blew out his cheeks and took a deep breath. "We are suddenly in a desperate state, and everything has turned bad at the same time. In a skirmish with a Saxon column that had advanced along the coast, our friend, Prince Yestin of Gwent, died two weeks ago. A number of important officers died with him.

Anarwd was forced to send our army to recapture the princedom and appoint new leaders."

"This is his Southern Army?" Dafydd asked quietly.

"It was the Southern Army when King Gruffydd was alive," Sir Maelgwn said, flexing his large hands. "But it's been impossible for the Prince to afford to keep a standing army. He has been forced to rely on his house guard and only mobilizes his reserves when absolutely necessary. It's planting time, and the men are on their farms. It takes time to raise an army, as you know," he nodded at Gwriad. "It takes even longer when they don't want to come. The men are war-weary, General; it's hard to remember that under Gruffydd we had nearly seven years of successful attacks on the Saxons. After we defeated them in 1039 at the battle of Rhyd-y-Groes, they were always on the defence. We attacked their border towns at will, and with the loot we were able to pay a standing army. That's over, General, and the soldiers need to feed their families. They no longer believe they control the borders, and each man thinks of himself first."

"I'm no longer a general," Gwriad said quietly. "Like Prince Anarwd, I don't have the money to keep a standing army either. The Army of the South West and Mid-Wales is no longer an entity." He refilled their cups, with the exception of Dafydd who rarely drank much wine. "Perhaps I had better explain our situation before you continue. It might affect what you hope from us."

Gwriad rested his arms on the table. "After the battle in February 1063, when King Gruffydd was defeated, we also lost the whole of the Northern Fleet, and much of the Northern Army. As you know, Gruffydd was killed in an ambush on his way down south, and the men lost heart."

"You weren't involved in the battle, I understand?"

Gwriad regarded Edwin for a moment, as if checking he was not making an insinuation. He nodded grimly, and took a long drink. "Gruffydd had ordered me to return to Deheubarth with my army, and to disband it for the winter. I did as he ordered, but Dafydd who was then his secretary alerted me to the problems between General Owain and his officers of the Northern Army. General

IN THE ASHES OF A DREAM

Owain was also in disgrace with the King, having murdered a northern lord in a drunken dispute.

In spite of the King's orders, Dafydd encouraged me to return to support the King. I managed to re-enlist much of my army, but by the time I was able to march north, the Saxon Earl Harold had defeated Gruffydd and retreated back over the border. The weather was bad and communications were confused, but I heard the King was regrouping in Conway. My men were tired, food was short and the travelling was difficult, and we were seriously delayed. By the time I reached Conway, Gruffydd had gone south with a small guard to regroup in Deheubarth, but was murdered in the mountains." He paused, and thoughtfully sipped his wine. "I returned home with my army, and I had no choice but to disband. Suddenly, the strength that Gruffydd had created in seven years dissolved. The ambitious princes of the north grabbed their perceived inheritances; the central organization ceased to be, and suddenly we're back to local lords defending their own birthrights."

There was a long silence as each man considered what had been said.

"What is the situation with the Southern Fleet?" Dafydd asked. He was keen to move on and discover the reason for the unexpected visit. Later, he would record the facts on a piece of his dwindling supply of vellum, an echo of a past age.

"Prince Rhodri ap Williams, Admiral of our fleet, is still a force to be reckoned with," Maelgwn answered. "He captures trading boats from Normandy and Brittany, and that helps to pay his men. But many of his sailors have returned to their homes since the death of the King. It seems like the heart has gone out of everything."

There was a grim silence as they all sipped their wine. "What else?" Gwriad's deep blue eyes fixed on Edwin.

"I have it on good authority, that the Saxon Earl Harold of Wessex is preparing to lead another army to destroy whatever forces we can gather. It is rumoured that he intends to invade us before the harvest. I have a viable defence force in Brycheiniog, capable of giving a bloody nose to any small Saxon force that wants to steal our cattle, but I don't have the men or the horses and armour to resist a full invasion. As I said, Prince Anarwd is restoring the security in Gwent, but he's worried that an invasion further north would leave us completely vulnerable. We need more soldiers, but more importantly, we need more generals." He looked straight into Gwriad's eyes. "We need your help, General Gwriad. You may not consider yourself a general any more, but Prince Anarwd does." He paused, and in an emotional voice added: "And so do I."

Dafydd cleared his throat. "What is this 'good authority' that makes you convinced that Earl Harold might try another attack?"

"It is the sworn authority of Queen Ealdgyth, former wife of King Gruffydd," Sir Maelgwn said.

Gwriad and Dafydd looked at him as though he was a lunatic.

"What!" Gwriad yelled, jumping to his feet and knocking over his chair. "Where on earth did you get this pig swill from?"

Dafydd stood up, "You may not be aware, but Ealdgyth, the former queen, fled to England shortly after Gruffydd's defeat, sought refuge with Earl Harold, and is living in his castle near Chester." Sir Maelgwn blanched, but remained seated. Dafydd continued, "She travelled from Conway, and took a boat from Caernarvon, and sailed to Llif Pwll, from where the Earl had launched his marine invasion. She was taken to Chester, and Earl Harold, having recently heard of King Gruffydd's death, offered her refuge, and married her to preserve her reputation and enhance his own."

Sir Maelgwn shrugged his hands. "I understand that once there, and realizing the error of her behaviour, she sent a messenger to Prince Anarwd, as a way of proving she is still loyal. She asked to be forgiven, and wanted her sister, your wife, to take her back."

Edwin smiled weakly. "She wants to be accepted back by her family, particularly her sister Angharad, and she wants you to have this information." He nodded slowly. "Yes, Gwriad, she wants Angharad to take her back even though she fled to Chester."

There was no reaction from the two brothers. Gwriad sat down and poured himself more wine, and Dafydd examined his fingers.

"In the meantime," Edwin said, "she has agreed to send news of any of her new husband's intentions."

IN THE ASHES OF A DREAM

"Suppose she was in league with Earl Harold, and wanted to ingratiate herself with her Saxon benefactor?" Dafydd said quietly. "Just think of the chaos she could cause if we believed her reports."

"She was the King's wife!" Edwin protested. "She was our Queen."

"Who slept with her servants!" Gwriad yelled. "She was a whore! She was no more a sister to my wife than my horse. She was never a queen or a mother. She thought only of herself. Unlike my wife, she was just a pretty butterfly who had no more intelligence than one." He took a deep breath. "Your news of her betrayal does not surprise me. But I would not trust any message she sent. Almost certainly Harold is behind this, and is using her for his own ends."

Edwin looked shocked. It had never occurred to him that the former Queen of Wales might be a traitor. Like most people in Wales, even those well connected in the nobility, he was unaware of what had gone on in Gruffydd's court.

"You think we have been given false information?" Sir Maelgwn glanced anxiously around the table.

"How did you receive this message?" Dafydd asked, his long fingers drumming gently on the table.

"The messenger came to me," Maelgwn growled. "I passed on his written message to Edwin."

"How did the messenger arrive?"

"He was a Welsh merchant who had contacts in Chester," Edwin said. "He rode up to one of our guard posts and asked to see an officer."

"And then? Did he return to the Saxons?"

"The officer took his message, with the Queen's seal, and the merchant returned the way he had come."

Dafydd smiled. "The officer recognized the Queen's seal?"

"Well," Maelgwn rubbed his chin, "the officer was told it was the Queen's seal, and it did look impressive."

"Do you know what the Queen's ring looks like when pressed into wax?"

"No, my Lord, I realize I took it to be genuine, even if it may not have been. It was on vellum and sealed with red wax and an impressive seal I took to be royal. I have only handled one such in my life." Maelgwn shifted uneasily in his seat.

"And you took this to Edwin?"

"Yes," Maelgwn said hurriedly, "and I rode with it to Prince Anarwd, who was still on manoeuvres in Gwent."

"What did he do?"

Maelgwn cleared his throat. "He broke open the seal, and read the contents. Then he handed it back to me."

"Did he question the seal?" Dafydd continued in his unemotional voice.

"No, my Lord. He accepted the message with my account of how it arrived."

"So, neither of you could be certain it was from the former Queen?"

Both men shook their heads.

"What did the message say?"

"Prince Anarwd showed it to me. The first part said that the Queen was writing from the home of Earl Harold near Chester, that earlier she had been afraid for her life, and had fled Wales to seek sanctuary," Maelgwn said. He spoke as a man in pain. "She wrote that Earl Harold had given her a place in his household, but that she was consumed with guilt. She said she wanted to warn Prince Anarwd that the Earl had decided to invade south Wales to destroy the only remaining Welsh army."

"What did the Prince do?" Gwriad said. He drained his cup of wine, refilled it, and passed the jug round the table.

"He sent a message for me to join him," Edwin said. "The three of us discussed the contents of the letter, and it was agreed that Maelgwn and I should contact you as quickly as possible."

"What exactly did Prince Anarwd ask you to do?" Dafydd looked intently into Edwin's eyes.

"He wanted us to assess the strength of your army; to agree plans for our joint forces, and to work out the best strategy for defending our borders."

Dafydd turned to Gwriad. "If this was false information what would be the purpose of sending it?"

"If it's false, then Harold could be trying to keep us worried.

IN THE ASHES OF A DREAM

After all, he must know we are not in a position to launch a major attack, but we could still be a powerful nuisance by launching small border raids. If he keeps us wasting time and money preparing for a non-existent invasion, he would be able to manipulate us with very little effort on his part. My first reaction is not to believe anything that purports to come from Ealdgyth."

Dafydd nodded at his brother. "I agree, I think this could be a clever ploy by Harold. He has achieved the defeat of King Gruffydd, and has become the hero of England. I suspect his attention will be focused on London and the ailing King Edward. The Godwinsons are the most powerful family in England, yet I have heard there is little love between the King and Earl Harold. I have learned that King Edward has promised the throne to Duke William of Normandy, known as the Bastard. This must concern Harold."

"Some of his family members, especially Harold's brother Tostig, are equally ambitious," Edwin observed. He was keen to get back into the conversation. "I agree with you. Now that Harold has defeated the best leader in recent Welsh history, he's likely to look to his own immediate future in London, which also means controlling his family."

There was a long silence as the men drank wine and considered their discussion. Gwriad suddenly broke the silence. "So, we'll play him at his own game! We'll attack him in force, and destroy his castle. If he has left for London, or has gone up north to control his brother Tostig, then his men will not put up much fight. It will show we are still strong, and will cause the ambitious Earl of Wessex some problems."

Edwin looked startled. His eyes were red with exhaustion and too much wine. "I thought you said...."

"This is what we'll do," Gwriad said with a dramatic emphasis, banging his fist on the table. "You, Maelgwn, will go back to Prince Anarwd and help him sort out Gwent. Then, your army will join up with Edwin's." He turned to Lord Edwin. "I want you to return to your mustering point in Brycheiniog and get your men together. Summon as many as you can. Promise them plunder," he paused.

"Promise them Saxon riches!" He roared with laughter. "Promise them anything, as long as they come ready to fight!"

The two visitors thumped their cups on the table and joined in with Gwriad's merriment. This was what they had wanted to hear. Dafydd remained silent, pretending to write, while trying to organize his thoughts.

"I'll mobilize our local men, and as soon as the crops are planted, we'll march to join you. We'll meet on a saint's day, so no one can confuse the date." He smiled condescendingly at Dafydd. "What saint's day do we have in mid-June?"

Dafydd looked thoughtfully at the excited face of his brother. He realized it was not just the wine speaking, and that Gwriad had some more political aim than just enriching some poor farmers. "I would suggest St. Dogmael? That would be the 14th day of June."

"Excellent! St. Dogmael it is then." Gwriad fetched another flask of wine. "What did he do to become a saint?" he asked. He had no interest in religion, but it enabled his brother to speak while he replenished the cups.

"A good question," Dafydd's long fingers embraced his cup. "St. Dogmael, sometimes called Dogfael, lived about four hundred years ago, and some say he cured children. Others say he was a hermit who lived somewhere in this area, and attracted a following with his holy sermons."

"Well at least he's local!" Gwriad said dismissively as he sat back in his chair. "St. Dogmael, it is then?"

"You're the General, I have no idea. Will you be able to muster our men and get them across country in time?" Dafydd sipped his wine. "You have only about five weeks." Edwin and Maelgwn nodded their heads but remained silent.

"As you all know, we have very few full-time soldiers," replied Gwriad. "Our army is made up of farmers, fishermen and servants who would like nothing better than a quick campaign, grab some loot and come back heroes."

"But will they get their ploughing and planting done, assemble, and march to Brycheiniog in five weeks?" Dafydd persisted.

"The weather's good. Many of the farmers are ploughing already. They'll get it done if I set a date and promise them the chance of becoming heroes and rich men. The march should be easy: no mud, they can live off the land; I might even have time to train some of them!" Gwriad drank deeply.

"What happens when we meet up? Maelgwn asked.

"We immediately march up through Powys, and cross into the Saxon lands opposite Shrewsbury, we sack it, and march up to Harold's fortified mansion near Chester, destroy it and make a fast retreat with our spoils. Harold's estate is south of the town. It will be a lightning attack: burn his home; raid the farms around the town of Chester, and return back before the Saxons can organize."

"You won't attack the town?" Edwin queried in a slurred voice.

"No. It's too well defended, and I don't intend to take provisions for a siege, nor do I have the siege engines. This is a raid with only two aims: destroy Harold's home in revenge for his attack on King Gruffydd's palace, and get enough loot to encourage the spirit of our men, and enable us to afford more regular troops. The Saxons might risk leaving the safety of their walls, but I doubt it, especially if Harold is absent. If our host is large enough, we will frighten off any counterattack." Gwriad looked pleased with himself.

"There is one problem to your plan," Dafydd said almost apologetically. "Bleddyn ap Cynfya is the new ruler of Powys, and his family claims historical rights to the royal throne of the princedom. He suffered under Gruffydd's rule, and he will see your army as an invasion. I doubt he will agree to you crossing his lands."

"I know Bleddyn," Gwriad made a dismissive gesture. "His father and our father, Cydweli, served together at the battle of Rhyd-y-Groes. Over the last few years, I have met him on a number of occasions when I was patrolling the southern part of Powys. He was always agreeable. I will arrange to meet with him in the next week or so." He winked at Maelgwn, who was having difficulty focusing. "He might even lend us some troops."

Dafydd raised his cup with slow emphasis. "To a unified Wales. May your plan meet with great success." He gave his brother a thoughtful look.

Everyone emptied his cup, and it was clear that the meeting was at an end. Both of the visitors, who were hardly able to keep their eyes open, staggered to the door uttering incomprehensible compliments. Dafydd opened the door, and ordered the guards to see them safely to their beds.

"I think you almost drank them into oblivion," Dafydd said as he returned to the table, where Gwriad sat looking remarkably sober.

"This is our chance to catch the Saxon bastard at his own game!" Gwriad lounged back in his oak chair.

"You forget, brother, the Bastard is a Norman Earl with the name of William. I think eventually we will find that he is more of a threat to Earl Harold than we will ever be."

"Whatever, isn't it?" Gwriad slurred his words. "If Harold's away from his estate, we will destroy his home." He stood up and banged his chest with his left hand. "I will make him sorry he ever burnt Gruffydd's palace." He sank down on his chair, and smiled drunkenly at Dafydd. "We are a fighting nation, brother, we need this."

"So, it's just revenge and loot?" Dafydd said. "The people are tired of war. They have lost their king. Do you intend to replace him?"

"Don't talk stupid, man. I have no wish to be a king!" He hiccupped. "I have no wish to be a general anymore either! But our countrymen need victory. We need to beat the Saxons, grab their livestock and their gold and give Harold a bloody nose." He took a deep breath. "I will do this, and I want your help." He grabbed Dafydd's hand. "Don't let me down, brother. I need you." He reached for his cup, knocked it over, and rested his head on the table. In a moment he was snoring.

Dafydd stood up and opened the door. "Rhys," he said to the remaining guard, "I want you to help Lord Gwriad."

The sturdy guard nodded and, with a broad grin, hoisted up the unconscious Gwriad, staggered with him across the room, and dumped him on the bed like a sack of turnips. As Dafydd left the room, Rhys was pulling off his Lord's long boots; it was a ritual he was well practiced in.

Dafydd knocked once on his bedroom door, not wishing to catch his wife and Angharad unprepared, and walked slowly into

IN THE ASHES OF A DREAM

the room. The women were both asleep in their chairs, and Alys, Teifryn's maid, was rocking the sleeping baby.

Angharad opened her eyes. She stood up and stretched. "How you men do talk," she said sleepily," and you say we prattle!"

She embraced Teifryn who yawned and hugged her back. Then she kissed Dafydd on his cheek and left the room.

"You go now, Alys," Teifryn murmured. "You must be tired."

Alys curtsied, gave the sleeping baby a final glance, and quietly left the room.

Teifryn began to remove her clothes, and watched as Dafydd stared out of the shuttered window.

"If only I knew what is best," he muttered. "What is my role?"

He had hoped that Gwriad had more in his mind than mere revenge and pillage. But the anticipated attack was to be short and bloody and, even if successful, would merely ensure a similar retaliation from the Saxons. It had ever been so. He contrasted the great changes King Gruffydd had achieved in his short reign. "In a short time Gruffydd created powerful armies, a strong fleet, increased trade, and for a brief time we had seemed invincible. Then, he was gone, and with his death we lost everything." He nodded to himself. "We must use this muster to regain our Welsh identity. Perhaps our hope could be to rally round Prince Anarwd's banner? We can be great again if we had someone who could unify us."

"Are you talking to yourself, husband, or is the wine talking?" Teifryn had moved up silently behind him. She wore a long, thin white shift that revealed her shape in the candlelight. Dafydd embraced her gently.

"I was sorting out the problems of the world, my love." He kissed her softly on her parted lips.

"At least you can recognize who I am, which is more than I imagine can be said for your brother?"

Dafydd ran his left hand down her back, feeling the outline of her spine. "Gwriad is never good at a meeting, especially one that happens after a feast." He took in a deep breath and his right hand cupped her breast.

"Did our visitors bring good news?" she giggled.

"Tomorrow I will explain all, and ask for your thoughts." He picked her up in his arms, and carried her towards their bed. "But, tonight we have other things to occupy our minds."

CHAPTER FOUR

"I am pleased to report the Welsh are no longer a problem, my Lord King." Earl Harold Godwinson bowed to the aged King Edward, who fixed him with a grim stare.

In his London palace, although surrounded by his court, the King still felt threatened by Earl Godwinson. God worked in mysterious ways. Edward had been certain that Harold would have been engaged in a long and bitter campaign with the powerful Welsh King, that would have kept him away from London for years and would have put a stop to his meddling. But, here he was, at the end of April, with the swagger and confidence of a victor, the most popular noble in England.

The King, known as Edward the Confessor, was happier in the planning of his new cathedral, Westminster Abbey, the largest religious structure ever built in Britain, than he was when dealing with the petty ambitions of his nobles. He had prayed earnestly to his God to relieve him of the constant plotting of the Godwinsons, and had been pleased with his idea, God's idea, that Harold should deal with the seemingly unending Welsh problem.

For nearly seven years the Welsh king had threatened the security of the West, and each year Wales had grown stronger. Yet, in a short campaign, in one of the coldest winters on record, Harold had defeated the seemingly invincible Gruffydd ap Llewelyn. Armies did not march in mid-winter, it was an indisputable fact, yet this upstart had succeeded and was now back in London. Edward had no doubt that the Earl would use his success to persuade the Witenagemot, the ancient committee that chose the Saxon kings, to name him as his successor.

"We are pleased with your success," Edward said, his face and tone of voice displaying anything but pleasure. "We welcome you back to London." There was a long pause as the King was wracked by a coughing spasm. It was a ploy Edward often used when he wished to give himself time to marshal his thoughts and embarrass the person who was preventing him from the comfort of prayer.

"However, I have some unfortunate news. It would appear that your brother, Lord Tostig, is being held hostage in Antwerp?"

"I am aware of that, my Lord King."

"I understand he has been held for a long time?"

"Indeed, my Lord King, nearly a year." Harold felt the moral high ground on which he had expected to stand, nay deserved to stand, begin to shift. The crafty old schemer was preparing to force him out of London once again. The glory and triumph of his victory was sinking behind a cloud of family disarray. Damn his brothers! They had been a constant impediment in his rise to power.

"Nearly a year?" King Edward sounded wounded, and there was a palpable gasp from the court sycophants. "Why have you allowed your younger brother to rot in a foreign jail? I understand it is only a small matter of a ransom?" The King sounded incredulous. "Surely the Godwinson family has the money to pay the ransom?" He was enjoying himself.

"My Lord King, I have been otherwise engaged."

"For which we are grateful," Edward gave him a sad smile. "But your own brother?"

"I will see to it immediately, my Lord." He bowed low and strode out of the court, his eyes daring any man to speak. There was a strange silence, like the pause between an in-breath and an out, but as the heavy door closed behind him the courtiers broke into a welter of character assassination, and the king smiled.

• • •

FOUR WEEKS LATER, AFTER A number of delays in rearranging his affairs, Harold sailed from Dover in the first large vessel he could charter. For days he had been gripped with rage, unable to shake off his frustration and disappointment. He had arrived in London certain of his welcome, and of enjoying his hero status throughout

IN THE ASHES OF A DREAM

England. He had been convinced he could persuade the aging King and the Witenagemot to name him as the successor to the English throne. Yet, he had been forced to leave London empty-handed. Damn Edward! Outwitted by a man whose strength lay in political cunning, and who had never fought a battle in his life.

Harold was a big man, possessing huge strength and a murderous temper. When the captain of the two-masted nef, the only seaworthy ship in port, tried to explain that it was unwise to attempt a crossing for a few days, as a storm was brewing, Harold threatened to dismember him. So terrified was the captain, that he sailed out on a rising tide, despite a near mutiny by the crew.

They had barely left port when the tempest forced them to reef their sails, and ride out the battering of huge waves. During the next two dark days, the captain and crew fought desperately to keep their vessel afloat, and eventually all of Harold's entourage was forced to bail, despite their acute seasickness.

"Where are we?" Harold demanded, his voice bellowing over the roar of the sea. "Shouldn't we be in Antwerp by now?"

"M'Lord, we be lucky t'be afloat!" The captain angrily responded. "This ship's not built for such seas." As he spoke a wall of green water smashed against the raised deck, drenching everyone in its path.

"Well, where the Hell are we?" Harold yelled. "You must have some idea!"

"I'm trying to get us to safety, m'Lord." The captain lent his strength to the two sailors who were battling with the rudder. The ship slowly regained its direction. "We should be in the bay of the Somme," he gasped, pointing at a dense fog bank ahead of them.

"Where's that?"

"Northern France, m'Lord. It be the only place we can get to!" He staggered as a rogue wave battered the lower deck, knocking down Harold's landsmen and threatening to wash them overboard. "The tide be taking us north, but with luck we'll get some shelter once we enter the bay." He turned to yell at the discombobulated courtiers and soldiers, urging them to bale harder.

"I need to be in Antwerp!" Harold raged.

"Be thankful ye still be alive, m'Lord. We might yet flounder!"

Slowly, the violence of the sea began to abate and the sailors were able to raise some sail, enabling the captain to gain greater control of his ship. When the thick mist lifted slightly, they were able to see the vague outline of a distant shore on their right.

"We've a chance, m'Lord," the captain gasped. He was exhausted, as was his crew, and he hated the arrogance of the man who had made him risk his vessel. "However, it be a dangerous bay with moving sandbanks. After such a storm, anything be possible."

"And if we hit a sand bank?"

"We'd be in great danger, m'Lord. The tide will change soon, and we could be grounded on an ebb tide." The captain looked anxiously ahead. "Pray God it don't happen."

At dawn, the wind dropped and the waves lessened in their intensity. The cob moved further into the bay and the tide turned, as the captain had warned, causing the boat to make slow headway. Sailors were posted at the bows to warn of sand banks, and mariners on both sides called out the changing depths, using a weighted marked rope. The cob edged towards the coast, and it was soon clear that the captain was heading towards a small fishing village.

From the cob they could see some small fishing boats pulled up above the highwater mark on a pebbly beach, and beyond was a collection of huts, with thin ribbons of smoke rising above. One of the boats had a short mast, but the others were rowing boats. When the cob was within shouting distance, the captain ordered the anchor to be dropped. There was evident relief from the exhausted crew.

"We must sail on to Antwerp!" Harold raged. "The storm has dropped. Now is the time to continue our journey."

"We'll anchor here until the next tide, m' Lord," the captain said firmly. "The sail needs attention, and my crew and I needs a rest, and some sustenance," he glared back at the Earl, "an' this be a safe anchorage."

Despite his murderous threats and even bribes of gold, Harold was unable to dissuade the captain from dropping anchor. He stared angrily at the curious villagers who had gathered on the

IN THE ASHES OF A DREAM

beach. Some carried weapons, but most waved and called out in a thick French accent.

"What are they saying?" Harold demanded.

"They want to know why we're here?" one of his officers translated.

"Tell them we're seeking a safe anchorage from the storm, and we come in peace." A gleam came into the Earl's eyes. "Ask them if we can buy horses. Tell them we'll pay in silver."

After some exchanges, it was agreed that a few horses could be bought, and that for an extra charge the fishermen would row them to the shore.

"Ask them how far it is to Antwerp?" Harold ordered; he was feeling happier now that he had an alternative to spending any further time on this leaking, uncomfortable hulk. The fact that he had insisted on sailing in a violent storm, and that he was alive only because of the skills of the captain and his crew, did not concern him.

"They have not heard of Antwerp, m'Lord," the officer concealed a smile, "It's possible none of them have ever left this area."

"Tell them to send a boat out, and I'll go back with them and talk to their headman." As the officer shouted back his instructions, Harold smiled grimly at the captain. "We'll soon be leaving your miserable boat, and you can turn tail back to London."

The captain slowly shook his head. "I wouldn't trust them, m'Lord."

"Why not?"

"They're Frenchies, m'Lord."

Harold let out a raucous laugh. It was the first time he had laughed for some weeks, and he felt better. "Frenchies!" He threw a money purse at the captain. Be happy with that," he warned. "I was thinking of not paying you at all, as you never reached Antwerp." He turned back to the officer whose name he couldn't remember. "You can come with me, and arrange for the horses to come over."

The largest boat on the beach was launched, and four men rowed out to the ship. Harold insisted on going first, and climbed down a rope ladder, and clambered awkwardly into the boat, his translator came next, and the boat immediately rowed back to the shore.

"What are they saying?"' Harold demanded, as they beached.

"They think you're an important man, and worth a lot of money." The officer seemed troubled.

"Good. I am an important man, and I will pay in silver for their horses, and for a guide."

They got out of the boat, and were immediately surrounded. Fish knives were placed against their necks, and in spite of Harold's protests, their swords were taken, together with their money purses and their daggers. They were manhandled to the largest hut, where the village elder explained, for the officer to translate, that they were prisoners and he was taking them to a powerful local lord. Without warning, their wrists were tied behind their backs and they were forced to kneel.

"Tell them, I am the future King of England, and I will destroy them if they don't take us to Antwerp!" Harold bellowed.

"The elder thinks that's very funny," the officer muttered. "He says he will do what he wants, and you will be taken from here and put in a dark place, until he hears from his Lord."

In spite of dire threats, which the officer thought it prudent not to translate, Harold and the officer were thoroughly searched, and thrown into a storage room without any windows, with a strong wooden door, and with a burly guard outside.

After much pleading by the officer, their wrists were eventually untied, they were provided with a waste bucket, and given some stale bread and water.

They spent two days in the dark hole, until the door was opened, their wrists rebound and they were frog-marched into the open air. They had trouble with the intense light, and staggered as they were propelled towards a large cart. Rough hands forced them aboard, where they sat facing each other, with guards on either side.

"What the Hell's going on?" Harold demanded. "Why have our men on the ship not rescued me?"

"I picked up some of their chatter. It seems the villagers have bows, and directed fire arrows at the ship. The captain was terrified and moved into deeper water." He paused. "I think the ship's gone home, my Lord."

"Gone home!" Harold was beside himself with indignation. "I'll kill that damned captain when I catch up with him! And what about my courtiers? Why have they not forced the captain to rescue me?"

"Your courtiers are not sailors, my Lord," the officer said pointedly. "Most of them are not even good soldiers."

Harold took a deep breath, and briefly considered the truth of the statement. "What's your name?"

"Lidmann, my Lord."

"How appropriate," Harold sneered. "Anything else?"

"They're taking us to their local Lord."

Harold sank into a black silence. The guards placed their hands on their knives, as they noted his size and obvious strength. Even though his wrists were tied behind his back, they were afraid of him.

Some hours later, after an uncomfortable and humiliating journey, where they were refused the chance to relieve themselves, they arrived at a fortified manor. It was a large wooden building inside a strong palisade of pointed stakes, with a strong reinforced gate. Around the outside of this fortification were numerous shacks and barns. The party passed through the heavily guarded gates and came to a halt outside the entrance to the main building.

"They say this is their liege Lord's palace," Lidmann whispered.

"Palace!" Harold jeered. "This is a pig sty!"

"I think it best that we don't upset them, my Lord," Lidmann cautioned.

"I'm the next King of England! I know what a pigsty looks like!"

Lidmann bit his lip. He did not think that the enraged Harold would see the humour of what he had said. "I think they intend to hold us hostage, my Lord, until they can exchange us for a deal of gold."

Before Harold could respond, they were manhandled off the cart, and frog-marched into the main hall. It was a large space, with heavy beams holding up a roof of wooden slats and reeds. A wide fire smouldered in the centre of the hall, and beyond the smoky space was a raised area with a carved chair, in which sat a tall, thin man with stringy white hair. He was draped in a dirty, faded cloak and had an unwashed look.

The local Lord, for that was who they assumed he was, stood up and began to yell and point his hand at them. They were pushed forward and made to drop to their knees.

"What's he saying?" Harold was beside himself with rage.

"He says you have invaded his lands, and he intends to make you pay."

They were both manhandled out of the hall with Harold threatening dire retributions, but as the Lord and his men did not speak English, Lidmann knew it was Harold's way of coping with the situation.

They were imprisoned for nearly a week in a large room with a small window and two straw paillasses on the floor. There was a large jug of water with two mugs, and twice a day their numerous jailers served soup and bread.

"It's an improvement, my Lord," Lidmann said, trying to be optimistic.

"Why are they keeping us here?" Harold growled. The room stank, and he was bored.

"I have asked them, my Lord, and they say we are being ransomed."

"Who to?"

"The guards don't know, my Lord, or if they do they're not saying."

Harold spent his days in a silent, dark fury, unable to believe that he had ended up in this degrading situation, and finding Lidmann's company disagreeable.

Finally, they were dragged out of their cell in irons and paraded past a crowd of hissing, spitting people who yelled untranslatable insults. In the main hall the local Lord ordered them to their knees, and glared down at them from his raised chair.

"Tell him I'm the next King of England!"

"I think he knows that, my Lord. He's been agreeing the ransom."

"Who with?"

IN THE ASHES OF A DREAM

"He says he's going to hand you over to Duke William of Normandy."

"What?" Harold took a deep breath. "Tell him I will agree to be handed over to Duke William, known as William the Bastard, and he'd better start treating me as a Lord, or I will have him beheaded as soon as I meet my friend William."

This information caused some concern among the Lord's advisers, who suddenly realized that they might be out of their depth in the political negotiations in which they were involved.

The Lord turned pale. "You know our Duke William?" he asked in halting English.

"Tell him I'm the next King of England! Of course I know his Duke William! And he'd better release us immediately. I want food, wine and fresh clothes, and a decent place to sleep while I await the reply from my friend." He placed emphasis on 'my friend'.

The iron chains were removed, and food and wine were quickly served, but the fresh clothes were more difficult to supply. "They don't appear to have clothes for someone of your size, my Lord," Lidmann said after some back-and-forth with the servants.

"They're savages," Harold said dismissively. He was secretly pleased that he was larger than any of them.

Eventually, clothes were provided, and by the time they had spent two nights in reasonable comfort, a messenger had returned from Duke William.

"I have orders to send you to Duke William," the local Lord declared, indicating a sense of relief in his voice. "You will leave immediately."

When Lidmann translated the Lord's words, Harold stood up and walked towards the embarrassed man, staring down at him. "Tell him I will let Duke William know of the…" he paused, "the welcome he has given me." He let out a great bellow of a laugh, and stalked out of the hall, leaving the discomforted Lord waving his arms as he urged his servants to see this ruffian out of his domain.

• • •

On his arrival, Harold had tried not to be impressed by Duke William's imposing castle: the fine stonework of the outer walls with their complex turrets, the huge gates and the wide moat. He realized this would be a difficult castle to capture. His fortified mansion near Chester, with its wooden palisade, and its narrow ditch did not bear comparison. Unlike most Saxon fortifications, this Norman construction had placed the emphasis on space, height and some degree of comfort.

William's great Norman hall was twice the size of his own. It was a stately, spacious room with wide, shuttered windows that were open to the sun. The lofty walls were decorated with large tapestries and heraldic flags, and there was a permanent, raised area for a grand high table at one end. Around a majestic fireplace, built into the inside wall, was a display of shields and swords, while a blazing, smokeless fire warmed the room. The two men sat in large, comfortable, carved chairs, with an elegant table between them. There were pewter plates heaped with food, and a large glass bottle of fine wine from which William had poured lavish amounts into their glass goblets. Two soldiers, in rich costume, and with ceremonial spears, stood guard at the either side of the massive door, while a row of uniformed servants stood attentively along one wall. It was an expression of power and taste, and made Harold acutely aware of the contrast with his ill-fitting clothes, and his one servant, the awkward Lidmann, who stood to attention behind him.

"Do you like my small home, Earl Harold?" William smiled with his teeth. He was enjoying himself. He was a tall, muscular man, not as large as Harold, but giving the impression of being at the peak of physical fitness. He lounged contentedly in his chair, and raised his goblet in a silent toast, aware that French was not Harold's first language.

"Indeed," Harold tried to appear indifferent as he drank his wine. He was not used to being beholden to any man, especially one who might challenge his right to the English throne. He was conscious of his own ragged beard and the cast-offs he was wearing, in contrast to William's short trimmed beard and his elegant clothes. He felt strangely ill at ease.

IN THE ASHES OF A DREAM

"So, you narrowly escaped drowning?" The Duke raised an enquiring eyebrow, and Harold understood they had passed the initial stage of pleasantries and were slowly moving towards negotiations.

"I was on my way to Antwerp to bail out my younger brother, Lord Tostig." He dismissed the affair with a boisterous laugh. "Young men are frequently stupid."

"I understand you have," William paused, "a difficult family?"

Harold tensed. He would have said his younger brothers were all a pain in the arse. However, he objected to anyone else making such judgements. "They have a lively disposition," he said, drinking deeply from his goblet. "How are you coping with your local problems?" He asked innocently, changing the subject.

"I have no local problems," William replied quietly. "Tell me about my dear cousin, the divine King Edward. I believe you call him 'The Confessor'?"

"He's well." Harold stuck out his lower lip. "I was at his Court before I left Dover to rescue my brother."

"I understand King Edward, my Christian cousin, reminded you of the fact that your poor brother had languished in captivity for a long time?" William filled up their goblets, and was pleased to see Harold's face was flushed. "I suppose I should congratulate you on defeating the Welsh King Gruffydd?" he sipped his wine. "But, then again, I understand it was other Welshmen who killed him?" He looked knowingly at his guest.

Harold took a deep breath. He realized that while he knew virtually nothing of what was happening in France, William had proved that he knew exactly what was occurring, and had occurred, in England and Wales. "My ships defeated his northern fleet, and the Welsh are in disarray," he drained his goblet, and slammed it on the table. A clear sign that he did not wish to discuss it further.

"Quite so," the Norman nodded sagely as he refilled Harold's goblet. "You understand, of course, that your holy King Edward has promised me, his cousin, the English throne when he dies? I will be the next King of England."

Harold's eyes bulged. "That's mere rumour. I have no

substantiated knowledge of this. Also you are only a distant cousin," he shifted forwards on his seat, "and known to be a bastard."

If this was intended to embarrass William, it failed utterly. William wore the term 'The Bastard', with as much pride as his title of Duke.

"He must surely have told you," William made a dismissive gesture, "that as he's your King, he can make such decisions?"

"The Witenagemot will decide who will be the next King!" Harold was tempted to knock William to the ground, but he noticed the Norman had a dagger in his belt. He stood up, towering over the Norman, and stretched the tension out of his neck. He forced a smile: "Thank you for your help in my time of need. I will get the next boat back to England, and relieve you of your obligation to me and my servant."

"And how will you get the next boat, my Lord?" William smiled like a cat about to catch a mouse. "You are my guest, and before you depart, I must ask you to sign this…" He snapped his fingers, and suddenly the doors burst open and the room was full of people.

Harold turned quickly to face a sea of humanity that flooded toward him. In the front was a group of religious clerics, led by a bishop who carried an important looking manuscript. Behind him were two monks: one carried some large, leather-bound books and the other a quill and an ornate ink holder. Behind them was an excited collection of expensively dressed men and women.

"As this is an important occasion, I have asked my Court to witness your signing, and for the Bishop to bless it."

"What am I signing?" Harold sank back into his chair and reached for his goblet, his mind racing. He knew exactly what William wanted him to sign, and that his reference to being a guest could quickly be changed to being the Duke's prisoner. He had been caught wrong-footed, and he knew he must salvage what he could: a passage back to England.

"I believe you and I can work well together," William gestured for the Bishop to place the manuscript in front of Harold, and the books and the writing materials were piled on the table. "King Edward has promised me the throne, and I want you, as the second most important man in England, to sign that you agree, and that

IN THE ASHES OF A DREAM

you will faithfully serve me." As a sop, he added: "Together, we can transform England, make peace with the Welsh and contain the Scots."

Harold pretended to read the Latin text, conscious of the fact that he was not well versed in it.

"You will notice that the Pope, via Bishop de Gascoigne here," he nodded his head at the Bishop, "sends his blessings to me, as the future King of England, and extols the decision of the holy Edward the Confessor." He patted the pile of books. "In these volumes is recorded evidence of various established rulings of the Church regarding primogeniture, and the just procedures to be taken when a king dies without a natural heir."

Harold had no doubt that this theatrical piece had been rehearsed the moment that William had known of his captivity in France. He shook his hand to indicate there would be no need to read out from these dreary books, which he was unable to contradict. "Duke William," he said ponderously, trying to sound as though he was in charge, "do I have your word that I will be transferred safely back to England, immediately I sign this document? And that you will arrange for my brother, Tostig, to be released from Antwerp?"

"Of course," William smiled at his courtiers, "we must trust each other." There was a ripple of laughter. He nodded at the monks, who quickly placed the inked quill in Harold's hand, and pointed to the place where he should sign.

Keeping a set face, Harold signed with a flourish. There was a moment of silence, and then William stood up and offered his hand to Harold, who rose slowly out of his chair, and clasped it in a powerful grip. The courtiers erupted in a burst of clapping and cheering, and on the surface it seemed like harmony had been restored.

CHAPTER FIVE

Jon awoke to the crashing of metal bowls and the powerful voice of Megan. His head hurt, he felt sick and he realized he had to find the jakes immediately. He staggered to his feet from his warm, but uncomfortable, sleeping place near the fire, and tried to walk quickly towards the outside door, weaving like a drunkard. He could hear hoots of laughter, which he assumed were aimed at him; but he did not care, he had to get outside.

He stood gasping with relief as his bladder emptied, holding on to the wall of the jakes, and unable to focus. He had never felt so sick, and no sooner had he finished with one problem, than his stomach heaved up the rich food he had eaten last night, and he fought to stay upright as he vomited uncontrollably.

"Enjoying yourself?" a voice called out.

Jon turned to face Sergeant Penn, the senior soldier, who had been kind to him yesterday. "I feel awful," he admitted. "Never felt like this before."

"I don't suppose you've eaten such fine food before," Penn grinned.

"Sorry. I'll try..." he turned away and vomited.

"When you feel better, come into the kitchen. We'll give you something to help." Penn waited until Jon turned to face him, and tried not to smile. Jon's eyes were swollen and bloodshot, his face was a yellowy tinge, and he stank.

"Before you come to the kitchen, get a pail of water and wash yourself, and swill out your mouth." He paused, "The Lady Angharad wants to see you. So, get a move on."

"The Lady Angharad wants to see me?" Jon panicked, realizing the memory he had of her wanting to see him today was not a dream. "Now?"

"Yes. Now, you dimwit! So get a move on. I'll see you in the kitchen!"

A short while later Jon staggered into the kitchen. His hair was plastered down, his face was red with rubbing, and his damp clothes showed that he had tried to remove any traces of vomit.

"Come over here," Megan said. "Sit down, and drink some water. Then, eat this bread." She cut a hunk from a large brown loaf, and winked at Penn. "I know you don't feel like eating, but you must put something in your stomach."

He sat down on a bench at the long table, and sipped the water. He carefully broke off a small piece of bread. His head was throbbing, and all he wanted to do was go back to sleep; he chewed slowly, remembering he would normally be stuffing it down. Megan stood by the side of him, and sniffed. "You can't see Lady Angharad smelling like a drunk, can you?"

"No, Ma'am," Jon replied miserably.

"Hurry up and finish that bread, then use this." Megan put a small bowl next to him with a bar of soap. It smelled pleasant. Jon stared at it, as if it might bite him.

"Never used soap before?" Megan shook her head sadly. "You use it like this." Jon watched anxiously as she wet her hands, rubbed the soap and worked up a lather. Then, she dried her hands on a rag. "Hurry up with that bread. Then wash your hands and face, as I showed you, and hurry up! Lady Angharad won't wait forever."

He forced down the bread, and drank all of the water, and felt strangely better after using the soap and drying his face.

"I think I can take him off your hands, Megan," Penn said as he stood up.

"And good riddance!" Megan said angrily, but she winked at Penn.

Penn led the way as they crossed the courtyard. There was plenty of activity: the visitors' horses were being groomed and saddled; soldiers were trying to shake off their hangovers under the critical abuse of their sergeants and servants were rushing to the jakes with buckets of night spoil. "Keep up!" Penn roared.

It was his job to get this so-called hero to the Lady before she complained.

"What does she want to see me for?" Jon mumbled. His head still ached and he had difficulty in focusing his eyes.

"How should I know?" Penn snarled, "I'm not the hero who kills monsters. Perhaps she wants to drink your blood!"

Jon stopped dead. "Drink my blood?" He stared at Penn with wide eyes, suddenly awake.

"Don't be daft. It's a joke, you moron." He looked at the boy's bewildered face and scowled, "She wants to train you to be useful, I should think." He was cross that Jon was so gullible, and subconsciously envious of the boy's good luck. "If you let her down, we'll all drink your blood." He smirked when he saw the troubled look return to Jon's face.

In the great hall, Angharad and Teifryn were seated in front of their spinning wheels, a daily routine that helped to clothe the household. They wore plain, woven dresses, with long shawls around their shoulders. Although they sat near the glowing embers of last night's fire, the hall remained cool. High, unshuttered windows allowed some weak light to enter the large space, but candles provided the real light for them to see by.

"I've sent for Jon," Angharad announced, breaking the comfortable silence. Teifryn looked up. "Last night's boar-killing hero," she added.

"Oh?"

"I'm going to train him to be my personal servant."

Teifryn nodded her head thoughtfully. She was used to Angharad's sudden bursts of enthusiasm.

"We have a personal servant that we share," she observed.

"Alys is your baby's nurse, and only deals with our clothes. I'm thinking of a young person to wait behind me at table, take messages..." she paused. "I'm going to have him trained as a squire, then he can be useful to Gwriad as well." She sounded pleased with her decision.

"I understand this boy knows nothing," Teifryn observed. "He has no skills. Wouldn't it be better to choose the son of a local landowner? At least he will know how to behave, how to

IN THE ASHES OF A DREAM

ride a horse, and almost certainly will have some experience with weapons?"

Angharad sat up straight and her eyes flashed; she never took well to contradiction, even from her best friend. "Jon has potential. He just needs a chance."

"I'm sure he does," she smiled. "Is he to be an adopted son?"

"No, of course not!" Angharad scowled at Teifryn, who opened her eyes wide and waved a finger. "You think you know me," she protested, "but this is just…" she was interrupted by a loud knocking at the door.

Sergeant Penn entered, and bowed. "I've brought Jon along, as you asked, m'Lady."

"Bring him in, Sergeant." She smiled, "then you may go."

"Yes, m'Lady." He bowed his way out and curled a finger at Jon. "Go in there and remember to bow. You can tell me all about it when you get back to the kitchen." He frowned as Jon passed him; he had hoped to stay and hear what Angharad wanted.

Jon entered hesitantly, carefully shutting the door behind him. He faced the two women, who were many paces away, and bowed. "M'Lady Angharad. M'Lady Teifryn." He was grateful that Megan had prepared him before he left the kitchen.

Angharad smiled at him. "Come over here, Jon." She indicated a stool. "Bring it over and sit between us." Jon took a deep breath and did as he was told; he was uncomfortable with the women on either side of him.

"Do you know why I want to speak to you?" She deliberately spoke slowly and in an encouraging tone: she wanted him to impress Teifryn.

"No, m'Lady."

"Haven't the other servants said anything to you?"

"Well, um, Sergeant Penn said you wanted to train me to be useful."

"Sergeant Penn is right, Jon. Would you like to be trained to be useful?"

"Oh, yes, m'Lady. I would, I really would!" He sounded so keen that Teifryn smiled, in spite of her doubts.

"Do you have any family?"

"No, m'Lady." He paused, but seeing that more was expected, he continued. "I never knew me mother. Me father said she ran away, and that she were no good. Me father, he took on Mistress Lewis to mind the house." He hesitated, "she were an old woman and didn't like me. When me father died, she sold the house and moved away to stay with another old woman."

Angharad kept silent.

"What did you do?"

"Mistress Lewis said I were to go to the castle." He shifted awkwardly on his stool. "Lord Gwriad said I could help in the kitchen."

"Do you like horses?" Teifryn asked, changing the subject.

"Yes, m'Lady."

"You're not afraid of them?"

"Oh, no! I think they're wonderful."

Angharad leaned forward. "Did your father teach you anything?"

"No, m'Lady. I didn't see much of him. It were my job to keep the house clean, chop the wood, collect the water, empty her pot...."

"Where was your house?" Teifryn cut in quickly, there were some details that she did not wish to hear.

"On this side of the river, down at the Gwbert. It weren't really a proper house."

"I know the Gwbert." It was a small collection of squalid fishing huts around a sandy inlet near the mouth of the river. She had ridden there with Gwriad and his house guard, on a cold, wet day in March. He had wanted to check on the small fishing hamlets that clustered in the bleak bays along the rocky coast. "They're on my land," he had explained. "They pay their rent in fish, but I'm really interested in any potential soldiers. Also it's good that they know who I am."

She realized Jon's early life had been miserable. "Your father was a fisherman?"

Jon nodded at Angharad. "Yes, m'Lady. But, he liked to be a soldier. I never saw much of him."

"Any friends at the Gwbert?"

IN THE ASHES OF A DREAM

Jon gave a humourless laugh. "No, m'Lady, they were just old people there."

There was a silence. Angharad looked knowingly at Teifryn, and turned towards the anxious boy. "I'm going to give you a chance to be useful, Jon. First, I'll send you to Father Williams. He will teach you to read and write. Sergeant Penn will teach you to use a sword, and he will choose someone in the stables who will teach you how to ride and care for a horse." She smiled at the excitement on Jon's face. "And I will teach you how to behave as Lord Gwriad's squire and as my personal servant."

Jon stood up, licked his lips, and tried not to cry out with joy. This was beyond his wildest dream. "Thank you, m'Lady! Thank you. I won't let you down. I promise."

"No. I don't think you will." She handed him a rolled piece of vellum, borrowed from Dafydd, with her seal on the front. "Take this to Father Williams, and listen carefully to what he says. Report to me before the meal tonight."

"Yes, m'Lady." He took the letter, bowed quickly, and disappeared out of the door.

"So, what did she want?" Penn asked truculently. He had been waiting about for longer than he had intended.

"I'm going to be trained to be Lord Gwriad's squire."

"Yea, and pigs will fly!" He cuffed Jon, sending him staggering away.

"It's true!" Jon yelled. "An' you're going to teach me how to use a sword an' all." He rubbed his ear. "An' you've got to find someone to teach me to ride."

Penn clenched his fists and advanced menacingly as Jon backed away.

"The Lady Angharad said you will train me, or you'll be in trouble."

Penn paused; he was not used to being challenged, but he valued his job. "What's that you've got?"

"It's a letter I have to take to Father Williams. He's going to teach me to read and write."

"Give it here, you little turd." He held out his large, dirty hand.

"The Lady Angharad said nobody was to touch this except

Father Williams." He backed away as Penn came closer. "Her said she would punish anyone who got in my way."

Penn stopped, and scowled at the skinny youth. It occurred to him that he did not need to see the letter; he couldn't read anyway, and he didn't want to upset the Lord's wife. "Just watch your step, that's all. I'll teach you to use a sword, but you'd better watch it. Alright?" He marched off towards the kitchen. He'd give his side of the story before Jon returned.

Jon watched him go, and then walked purposefully towards the main gate. The two soldiers on duty gave him exaggerated bows as he passed them. "We bow to the great monster-killer!" Hywel taunted.

"Off to kill another wild animal? An' just with your bare hands?" Rhodri sneered, noticing Jon had no weapon.

Jon grinned at them, and waved his hands. He was so happy, he would not have minded if they had spat at him.

• • •

St. Dogmael's Day was typically supposed to be fine and sunny, and what was expected for June 14th, but instead it was wet, cool and windy at the muster in Brycheiniog, and the inclement weather continued during their two-day march into Powys. The rain was pelting down with a ferocity that matched the intentions of the Welsh army that moved, like a dark cloud over the land. They were near the town of Shrewsbury, and had advanced through Welsh princedoms with ease. Prince Bleddyn ap Cynfya, the self-appointed ruler of Powys had not only agreed to the army crossing his supposed territory, but to save face, had agreed to add some of his men to the invasion.

"He knew we would knock him off his petty throne if he disagreed," Gwriad muttered as he smiled at the youthful Prince. He and Dafydd bowed formally and turned to leave the great hall.

"We can use his 200 men," Lord Edwin Ap Tewdwr agreed as he gave a mock bow to Bleddyn and joined them. "With luck and a semblance of organization we should be able to loot Shrewsbury, march on up towards Chester, destroy Earl Harold's home, and get back to our homeland before the Saxons can organize a counterattack."

"You're beginning to sound like an old man," Gwriad mocked. He liked Lord Edwin, but his cautious manner reminded him of Dafydd's approach to life: think carefully before you act, and then think again. "I would like it if the bloody Saxons sent an army against us. Then, we could prove that we're still a force to be reckoned with. They think, after the defeat of Gruffydd, that we're beaten. We need to show them otherwise."

"Good idea," Dafydd responded drily. "Just make sure you do beat them. Another defeat would cause us a real problem."

As they walked purposefully back from Prince Bleddyn ap Cynfya's stronghold, the thick glutinous mud clung to their boots. They all wore body armour with heavy, ankle-length cloaks to protect them from the insistent rain, and in spite of a sharp wind were soon dripping with sweat. In front of them, tired horses were struggling to pull heavily-laden supply carts up a steep slope, while camp followers: the cooks, the slaves and the loose women were pushing from behind. The troops had made good time, and hundreds of soldiers clad in an array of armour and carrying a variety of weapons were camped at the agreed meeting place. Two large cavalry sections were situated at either end of the camp. The army seemed ready.

The original muster at Brycheiniog had been as successful as Gwriad could have hoped. With his brother's help, he had managed to assemble his army and had arrived at the agreed place three days before the appointed date of June 14th. All of the officers had horses, but fewer than a hundred of his men formed a cavalry unit of scouts. "Thank God that Prince Anarwd has been able to send a stronger cavalry wing," Dafydd observed.

"In this type of campaign it's numbers that count, and I think you'll find we have enough foot soldiers," Gwriad said confidently.

After passing through a well-manned checkpoint, and aware of numerous mounted scouts on nearby hills, they had approached a dense cluster of tents arrayed in military fashion on a low, treeless hill where Lord Edwin had camped with his army of local men. There were dozens of mountain horses in a fenced enclosure, and

Gwriad was impressed with the way Lord Edwin had prepared the area.

"You've done well, Edwin." He said, embracing the taller man, and waving a hand at the camp.

"I've been defending this area with Maelgwn for more than a year," Edwin said. "This is a well-used military camp."

"Of course," Gwriad tried to curb his enthusiasm. "But it's a welcome sight to see this organization."

Sir Maelgwn ap Owen arrived the next day having marched from Gwent with the bulk of Prince Anarwd ap Tewdwr's battle-hardened Morgannwg army. In total there were nearly 1,000 men, who set off the next day for Powys.

"Wouldn't it be fine, if once again, we had an organized standing army?" Dafydd said reflectively as he noted the differences between the experienced soldiers and the new recruits spread out before them.

"Let's be glad we have an army at all," Edwin replied. "Although there are many who are poorly equipped, and some who are either too old or too young, we do have a large core of experienced men who have good weapons and armour. And our cavalry section is larger than I had expected, thanks to Anarwd's generosity."

Gwriad agreed, "Yes, we have a host of men who have answered our call. Some of them fought under Gruffydd, some have fought recently with Prince Anarwd, and many with you. But, I agree, most of my men are raw farm boys who are seeking excitement, loot and a quick return back to their farms. Some have no military training at all, and as soon as the enemy fights back, they'll race off over the border like rabbits. The problem is that as soon as some start to run, an army falls apart."

"So? What do you intend to do?" Dafydd was sure his brother had thought about this before they had set forth.

"I intend to speak to the sergeants and tell them to pass on the fact that there is a second Welsh army coming up behind that will kill any deserter that tries to get past them." Gwriad gave one of his impish smiles. "The fact that we don't have a murderous second army doesn't matter," he laughed, "just as long as they believe it exists!"

IN THE ASHES OF A DREAM

Maelgwn gave a bellow, and slapped Gwriad on his back. "We'll be fine, my Lord, as long as they remember they have come to fight and not just to steal and womanize!"

General Gwriad was given overall command and gave his customary orders that no Saxon civilian was to be attacked. He had instructed the sergeants to warn the men that rape was different to pillage, and any man who assaulted a Saxon woman would be put to death. "It's like putting sweetmeats on the table in a room full of children and telling them not to touch any while the adults are away," he quipped.

"But, it makes you feel better," Dafydd said. "I remember your first invasion with King Gruffydd ap Llywelyn. He believed that Welsh soldiers wouldn't commit the atrocities that the Saxons had in the past, and when his troops set fire to villages he blamed it on our soldiers from the south, although you and the other officers knew it was his northern men who had done it."

"Nothing changes, Dafydd, but we have to try." He was silent for a moment. "I still like to think that we are better than they are, and that when we invade them, we are getting a justifiable revenge on the Saxons for their constant attacks on our people."

"How far are we away from Shrewsbury?" Dafydd asked, changing the subject.

"In this Devil's rain, and with the problems we are having with the wagons, I think we might be lucky to be there by late afternoon," Maelgwn said, wiping rain from his eyes. He was wearing a domed helmet that prevented the hood of his cloak from covering his face.

"So, they will be ready for us?" Dafydd queried.

"No," Gwriad said harshly. "They're not expecting an attack, and this weather will deter their scouts. They'll think twice about a worthless patrol. With luck we should be able to attack them before dusk, overwhelm their defences, and spend the night ransacking the town."

Maelgwn nodded in agreement. "We have a plan to get into the town. If it works, then we should have no problem marching on towards Chester by this time tomorrow." He clasped his long sword, "And with luck, we should be under cover tonight, and dry for a change!"

"Men rape women at night," Dafydd said quietly. He could not resist reminding his emotional brother that there would be consequences to an evening invasion.

"I will order the sergeants to publicly behead the first soldier found guilty of such a crime!" Gwriad responded passionately. "We will grab their wealth, but I will not allow rape!"

Dafydd nodded. He was convinced his brother wanted to believe that this army would be different to any other, but Dafydd knew, and he suspected his brother really knew, that the Saxon women of Shrewsbury were in for a rough night if his soldiers captured the town.

"You should speak to the sergeants," Dafydd said, "and more importantly, you should remind the officers of their duties. They are the ones to enforce order."

"I know that!" Gwriad snapped. "I don't need your advice on military matters."

Maelgwn nodded in agreement. He observed the pent-up energy and forceful character of Gwriad and the quiet strength of the thoughtful Dafydd. He understood how they were considered to be a powerful family.

• • •

THE ATTACK ON SHREWSBURY WAS only a partial success. The town was easily captured and the Welsh army fought bravely, but not always with any sense of co-ordination. Many more Welsh soldiers died than was necessary because they had felt the need for personal recognition. Their heroism was great, but many had died needlessly.

The Saxons had been caught off-guard, unaware of the Welsh incursion. As dusk began to fall and objects became indistinct, a line of heavily-laden carts, each hiding a small group of fighters beneath a root crop and driven by Saxon-speaking farmers, approached the town. It was raining heavily as the drivers reached the closed gates, and they began to yell at the guards, complaining about the weather, and cursing them for their slackness.

IN THE ASHES OF A DREAM

"Let us in for the love of God," they moaned loudly. "You know us, you bastards! We're your neighbours and we're drowning out here! We have turnips and swedes. What are you afraid of? You nipple-suckling half-wits! Open up!"

The unsuspecting guards unbarred the gates, and once the heavy carts had passed through, the hidden soldiers jumped out, overwhelmed the opposition, and kept the gates open while the Welsh army surged through.

The next hour turned from a rapid advance by determined Welsh troops through the narrow streets of the quiet town, into bloody hand-to-hand fighting as the inhabitants became aware of the screams of their neighbours. The Welsh troops raced further into the large town and met increasingly strong opposition. Once the warning was out, the Saxon barracks emptied quickly, and professional Saxon soldiers streamed onto the streets to protect their town. It was only the overwhelming numbers of Welsh fighters that won the day, but with unnecessary losses.

"We have control of the town, General Gwriad," an exhausted officer reported, as darkness finally descended on the town. "The regular Saxon soldiers are either dead or have gone into hiding. There is no further organized resistance."

"You've done well," Gwriad replied, conscious of the fact that he had spent much of the attack trying to enforce discipline on his disparate army. "You will be rewarded after this is over."

His reserve troops had been used when young Welsh farmers had tried to retreat with their loot after meeting their first resistance, and many Welsh soldiers had disregarded orders, setting fire to the tightly packed, thatch-roofed houses, and adding difficulties as the officers directed the capture of the town.

Outside his newly established headquarters, Gwriad could hear the screams of women and the hysterical cries of children. "Tell the officers I expect them to keep order!" he bellowed.

"M'Lord." The young officer bowed and left. He knew it was an impossible order, and suspected the general did as well.

Slowly, the other commanders gathered together in Gwriad's makeshift headquarters: a partially ransacked inn, which had been saved from destruction by Dafydd and some proven sergeants, who had forced the looters to return to the fighting.

"You have high expectations, my Lord," said Lord Edwin ap Tewdyr, when Gwriad complained of the attacks on civilians. "These are soldiers who are risking their lives. You can't expect them to become violent killers one moment and saints the next."

Edwin was breathing heavily. He had led the cavalry charge into the centre of the town. His men had broken the back of the main opposition, and then he had withdrawn his vulnerable horses to patrol outside the walls, leaving the foot soldiers to fight their way through the crowded, narrow streets. He raised a mug of beer. "To victory, no matter what the cost."

Gwriad glanced guiltily at Dafydd, then raised his mug, drank deeply and added: "To the rebirth of a strong Wales! And may we get our revenge on Harold Godwinson!" The generals drank deeply and refilled their mugs. It had been a long day, and although the town had been captured relatively easily, the tension had been extreme. Maelgwn had been active in capturing the main barracks, and although Gwriad had been aching to be involved in the action, he had been kept busy with constant demands on him as the overall general. Now each, in his own way, was unwinding from the combat, and prepared to forget the incidents that had found him lacking. With the absence of women, alcohol was the best way of blocking out the horrors they had experienced. However, they had won, and at that moment it was all that mattered as they exchanged ribald jokes.

Dafydd appeared not to be listening. He was staring in a fixed manner at a map sketched out on an ancient piece of vellum. "We must act fast tomorrow if we are to destroy Harold's castle," he said. His words sounded like a church bell's call to service.

"Tomorrow. We will deal with that tomorrow," said Lord Edwin, his words slightly slurred.

"No!" Dafydd roared, his voice drowning out the screams and drunken laughter outside. "We came here to get revenge on Earl Harold, who defeated our King, destroyed our security and reduced us to a mere collection of competing princedoms… the way we have always been." He glared at the other men who had been awakened from their complacency. Dafydd was not known for his anger. "We need to plan now! Tomorrow will be too late."

Gwriad nodded solemnly and finished his beer. "Indeed."

"Do not imagine that we can get our army back into a fighting force starting at first light tomorrow!" Dafydd had his blood up, and it was so unusual that Gwriad and the generals listened. "Within another hour, the men will be too drunk to march, and it will take a whole day to get them sobered up. If they sense they can disobey us, they will grab their loot and return home." He stood up, and they were all aware how tall he was.

"Once the Saxons know that we have looted Shrewsbury they will be out in force to defend their key towns and homes." He nodded towards Lord Edwin. "I know your cavalry prevented any of the town's people from escaping during the attack, but don't think that nobody has escaped under the cloak of darkness to raise the alarm. Unless we are away long before first light, we will find ourselves prone to ambush, and our chances of achieving a surprise attack on Harold's fortified manor will be nil. We will have thrown away our chance of revenge because we wanted to celebrate a small victory."

There was an uneasy silence. Gwriad lowered his mug of ale, and sniffed loudly. "You're right, Dafydd, we're acting as though we've already done what we set out to do." He stood up and patted his brother on the shoulder. "Maelgwn, get your sergeants together, and get them to round up the men, and threaten them with death if they're unwilling. Tell them we leave in one hour, and anyone who's left behind will fall foul of the townsfolk. Edwin, get your men back on their horses, they can patrol the main streets. I want the army formed up outside the main gate within the hour. Dafydd, find the officers and tell them what we have decided."

The sergeants, with men they could trust, began the difficult task of rounding up their soldiers, many of whom were already drunk, fight crazed, and were initially reluctant to leave the pillage and rape they considered their just rewards.

The surviving Saxons had gone to ground, hiding wherever they could, and leaving their streets to riotous Welsh soldiers and mangled corpses. For the inexperienced men, who had never left their villages before, this small victory was the greatest adventure of their lives. Few of them had distinguished themselves in the attack on the town, but all were keen to get drunk and take back trophies to their villages.

Those who had been part of Gwriad's former army and those who had fought with Sir Edwin and Prince Anarwd were battle-hardened, and more able to hold their drink. They stole only small things of value that they would not be forced to leave behind. It was these men that were the sergeants and the trusted troops, who violently rounded up the dross of the army.

Eventually, the main body of the soldiers was forced out of the burning town and assembled in ragged columns outside the main gate. Those who protested were severely dealt with by the sergeants who were quick to lash out with clubs, and the cavalry had no hesitation in using the flats of their swords on any who tried to desert. For many of the inexperienced soldiers, this was a frightening turn of events.

Lord Maelgwn had arranged for the destruction of the Saxon barracks, which were soon burning fiercely in the centre of the town and igniting all the surrounding buildings. As he returned to the main gate, with a platoon of hardened troops, he gave his final orders: "Pour oil on the gates! Light them when we leave!" He gazed back at the destruction, hearing the thunder of the burning houses, the screams of women and children, and the manic laughs of the remaining drunken soldiers.

"That will teach the Saxons!" he shouted to his men, as he rode his horse out of the town to join General Gwriad. Behind him, he heard the satisfying whoosh as the oil-soaked gates went up in flames.

He joined the other three generals who, surrounded by their mounted officers, waited patiently while the sergeants enforced a rigid silence. A large moon illuminated the scene as the clouds thinned and the rain abated. Gwriad rode his horse slowly forward to a space where the majority could see him. He looked impressive in the flickering light: his armour gleamed, and he carried a flaming torch in one hand and his drawn sword in the other.

"You are all brave Welshmen!" he bellowed. The officers raised their swords in the air and cheered, and this was taken up by the troops, even those who had been reluctant to leave the town.

"Now we're going to destroy the home of the Saxon devil who burnt down the palace of our great King Gruffydd ap Llywelyn. We will have revenge in his name!" A mighty roar went up from the troops, some of whom were so drunk they could hardly stand.

"To achieve that, we must march while it is still dark!" Gwriad's powerful voice carried over the heads of the assembled army. "We will burn down his home! Destroy his farms! Steal his goods and his animals!" This was greeted with cheers and the thunder of weapons on shields. "Then, with your riches, you will return like heroes back to Wales! Back to your homes and families!" The Welsh soldiers roared. This was what they wanted to hear: their chance of getting back to their villages with more riches than they could earn in a lifetime.

"But first, you have to earn the right!" He waved his sword. "We will march under the cover of darkness, and attack Harold's home before the Saxons know where we've gone! That means you have to march fast, move quietly and look after your weapons! Don't let me down! Don't let yourselves down! Don't let Wales down! And victory will be ours!"

After prolonged cheering, during which many sobered up, and some latecomers were bullied into line, Gwriad and his generals led the army north towards Chester. Edwin sent elements of his cavalry ahead to act as scouts, and others rode in groups behind the individual marching columns, prepared to punish any who attempted to desert. The supply wagons followed on behind with tethered goats and caged fowl stolen from the town, and a small herd of cattle was driven forward by the remaining cavalry who were also acting as rear guards.

Dafydd and Maelgwn had discussed the best route to take, and Gwriad had agreed. "We'll have to risk using their roads whenever possible. I know we are more likely to be noticed, but it's the only way to travel quickly, and the longer we're this side of the border the more likely we are to meet some strong opposition."

"I agree," Dafydd said, "but I don't think we'll get to the Chester area before midday. I've looked at our maps; they all seem to indicate that it will be a long march, longer than we anticipated. On horses we could make it by dawn, but the marching men will be exhausted by midnight." He turned towards his brother. "Before long you will have to call a halt and give the army time to rest, or we won't have a fighting force once we reach Harold's home."

"When we stop, the men must be fed and the animals watered," Lord Edwin said. "An army marches on its stomach. If we expect these men to fight tomorrow, they must be rested and fed."

"Of course," Gwriad answered curtly. He had been hoping that they could march throughout the night and attack at first light. He was worried about being caught in an ambush. "Make sure the scouts have located Harold's manor. We must march directly toward his lands." He rubbed his unshaven face. "Harold's manor is south of Chester. We cannot take Chester; it's too well defended. Nor will we be able to fight off a direct attack from the city's garrison, if they decide to leave their safe walls." He grinned. "I think we can do this, as long as we attack before they expect us. Nobody in their right mind will leave a walled city against unknown enemy forces."

The marching army had not encountered many inhabited places, and those they passed were dark and quiet, with their owners sheltering behind barred doors and praying to their gods that the soldiers would pass. The officers enforced a ban on attacking isolated farms, to ensure the army kept together.

After some hours, it was a reluctant Gwriad who called a halt at a large cleared space, near a fast-flowing stream. It sloped gently and the ground was firm, allowing the men to erect tents. "We'll camp here until first light," he told his officers. "The men can light fires and the cooks can roast the animals we took from the Saxons."

It was a clear, dry night, and the inexperienced men sank down in the grass, grateful for a rest and the chance of food. Many immediately fell asleep, still recovering from the alcohol and exhausted by the fighting and the enforced march. In contrast, the professional soldiers built fires, erected tents, refilled their water bottles and waited patiently for the cooks to provide the food. Within an hour, the roasted meat was being doled out on stale bread platters with a covering of thick soup. Long lines of men formed up, carefully controlled by their sergeants.

Eventually, everyone was fed, the fires died down, and new sentries were posted. "At first light, sound the trumpets," Gwriad ordered. "We must reach the Chester area before the Saxons know where we're heading."

He joined the other generals in his tent. "Things are improving, even the weather is on our side, at last!" he yelled, as he burst through the entrance. There was a sound of snoring, and he realized he was the only one awake.

. . .

At first light, the trumpets sounded and the sergeants rushed about screaming abuse and kicking out at any soldier who was not on his feet.

"The scouts have returned, m'Lord," Sir Maelgwn announced, bursting in to the command tent. "They've found Harold's manor, it's well fortified, and there seemed to be plenty of soldiers on guard."

"Could the Saxons have been warned already?"

"It's possible, but the scouts didn't report any unusual activity in the area. Certainly, they didn't see any large movement of troops."

"We're ready to march," Dafydd said. "We could be there by midday." He noted Gwriad's worried face. "I don't think the Saxons can have mustered their forces yet, although it's likely that those defending Harold's fortification, might be prepared for us."

Gwriad nodded. "Send out fresh scouts to patrol on all sides as we march. I agree, Dafydd, I don't think the chance of an ambush is likely, as long as we move quickly." He winced as he remembered that if it had not been for Dafydd they might still be trying to assemble their men outside Shrewsbury.

He turned to Lord Edwin: "I want you to keep your cavalry in reserve and defend the supply train; Maelgwn, keep the scouts constantly reporting. I want some on long-range reconnaissance and others keeping close to the army."

As the two men marched off, he turned to Dafydd: "What's the matter with me? Edwin and Maelgwn don't need to be told to do what they've already been doing."

"You're just worried." Dafydd placed a hand on his shorter brother's shoulder. "We both know that so much of this attack depends on good luck. We've been lucky so far, even the weather's improved."

"We lost too many men in yesterday's battle. Needless deaths. If it hadn't been for the cavalry and our seasoned soldiers, the army would have fallen apart." He buckled on his sword, lost in thought. "If we meet strong resistance today, we could have a problem with deserters."

"When we're within sight of the manor, give one of your speeches," Dafydd said encouragingly. "Tell them that if they fight well and break through the manor's defences, they'll be rich men. Remind them that if they get drunk we'll leave them behind and the Saxons will cut them in pieces." He picked up his helmet. "It would be good to have the men march back into Wales like an army and not a defeated mob." He looked out at the soldiers forming up in ordered lines under the supervision of the sergeants, who raced around like sheep dogs, yapping at their heels. "Perhaps, we won't have to fight?"

"Not fight?" Gwriad queried.

"I'll tell you my idea as we ride ahead." Dafydd said. "We might be lucky again."

CHAPTER SIX

"**W**ell, look at our monster-killing Jon, in his new tunic!"
"Our Lady Angharad's little puppy!"

Jon glared at the two youths who had suddenly appeared as he was saddling up the horse that Lord Gwriad had given him. He knew the tall, flaxen-haired youth as Owen, and the thickset, bullying one, as Davis. Most of the time he was able to avoid them, but this was not the first occasion they had tried to provoke a fight.

It was many weeks since he had killed the boar, and become Lord Gwriad's squire, but he was still in training, and spent his time with the Lady Angharad, Father Williams and Sergeant Penn. When the Lord had departed on his campaign against the Saxons, Jon had been denied the chance to go with him. Although Lord Gwriad had been willing to take him, Angharad had protested Jon's lack of training. "He's not ready," she had argued. "Let Penn and Father Williams work on him. He will be of more use to you on your return."

Although Jon had been desperate to accompany his Lord, his inability to do so had been interpreted by some as evidence that he was weak, and only suitable as the Lady's pet.

"I see you, Owen, and you, Davis," he said quietly.

Jon had known that eventually he would have to fight them. It was the one thing they respected, and he knew it was only their fear of Angharad that had held them in check. In recent days he had felt more confident; he no longer feared Penn, and only yesterday had matched him sword for sword in his training, and had heard him muttering: "Bloody Hell, I'm getting too old for this."

Jon had put on weight and muscle with his regular meals and exercise, and he no longer felt inferior to those around him. Even Father Williams had been pleased with his progress. Jon felt the time had come.

"What did you say?" Owen growled, moving to the side of the stall, where Jon was tightening his horse's girth. Because of the animal, Davis could not enter, and watched in open-mouth anticipation as Owen rushed forward, his hands formed in fists. There was a brief tussle, and Owen staggered back and collapsed on the muck in front of Davis. He sat holding his face with both hands, and groaning; there was blood trickling between his fingers. "He's broke m'nose," Owen whimpered.

"I'll get you!" Davis yelled and, pushing the horse to one side, he attempted to attack Jon, who was still marvelling at the effect of his random punch. Unfortunately for Davis, the horse was upset by his action, and as he tried to level a punch at Jon, it moved against him and stamped down on his foot. Davis let out a cry, jumped back on one foot and tripped over Owen. The two youths lay tangled in straw and horse turds.

Jon backed his horse out of its stall and yelled, "Move out of my way, or my horse will trample you!" The two youths quickly rolled over in the muck as Jon led his horse out of the stable. "I wouldn't try that again!" he yelled as he mounted his horse. He smiled as he heard the muffled cursing from the stables. It was a great day in his life, and he felt certain that the story of the fight would soon get around the castle. He was confident that Owen would not risk another encounter.

When he reached Llanduduch, he felt as happy as he had ever felt. A fisherman doffed his cap to him, and he realized that being the rider of a horse conferred on him a huge social advantage: only powerful people owned a horse. He pulled up by the side of the man.

"Is that you, Jon?" the fisherman asked, scratching his head. "I remember you when your father were alive." He replaced his hat. "He'd be proud to see you now, boy."

"My father never cared for me," Jon answered quietly. He

IN THE ASHES OF A DREAM

dismounted from his horse, and offered his hand to the man. "You're Jenkins, aren't you?"

Jenkins took his hand. "You've changed, Jon. Hard to believe it's you." He stared hard at Jon, and smiled. "Good for you, boy."

"You were one of the few people who was ever kind to me," Jon said. He felt strangely emotional. "The Gwbert was a sorry place, and I was the bottom of the pile, but you always treated me well."

"It were nothing, isn't it," Jenkins muttered. He seemed lost for words. "Mistress Philips died last week. There weren't many as had a good word for her." He shuffled his feet. "I knows she treated you bad."

"That's all passed," Jon said. "Lord Gwriad is training me as his squire."

Jenkins looked amazed.

"If you ever need my help, Jenkins, let me know. I'd like to repay your kindness to me."

The fisherman nodded, straightened his shoulders, and without a word strode off to his hovel. Jon rested his head against the hot belly of the horse, conscious of the fact that he had made an empty promise to the man and, without meaning to, somehow had insulted him.

Later, in the warm house of the priest, he tried to explain what had happened. Father Williams nodded and refreshed his own wine. "You have to understand, Jon, Jenkins is older than you, much older. He is a naturally kind man, but here you are, once the lowest in the social order, offering to help him." Father Williams patted Jon's hand. "This man has very little except his pride: which is based on his ability to feed himself and his family. You have shown him what might be possible, and then you, who had been a person whom he could use as a measure of his own success, offered to help him." Father Williams slowly shook his head.

"But I meant it!" Jon protested. "I wanted him to know I would help him if he needed help."

"Jenkins did not see it that way. He thought you were lording it over him, and he never believed you would ever help him to keep his house and feed his family."

Jon stared miserably down at his hands. "What can I do to

make it better? Jenkins is a good man, I would like to repay him, in some way, for his friendship."

Father Williams sipped his wine. "What did Jenkins do for you? Did he help you to leave the awful hovel in which you lived? Did he offer to speak to the odious Mistress Philips about the way she treated you? Did he speak to your drunken father? No, he was just kinder to you than most other people. Your thanks were enough." He passed some bread and water to Jon. "In Confession, I will try to explain to him that you meant well." He reached for one of the books by his side. "Time for reading." He burped quietly as he passed the book towards Jon. "Today, we'll start on Ovid, and then you can practise your writing while I have a nap."

• • •

WITH THE SERGEANTS SCREAMING ABUSE, and the cavalry urging them to close ranks, the Welsh soldiers formed up in powerful cohorts and in full view of the soldiers defending Harold's fortified home, but out of the range of their arrows. The fortification was bigger than the Welsh officers had expected, and it was clear that it was a refuge for local farmers. The roofs of numerous buildings could be glimpsed beyond a strong palisade, with a deep ditch in front; the main gate was strong and appeared well defended. It was after midday, and Gwriad was becoming increasingly concerned that a strong Saxon force could be on its way from Chester.

"Send them our proposals," Gwriad ordered, and watched anxiously as five riders approached the fortifications with a white flag. "I hope this works," he turned to his brother, "or I might lose some good officers." He tried to make a joke of it, but both knew that a lot depended on their successful negotiations.

"What about Ealdgyth? Do we leave her here?"

"If she's in there, which I doubt, I intend to leave her. She has no place with us anymore. Angharad considers her a traitor and despises her cowardliness, and I don't intend to take her hostage, in case Harold doesn't want her back." He gave a scornful laugh. "Knowing Ealdgyth, she will have left as soon as she heard we were coming. Unlike the others in there, she has nothing to lose." He patted his horse. "I imagine her use to Harold will have vanished with the failure of the letter."

Dafydd watched intently as the small band approached the main gate. "We have offered the Saxons the chance to live. If you were in that basic fort and saw our huge army in front of you, would you fight to the death for a leader who was not there, or would you agree to leave the fort and live?" He sat motionless on his horse. "Our problem will be ensuring that the Saxon warriors can evacuate safely, and that we protect their women and children."

He shook his head in disagreement. "Our biggest problems will be destroying Harold's home before we get ambushed, and then achieving an ordered retreat. We might have to fight before we reach the border." Gwriad shifted excitedly on his saddle.

"If the Saxons agree to leave that fort, there are many of our men who will be seeking their blood," Dafydd predicted.

"The sergeants have been warned," Gwriad said dismissively. "Let's just hope those Saxons agree." He gazed up at the overcast sky. "If they decide to fight, it could be dark by the time we overwhelm them. It makes it difficult to arrange an orderly retreat."

"They'll choose our offer. They've farmers, servants and children in there, not just soldiers," Dafydd said.

They sat silently watching the events. There was a brief exchange of words at the gate, and a long pause. Eventually, one side of the main gate opened and the Welsh officers disappeared inside. After another long pause, the Welsh officers reappeared and galloped back. "They have agreed to your proposals, my Lord," the senior officer gasped and nodded his head to Gwriad. "However, they ask to be allowed to keep their weapons to defend themselves and their families."

Gwriad looked at Dafydd and Lord Edwin. "I'm against them keeping their weapons," he said. "They could use them to attack us as we retreat."

"They won't agree to leave the fort otherwise," Dafydd said quietly. "If you were in their shoes, would you walk out into an army of Saxons, with your family and no weapons?" He shook his head. "Let them feel safe. Let them keep their weapons. I'm certain they want to survive rather than die for a Lord who isn't here."

"I agree," Lord Edwin nodded. "I don't believe they'll risk their lives against such a large army. Let them keep their weapons."

"Indeed," said General Maelgwn. "We came to destroy Harold's mansion and grab his wealth. Let them keep their weapons." He pointed to the cavalry. "Our men can shepherd them along part of the road to Chester. They will also be well-placed to warn us of any Saxon counterattack."

Gwriad nodded thoughtfully, pursed his lips and stared at the fort. He turned to the officer. "Go back and tell them we will agree to their request, but they must understand that for their own safety, they will stand together over there," he pointed to some water-logged fields at the side of the fort. "After we have ransacked this place and set it alight the army will then retreat, led by the scouts, and the cavalry will guard the prisoners until we are out of sight." The officer saluted. "Remind them they must not take any goods with them, and that includes jewellery. Tell them we will kill anyone who disobeys!"

Edwin walked his horse alongside Gwriad's. "I'll use the cavalry to escort them from the fort to the field; we'll have more control than if we allowed the foot soldiers to guard them."

Gwriad nodded, and as the officer and his party turned their horses to leave, he stopped them. "Tell them they must leave the fort immediately, and all weapons must be carried on their backs or in their belts. Any person who takes a weapon in his or her hands will be killed. Make that clear!"

The officer saluted again.

Edwin moved off with him. He was relieved there was to be no unnecessary shedding of blood.

"It'll be difficult letting some men loose to plunder the main buildings and animal sheds, while expecting others to stand back and prepare to destroy the fort," Dafydd said quietly. "It would be different if they all had to fight their way in, but the buildings will be empty, and to many of them this is their big chance for unimagined wealth. We know there will be very little there, but they don't. They could easily become a mob, fighting each other."

IN THE ASHES OF A DREAM

Gwriad glowered, then his face relaxed. "You're right. I hadn't thought it through."

"Here's what I suggest," Dafydd said in a low voice that others could not hear. "While the cavalry escort the Saxons to the field, order the officers to get our men to form up in approximately three groups. Instruct the officers and their sergeants to spread the word that they are one of three groups. Tell them we have drawn lots: that always sounds fair." He coughed apologetically. "When they are in their groups, tell them only group one will be allowed to pillage the town. Group two will round up all the animals and the farming tools, and group three will be allowed to attack any Saxon settlements on our way back to the border. We, that means you and I, will reward the cavalry."

Gwriad stared at his brother in disbelief. "Are you mad?"

"Can you come up with a better plan that will prevent our soldiers fighting each other for something to take back to their families?" Dafydd's voice had become louder and more assertive. "You don't have the money to pay them, and at this moment we are likely to release an army of excited men who will destroy the fort, the citizens and each other!" Dafydd had suddenly become a dominant force whose logic seemed irrefutable. "Without order, our army will destroy itself, and your dreams of a powerful Wales will be over!"

Gwriad glared at his brother, looked away, and took a deep breath. Then, suddenly, he was issuing planning orders to his officers in a cool, detailed voice, and the plan was Dafydd's.

· · ·

HOURS LATER, THE TIRED SOLDIERS of the straggling, retreating army were forced to halt when they were still some distance from the Welsh borderlands. It was pitch black, except for the occasional glow of distant fires, and the weather had changed again. Rain, which had started as drizzle, had become torrential, turning the ground into a quagmire. The men were struggling across rough land, over bare, rock-strewn mountains and through fast-moving streams. This alternated with densely-treed forests in steep, narrow valleys. It was impossible to continue until dawn arrived.

The third group had marched away quickly, as soon as the fort was in flames, keen to find any Saxon farms and hamlets before nightfall; they had had mixed success. Their officers had agreed to allow them to disperse in manageable platoons that had soon become confused and dissipated. Some had discovered empty hovels where the owners had recently fled for their lives, leaving the remains of a meagre meal and little else. Others had met with spirited opposition, where Saxon warriors, aided by their wives, had fought to the death, and in some cases repulsed the disorganized rabble that some elements of the scattered third group had become. The scouts had eventually managed to locate most of the disparate Welsh soldiers, and lead them to their gathering point on a bare, low hillside. Around them, the dark landscape was faintly illuminated with the red glow of burning hovels, and Gwriad was concerned the fires presented a clear signpost to any Saxon soldiers as to the Welsh army's whereabouts.

With the arrival of the supply wagons, some covers had been erected, but the majority of the soldiers stood or squatted in small groups, enduring the rain, and stoically waiting for dawn. They cursed the weather and their officers, and boasted about their success or moaned about their lack of it.

The second group had arrived next, encumbered by farm animals and urged along by their officers. Although some had benefitted from stealing carts and farm horses that they could ride, the majority were dragging unwilling cows and pigs, or carrying terrified chickens and ducks. Young farmers carried captured pitchforks, spades and rakes, while others worked in teams to push heavy handcarts and drag ploughs.

The first group, the last to arrive, had wanted to stay longer in the doomed fort. For them it had been a once-in-a-lifetime chance to find instant riches, and they had been unwilling to leave when the trumpets sounded. Earlier, the officers, under Gwriad's orders, had entered Harold's mansion with an elite squad of soldiers, before the rest were allowed in. They had collected the silver ornaments, the pewter plates and goblets, and the fine linens, together with Harold's collection of weapons. "This will help pay towards the cost of this expedition," Gwriad said firmly. "Find a wagon, and take this stuff away beyond these fortifications and guard it. I will reward each of you." He and the officers then left the building, allowing it to be ransacked by the rest of the soldiers.

The men struggled to get through the doors, racing about like demented children, grabbing chairs and stools and, finding them too heavy, and dropping them for easier loot. The well-stocked kitchen was quickly stripped, and the food devoured. A few soldiers had found the wine cellar and, unable to resist the opportunity, had drunk themselves unconscious, and had been unable to escape when the building was torched.

The nearby structures had been cleared of everything of value, but it was not until later that it became clear that the captive Saxon women had hidden their gold ornaments on their bodies, confident that they would not be searched. When the trumpets blared, the Welsh soldiers had reluctantly fled the fortification as oil covered structures went up in flames and the wooden ramparts were consumed by the fire. For some it had been a bitter disappointment.

The encircled Saxons had watched the destruction with mounting anger, and only the presence of women and children had prevented them from attempting a breakout.

Eventually, the Welsh officers had managed to achieve some semblance of order and marched the last of the men away, along with a few heavily loaded wagons. The cavalry continued to circle the prisoners long after the last flickering torch light had disappeared into the darkness.

Lord Edwin ordered a Saxon-speaking soldier to tell the male captives to sit down on the waterlogged field. "Tell them they must not move until we are out of sight." The Saxon men reluctantly obeyed; they wanted revenge, but they also wanted their families to survive.

"It's almost dark," Edwin observed. "Time to move off." He looked at the flattened earth, the mud and the deep ruts of the wagons that led towards the west. "It's never difficult to follow an army." He urged his horse forward and was quickly followed by the majority of his cavalry, although some had to fight their way out of the field, as Saxon soldiers tried to rush them.

• • •

Harold had insisted on returning to Dover. He could have ordered the ship to sail up the Thames to London, but he was unsure of the political situation, and docking at Dover allowed him time to send out messages to his supporters and quickly assemble a small guard.

"What will you do now, my Lord?" Lidmann asked tentatively, as they rode quickly towards London. He had lived for days in a state of fear. He was not a brave man, and had only accompanied Harold on his trip to Antwerp because it had seemed a relatively safe way of advancing his ambitions. His mother, Aethelinda, who had survived his father, was a proud and authoritarian woman who had predicted that Harold would be the next King of England, and that her only son must use, to his own benefit, his late father's reputation with Earl Harold.

"Your father's name will mean nothing once Harold is King," she had insisted. "You must show the Earl how you support him while he is still a hopeful for the throne." His mother was always right, and Lidmann had ingratiated himself with Harold's small group of supporters. Going to Antwerp had seemed a logical move,

"Do?" Harold bellowed. "I will report to the King, and tell him I have arranged for my brother's release!" He roared with laughter.

Lidmann nodded enthusiastically. His legs, unaccustomed to riding for some weeks, were aching, and he was finding it increasingly difficult to keep up with the Earl. Over the weeks in prison, and during the following journey, he had found Harold to be a bully, given to violent tantrums and capable of changing from a friendly, hospitable man to a roaring, violent demon. Lidmann suspected he had not measured up to Harold's expectations, and wished he had never agreed to try to be part of his inner circle. "And then?"

"We'll go back to my home near Chester, and wait for the self-righteous old bastard to die." He turned to Lidmann, who was unable to prevent the shock on his face. "Everyone dies you know, no matter how holy they might pretend to be!" He suddenly glared at Lidmann. "When we get back to my home, you can return to yours. I've been grateful for your support, but you're not the sort of tight-arsed fart I would have chosen to be my companion." He gave a dismissive laugh and galloped off, leaving Lidmann, and the rest of the Earl's party, to follow.

Lidmann sniffed as he tried to keep up with the rest of the company: his head was thumping, and his tired legs were on fire. Worst of all, he realized that his awful experiences with Harold had counted for nothing. "I hope he falls off his bloody horse," he mumbled, knowing that his mother would not have been impressed.

• • •

"I've just had a messenger arrive with a letter from Dafydd!" Teifryn said excitedly, as she rushed into the main hall.

"Hush, love," said Angharad gently, "your baby sleeps." She carefully returned the sleeping child to its crib; she enjoyed being a surrogate mother, and was grateful to Teifryn for providing her with the chance. She gave a final lingering smile at Tegwen. Dafydd had chosen the name, and Teifryn had agreed, and the child showed every chance of being, as the name implied, lovely.

"They've sacked Shrewsbury, and burnt Harold's fort to the ground!" Teifryn said enthusiastically, "and they're on their way home."

"Thank God for that." Angharad stared at the fire. She took a deep breath and exhaled in a long-drawn-out sigh. "I didn't want Gwriad to be involved in this. We have few enough soldiers we can rely on; we're still recovering from our defeat. If Lord Edwin hadn't arrived, Gwriad wouldn't have thought of doing such a risky attack." She turned to Teifryn. "I know Dafydd wasn't very keen."

"No, you're right, but they're brothers, and Dafydd has always looked up to his older brother, and sees his role as Gwriad's right-hand man."

"It's true," Angharad sighed. "I also know that when Gwriad is not doing something physical, he drinks too much. But I'd prefer a drunken husband to a dead hero," she laughed. "At least he's sober most of the time."

"It's a truth; they're like two halves of the same coin: each providing what the other lacks."

"How long has the messenger taken to get here?"

"He says it was five nights ago, including the evening when he set off."

"So, they were still in Saxon lands when Dafydd sent the message?" Angharad twisted the ornate gold ring around her finger. "Things could still go wrong."

"That's not like you." Teifryn placed her arm around Angharad's waist, and rested her head on the older woman's shoulder. "You're normally the optimistic one who will take on the world."

"I never wanted them to go. I had a dream about this campaign," she turned to look into Teifryn's eyes. "I never told you, because it was too vivid."

"Go on."

"You and I were running away from something, it was dark, and we were lost. We were taking it in turns to carry Tegwen. There was a lot of noise, and an awful thing was catching up with us." She stopped and rubbed her face. "It's has been on my mind." She walked back to the fire.

"Do you believe in dreams?"

"Sometimes. I've had this one twice. It's so vivid, I wake up with my heart pounding."

"Well, you haven't woken me," Teifryn jested. She preferred sharing a bed with Angharad while the men were away.

"That was what convinced me I had not been screaming. In the dream we were both screaming." She paced about. "When I was a small girl I used to get powerful dreams, and I would tell my mother about them. I dreamed my dog would be killed by wolves, and it was. I dreamed that men would attack our house, and two outlaws did try to break into our home, but my father and his servants killed them."

"Did you tell your mother of your dream?"

"Yes. She told my father, who joked about it and called me his little witch. But after it happened, my sister, Ealdgyth, who was jealous of me, told other children in the village, and they would yell out that I was a witch. There was one particularly, spiteful girl, Ealdgyth's best friend, who threw cattle dung at me. I was so cross, I grabbed her and threw her into the village stream and threatened to drown her if she ever called me a witch again." Angharad gave a sad laugh. "Then, I caught Ealdgyth in the stables, where she was hiding from me. I tied her hands behind her back and roped her to a post. Because it was summer, I knew she was not wearing any undergarments, so I dragged her smock over her head, and said I was going to get all the boys to have a look."

"You didn't, did you?" Teifryn stared at her, appalled by the thought.

"No, but she didn't know that. I left her sobbing away, and unable to see if anyone was there. Just to teach her a lesson, I ran backwards and forwards, yelling: 'Come and have a look, boys!' Then I untied her and told her that if she ever called me a witch again, I really would involve the boys. We were not loving sisters."

Teifryn started to giggle. "I'm seeing you in a different light. But then again, when I think how Ealdgyth turned out when she was a grown woman, I think you had every right to stand up for yourself." She paused as the baby moved, burped and went back to sleep. "Did your father get to know about it?"

"Oh yes, but he never involved himself in childish things. My mother was the one who was outraged when Ealdgyth told her. It was the only time she ever thrashed me, and for good measure she thrashed Ealdgyth as well."

"It's not nice to call someone a witch." Sometimes Teifryn sounded like a young girl. "When a woman calls another woman a whore, the men just grin, but you call some old woman a witch, and things get nasty, very quickly. Some priests encourage it; it's frightening."

"It's ignorance that's what it is, and it's not only old women who are accused. Some men can't abide being shown up. The wise women are healers, but some priests and some so-called doctors feel threatened by their knowledge," she shrugged. "At least we have an intelligent priest. Father Williams is a good man, although

I suspect he doesn't believe everything he teaches. Did Dafydd say anything else?" she asked, changing the subject.

Teifryn held up the scroll. "Dafydd also wrote that he was sure the Saxons would seek revenge, but he was convinced they wouldn't come this far. However, he did warn us about the chance of a Pictish attack; it's that time of the year."

"The last attack was on Llanduduch in 1052. That's when our husbands helped defeat them. Just think, that was only 12 years ago, and they were just boys." Angharad grinned. "My husband's still a boy!" She raised her eyebrows. "In some ways."

"Do you think we should remind Father Williams of the possibility?"

"It wouldn't do any harm. I'll send Jon with a message." She quietly opened the main door. Outside Rhodri was sitting on the step, his spear by the side of him. His eyes were closed as he dozed in the afternoon sun. "I'm so glad you're looking after our safety!" Angharad roared.

Rhodri jumped to his feet, tripped on his spear and staggered awkwardly down the remaining steps. "Sorry, m'Lady. Very sorry. Just um…" he stuttered into silence.

"Who's guarding the main gate?"

"Um, Davis and Owen, m'Lady." He adjusted his helmet.

"Where's Hywel?"

"Hywel?" He did a good impression of never having heard of him. "Um. Oh, Hywel? …Yes, he's gone to the jakes, m'Lady."

"So, I wouldn't find him in the kitchen then?"

"The kitchen?" He looked away, unable to meet Angharad's angry stare. "He… um, he might have looked in, m'Lady."

"Tell him to report to me as soon as he returns, and if he can't find me, he's to keep looking until he does! You will both take on extra guard duties until you begin to behave like guards!" She sounded outraged, but in fact she was enjoying herself. She noticed Davis and Owen suddenly appear at the open main gate, and faces looked out from the stables. "I want the gates closed at all times!" she roared. "You will all assemble in the courtyard before supper, except for Megan the cook!"

IN THE ASHES OF A DREAM

She stormed back into the main hall, slamming the door behind her. Teifryn stared wide-eyed and Tegwen protested loudly.

"I enjoyed that," Angharad said. "Every time Gwriad is away, the castle goes to pot. The boys are sulking because they wanted to go on the raid. It never occurs to them that they might have got themselves killed or have lost a limb. Penn is delighted to have stayed; he's born lazy and he finds even training Jon too much like hard work. We have a few older men who do their best, but the castle is undermanned, and there are only a handful of useful men left in Aberteifi. I'm convinced Gwriad never considered the fact that we might get attacked while he and his little army was away. Enthusiasm and alcohol is a deadly combination."

"We haven't been attacked for 12 years, I think it highly unlikely we'll be attacked in the next week or so."

"That was because of Gruffydd ap Llywelyn. Our enemies were afraid of us when we had a King who ruled the whole of Wales, but now they see us as a defeated nation, and easy pickings for the sea wolves." She shook her shoulders, releasing the tension. "Anyway, it will be a useful policy to get everyone worried, it'll keep them on their toes."

CHAPTER SEVEN

The weather improved in the early hours of the morning, promising a warm, sunny day. As a pink dawn illuminated the camp, a tired scout galloped towards the guards, and was taken immediately to the officers' tent. Maelgwn was standing outside, stretching his aching limbs after an uncomfortable night. He watched, suddenly alert, as the rider climbed slowly off his horse and staggered as he attempted to walk towards him.

"Help him!" he ordered two guards, and opened the flap of the tent as the exhausted man was supported and led to a campstool just inside.

Dafydd grabbed a leather canteen and the scout drank gratefully. He cleared his voice and tried to get up as Gwriad approached. "Stay seated," Gwriad said quietly. "Give me your message."

"There's a large force of Saxons approaching from the south, m'Lord," he paused as a fit of coughing racked his body. He drank from the canteen, and continued on: "I reckon they've come from the Shrewsbury area. Mainly marching men, carrying banners and well armed.

"How many?" Gwriad's voice betrayed his anxiety.

"Maybe two hundred or more. I can't be certain. I came across them before dusk. I trotted over a hill, and there they were, coming towards me." He began to cough, drank some more, and continued. "They were marching fast. I had little time to look carefully; 'cos they were only about 500 paces away. Then, some riders saw me, and I galloped off. They gave chase for a while, and gave up when it got dark."

"How far away do you think they were?"

"If they knew the area, and marched all night, they could be

IN THE ASHES OF A DREAM

here shortly. I got lost in the dark, m'Lord, and it were difficult to find you."

Gwriad nodded. "Good man. You've done well." He patted the scout on the shoulders. "Get him some food and somewhere to rest." He breathed out loudly as the guards helped the scout out of the tent.

"Our worst nightmare," he said, grimly. "We could be caught between two armies."

"Two hundred men!" Maelgwn made a dismissive noise. "We have nearly ten times that many."

"We lost many good men at Shrewsbury," Dafydd cautioned, "perhaps more than we think. Our men are tired and burdened down with their bits of loot. They're not an army I would chose to take into battle, but," he opened his hands, "we appear to have no choice."

Gwriad nodded his head. He turned to Lord Edwin, "I want you to divide the scouts. We've been concentrating on the north, now we must focus on the south. The scouts must locate the enemy and keep me supplied with the latest news. We must know how long we have." Edwin nodded and prepared to leave.

"Round up the sergeants immediately," he said to Maelgwn, as he fastened on his sword, "I want to speak to them, then I want you to be in charge of moving the camp. It'll be a problem getting the supply wagons moving, and keeping the animals together." He punched him gently on the chest. "I can only ask you to do your best, Maelgwn."

"I won't let you down, my Lord." He grabbed his helmet and strode out of the tent. The prospect of action excited him.

"Dafydd, we'll take a small force of the cavalry, and gallop ahead. I want to judge the lay of the land for myself. We'll leave as soon as I have spoken to the sergeants. Edwin, you'll be in overall charge while I'm away." Dafydd could see he was suddenly enjoying himself.

"Don't be too long, Gwriad," Edwin observed. "The men lose heart when they see their general galloping away before a battle."

Gwriad glared at Edwin who smiled back. "Just a plea for you to get back soon, my friend." He strode out of the tent and began calling for the scouts.

"He's got a good point," Dafydd said as he signalled for a guard to help him don his chain mail. "Perhaps it would be best if you took General Maelgwn. I'll stay here and support Lord Edwin. The fact that he used their formal titles was not lost on Gwriad.

"You're right," he said, and hugged his brother. "I'll feel happier with you in charge while I'm away," he coughed, "you know what I mean."

• • •

THEY WERE WITHIN SIGHT OF Offa's Dyke, known to the Welsh as Clawdd Offa, where it snaked between the borders of Wales and Saxon lands. In some parts, the ancient earth mound was more than twenty paces wide and one and a half times the height of a man, and ran from the edge of the northern coastline of Wales near Chester, south to the start of the Severn estuary. On the Welsh side was a deep ditch, and on the Saxon side the excavated material formed a high barrier from the top of which much of Wales could be seen. In parts, farmers had, over many years, cleared gaps through which they could move animals, as unlike their rulers, they lived in relative harmony with their neighbours.

Gwriad and Maelgwn sat on their horses and looked down from a steep hill, while the guard waited impatiently below. It was warm in the midday sun, and the clear air allowed them to see for miles. On the Welsh side, a wide section of the dyke had been demolished, and the ditch had been partially filled in. "Wherever there's high ground along the route of the Dyke, you notice it's always been built along the low ground on the Welsh side," Gwriad said, "allowing the Saxons to hold the tactical advantage. This is ideal ground for an ambush, and we must ensure that we either get the whole army over and well beyond our borders, or we must choose to hold the high ground on this side if we have to fight two armies." He pointed to the gap in the dyke. "This would be a good place to cross."

"Indeed," Maelgwn nodded thoughtfully. Looking back down a wide valley, he could see the black smudge of their army in the far distance. "We're heading west as fast as we can, and while it's possible that the Saxons could attempt to attack us on both sides, we've seen none of their scouts."

"Last night our retreat was clearly marked with burning farm buildings. It won't be difficult for them to follow." Gwriad stared hard at the hills to the south. "I want you to take the majority of this guard, and find a suitable place where the cavalry can assemble. It must be near here and to the south. It should allow them a clear view of the advance of any enemy forces, but provide them with some cover and the chance of ambush. When you find such a place, send back some riders immediately to guide me back. In the meantime, if you see any sign of Saxon formations, return at once and leave a small force to shadow them."

"What will you do?"

"I'll return and give Edwin command of the rear guard, mainly archers, and he'll defend the wagons. When you return you'll command the foot soldiers. If you're forced to remain here, Dafydd will take charge of the army. If you see the enemy, you'll return and take over while Dafydd and I lead the cavalry, and try to ambush the Saxon force that we know is somewhere over there."

He led the way down the steep hill, chose three men that he knew, and galloped back down the valley towards his distant army. Maelgwn instructed his troop, and led the way south up into high ground, with Clawdd Offa on their right.

• • •

JON WAS FEELING PLEASED WITH himself. It was one of those perfect days, when his unhurried ride to Llanduduch had been enhanced by the feel of the warm air, the sounds of the birds and the constant, and reassuring, roar of the river. When he reached the village a fisher girl of about his own age had smiled at him, and to cap it all, Father Williams continued to be pleased with his progress.

"You're looking well, Jon," Father Williams observed as his pupil entered the warm house. "Exercise and education are a fine combination. It's hard to recognize you as the skinny waif I first met." He indicated a stool. "You've taken to writing remarkably quickly, and your reading is coming on." He sipped his wine. "If I didn't know who it was, I'd have said you must have a good teacher." He chuckled.

"Oh, I have Father. The best!" John answered passionately, unaware that the old priest was teasing him.

"Thank you, my son." He turned to look down at the village. "Were the boats out when you arrived?"

"Yes, Father."

"What was the tide doing?"

Jon stared quickly out of the window. "It was coming in."

"Where are the fishermen, do you think?"

"They'll be returning on the full tide."

"Why?"

Jon frowned. "Because it's easier to get up river at full tide, Father."

"Exactly." The old priest rose slowly from his chair and walked outside, beckoning Jon to follow. He paused in front of the church, and both stood in the sun and enjoyed the panorama. Below, was the ancient village with its disparate houses that appeared to be scattered willy-nilly about the steep hillside. Although most had solid slate roofs, the majority were poor wooden hovels with a single room, and only a few houses had their sleeping quarters on a second floor. These households, if they possessed animals, would keep them overnight in the lower level, providing both security against wolves, and animal heat in the building. The occupants soon became immune to the smell.

On such a peaceful day, the village looked idyllic from above, with its colourful blue roofs, its grassy centre around a communal fire pit and its winding path that led down to the steep bank of the river. At the lower end of the village, they could see the partial stockade that fortified the stone steps descending to a shallow harbour where the fishermen's small boats were kept.

Even at full tide, the only way for a surprise attack from the river was up the stone steps, as the clinging mud and the steep banks prevented any other approach.

"Our river provides security against attack on an outgoing tide, but it's ideal for a fast passage upstream on a flood," Father

IN THE ASHES OF A DREAM

Williams glared down at the distant flood plain that resembled an inland lake and, beyond it, the placid blue sea shimmered in the sunlight. "It's the same for our fisherman: they leave on the ebb tide, but must stay out until the flood tide is well advanced." He turned to Jon. "Where is the big danger do you think?"

Jon raised his eyebrows. "I don't know, Father." He realized that more was expected of him. "Um, well…" He suddenly understood: "If raiders attacked on a day like today, there would be very few men to fight them off. They'd all be fishing!"

"Exactly. Well done, Jon. However, there is an even worse scenario," he paused, noting Jon's look of incomprehension, "a worse thing that could happen to us. What is that?"

"Worse?" Jon shook his head.

"On a day like this one, when the men are fishing in the bay or waiting to return up river, they would be easy prey to any raiders. Those wolves, in their long, multi-oared fighting ships would easily destroy our men in their small boats. And remember, our fishermen have only their knives and no armour, and these murderers are dressed for battle."

"I thought Lord Gwriad had provided them with weapons?"

"Have you ever been out fishing in those boats?"

"Once or twice. I went out with my father," Jon swallowed.

"Did you enjoy it?"

"No. I was scared," he admitted. "Those small boats can easily turn over. I was certain we were going to drown."

"Can you imagine the fisherman wearing armour or carrying weapons in those boats?"

"No, Father," he paused. "Then, with our fishermen destroyed, the raiders would know the village was undefended, and would be able to attack before a warning was given." He looked uncomfortable, no longer feeling pleased with life. "What can be done?"

"What indeed." Father Williams burped gently. "We're better off if they attack at night. Our men don't fish at night, and we can defend ourselves. But, today would be a perfect time for them."

"What does Lord Gwriad suggest?"

"Unlike me, I doubt if he's thought about it." Father Williams scanned the distant horizon one last time. "I want you to return to the castle, and tell Lady Angharad about our conversation. She can raise it with her husband when he returns." He turned to walk back to his house. "Although I think Lord Dafydd will take it more seriously."

"When do you think they'll return, Father Williams?"

"Who knows? Let's hope they do return."

"Is there a chance they might not?" Jon asked anxiously.

"Indeed there is." The elderly monk glanced at the boy's worried face. "I tend to forget how limited is your experience of life, my son. Eventually, I'm going to let you read Tacitus, when you are able. He will give you the history of the Roman campaigns. In the meantime, I will start to explain to you how wars are conducted and what might happen in our Lord's little raid on the Saxons. Oh, yes," he looked reflectively down at the river, "and I'll explain to you how the Pictish warriors could attack the castle. We'll start tomorrow."

• • •

It was late morning when Maelgwn and his guard reached a high, bare summit overlooking a range of lower hills. In some valleys, the recent rain had turned small creeks into cascading torrents, swelling the shallow streams into short-lived rivers. "Rest the horses," he said as he climbed wearily off his mount. It had been many days since he had slept well, and he had been riding for hours.

His horse guards were grateful, and immediately dismounted, sank down on the ground, and drank deeply from their leather water flasks. It was hot, and the clear blue sky had almost magically replaced the storm clouds of yesterday. "We'll water the horses when we get lower," he said as he paced slowly about, exercising his tired legs. "Keep your eyes open for any sign of movement, Meredith!" he ordered, nudging a soldier who was lying on his back. "We're here to find the enemy, not sleep, man."

"Yes, sir." The soldier got to his feet and stretched. He yawned loudly, rubbed his eyes and suddenly came awake. "Over there, sir!" Everyone stared in the direction he was pointing.

IN THE ASHES OF A DREAM

"It's just a herd of deer, Meredith!" a soldier mocked. "There's a reason men like you can't see properly."

Meredith ignored the insult. "I know they're deer, Evan, but what's making them flee like that?"

"Good work, Meredith," Maelgwn slapped his back as he raced for his horse. "Get your horses out of sight, and then crawl back. Take off your helmets and keep your heads down." They quickly hobbled their horses behind the summit and crept back to their vantage point. "If it's the Saxon army, I want Dai, Reece and Meredith to stay and shadow them. The rest of you will come with me. Meredith, you're in charge while I'm away. Get some idea of where they're heading, and report back to the place where we stopped earlier, near the Dyke. Lord Gwriad should reach there by late afternoon." He shuffled back to observe the soldiers who were lying next to him; his heart was pounding with excitement. "Don't move! Just keep your eyes open. We're hundreds of feet above them." He realized he was giving unnecessary orders, and shut up. He licked his dry lips, and wormed his way back to the edge.

They lay like corpses, watching the herd of deer vanishing into a small valley to the west of the hilltop. After a short while, two horsemen appeared like distant shadows at the far end of a long valley to the south. Their progress was slow, as they picked their way through the fast-flowing stream that was racing towards them. The valley sides and the twisting stream were strewn with rocks and the occasional boulder, and in some places stunted trees and hawthorn bushes added further complications to their advance.

"If they're scouts, they've chosen a difficult route," one soldier observed.

"I reckon they've taken a short cut to try and cut off our retreat," Meredith said. "I don't think they expected the water to have risen so quickly."

"If their soldiers come this way, they're going to find it hard going," Maelgwn agreed. "That should slow them down."

At that moment, the sun glinted off a mass of helmets that slowly increased in number. They were about half a mile behind their scouts.

"Right! That's them!" Maelgwn could not keep the excitement

out of his voice. "Everyone move back and mount up. Keep out of sight!" When he reached his horse, he turned to Meredith: "Get some idea of their numbers, and don't let them see you!" He led his horse slowly down the steep slope they had climbed only a short time before, and his small band followed in single file.

When they returned to the place near the Dyke, where they had gathered earlier, Maelgwn rode up to the top, and was relieved that there was no sign of the approaching Saxons. He turned his horse to the east, and was soon in the wide valley with the dark mass of the Welsh army far away. The valley had small hills with flat grassy areas, and heavily-treed copses, an ideal place for an ambush. As they moved down, they were comforted by the knowledge their army was somewhere ahead of them. There had been no sign of Saxons, neither farmers nor warriors, and Maelgwn urged his tired horse into a gallop, dismissing the danger and determined to give Gwriad as much time as possible to prepare for the inevitable battle. The Welsh army suddenly appeared below, and at the same moment a small force of cavalry blocked their path.

After a brief welcome, Maelgwn and his troop made their way down towards the sprawling mass of marching men that was the Welsh army. In the front were Gwriad and Dafydd sitting on huge horses bred for war and trained to use their front hooves with deadly effect. Behind them rode two standard bearers carrying flags with large red dragons on a green and white background. Gwriad, like his brother, wore a chainmail vest with polished leather body armour and a domed metal helmet that was lined with leather. He carried a long sword in his belt, and a round shield was attached to his saddle. Unlike his brother, he wore a bright red cloak, so he could be seen by his troops, although he was aware it made him an obvious target for the Saxons. "A leader must look like a leader," he had often said, "especially in a battle, when you're expecting men to die for you."

Behind the two brothers the cavalry were riding in impressive formations, most were experienced troops who took pride in their uniforms and the upkeep of their horses and their weapons. They carried long spears, round shields made of cow leather on wooden frames, and heavy swords designed to inflict maximum damage

IN THE ASHES OF A DREAM

with a single blow. Their basin-shaped helmets reflected the area of Wales from which they came, as no blacksmith used exactly the same design, and their iron shod long leather boots, were a defence in dense fighting.

Behind them were the marching columns, each man carrying his long heavy panel-shaped shield on his back. Many had red dragons painted on the thick cow's leather, with metal studs fitted around the edges and designed to make these both offensive as well as defensive weapons. The soldiers carried long spears, and once these had been thrown or become locked in a shield or body, they relied on short stabbing swords for the close-up fighting of the shield wall. Many in the columns had no experience of this type of fighting, and hoped to get over the border before they might be called upon to stand shoulder to shoulder in a solid line of men, and fight to survive.

Beyond this appearance of order and discipline came the lumbering wagons, surrounded by a large rambling crowd of camp followers and those considered to be useless in battle. They herded the animals and pulled laden carts filled with the combined plunder of the two attacks and the camp supplies. The men carried assorted weapons, including scythes, pitchforks and long knives, in the knowledge that they might have to defend themselves if a Saxon army came up from behind.

A strong section of archers marched at the back. They carried long bows, and wore light armour. Most were armed only with short swords or knives and relied on the speed and accuracy of their archery to protect them. At various distances, scouts maintained a constant vigil, and reported to Lord Elwin who, with a group of officers, maintained order while continuously driving them on towards safety.

There was a sense of optimism among the marching men as they neared the border, and the welcome sunshine and the bravado of the cavalry raised their morale. Gwriad stopped the advance when Maelgwn was seen approaching. The forced march had lasted hours, and the soldiers were grateful for the short rest, taking the opportunity to relieve themselves and drinking whatever water remained in their flasks.

After he had received the report, Gwriad gathered his officers together and gave his final orders. "Good work, General Maelgwn. You're in charge of the main army while I'm away, and Lord Elwin will control the rear guard. Keep in constant touch with each other. We must get our men over the border before dark."

He walked his horse to a small rise and stood up on his stirrups from where he could be seen by the cavalry in their ordered ranks, and by many of the soldiers. "We have located the enemy soldiers!" he roared, and waved his sword in the air. "This is what we wanted! Now we have the chance to show the Saxons we are not a spent force, and that we can beat them in battle. So far we've had it easy. Now we fight! We fight for Wales!" There was a huge roar of approval and a beating of swords on shields.

This was indeed what his brother wanted, although Dafydd suspected many of their soldiers would be grateful just to return home. They had destroyed Saxon houses, stolen their property, and even had revenge on the hated Earl Harold, but now they were tired and longed for their wives, their families and their farms. But burning towns was not enough for Gwriad; he needed to show the Saxons that the Welsh could still fight. Secretly, he lamented the fact that he would not cross swords with Earl Harold.

He smiled at Dafydd. "I'll see you near the Dyke!" he yelled, and with the trumpets blaring, he led the cavalry in a dramatic charge towards the mountains.

• • •

"What have you been learning with Father Williams?" Angharad asked as she and Teifryn sat at their morning spinning. She had set Jon to clean and sharpen the spears, knives and swords that decorated the main hall, and unless prompted, he never spoke. She was not sure whether he was in awe of her, or just naturally shy.

"He makes me read and write, every day, m'Lady, but he's also been teaching me the history of war." The way he spoke the words made her realize the title came from the mouth of the priest.

"Are you finding it interesting?"

"Oh yes, m'Lady!"

IN THE ASHES OF A DREAM

His enthusiasm was so evident that Teifryn looked up. "What have you learned?"

"Father Williams has taught me how the Romans fought. All about their armour and their weapons and why they won so many battles. He said that more people die in war through disease and hunger than in battle."

"Did that surprise you?" Angharad stopped spinning. It was such an obvious fact, but one she had never thought about.

"Well, yes, m'Lady. Father Williams says that the number of soldiers killed in battles was less than those who died later from their wounds."

Teifryn shuddered. "I hope our husbands have not had to fight."

Angharad smiled sympathetically at her friend. "With luck, they should be back soon." Although she cared for Gwriad, it was not the same: her husband had always been involved in dangerous things, and if he was not fighting or hunting he became bored and drank too much. The contrast to his brother David was like night and day. David was a devoted husband, a caring father, and a man who was never happier than when he was reading or writing reports. He was not a violent man, although he was not afraid to defend what he considered right, and she knew he would be supporting Gwriad on their campaign, and trying to balance his brother's wild nature.

"What else have you learned?" Angharad asked; there was no point in worrying about something they could not influence.

"Well, m'Lady, he was telling me how a Castle like this could be attacked, and how to defend it."

"Was he now?" Angharad smiled. This was typical of the subtlety of the old priest. She knew he worried about how vulnerable they all were to Pictish attacks, especially at the present time when the seas were calm and the soldiers were away. Rather than worry her directly, he was ensuring that some ideas would filter back, just in case. "Why would the Picts attack a castle when they could more easily attack villages and farms?"

"Father Williams said that small castles are not difficult to capture, and that they have more… plunder," he had difficulty with the word. "He says that poor villages and farms don't have much plunder."

"I find it hard to believe that the Picts would attack a castle, when they could have easier pickings," Teifryn mused. "How would they capture a castle? They can't lay siege to us, they don't have enough men for a lengthy attack."

"Well, m'Lady," Jon's enthusiasm for the role of instructor was amusing, "they would attack the gate. These men have proper armour and they would use a battering ram, and once in they would quickly capture the castle."

"You make it sound easy Jon," Angharad glanced at Teifryn's worried face. "What did Father Williams say about defending this Castle?

"He said we should have extra oak bars to put across the gate, m'Lady, and we should have heavy stones piled along the wall above the gates." He began to count on his fingers. "Oh yes, you should have boiling water to pour down on them, and have archers on both sides." He paused and screwed up his face. "Check for any weak places around the wall: trees that are too close, and… oh yes! Father Williams said to send out for help at the first sign of the enemy."

"Well done, Jon. I want you to tell Father Williams, when you see him tomorrow, that you have told me. Say that I appreciated his advice," she saw his face cloud over, "and that I liked his advice."

CHAPTER EIGHT

"Father Williams! Father Williams!"

The elderly priest awoke with a start. He had been dozing in a chair outside his house, enjoying the warmth of the sun, and sleeping off the effects of his lunch. This was his favourite spot, from where he could observe the goings-on in the village below, and he often knew in advance what his congregation might come to confess. Before he dozed off, he had been watching the wide river as the tide moved towards the flood, with its swollen estuary, and the placid sea behind. This was a fine place to sit as he waited for Jon to come for his daily lesson.

He rubbed his eyes, turned his head and focused on a young girl who was racing down the hillside like a mountain goat. "Is that you, Megan?"

"Father Williams!" she screamed. "The raiders have come!" Megan slewed to a stop in front of him, hardly able to speak, and pointed dramatically towards the sea. "I been collecting herbs for my ma, and then I saw 'em."

"Well bless me!" he said as he stared at the bay. "Is that a longboat?" He screwed up his eyes and tried to focus on the black dots on the sea.

"There's two of 'em, Father! They're attacking our fishermen!" she wailed.

He could just make out two large, multi-oared longboats each with a single, square sail. They appeared to be quickly approaching the small fishing vessels containing many of the men of the village. "Is your pa out there?" he asked gently.

"No, he's hurt his leg. I been collecting herbs for my Ma, for a poultice for him."

"Well done, Megan," he smiled encouragingly. "Now, I want you to run down and warn the rest of the village. Then, I want you and your best runners to race to Aberteifi and warn them. If you meet Jon on his horse, tell him I want him to gallop back to the castle immediately. You understand, Megan?"

The girl was nodding furiously. "I will, Father. I will." She turned and ran down the steep hill, and in moments he could hear her yelling her warning.

He rubbed his face, and after a moment of thought, hurried towards his house. Once inside, he opened a large polished box, and drew out a lengthy bundle tightly wrapped in woollen rags. He stared at it and paused, lost in memories, before feverishly unwrapping a magnificent sword.

It was a deadly weapon that was also a work of art: the creation of a master smith. The long blade gleamed in the firelight as though it had just been polished, and it was sharpened to a fine edge. On either side of the blade was a deep grove or fuller, that enabled the sword to be lighter and wider using the same amount of metal as a normal sword. His fingers moved lovingly down the fuller; it amused him that some fools called it the blood groove.

The hilt comprised a highly decorated, slightly curved cross guard, an ornamental pommel inlaid with semi-precious stones and between both the long grip was wrapped with silver and copper wire to prevent the hand slipping during a fight; it also added beauty to the weapon. As a young man, he had captured it in battle before he chose the spiritual world and forsook violence. Since then, he had kept the sword in perfect condition. It was his last tangible memory of his much earlier life.

He raised it above his head with his left hand, and swung it around, and then used both hands to practise some movements. The sword felt heavier than the last time he had held it. He tossed away the scabbard into the open box and hurried to the door. Outside, he could see the two Pictish longboats racing through the distant estuary, making the most of the full tide, and he knew they would reach the village before the incoming flood lessened.

He grabbed a walking stick with his right hand and, carrying

IN THE ASHES OF A DREAM

the sword on his left shoulder, he began the steep descent as quickly as he was able. In moments he was in the village centre.

"What shall we do, Father?" an old man asked anxiously as he limped out of his hovel. "Should we run for the woods?"

"No, my son, we should always oppose evil. God will decide." He looked about as the villagers emptied out of their homes. There were a few younger men who had decided not to fish that day, but most were mothers, children and elderly folk. He could sense the panic in the air.

"Gather round!" he called out. "We can oppose these murderers. We will not allow them to destroy our homes and our lives!" He raised his sword, which they had not seen before, and a gasp went up from the villagers. "Some of your men may have died today at the hands of these invaders, but with this sword and God's help we will defeat them!" There were some half-hearted cheers, but some women were sobbing.

"We defeated them twelve years ago, and we'll do again!" He tried to encourage them, but it was clear that many felt unable to overcome their fear and their sense of loss.

"Twelve years ago, Lord Gomer and his soldiers was here to protect us, Father," a woman called out.

"That's true, Deryn, but you will remember that the Pictish wolves attacked in the early morning when we were sleeping, and we still won."

"There's very few men here, Father," another woman called out. "How can we fight armoured soldiers?"

"Well done, Rhiannon. You ask the right question, and here's the answer." There was a sudden stillness as everyone waited to hear what Father Williams had to say. He was respected as a priest and loved as a man, and his reputation prevented the panic that would otherwise have overwhelmed them.

"We have the fortification that Lord Gwriad helped us build, and some of you have had some training in recent months. Now, this is what I want you to do: everyone is to find a weapon. How many of you have bows?" A handful of adults raised their hands. "Bring knives, scythes and especially bows. Hurry now!"

As the older villagers rushed off, Father Williams called the children together. "How many of you have slings?" Most of the boys raised their hands. "Good, now I want you boys to collect sling stones and place them in piles at the top of the steps, behind the fortification. Off you go!"

"Now you girls, I want you to find as many big stones as you can." He saw the look of confusion on their faces. "About the size of my head will do!" They laughed and ran off, keen to help.

He gathered the men with bows around him. "How often do you use your bows?" Some looked embarrassed. "I don't care if you've been killing Lord Gwriad's game!" he said encouragingly. "I just need to know how skilled you are." It was quickly agreed that five of the men, two quite elderly, were good with their bows and three others had some limited experience. "Get all your arrows together, and you five, I want you to soak rags in oil and bind them to the shafts of about five arrows each. Get some women to help you, and bring out all your cooking oil."

As villagers reappeared with any weapons they could find, he sent them to gather more large stones, and start a large fire near the top of the fortification. Then, he gathered them all together.

"I want you all to get some form of helmet, hat or any sort of head cover. I want your children to look older, and when they first arrive, I want you to yell and wave weapons. From down there on the river, I want them to think we have more fighting men than we have."

Suddenly, the first of the long boats appeared round the bend, its oars cutting into the water, and its sail being driven by a breeze from the sea. "Now listen," Father Williams spoke calmly, "this is what we'll do. When the ships are near enough for your arrows to reach them, light your arrows, and fire them before they become too hot. Aim for their sails, and don't fire too soon, we can't afford to waste any arrows."

"If that does not stop them, I want you to pour your cooking oil down the stone steps, and if they reach the steps, set light to the oil by throwing down burning embers. When the fire dies down, and they start to climb up, start hurling down the big stones, and I want you boys to use your slings from both sides. Finally, we'll fight them with our weapons!" He raised his sword. "We'll fight them, and we'll win!"

• • •

MEGAN RAN BARE-FOOTED ALONG THE twisting path that led to Ceredigion; she had never worn shoes in her nearly fourteen years, and was unconcerned with the rough surface. To her left, the river was swelled by the high tide and appeared to be motionless, its outward flow prevented by the dam of sea water that was slowly reaching its climax. At this time, the river was like a long placid lake, reaching up and caressing the grassy banks and, in places, overflowing into small depressions along the way. But, once the tide turned, the water would rush out like the breaking of a dam, and in a short time the brown, muddy banks would be revealed and the power of the river would return.

She stopped to glance back, and was pleased to see that none of the other three girls were in sight. Megan was the acknowledged runner in the village, and she was determined to be the one who would bring the news to the castle. Also, there was the hope that she might meet Jon as he travelled to Llanduduch for his lesson with the priest. She would give him Father Williams' message, and perhaps he would allow her to ride with him on his horse. She had never ridden a horse, and had no idea how unsuitable her shift would be, but it was her dream ever since he had smiled at her in the village.

She turned a corner, and there was the bridge in the distance, with the stone castle beyond on the other bank. She increased her pace, and was delighted to see Jon crossing the bridge on his big horse. She waved to him, but he did not appear to see her, and urged his horse into a trot, and disappeared behind some trees.

Megan stopped running and waited until Jon appeared from around a bend. "Jon! Jon!" she called and stood in the middle of the path, waving her arms.

Jon stopped his horse and quickly dismounted. "What's the matter?" he asked, both concerned and delighted that it was the girl he had noticed in the village.

"Two longboats are coming up the river!" she screamed. "Father

Williams said you must warn the castle, and to take me with you," she added.

"Have you ridden a horse before?" She shook her head. He jumped into the saddle, and with apparent ease lifted her onto the horse and set her before him. He noticed, as he did so that her shift had risen up on one side, revealing a pink and grubby bum. "Pull down your dress," he said awkwardly, as he turned the horse towards the bridge. While he felt good entering the castle with this girl, he did not want the guards making rude comments.

"Open up!" he yelled. "Long boats are attacking Llanduduch!"

Davis looked down from the parapet and saw Jon with a girl. "What're you up to, Jon? You can't bring her in." He was uncertain about Jon, but didn't want to get in any trouble with Lady Angharad. Since the incident in the stables he was no longer as confident as he'd been. Owen joined him, and couldn't believe his eyes. "We're not opening the gate until you get rid of that girl!" he yelled.

"Open the gates! The longboats are attacking Llanduduch. This girl has a message for Lady Angharad!"

It had been a quiet afternoon, and the sudden shouting brought people to the gate, including Penn who, when he had heard Jon's message, screamed at the confused youths. "You halfwits! Let them in, and sound the alarm!"

Angharad and Teifryn heard Megan's excited message, and asked her some questions. Jon watched with interest as Megan overcame her embarrassment and spoke out clearly. "Father Williams was going to fight the invaders, m'Lady."

"And there were two longboats?"

"Yes, m'Lady. They attacked our fishing boats in the bay. M'Dad was not out fishing 'cos—."

"Thank you, Megan. Did you get a chance to see how many men there were in the longboats?"

Megan nodded, and screwed up her face as she brought up a clear picture in her mind. With her eyes closed, she began to speak: "The first boat," she stopped as she moved her fingers, "had this," she raised a hand, "and this," she raised two fingers, "on each side." She kept her eyes closed, "and this many at the front," she raised a hand, "and this many at the back," she raised two fingers.

IN THE ASHES OF A DREAM

"Twenty-one in each boat," Teifryn said quietly.

"Well done, young Megan," Angharad opened her arms and embraced the delighted girl. "Jon, take her over to the kitchen and make sure she's well fed, and tell Penn to come to me immediately."

"They have a minimum of forty-two well-armed fighters against our peasants and a handful of so-called soldiers who have never fought a battle." Angharad gazed thoughtfully into the fire, then rose quickly and opened the door. Rhodri was standing on guard outside the hall, and he jumped to attention as soon as he saw Angharad.

"Well done, Rhodri. Now, I want you to find Owen and the two of you must run down to Ceredigion and warn everyone."

"What about, m'Lady?"

"Rhodri! Have you been dreaming? There are longboats in the river! Get everyone to come up to the castle immediately. Find Owen!" Rhodri had been in the jakes when Jon and Megan arrived, and he ran off, as though a hornet had stung him. "Owen! Ring the warning bell! And keep ringing it!" she yelled.

Penn arrived panting and still buckling on his sword belt. "Penn, get everyone organized! Make sure they have weapons. I want everyone who can use a bow to line the bridge, and then retreat to the castle. Get the servants to pile large stones on the walls. Tell the kitchen to boil water, use pans and buckets, and to bring them to the gates if we're attacked, and tell Megan she is to help you organize the local people when they arrive. Get her to supervise the women." She rushed back inside. "Teifryn, I want you and your child to stay upstairs, that is your duty. Keep a watch on the river from my room, and I'll send young Megan to act as your messenger."

She raced up to the sleeping quarters, and opened Gwriad's long box. Inside was his formal armour that he had worn for Court functions at the time of King Gruffydd and had not worn since. She stripped off her dress, put on tights, and a leather jerkin, and her own long boots. Alys helped her buckle on a leather breastplate, and place the heavy domed helmet on her head. Finally, she strapped on one of Gwriad's spare sword belts. His gauntlets were too large for her hands, and she tossed them back.

"You look like a war lord," Alys said admiringly.

The bell continued to toll, and as she descended the stairs, a new sound was growing in volume: the clamour of people. She took a sword off the wall, and walked into the courtyard as dozens of frightened peasants streamed through the gates, many driving their livestock before them. Penn and the older Megan were doing an efficient job of allotting jobs and positions, and the children were told to mind the animals.

On the walls, some older men were setting up defences, while on the bridge a blacksmith named Rhys was showing some nervous archers where to position themselves, and instructing them how to make the best use of each of their meagre supply of arrows. "Aim for the men at the back of the boat to start with, but I don't think they'll come this far, they'll almost certainly beach down there, by the village, in which case you all retreat back to the castle."

Finally, the last person limped up from the village, the other girls from Llanduduch panted across the bridge and the gates were closed. The animals were corralled and most of the preparations completed, and anxious people lined the walls, staring down the river, each wanting to be the first to see the longboats, yet hoping they would not appear.

"What do you think is happening at Llanduduch, m'Lady?" Jon asked excitedly as he tightened Angharad's armour. He felt very much in awe of her, for with her high boots and her helmet she towered over him.

"One of two things, Jon. Either, they're attacking the village and whatever occurs there, they may decide to leave before the falling tide makes the river difficult. Or, they may bypass the village, especially if Father Williams has organized the defences, and they'll race up to attack our village. They will only attack our small castle if they think they can win."

"If they attack Ceredigion, will we leave the castle to drive them off?" He had dreams of leading an attack on the raiders, and being a hero.

"No, Jon. Hopefully our castle will save our lives; we would never risk leaving it to drive off an enemy. It would be like sheep leaving their secure pens to attack wolves."

IN THE ASHES OF A DREAM

Jon winced and nodded his head. "Perhaps they might decide to stay, and not leave on this tide?"

Angharad nodded thoughtfully; it was not something she had considered. All the reports of coastal attacks had spoken of lightning raids. "I suppose it depends on how desperate they are. These warriors have come from a place where life is hard. They're looking for food and easy plunder. They want to attack our women, and they enjoy killing our men. What they try to avoid is determined opposition, for if they lose too many warriors, they can't operate their longboats."

"What would you like me to do, my Lady?"

"Go down to the bridge and ask Rhys what he advises. I think my idea of placing the archers on the bridge was not a good one."

• • •

It was late afternoon as they approached the hills before the dyke, and Gwriad sent out groups of riders to search for any sign of the Saxon army. He looked anxiously around; in other circumstances he would have enjoyed the panoramic view. In front of them the valley narrowed, and on each side smaller valleys twisted away into high treeless hills sprinkled with sheep, while to the north the snow-covered tops of tall mountains contrasted with the blue sky. In the lower parts, small streams and dense clumps of trees lined the sides of the valleys.

Dafydd rode up alongside his brother, and they slowed their sweating horses to walking pace. "These narrow valleys lend themselves to shield walls," he observed, screwing up his eyes into the western sun.

"Yes," Gwriad agreed, "a small army could try to prevent us from passing. The sooner we locate their forces, the sooner we can complete the withdrawal."

At that moment, a trio of horsemen appeared ahead, galloping fast towards them. Meredith pulled up in front of Gwriad. "General Gwriad, a Saxon army has taken up positions to stop us reaching the border."

"How far from here?"

"Not far, General. Just over this ridge, the valley narrows, and they have taken up a shield wall that reaches both sides." He pointed to a distant hill, where two horsemen could just be seen. "They know where we are."

"How many?"

"More than two hundred foot soldiers, General, and a handful of horsemen."

Gwriad dismounted, and Dafydd and Meredith joined him. He used a spear to scratch out a map on the ground of the immediate area. "Here's our main army behind us; here's the border with the dyke here, and we're here." He turned to Meredith, "Show me where the Saxons are, and how we could by-pass them."

As they discussed the possible routes through the hills, other scouts returned and confirmed the position of the Saxons. The cavalry dismounted and stretched their legs and watered their horses, while behind them the dark mass of the distant army slowly advanced.

"This is the most likely way to enable us to get past the shield wall of the Saxons," Dafydd said, pointing to a hill to their right. "However, the scouts make it clear that it's a small, narrow valley in parts, and would be unsuitable for the majority of our cavalry."

"True," Gwriad said, "which is why I want you to lead a section of the cavalry through this narrow path and attack the Saxons from the rear, after I have begun an attack from the front. With luck we should be able to shatter their shield wall and drive them away." He smiled excitedly at his brother. "I won't attack until you're in position, but then you must come down fast."

After final agreements, Gwriad led his men at a slow pace up to the ridge, while Dafydd galloped off with about fifty of the cavalry, hoping the Saxon scouts would not discover them.

Towards the end of the valley, the Saxons had chosen a place where fallen rocks had blocked both sides, allowing them to form their defensive wall and have a smaller reserve line behind them. The valley floor was uneven, and parts of the shield wall were lower or higher than the main line, weakening the defensive posture. The officers had been anxious to get their men in position before the Welsh cavalry attacked, and although this part of the valley was not ideal, it did allow them the chance to block an attack.

IN THE ASHES OF A DREAM

They waited patiently, with the sun beating down on their right flank. The scouts had warned them the Welsh cavalry was close, and although they were exhausted by their rapid march, the excitement and fear of battle banished the men's weariness. They stood with their long shields locked together, and their spears held out in front, confident that they could withstand the shock of the charge. Once their spears were used, they would rely on their short swords.

A cry went up from one of their few horsemen, as a dense wave of Welsh cavalry appeared suddenly over a distant rise, and began to advance at a trot. When they were about three spear lengths away, the horsemen in the front stopped as if to allow those in the rear to catch up, and then they all became motionless. In the centre of the front rank was an impressive soldier in shining armour with a red cloak, who sat like a statue on a huge warhorse. He carried a long sword that he rested on his shoulder, and a small round shield. Next to him was a soldier carrying a large flag with a red dragon.

"What are they waiting for?" a Saxon officer growled nervously. In his mind, the Welsh had lost the advantage that they could have had if they had charged immediately.

The Welsh horses shifted nervously, but their riders had no difficulty in controlling them. Nobody spoke, and each horseman stared ahead as though the Saxons were not formed up in front of him. It was an impressive display of discipline, and had an unsettling effect on the Saxons, who began to beat their spears on their shields.

Gwriad swore under his breath as the Saxon ranks began to shuffle forward to the sound of their drumming. If they advanced much further, he knew he would have to turn his cavalry and retreat further back, for soon the Saxons would be would be too close for him to charge effectively. At that moment he saw Dafydd's section descending quickly from the high ground further up the valley

"Prepare to charge!" he told his nearest riders; the message was quickly passed back. Gwriad saw the Saxons hesitate, and stood up in his saddle. "Charge!" he roared, and his trumpets sounded.

When the sea of armoured men and horses was unleashed, their spears and deadly hooves presented a terrifying sight to the shield-bound Saxons. Some threw their spears, but most placed their shields on the ground and tried to stand sideways, leaning against them to withstand the initial charge, with their spears pointing out. A few tried to move back behind others for safety, and were sworn at by their officers, and in moments the two sides clashed in a melee of men, weapons and horses.

There was vicious fighting, as the cavalry used their spears and the power of their horses to try to break through the shield wall. Soon they were using their long swords and small shields to protect their horses, and those animals that were experienced in battle were terrifying in their use of their iron-clad hooves to break down the Saxon shields. But, in spite of the power of the charge, most of the wall held and Saxons from the reserve rushed in to close the gaps.

Gwriad, who had escaped injury, ordered the trumpets to sound the withdrawal to enable his men to regroup and prepare for a further attack. There had been losses on both sides, and although the Saxons had lost the most men, their shield wall was still holding. A cheer went up from the foot soldiers as the Welsh pulled back, and they beat their shields defiantly.

It was at that moment that Dafydd's cavalry raced up from behind. The Saxons were slow to comprehend what was happening, and as they turned to face these fresh troops, Gwriad ordered a second charge, and the formerly-indomitable shield wall collapsed as a hail of spears decimated the Saxons from behind. As they retreated they tried to form into smaller defensive circles, each man fighting for his life. Those who were unable to find others to defend their backs were cut down as battle-crazed Welsh cavalrymen galloped around the scene of battle, seeking revenge.

Gwriad's standard-bearer fell to the ground as a stab to the heart killed his horse, and he lay trapped under the dead animal, unable to free himself. The soldier who had stabbed his horse snatched the flag from him, and with a cry of victory rushed off towards a group of Saxons who were led by a huge officer with a decorated helmet. The officer was conducting an organized retreat

IN THE ASHES OF A DREAM

with perhaps thirty men, and stopped to yell encouragement to the hero with the stolen flag.

Near the centre of the fighting, Gwriad was attempting to bring some order to the last part of the battle, when he saw what had happened. Without a second thought, he raced after the retreating soldier, and was able to cut him down with his long sword just before the soldier reached the safety of the Saxon's line. Gwriad was single-minded in his determination to recapture his flag, and he transferred his sword to his shield hand, leaned down on his right side and grabbed the heavy flag from the grip of the dying man. In doing so, he took his attention off the Saxon group to his left.

His moment of elation as he grasped the flag was instantly replaced by anger, fear and confusion as his horse crashed down to the ground with a spear in its neck. He threw himself out of the saddle, and managed to avoid being trapped under the convulsing horse, whose powerful death throes prevented the Saxons from attacking him while he was down.

Gwriad staggered quickly to his feet, dazed and unbalanced. He had lost his helmet and, throwing his shield aside, defended himself as best he could with random two-handed blows at the advancing Saxons. They recognized their chance to kill the Welsh leader, and sacrificed their defensive shield wall as they charged forward towards him. Immediately, the fresh cavalry led by Dafydd swept in and prevented the remaining Saxons from reforming their defensive wall, and all around Gwriad a series of vicious, individual fights developed.

A giant Saxon, known to his men as Draca, fought his way towards Gwriad, cutting a bloody path towards the Welsh officer who, he believed, was most certainly responsible for the attack on Shrewsbury, where his younger brother had died. Screaming Saxon oaths, he rushed at Gwriad, a long shield in one hand and a heavy double-edged axe in the other.

Gwriad was panting fast, trying to regain control of his senses, and aware that his fall from his horse had upset his vision. He swung the long sword in a two-handed arc, trying to keep his enemies away while he recovered. In a confused moment, he realized that the sword-wielding Saxon, against whom he had been sparing, had been replaced by a huge warrior with an axe.

He closed one eye to focus, and jumped back to avoid a mighty axe blow to his head. All around him his men were fighting well, and the number of horses seemed to be increasing. He glanced back to avoid tripping over a corpse and as he did so, the giant slammed his long shield into Gwriad's face with brute force. Without his helmet that would have taken much of the blow, Gwriad was knocked unconscious, and fell backwards, dropping his sword and collapsing senseless onto the ground.

The giant rushed forward to deliver the deathblow. He raised his arm above his head, and knew nothing more as a spear from a cavalryman was thrust into his armpit, and down through his heart. With his death, the fight went out of the remaining Saxons, and they began a fast retreat back the way they had come. Some of the cavalry were keen to pursue them, still burning off the blood lust, but most were happy to have won the battle, and rest themselves and their horses.

When Gwriad fell to the ground, his soldiers fought off any further attackers, and immediately surrounded him. There was no doubt his red cloak had identified him in the heat of battle, both to the enemy and to his men.

Dafydd took command of the battlefield, and having ensured that the Saxon retreat had disintegrated into a rout, he rode up to check on his brother. "Is he alive?" he asked anxiously, as he dismounted.

"He's breathing, m'Lord, I reckon he got a smack in the face," one of the officers observed as he picked up Gwriad's helmet.

"Thank the Gods," Dafydd said quietly, as he looked down at his blood-soaked brother. He stretched slowly, his body was aching and he was overwhelmed with a sudden feeling of tiredness. He directed a soldier to untie his leather breastplate, and after removing his helmet and his gauntlets, he knelt down by Gwriad.

"Well, that's something to boast about when we get home," he observed as he noted his brother's battered face. His nose was broken, and his eyes were a mixture of blues, blacks and browns.

His lips were bleeding and there was a bloody welt on his left cheek.

The men slowly dismounted and sat about in small groups, some just collapsed on the stony ground, utterly exhausted. Only a few were still driven to chase down isolated Saxons, and even fewer felt the need to go among the bodies killing those who were still alive and stealing anything of value.

Dafydd gave instructions for Gwriad's armour to be removed, and for his face and hands to be gently washed. His older brother lay still on the ground, breathing heavily, and Dafydd wondered how soon he would recover. The main army was now in sight, and Dafydd began to hope that they might complete their withdrawal to the Welsh border before nightfall.

He asked for details of the deaths and injuries, sent back messages to the main army and finally sat down next to the unconscious Gwriad. Dafydd slowly sipped water and pondered on the monstrous face of his brother. Somehow, it seemed to symbolize the irony of war, in which even the victors suffered and the eventual successes were mere shadows of the earlier dreams.

However, when the other officers gathered around, it was slowly apparent that the awful sense of anti-climax had given way to a growing sense of victory. "We showed them we can still fight, and we've got our revenge on that Earl Harold," one officer said.

"Not only that," another cavalryman added, "but we've shown who our best troops are!" There was a loud chorus of agreement. When the army was about half a mile away, Dafydd ordered the cavalry to reform and resume mounted patrols, and there was no complaining: it was a time to look proud, and the cavalrymen were keen to show their military supremacy.

General Maelgwn and Lord Elwin rode up and gazed down with alarm at the unconscious Gwriad. "I'm hoping he'll recover soon," Dafydd said awkwardly. He was unused to his elder brother not being in command.

"How many did you lose?" Maelgwn asked.

"About twenty dead and more than fifty injured, some badly."

"And the enemy?"

Dafydd shrugged, "I haven't counted. A lot. The main thing is we won, and now it's time to get home."

"You did well," Lord Elwin patted Dafydd's shoulder. He looked round the battlefield with its corpses, its dead horses and the cries of the wounded. "I'll arrange for the corpses to be burnt in separate pyres."

Nearby, injured Welsh soldiers were being placed close to each other, ready for the approaching wagons, and further off a large group of Saxon captives were being guarded; some were injured, but all were standing. Those that had been seriously injured were no longer alive. "We'll march them to the border, and release them," Dafydd said in a voice that brooked no argument.

He turned to Lord Elwin, "I want you to organize enough carts and wagons for those who can't ride. I want Lord Gwriad to travel in a cart by himself, and if we have some camp followers who have healing abilities, tell two of them they can travel with him." He shook his head. "They'll be pleased not to have to walk, but when he wakes up he'll be poor company." He laughed. "In fact I feel sorry for them!"

CHAPTER NINE

The Pictish vessels moved silently through the water towards the small village perched high on the bank of the river. The complete destruction of the villagers' small fishing fleet had been accomplished with ruthless efficiency, and there was a chance that the village's inhabitants were still unaware of the disaster that was about to happen to them. The raiders had ignored the cluster of poor hovels that was Gwbert, in order to make the maximum use of the tide.

As they drew closer, there seemed to be no movement, and apart from a large fire, the village appeared uninhabited. The leader nodded to his helmsman, and gave the order to stop rowing. The second boat, five lengths behind, also shipped its oars. The quiet river was at full swell, and the sleek craft cut silently through the limpid water, their single sails producing some forward motion in the light airs.

As the first boat approached the shore, a crowd of people suddenly appeared at the top of a steep pathway leading to the village. They were yelling and beating drums, and there were more of them than the Pictish leader had expected. He was convinced he had killed most of the adult fishermen in the bay, and the inhabitants' numbers and their intention to defend their village surprised him: when long boats appeared, peasants usually ran away.

At that moment, a flight of flaming arrows descended on his boat; a few hit his sail, and others caused injury to his crew. "Fast to the shore!" he yelled, noting that his sail was burning. Immediately they touched the bank, the raiders attended to the burning sail, as a second flight came down.

The leader realized he was like a sitting duck, and immediately jumped into the muddy river and led the majority of his men ashore, while the others put out the fires. In front was a steep rocky stairway, but with his armour, his weapons and his experience, the leader did not hesitate to lead the charge up to the waiting peasants. He reached the fourth step when he was suddenly aware that they had become very slippery, and before he could react, the staircase burst into flames.

"Back!" he yelled, screaming with pain as his bare legs were enveloped in fire. He pushed his way back to the river where he jumped into the cool water. Two others of his men were also burnt, but the rest had managed to avoid the flames that quickly began to subside. Another flight of burning arrows descended on his boat, and although his men had taken down the sail, the arrows were still causing concern.

Holding their shields above their heads, the Picts launched a further attack up the slippery steps, led by the second in command, and they were within a few steps from the top when heavy stones crashed down on them, smashing down their shields and causing the front warriors to fall back on those behind them. Another load of stones rained down on them, and their advance halted. Sling stones and more arrows thudded into them, and in spite of their armour and shields, their attack faltered.

The leader was still standing in the cooling water, enraged as his men retreated, but physically unable to lead them. Some were being helped back to the boat, and at least two had sustained serious injuries. As they retreated, only a few more arrows descended, and it seemed that the villagers were running out of defences.

The second boat glided into the bank, and the fresh warriors, having seen what had taken place, needed no encouragement to begin a fast assault up the staircase. A hail of stones and slingshot rained down on them, but using their long shields, they were able to battle their way up to the top of the stairs, a few hurling their spears at the massed villagers. But instead of pouring into the village as they had imagined, they found themselves contained in a narrow passageway with high oak walls that curled in a half circle. The defenders were raised up above their heads, and fought back with all manner of weapons.

The first warriors were beaten down, overwhelmed by the ferocity of the defenders, and particularly a monk who blocked the exit and wielded a long sword that cut effortlessly through their armour. The passageway was soon blocked with the bodies of the raiders, and as the defenders were able to fight from both sides, the Picts found themselves overwhelmed. This had never happened to them before, and in a full defensive movement, they backed down the staircase dragging their injured and leaving their dead behind.

Back at the river, they piled back aboard their vessels and rowed out beyond the range of occasional arrows. There was a sense of disbelief as they tried to come to grips with their disaster. The first boat had lost a quarter of its crew, either dead or severely injured, and its sail was badly damaged. The second had smaller losses, but its captain had been the first to die at the stockade. The tide had turned, and the dispirited crews were content to let the boats be taken out by the changing tide as they assessed their damage, and the number of men still able to row. There was no thought of revenge, merely survival.

Back at the village the peasants were lamenting the loss of many of their fishermen friends and relatives, but it was also a time to celebrate their unexpected victory. Many had never been involved in any fighting before, although some still remembered the last attack by the Picts, but at that time they had left the real fighting to old Lord Gomer and his soldiers.

Brother Williams was everyone's hero, but now the fighting was over, he was exhausted. He gathered everyone together and made a brief speech in which he praised their courage and their determination. "You've made history and the Picts won't be back in a hurry!" Everyone cheered. Then, he arranged for those who were able to make their way down to the bay to search for the bodies of their loved ones and pull them above the high tide mark. "I'll arrange for the people of Aberteifi to help us bring them up to our church tomorrow. It's possible there may be some survivors."

He gratefully drank some beer that he was given. "I must lie down and sleep for a bit," he smiled. "I haven't used my sword arm for a long time!" There was a roar of good-natured laughter, and more cheering. "Those who don't go down to the beach, should build a big fire, and we'll have a feast this evening, and we'll honour our dead and celebrate our victory!" With that, he turned and slowly made his way up the steep hill to his cottage, aided by a boy who proudly carried his sword.

Once their priest had reached his house, the peasants quickly turned from relief and celebration to revenge. They stripped the bodies of the Picts, and threw them in the river, where they floated out on the tide. The young people tried on the armour and the helmets, and proudly waved the captured weapons, while others built a big fire in the centre of the village. The adults drank their beer, and prepared for the sad journey to the beach.

As the sun began to set, and the river roared unchecked past the castle, it slowly dawned on Angharad that the Picts weren't coming. She arranged for Penn, Jon and some of the men from the village to take the remaining horses and travel down to the Llanduduch to see what had happened. "I hope the villagers managed to escape into the forest," she said but her voice betrayed her optimism. "I expect the village is destroyed, but be careful, the Picts might still be there." She took off her helmet, feeling suddenly foolish. "If there are injured people, some of you return and use your horses to take the carts back to collect them." There were so many instructions she felt she should give, but she could do nothing until she knew what had happened. She made a face at Teifryn and put her sword back on the wall; Gwriad and Dafydd would have known what to do.

• • •

JON HAD GALLOPED OFF WITH Penn and the village men, leaving the anxious Megan behind. The cook had fed her, and taken the young girl under her wing. "Don't you worry about your Da, he'll have fled to the forest, and you can stay here and help me in the kitchen while your home is rebuilt."

After darkness fell, one of the Aberteifi men returned from Llanduduch with the wonderful and unexpected news. "Father

IN THE ASHES OF A DREAM

Williams led the villagers to a victory over them Picts, and they was driven off. They defeated 'em!" he yelled. "They defeated 'em!"

There was a huge roar of approval, as everyone in the castle rejoiced. "Where's Penn and the others?" Angharad asked.

"Penn and the rest of 'em have gone down to the bay to 'elp find the bodies of the fishermen. They'll stay the night, and come back tomorrow," he said.

"I can't believe this," Angharad said as she hugged Teifryn. They had spent much of the day in a state of anxiety, and suddenly everything had changed, and she was no longer responsible for the security of the castle and the two villages. "What a relief! We didn't lose either of the villages, and nobody from here was killed."

"They lost most of their fisherman from Llanduduch," Teifryn said quietly, "and all of their boats. They're going to have a hard time."

Angharad bit her tongue. She had not forgotten, it was just it could have been so much worse. "Tomorrow, we'll travel down and congratulate Father Williams, and attend the burial ceremony. When Gwriad and David return, they'll know how best to help them."

She went outside and gathered the assembled villagers and castle servants, and gave them all the news that she had. "Tonight, those in the castle can celebrate, while you villagers return to your homes. Tomorrow, we'll have a big fire in the village." She paused. "And tomorrow, you may hunt as you wish, and we'll have a feast around the fire." There were enthusiastic cheers as everyone returned to their places.

Angharad made her way to the kitchen. "At this late time," she said to the cook, "we'll celebrate on soup, and anything else you can find." She laughed, "We're lucky to be celebrating."

"Don't you worry about that, m'Lady," Megan said with her usual firmness, "even if we'd been besieged, I would 'ave still 'ad to produce something to eat." She nodded towards a bevy of women who were busy preparing food dishes, and outside the back door, servants were roasting chickens on the spits.

"I never doubted you, Megan," Angharad felt wonderfully supported. She noticed the young girl from Llanduduch working with the women. "I see you've got your name-sake working for you?"

"Just for tonight, m'Lady. I thought she might lose her home and family, and I was prepared to take her on. But I reckons she'll be keen to get back to her village now she knows they're safe."

"Yes, I can use her." Angharad called her over, and young Megan looked worried, wondering what she had done wrong. "At first light, Megan, I want you to run back to your village. Tell Father Williams that Lady Teifryn and I will be there by late morning, and that I want him to conduct the burial service when we arrive."

"Oh yes, m'Lady. I can run there now if you like!"

Angharad tried not to smile. "No, Megan, I want you to run back tomorrow, and you are not to leave here until it's clear daylight. Do you understand?"

The girl nodded solemnly. It was not just the importance of her role that pleased her, but she knew that Jon would be there when she arrived.

• • •

ANGHARAD AND TEIFRYN, WITH TEGWEN and her wet nurse, arrived on horseback before midday. They rode at the head of a long column of peasants. Below them, the tide was coming in, but it would be a while before the estuary would be filled, and the river was still roaring.

Father Williams was standing outside his home to meet them, and after the formal greetings Angharad spoke: "Father Williams, I had no idea you were a military mastermind!" She placed her hand on his arm. "Before we go down to the village, I want you to show me your sword."

The priest bowed. "Of course, my Lady, but after showing it to you, I hope I may never have to handle it again."

Angharad looked in awe at the weapon. "How did you come by this?"

"In a battle, my Lady," he said vaguely. "It was a long time ago, and it convinced me I needed to join the Church." He removed it carefully from Angharad, and replaced it in his long box. "God works in mysterious ways," he murmured.

IN THE ASHES OF A DREAM

They walked together slowly down the steep path to the centre of the village. Behind them came Teifryn, who found the path a challenge and had not been to the village since her pregnancy; her wet nurse carried Tegwen, who gazed about with interest and behind them came the rest of the folk from Aberteifi.

In spite of the warmth of the day, a large fire was burning in the communal fire pit in the middle of the village. Above the fire, a row of rough coffins lay on the hillside, a powerful reminder of the horror the rest had experienced. The villagers were gathered on the far side, and many were weeping; the exhilaration and relief of yesterday had been replaced by sadness and a deep sense of loss.

Father Williams stood on the hillside facing down on the row of coffins with Angharad and Teifryn standing beside him. On the other side, facing the mourners, the people of Aberteifi formed up, many feeling awkward and emotional, for some were related to the men who had died.

The priest held up his hand, and stillness descended on the villagers. There was just the roar of the river and the sound of the single church bell, which Father Williams had arranged to be tolled by Megan, in recognition of the role she played in saving the village.

After a short time the bell went silent and he began the burial service. At the end of his prayers, the villagers sang a traditional song that they all knew by heart, and the coffins were carried up the hill to the small graveyard next to the church. A line of graves had been dug, clear evidence of the frantic activity shown by the villagers and the men from Aberteifi, including Jon. Once again, those from Llanduduch stood together on one side and the visitors on the other.

Father Williams was aware that none of the villagers could read, and that the wooden grave markers were symbolic. He had arranged for each family to place personal items on the coffins, and before each coffin was placed into the ground, the items were removed, and replaced on top of the covered grave. He said a final prayer. The bell began to toll, and everyone moved quietly down to the empty village.

The wake began slowly. Drinks were handed out, and food was

cooked, much of it brought from the castle and people moved about muttering their sadness, and promising to help those families that had lost their providers. The children stood quietly at first, but like all children soon began to play, and the adults gradually moved to the telling of funny stories about the men who had died. Alcohol was consumed, tongues loosened, and food was passed around.

Father Williams said some encouraging words, and praised the villagers for their courage in saving their homes and their loved ones, and for their determination to defeat the devil's agents who had murdered their menfolk. "This victory will be remembered for years to come, and whenever you meet strangers you can say 'I come from Llanduduch, and I helped defeat the Picts!'"

After the cheering had lessened, Angharad gave a short speech in which she also praised their bravery, acknowledged their great losses and promised to have a new boat constructed so that they could soon get back to fishing in the bay. "I know you have coracles to fish with in the river," she said, referring to the small single-person round boats that the older men used, "but I will have a boat built that will be safe in the sea, and provide you all with food." There was a huge outburst of cheering, and everyone began to celebrate in earnest.

"Well, time to go," Angharad said to Father Williams, who nodded enthusiastically. They walked slowly up to his cottage with Teifryn and Tegwen's nurse trailing behind. Six of the castle's soldiers, including Penn and Jon, were ordered to accompany them back, and were less than enthusiastic. For the men, it had been a chance to socialize, and for Jon it had been an opportunity to talk to Megan.

"That was a very generous gift," Father Williams said.

"Lord Gwriad will think it a good investment when he's able to collect rent next year," Angharad smiled. "Lord Dafydd will certainly see the sense of it."

The priest laughed. "You're beginning to sound like my Bishop." He handed them mugs of water. "Today was a sad day for some of the villagers, but like all such events there is always something good that comes from it. Llanduduch has achieved a victory that

IN THE ASHES OF A DREAM

few small communities ever achieve: they have not only beaten back the Pictish robbers, but they have proved to each other that they are a capable of working together in harmony." He winked at Angharad. "It won't last forever, but I think I will have fewer complaints at Confession for some time to come."

They made their way back at the speed of the marching soldiers, and the sleeping baby, and by the time they reached the bridge the light was beginning to fade. "Something's up," Angharad said urgently, waking the dozing Teifryn. They all stopped at the far bank and stared at the castle. The main gates were open, there were no guards on the walls and there were lights everywhere. They paused on the edge of the bridge looking up at the castle, suddenly terrified.

The soldiers moved unwillingly to the front. "Find out what has happened," Angharad said forcefully. The six of them, with drawn swords, moved slowly up to the open gates, paused and let out cries of joy: "The Lords are back! They're back!"

Angharad raced her horse towards the gates, yelling "Gwriad!" She was pulsating with excitement, and giving herself up to the joy of having her husband back. It was also the relief of being able to hand over her responsibilities: the last two days had been difficult, and now she could relax.

She jumped off her horse as she entered the courtyard and almost collided with Dafydd. "Welcome back, Dafydd!" she hugged him quickly, and looked anxiously around, her excitement draining. "Where is he?"

Teifryn had also dismounted and sank into her husband's arms, demanding his attention.

"He's up in your bedroom," Dafydd said, trying to deal with the different emotions. He kissed his wife as he tried to explain. "He's injured, Angharad. His face is a mess, and he was unconscious for two days. He's only just beginning to understand things, and he's been drugged to ease the pain."

"Oh! No!" Angharad exclaimed. She pushed through the welcoming crowd and ran towards the great hall, choking with anxiety.

"I'm so sorry!" Teifryn called out after her. She took her arms from Dafydd's neck and began to follow.

Dafydd grabbed her shoulder. "Leave them be, Teifryn. Gwriad has been badly injured. His face is unrecognizable, and Angharad will be shocked when she sees him. We must give them time." He embraced his wife. "I've done everything I can for him. The Wise Woman has treated his wounds and given him something for the pain. He won't know anything until tomorrow."

He walked over to the wet nurse and took his child in his arms. Around them, people stood in subdued groups, as each side began to tell their stories. "Let's go to our room," Teifryn said quietly. "I've missed you, Dafydd, and I'm so glad you're returned unharmed." She took back the baby, as Dafydd gave orders to the servants, and put Penn in charge of the soldiers.

"I've heard about the Picts," he said as they crossed the hall, "at least, one version of what happened, and I have so much to tell you." He led the way into their room and waited until Tegwen had been placed in her crib. As Teifryn turned to him, he took her gently in his arms. "But first let's not say anything."

"Yes," she said as her arms went around his neck, "we have a lot of catching up to do."

• • •

HAROLD WAS LESS THAN A day away from his home, when the weather unexpectedly changed, and what had been an enjoyable ride became a tedious rain-drenched journey. A sharp wind buffeted them, the road turned to mud, and their expensive clothing proved inadequate to the conditions.

Eventually, they reached a cheerless inn, situated in a small impoverished hamlet. Harold dismounted, bellowed loudly for stable boys, and barged into the building. Inside, a smoky fire provided some meagre heat, and the dim lighting did not conceal the poverty of the place. A group of ruffians were sprawled on benches near the fire joking with a young, slatternly girl, and behind a makeshift counter an old man was dozing.

"Get out!" Harold bellowed, pointing at the men.

"Says who?" The largest of the gang got to his feet and, suddenly

IN THE ASHES OF A DREAM

realizing that he was facing a man bigger than himself, rested his hand on a dagger in his belt.

Without warning, Harold punched him in the face, and the man dropped like a stone. At that moment, the other members of Harold's company walked in, and the gang of thugs, who until then had felt they owned the place, quickly departed, dragging their leader out of the door and into the torrential rain. The girl screamed and fled behind the counter, where she and the old man stared wide-eyed at the rich folk who had invaded their inn.

In a short while the fire was blazing, and grubby mugs of weak beer were served. Harold tossed some coins on the counter and ordered the peasants to produce whatever warm food they could. The girl sent out for help with the food preparation, and eventually hot soup and brown bread followed by slices of roasted venison were served. None of Harold's party asked how venison came to be available.

While their clothes steamed, Harold and his men slowly began to relax, and jokes replaced complaints. "I can't wait to sleep in a decent bed, and eat some legal food. Never has pee water tasted so good!" he joked raising his thick eyebrows.

It was at that moment that two soldiers burst into the inn, and seemed shocked to find Harold and his group occupying the cramped interior. For a moment, they stood dripping in the doorway, the light behind them fading, unable to understand what they were seeing.

"We've urgent messages for Earl Harold," one of them gasped. It was clear he had no idea to whom he was speaking, but these looked important people.

"Come in," Harold stood up. "Close the door. I'm Earl Harold."

The soldier who had spoken looked terrified, and turned to his partner for support. The other soldier muttered something, and shook his head, and unwilling to speak, stared fixedly at the floor.

Lidmann realized the men were both shocked, exhausted and seriously out of their depth. "Just tell the Earl what your messages are," he said gently. "You'll not be punished if you are the bearers of bad news."

The soldier nodded and chewed on his lower lip. "M'Lord, I does bring bad news." Harold scowled, and the soldier's eyes bulged; he took a deep breath. "The Welsh 'ave sacked Shrewsbury, m'Lord."

There was an immediate hubbub among the group, and Harold swung round on them. "Quiet!" he ordered. "When did this happen?"

"Four days ago, m'Lord. We was part of a small relief force, and tried to cut 'em off, but it took two days to get our force together." He closed his eyes as if in anguish. "We tried to ambush them near Offa's Dyke, and lost many men." He anxiously rubbed his hands together, and looked as though he was going to say more, but merely opened and closed his mouth like a fish.

"I think you have another message?" Lidmann said encouragingly.

"M'Lord, I 'ave been ordered to tell you that..." he groaned. "They've attacked ye castle, and burned it down!"

Harold stared balefully at the soldier, his large hands opening and closing. A muted gasp came from his assembled company, as they waited for the inevitable explosion. To their surprise and relief, Harold turned away, sat down on a bench, and stared into the fire. The soldier swallowed loudly, and nodded hopefully at his partner.

Lidmann signalled for the girl to fetch them some beer, and indicated they should move away from the door. Nobody said anything and the tension increased. "When did this happen?" Harold continued to stare at the fire.

"Two days ago, m'Lord."

"How many of my soldiers and servants were killed?"

The soldier turned to look at the other man who once again looked at the floor. "I don't know, m'Lord. That be the messages I was to get to you, or to anyone who could find you."

There was a long silence, and then Harold walked slowly towards the old man. "You have rooms?"

"Yes, m'Lord." The old man kept licking his lips.

"Give me the best one. Make sure the girl puts on clean sheets."

"We'll do our best, m'Lord."

"Call me when it's ready." He spoke in measured terms and everyone in the room felt as though they had seen the lightning and were waiting for the thunder. He turned to face them, "The rest of you can use the other rooms or sleep down here." Harold slowly stared from face to face. "We leave at first light. Get it arranged." He finished his beer and drank another, his back to the company. No one spoke, each man appearing to meditate over his mug. Eventually, the girl reappeared and announced timidly that the bed was ready. He left without a word.

There was silence in the inn until they heard his footsteps in the room above, and then cautious whispers broke out.

"What do we do now?" They knew Harold was unpredictable, but the majority believed he would be the next king, and that they would be wise to support him. None knew of Lidmann's dismissal, and after his imprisonment with Harold, it was assumed he was a rising power. They had noted the way he had dealt with the soldiers, and how he was befriending them. They inched closer.

Lidmann bought the soldiers fresh mugs of beer, soup and bread. "You had more to tell Lord Harold about the destruction of his home, didn't you?"

The soldiers froze, and looked guilty. "More, m'Lord?"

"Tell me what happened to Lord Harold's soldiers and servants. I will not have you punished. After you have told me, you can finish your meal and leave."

The soldiers stared at each other. "We heard that the Welsh surrounded Earl Harold's castle with a big army, and the defenders were sure they would all die," the second soldier was suddenly keen to speak. "Then, the Welsh leader promised they would all live if they left the castle without fighting."

"So, they all surrendered? Even the soldiers?"

"Yes, m'Lord. There were just a few guards. Most were servants, local people, an' farmers seeking refuge."

"Where are they now?"

"They've gone back to their homes and farms, m'Lord", he paused, "them what haven't been destroyed. The servants didn't know what to do, and the soldiers fled."

"What about the Earl's wife, the Lady Ealdgyth?"

"I don't know, m'Lord, she weren't mentioned," the first soldier said.

Lidmann sipped his beer. "Where are you from?"

"South of Shrewsbury, m'Lord. We serve the Lord Eadric."

"The attack on Shrewsbury was five days ago?"

The soldier counted on his fingers. "Yes, m'Lord. The weather's been bad, and we didn't hear nothing about the attack until late in the day after it 'appened. We got to Shrewsbury the following afternoon. The town was badly damaged, and there were many dead, including a lot of Welsh soldiers."

"Some of 'em were badly injured, m'Lord," the second soldier added. "Under torture they said they was going on to destroy Earl Harold's castle. We marched the next day, and then got news the Earl's castle had been attacked. We then changed direction, and with some of the Shrewsbury soldiers what had survived the attack, we marched towards Offa's Dyke to cut 'em off."

"We fought hard, m'Lord," the first soldier added looking at his empty mug. "Them that survived, like us, were sent out to spread the news."

"You've done your job." Lidmann handed each a silver coin. "Now leave before the Earl comes down to question you further."

The soldiers nodded their way out of the door. The rain had eased, but a sharp wind was still blowing.

"What now?" one of the nobles addressed Lidmann, and the rest gathered round.

"We rise early," Lidmann said. "I think the Earl will want to inspect the damage and give instructions on the rebuilding. He'll almost certainly head back to London." He was convinced Harold would not risk retaliating at this time: it would take too long to build up enough forces, and it was almost certain the Welsh would have retreated back to their farms now they had punished Harold for the attack on their late King's palace. "I'd prepare yourselves for many hours in the saddle if I were you!"

He smiled to himself; perhaps he might yet snatch a reward from this disaster.

• • •

THE SUN WAS HIGH IN the sky when Harold and his company reached the site of his previously fortified home. He sat motionless n his horse, unnaturally still, only his eyes and the set of his mouth

IN THE ASHES OF A DREAM

revealing the anger that he felt, and his followers thought it wise to keep their distance.

In front of them was a picture of destruction: the huge gates had been reduced to large cinders, still giving off thin tendrils of smoke in spite of the heavy rain of the previous days, and much of the former wooden fortifications were either destroyed or badly damaged. Beyond the gates, the great hall was totally demolished as were most of the other buildings, and the stench of burnt timber, thatch and tar hung in the air, made worse by the heat of the day.

After a long, tense pause, during which nobody spoke, Lidmann moved his docile animal up quietly to a few paces behind the Earl's large, tempestuous horse. "What are your orders, my Lord?"

"Where is everyone?" Harold said in a dangerous whisper.

"I think they're fearful, my Lord."

Harold glanced round at Lidmann, glared a warning at his other followers and walked his horse slowly towards the wrecked gate. "Where are those two soldiers?"

"They left in the night, my Lord."

"Why is there no evidence of fighting?"

Lidmann licked his lips. "The Welsh General promised them safety if they left your castle without fighting."

"How do you know that?"

"The soldiers told me after you'd gone to your room."

Harold nudged his horse forward. "Stay back!" he growled at Lidmann. Slowly, he rode his horse around the remains of his former home that was reduced to burnt beams and ashes. Nothing of value remained.

He knew, once again, it was his fault. If he had put a Knight in charge of his estate, this would not have happened; his soldiers and servants would have fought, and perhaps beaten off the attack. He had not thought it through. After the King had mocked him, he had been driven by anger to react immediately, and in his attempt to achieve the instant release of his least favourite brother from his imprisonment in Antwerp, Harold had defied the elements, resulting in his own imprisonment, the disastrous climb-down with the Norman Bastard, and now this.

However, he resolved in the end it was all Edward's fault. Perhaps God was on his side? The old rogue, who spent all day on his knees, was determined to prevent him from becoming the next king, but Harold was equally resolved to inherit the crown. Apart from anything else, Edward had been married to Harold's sister Edith of Wessex, who had died without having children.

As Earl of Wessex, he had agreed to marry the recently widowed Welsh Queen Ealdgyth, who although a previous Queen, had yet to prove her value. He had a greater claim to the Saxon throne than William the Bastard, and Harold realized he must get back to London as quickly as possible, to regain his reputation and to find a way of influencing the aging, religious fanatic before his God finally claimed him.

He approached Lidmann. "Where's my wife?"

"Nobody knows, my Lord. I heard that she fled the area before the Welsh arrived."

"How surprising," he muttered, and walked his horse around the edge of his former fort, trying to assess what, if anything might be recovered.

Lidmann looked around, and saw a small group of people emerging from behind some distant trees. He trotted over and they bunched together nervously.

"Were you in the fort when the Welsh arrived?"

They looked guiltily at each other. After a brief, almost comic, mime, a tall thickset man with a full beard stepped forward. "We were, m'Lord."

Lidmann smiled down from his horse. The man looked like a leader. "Why were you there? Were you a servant?"

"No, m'Lord, I'm a farmer. I and my family wanted protection from the Welsh." He scowled. "They burnt my farm and stole my animals."

"Too late now for this year's planting and not the best time to buy animals?" The man nodded. "Always assuming you have any money?" The man nodded again.

"I intend to rebuild Earl Harold's home, and I will allow you and your friends the timber you need for your own homes if you will do as I ask." He leaned down from his horse and gave the astonished

IN THE ASHES OF A DREAM

man a silver coin. "I want you to find the Earl's servants, and any skilled people who are willing to help. Let them know I will pay them for their work. Meet me here tomorrow."

As he rode slowly towards the gutted fort, Harold reappeared from behind the remains of the palisade. Lidmann quickly explained what he had arranged, knowing that his future was either secure or truly in tatters.

As he listened, Harold felt his anger drain away. "I've misunderstood you, Lidmann," a thoughtful smile crossed his face. "I'm going back to London, and I'm leaving you in charge. Get all the builders you can find. Here's some money," he handed him a small pouch. "There's enough there to get started. I'll make arrangements to send you more." He gave a bellow of a laugh. "Hire some soldiers, and administer the law while I'm away. Do this well, and I'll give you a title!" He turned his horse, and galloped towards his amazed followers. "To London!" he bellowed. "We're going to London!"

The courtiers groaned, glowered resentfully at Lidmann, and urged their tired horses back up the road they had just come down.

CHAPTER TEN

Three months later, Harold returned to his former home to find it partially rebuilt. He arrived midday, dressed in travelling clothes, with only a small guard, which he left at the local tavern. "I'll pay for everything," he had promised, "but anyone who gets drunk will get chucked in the river." With that threat he had walked down to the building plot.

Lidmann had been expecting his arrival for the past two weeks, as reports from London had indicated that Harold had received a frosty reception from King Edward. "Did you not claim to have settled the Welsh problem?" he had asked with a pained expression on his wizen face. "Perhaps, you need to return to the Welsh border and assert your authority."

Harold had spent his time in London trying to solidify his support among the other Lords, and he was aware that the King's acid comments were greatly enjoyed by the envious and those who had long time disagreements with his family. He had been amazed at how quickly his hero's reputation had faded. After defeating the Welsh King, Harold had become the idol of the nation, but the dismissive reaction of Edward, coupled with his French imprisonment had tarnished his image. Finally, the recent attacks on Shrewsbury and the destruction of his home near Chester had made him an object of ridicule in the King's Court. As one courtier jested: "When are the Welsh not defeated? When Harold defeats them."

"My Lord," Lidmann bowed, "I had not expected you, else I would have arranged a formal welcome from the men," he waved his hand towards the teams of industrious workers.

"You seem to have made good progress," Harold remarked,

IN THE ASHES OF A DREAM

aware that Lidmann was being diplomatic. "I didn't come to delay the work. Walk with me and explain your plan for my new home."

After nearly an hour, Harold was satisfied with the design of his house, after making some minor changes. "I understand you have established a new system of laws that are not as harsh as those that formally existed, and you have upset the Church?"

Lidmann swallowed before he answered. This was a subject that he knew he might be severely at fault. "I needed to find workers for this construction. After the Welsh raid, many of the people were without homes, without food and were living rough in the forest. I needed to gain their trust, I encouraged them to cut down trees and build their own homes."

"And the forest belonged to the Church?"

"Yes, my Lord. The Church had not helped these people. I felt the Bishop did not need the trees, but my workers did."

Harold stared impassively at Lidmann, who began to think he was about to lose his position. "Well done!" Harold roared with laughter. "That was masterful! The Bishop is a constipated old rogue. You did well." He looked around, "And the royal deer?"

"The people were starving. These were the people I needed to rebuild your palace," he placed an emphasis on the word palace, "and I gave them permission to hunt and feed themselves and their families."

"I agree." Harold smoothed his beard thoughtfully. "But tell them that when their harvests are in, the hunting stops."

Lidmann bowed his head. "I have recruited a notable builder, and I have hired six soldiers to guard the area, and help administer justice." Harold raised his eyebrows. "My Lord, you said I was to keep order, and it has been necessary for me to be severe in some of my punishments." Harold nodded. "After the Welsh attack, some people thought they could steal from others and abuse their women. Two brothers were found guilty, and I had them hanged."

Harold shrugged. "Anything else?"

"An elderly woman was claiming she had a dream that you would be the next King of England, my Lord. She was yelling it to anyone who would listen at the market."

Harold's face became grim. "What did you do?"

"I gave her a coin, and said she could do this at every market."

Harold gave a roar of laughter. "I misjudged you, Lidmann. Keep this up and you'll be well rewarded." He handed Lidmann a bag of money. "Send a message to London as soon as I can live in this place. You can leave a message with Lord Rochester." He paused and grinned at Lidmann, "The old woman's right. I will be the next King." He gave his servant a companionable smack on his thin back. "Where're you staying?"

"With an elderly widow, my Lord. She provides my meals and washes my clothes," he paused. "It's not much of a place, but it keeps me out of trouble."

Harold looked at him strangely, and then realized he was trying to make a joke. "Take me to the nearest decent inn, Lidmann."

"There's no such thing around here, my Lord. But I'll take you to a place where they won't poison you."

Harold laughed; he was feeling in better humour than he had done for weeks. "Good. Take me there, and you can tell me everything that has happened since I was last here."

• • •

JON ARRIVED AT FATHER WILLIAMS' cottage, and frowned as he saw the priest sitting outside in the sun and clearly waiting for him. On rare occasions, the priest had been out walking or visiting the sick and elderly in the village, and Jon had taken those opportunities to meet Megan. He went to great lengths to make his meetings appear accidental, and would have been surprised and embarrassed to know that he was the talk of the village and was known as 'the young Lord from Gwbert.' He had also been the reason why a neighbour had said to Megan's mother: "It's about time your Megan wore something under her shift."

It was late summer, and the elderly priest was reading a Latin scroll from his collection. "Come and sit down, my son," he smiled and indicated a rock near his chair. "How are things up at the castle?"

"Not very happy, Father," Jon said as he tethered the horse and sat down. "Lord Gwriad is still limping about, and although his face is improving, his nose is still odd, and his eyes are still red with black areas around them." He looked out towards the bay, and appeared to want to say something more, then paused. The priest said nothing, but after a moment, he cleared his throat and rested his hand on the boy's shoulder. Jon turned to face him, and the priest raised his eyebrows in an encouraging manner.

"Lord Gwriad is not the same man he was when he went to fight the Saxons," he said in a rush.

"In what way?" Father Williams rolled up his scroll.

"He shouts at everyone, Father. He doesn't laugh any more, and he's started to hit people."

"Who does he hit?"

"Mostly the servants, but I saw him hit the Lady Angharad yesterday."

"What did she do?"

"She walked away and pretended it hadn't happened."

"Anyone else?"

"Yes, Father, I saw him hit Lord Dafydd."

"When?"

"Today. Lord Dafydd had arranged a meeting in the great hall with some of the officers who had been part of the army that attacked the Saxons. There was General Maelgwn there, but Lord Gwriad did not appear. Then, suddenly, he burst in and accused everyone of treachery." Jon stopped speaking and took a deep breath.

"Go on," Father William murmured. "I need to know."

"Lord Gwriad was shouting, and everyone stood up, and he went up to Lord Dafydd at the head of the table and punched him in the face." Jon sniffed. "He would have given him another punch, but General Maelgwn prevented him, and wrestled him out of the room."

"Is Lord Dafydd injured?"

"No, Father, not much, just a swollen lip."

"What did they do with Lord Gwriad?"

"They locked him in a store room, Father, until the Wise Woman arrived and made a potion that they managed to get him to drink. He slowly calmed down and was taken up to his room.

Lady Angharad and Lady Teifryn were crying. Everyone thinks he's gone mad."

Father Williams did not reply, but walked slowly back and forth, deep in thought. After a while, he indicated for Jon to walk with him. "When did he first start to seem different?"

"Well, Father, he hasn't been the same since he returned. To begin with he was in much pain, and the Wise Woman drugged him and for the first few days I didn't see him. When he appeared, he was limping, and his face was frightening. His nose was badly broken, and he had trouble speaking, and he had a wild look in his eyes," Jon took a deep breath. "He didn't know who I was. I reminded him I was Jon, his squire, and he looked blankly at me and walked away without a word."

Jon scuffed his boot in the grass, lost in his memories. "Then, he started getting very drunk, and passed out in the hall. But he was not enjoying himself, he didn't laugh or joke with people, he just glared at everyone, and if you spoke to him he either ignored you or swore at you. He did not seem to know his brother, or his wife."

"Why did you not tell me this before?"

"It seemed disloyal, Father."

The priest nodded, quietly taking note of the great increase in Jon's vocabulary, which seemed to match his increase in height and weight.

"Disloyal?" Father Williams shook his head. "You must always remember that you can tell your priest anything. It is not being disloyal. I know you want to be a good squire, but most squires start their training when they are much younger than you. Most squires are the sons of lords and landed gentry, they know how to behave, they don't have to be taught. You cannot be expected to become a squire overnight. Also, you have been relying on Penn for your weapons training and Lady Angharad for your knowledge of what your duties are around the castle. You had little chance to get to know your Lord before he went on his campaign, and you have had no chance to mix with other squires. You must rely more on me."

IN THE ASHES OF A DREAM

"Thank you, Father Williams." Jon felt like bursting into tears. "It has been difficult."

"Let's change the subject. Come into the cottage and we'll have some water and something to eat.

They went inside and sat down near the fire, which was always burning. Father Williams handed Jon a mug of water, poured himself some wine, and shared some bread and cheese. "Tuck in, my son, you need to keep your strength up." He smiled and Jon felt himself relaxing.

"I understand you never knew your mother?"

"No, Father, she ran away when I was just able to walk."

"Did you ever get to know anything about her?"

Jon shook his head. "I asked the old lady who lived in my father's house about my mother, and she would only say bad things about her. I discovered she did not come from Gwbert. That was where my father came from."

"What did he say about your mother?"

"Most times he wouldn't speak about her, and I rarely had the chance to be with him." He shrugged. "He did some fishing, but most of the time he was soldiering for Lord Gomer, so I hardly ever spoke to him."

"Did your mother work?"

"The old woman said she worked up at the castle. That was before she met my father."

"Where did she come from? Was she born in Aberteifi?"

"I don't know, Father."

The old priest helped himself to some more wine. "Jon, I want you to tell Lord Dafydd that I would like to visit with Lord Gwriad tomorrow. I want you to ask him to send a cart, as I am not so good on a horse anymore."

Jon jumped to his feet. "I will, Father!"

"Sit down, Jon, there is one other thing I want to discuss with you."

"Father?" Jon felt his cheeks begin to flush.

"I understand you have become quite fond of a young girl in this village named Megan?" He sat back on his chair and looked fixedly at Jon, who felt he was going to burst with embarrassment.

"I, um, have met her, um, once or twice."

"You want to become a squire?"

"Yes, Father."

"You have a long way to go in your training, and you can never become a squire to a Lord if you fool around with a fisherman's daughter."

It was such a blow that Jon did not know what to say. "I... I don't fool around, Father."

The priest looked at the boy's anguished face and knew he spoke the truth. "I know, Jon, you are just enjoying the company of a friend. But she is a young woman who is, although she does not fully realize it, looking for a husband. There will come a time when the fact that you are male and she is female will come to the surface. You must stop seeing her now. Do you understand?"

"Stop seeing her?" Jon echoed. It all seemed so unfair.

"Do you not know the whole of Llanduduch is talking about your love affair? Do you not know you are called 'The Young Lord from Gwbert'?"

Jon stared in horror at the priest. "That's not true, it's not a love affair!"

The priest helped himself to more wine. "I believe you, Jon. But if you are to save this young woman's reputation you must not see her again. When you come for your lessons in future you must not go down to the village. She will be upset to begin with, but she will soon get over it." He got to his feet. "Go straight back to the castle and give Lord Dafydd my message."

They walked in silence back to where Jon's horse was quietly cropping the grass. The priest handed Jon a small book. "After I've visited Lord Gwriad tomorrow, I will have time to talk to you about this book."

Jon nodded, unable to speak, and slowly rode back to the castle. He felt utterly miserable. In a few short minutes his once happy world had fractured. What would Megan think when he never saw her again? He hadn't done anything that he could feel guilty about; they had just talked. For a few wild moments he thought of running away and taking Megan with him, but slowly the real world closed in on him and he returned to the castle to give his messages and take up his role. "I'm a squire," he muttered, "and squires must suffer."

• • •

THE NEXT DAY, JON ARRANGED to have sword practice with Penn, to avoid being sent with the wagon to collect the priest. When the wagon returned, Jon made himself scarce in the nearby orchard, where he pretended to read the book Father Williams had given him. However, he was unable to concentrate on the words, as his mind dwelt solely on the unfairness of life and the embarrassment of his situation.

After a short while, he heard Penn calling his name. Knowing that the sergeant would never seek him out unless ordered to do, Jon reluctantly returned to the castle.

"Penn's looking for you," Owen said smiling evilly as Jon walked slowly through the gate. "I wouldn't want to be in your skin. He sounded really mad." He made tooting noises.

"Remind me to thump you when you're next off guard duty," Jon growled as he passed the grinning youth.

"Where've you been?" Penn yelled as Jon walked up the steps towards the hall. "The Lady wants you."

Jon pretended he hadn't heard and continued to approach the doors. He was not going to explain. Why should he? He stuck out his jaw and was so wrapped up in his own importance that he did not see the punch coming. He staggered on the steps, his right ear ringing, and turned to face Penn whose anger was turning to satisfaction. "Just watch yourself, you little turd. You may be training for a squire but you're still under my control." He smirked as Jon screwed up his eyes to clear his head. "Even if you are the 'Young Lord from Gwbert'!" He roared with laughter.

A moment later the old soldier was lying on the ground, his jaw aching and blood in his mouth. Penn had never had anyone fight back, and he watched with disbelief as Jon rubbed his right fist, walked up the steps to the door and disappeared into the Hall.

Owen stared in amazement from above the main gate. "Wait 'til I tell Davis," he muttered. "He won't believe it."

Inside the hall, Angharad, Dafydd and Teifryn were sitting

around the fire. "Come over here, Jon," Lord Dafydd said. Jon crossed the floor, wondering if he was about to be criticized, yet again, for his meetings with Megan. Did everyone in the castle know?

"Father Williams is examining Lord Gwriad," Dafydd said. "As you are his squire, Father Williams wants you to be there." The women gazed solemnly at him but said nothing.

"Yes, my Lord," Jon gave a small bow. "Shall I go up now?"

"Yes," he seemed uncomfortable, as did the two women.

Jon bowed and left the room. As he climbed the circular steps, his mind was racing. What was Father Williams up to?

When he entered the room, Lord Gwriad was sleeping, a servant was carefully washing his face, and the priest was sitting in a chair by the window, writing at a small table. He turned as Jon entered. "Ah, Jon!" he smiled benignly. "I hope I haven't dragged you away from something important?"

Jon felt his face redden. "Oh no, Father. I was just reading the book you gave me."

"Indeed. We'll discuss it later." The priest pointed at the sleeping Lord. "I want you to stand by the side of him and tell me in exact detail what you see."

"What I see?" Jon echoed.

"Yes, I want your report of exactly how you see Lord Gwriad, as he is at this moment. I have examined him, and now I want you to tell me, as his squire, what you see."

Jon was sure that this was some sort of game, a way of making him appreciate his role as a squire. But he knew he had no choice. "Lord Gwriad has a broken nose," he began awkwardly.

"That is true. However, I will want you to tell me as accurately as you can, how it looks, how badly is the nose broken, and what ideas you have for helping your Lord to recover."

Jon swallowed, chewed on his lower lip, and began again. For a long time he listed every aspect of Lord Gwriad's face and head, and throughout the process the priest kept asking probing questions, such as: "Have you seen eye sockets as badly damaged as these?" and "Can you imagine the damage inside the skull?"

Throughout the session the priest would suddenly write

something down. "Well done, Jon. You now know, in great detail, the face and head of the man you serve as squire. Most people never get the chance to know another person's features as well as you now know Lord Gwriad's." He smiled. "Come and sit here." He indicated a small stool, and when Jon had sat down, stared into his eyes.

"Do you think Lord Gwriad's broken nose is the reason he's become a changed man?" the priest asked.

"No, Father, it's changed the way he looks, but not the way he acts."

"That is the correct answer," the priest nodded thoughtfully. "Now, I want you to tell me everything you have noticed about the change in Lord Gwriad. Begin from the first moment you saw him, up until the time you told me about his behaviour."

Jon described, step by step, the gradual increase in violence in Lord Gwriad's behaviour. At times the priest would interrupt to clarify a point, and at other times he would ask Jon to repeat it. Finally, he was satisfied.

"You've done well, Jon. You have an outstanding ability to notice things, and to remember them. Now I'm going to ask you a few final questions." Jon breathed a small sigh of relief. "If you broke your foot, would you continue to use it?"

"No, Father."

"What would you do?"

"I would try not to use it until it healed."

"Would you agree, that the blow to the head did more damage than the obvious broken nose and black eyes?" Jon nodded. "So, it would appear that Lord Gwriad's brain has been damaged?" Jon nodded again. "So, what would you think should be the cure?"

It suddenly seemed obvious. "He should rest his brain!"

"Exactly." He turned to look at the snoring body. "We must give him a sleeping draft, to rest his brain. But we can't do that for ever, for it's bad for a body to be inactive for too long."

Jon nodded; he was immersed in the logic of it all, and proud to be treated as a grownup. "So, we have to keep him drugged for as long as possible, and then see if he's better?"

"You are correct," the priest confirmed. "But what happens if he is still violent?"

Jon chewed his lower lip. "I suppose we have to drug him again?"

"Unfortunately, we have no other way. So, eventually he either gets better, or he will never improve. During the time I was serving in Spain, I met Arab doctors who could do amazing operations on the head. I never had the opportunity to work with them, but I did pick up some of their knowledge." He stared sadly out of the window. "So, we will do the best we can, and I will pray for his recovery."

He stood up, and walked over to the sleeping man, whose broken nose caused him to snore like the bellowing of a bull. "I can't stay here. I have my own responsibilities." He put his hand on Jon's shoulder. "The Wise Woman will keep him drugged on my orders. Then, she will slowly reduce the drug so that he will have periods of consciousness. I want you to observe him closely during these times. Eventually, he will be fully conscious, and you must watch him and help him in any way you can. That is your job. But, you will also keep up your lessons with me, and you will make a full report at such times. We don't know how or even *if* he will mend."

"Thank you, Father. I'll do my best."

"I know you will. Stay with him now until Lady Angharad comes up. I will tell them what we have agreed," he smiled. "This could be an important time in your life, so make good use of what I have taught you."

. . .

HAROLD GODWINSON HAD INHERITED THE Earldom of Wessex after the death of his father Earl Godwin in 1053. At that time he had become the most powerful man after King Edward. Harold's father had dominated the weak King, who had married his daughter Edith of Wessex, and Godwin had insisted in 1044 that Edward make his eldest living son, Harold, the Earl of East Anglia, Essex and Cambridgeshire. As well as these powerful Earldoms, Harold also owned property on the edge of the great Forest of Arden, south of Birmingham, and it was here that he had arranged to have a family gathering.

The light was fading as the riders entered the fortified yard that surrounded the rambling mansion. It was raining hard, and the cold wind of late autumn cut through their damp clothing. A host of servants rushed forward to take control of the lathered horses of the nobles and their followers, leaving the strong guard of mounted soldiers to fend for themselves. A single deer was the sole result of a disappointing day's hunting, and the tired hunters were cold and looking forward to warmth, roasted meat and mulled wine.

"Lords, gather in the main hall when you're ready, and refresh yourselves!" Harold bellowed. "Leofwine and Gyrth, come with me!" He led the way through the main doors into the wide hall with its great roaring fireplace and up the stairs to his bedroom. It was an airy room, with a huge bed, and an array of trunks and large boxes. At one end was a blazing fire, around which were an assortment of oak chairs, and a small table with jugs of wine and plates of food. At the other end was a single shuttered window above a large table on which was a collection of maps and scrolls, and next to it a jumble of weapons.

The brothers walked in and quickly established themselves around the fire. Harold handed round mugs of wine, and using a thick glove, withdrew a hot metal poker from the fire and plunged it into his drink. The red wine steamed and hissed, and the men gave a unanimous grunt of approval. When all the drinks had been heated, they sat back and sipped their drinks, with pieces of roasted chicken in their hands.

"Anyone looking around this room would not guess that you're a married man, brother," Leofwine, the youngest of the men jested.

"Do not ruin this moment," Harold growled, although he was not annoyed. Leofwine was his favourite brother, and although the shortest, he was the best swordsman of any of them. Always friendly, and a great supporter of the family's name, he was not ambitious, and was happy to rule an area to the south-east of London. He adored his wife and had more children than Harold could remember.

"Come on, Harold, tell us what's happened to your wife, the

Welsh ex-queen," Gyrth, his second youngest brother said. He spoke with an impressive sense of authority, and as Earl of East Anglia, a position he had inherited once Harold became the Earl of Wessex, he had increased his political influence in recent years. Although the jealous might insinuate that it was all due to his powerful family, most would agree it was his intelligence and diplomatic skills that had been responsible. As a younger brother in a powerful family, he saw his position as another asset to the Godwinson family. His constant support of King Edward and his enthusiasm for the building of Westminster Abbey, the largest church in England, had been reciprocated, and Edward considered him a friend, even though he was Harold's brother.

"If you must know, I've placed Ealdgyth in a nunnery."

"You didn't ask for my help?" Gyrth looked surprised. "I could have helped you place her in a wealthy London nunnery, where she could have lived in comfort."

"That was exactly why I did not ask for your help." Harold finished his wine, poured more into his mug and went through the process of heating it. "Ealdgyth is a monster, and I am surprised King Gruffydd put up with her. It's hard to imagine how he was attracted to her in the first place." He stared reflectively into the fire. "I only married her because I thought it might be a good political move, and because she pleaded with me to help her maintain her reputation after the death of her husband. Ha! She has no more reputation to maintain than our local drabs, and she's been of no political help to me whatsoever. To add to it, she fled when the Welsh attacked my home, and then she suddenly reappeared in London, claiming wealth and prestige in my name. In the short time, before I removed her, she had quickly made a reputation as the court harlot."

"That must have pleased our holy King!" Gyrth remarked quietly. He was well aware of the on-going friction between the King and Harold.

"As you can imagine, yet another juicy anecdote for our blessed Edward." He looked at Gyrth and smiled. "What with Tostig and my cloistered wife, I am grateful to have two reliable courtiers in the family." He raised his mug as a tribute to Leofwine and Gyrth.

IN THE ASHES OF A DREAM

Leofwine laughed. "I must ensure that none of my human weaknesses are revealed. At least not until you become King!" He looked at Harold and frowned. "There seems to be no end to Edward's Norman addictions, and I gather he's in constant touch with Duke William."

"New Norman fashions, new Norman merchants at Court, and Norman architecture, exemplified by Westminster Abbey," Gyrth said as he selected a chicken leg. "It's not surprising, I suppose, after all Edward spent more of his early life in Normandy than in England, and although he's got Saxon blood, the rest of him is Norman." He paused, "You must admit however, the new cathedral is an architectural wonder."

"It's Norman!" Harold complained.

"As long as the next King is not a Norman," Leofwine raised his cup in salutation.

Harold scowled. "I hope to persuade Edward that the future of the Saxon line can only be continued if he tells the Witen that I must succeed him." He finished his wine. "If only he'd been a man in his bed, we'd have had no problems with inheritance."

"True," Gyrth said, "but you could argue that our sister Edith has done us a favour. As Edward's long-suffering wife, her progeny would have put you and our family out of contention for the crown. Also, Queen Edith would have had little influence in protecting our family from the machinations of the powerful enemies who would side with any child born in the direct line of the Saxon Kings."

There was a pause as Harold reflected on this point. "I would have been happy to remain the most powerful Lord in England if I were supporting a true Saxon King. But there is no way that I can allow the Norman Bastard to rule. He'll bring his land-hungry lords into our country, and bit by bit the Saxon gentry will be removed, and we will all become Norman vassals." He clenched his fists. "As King of England, William will demand my allegiance, and once in command, he will find fault with me, even if I am loyal to him, and my days will be numbered." He looked at his brothers, "Then, you will be removed from power, and the name of Godwinson will disappear."

"You have some strong bargaining powers with Edward," Leofwine refilled his mug. "He married our beloved sister, and our father welcomed Edward back from his long banishment in Normandy. You are the next logical king when Edward dies. Although he may prefer his Norman friend, the Witen is solidly Saxon, and once dead, Edward's wishes will be ignored."

"However, your unfortunate meeting with William, when you were little more than his captive, does complicate the issue," said Gyrth, glancing at Leofwine, and giving an apologetic shrug. "He, and the Holy Church, have your agreement in writing, sworn over a particularly venerated bible stating you agree that he is to be the next King of England. Furthermore, you swore to be loyal to him, and worse still, this agreement has, as you know, received the blessing of the Pope, and has been announced in every church, monastery and nunnery throughout England, and throughout the Christian countries of Europe."

"I was broadsided," Harold muttered. "Whatever else I might accuse William of, he's a great planner." He looked at Gyrth. "The power of agreements fades over time, and when our weak King dies, I am certain the Witen will choose me. I intend to let it be known, that when Edward was on his deathbed he changed his mind and proclaimed that I would be the next King of this country." He glared at his brothers. "We are all in this together, and we either succeed or we lose everything."

There was a long silence as the men sipped their wine. "I hope our brother, the Earl of Northumberland, agrees with us," Gyrth said. "Tostig is not known for being reliable."

"He wants the throne himself," Harold said. "We all know his ambition exceeds his abilities. As the second brother in this family," he corrected himself. "As the second in line following the death of our eldest brother, Sweyn, during his disastrous pilgrimage, Tostig has never been content. I'm aware of his pathetic efforts to involve the King of Norway." He poured another mug of wine. "But whether King Harald Hardrada is prepared to risk an invasion remains to be seen."

Gyrth nodded at Harold. "There is no doubt that England is seen by a number of our neighbours as a plum waiting for the picking. A King without at least one son puts his country in the focus of every ambitious leader. I think you should keep a close eye on Hardrada, especially as Tostig has been staying in his Court, and some legal prelates argue that Hardrada does have a claim to the English throne, no matter how weak."

"Tostig's visiting William," Leofwine added.

"That's a puzzle to me," Harold said. "The Norman Bastard will never share power with him. As Earl of Northumbria, he has advanced as far as he is likely to go, and he's even making a mess of that."

Gyrth gave a humourless laugh. "He was appointed to that position because he swore he could contain the Scots and bring prosperity back to Northumbria. The Scottish threat has become worse, and his people hate him. Not a good recommendation for leadership."

Leofwine produced some dice. "The leadership game is on hold until Edward dies, then the players will reveal themselves." He looked knowingly at his two brothers.

Harold refilled all the mugs. "To our best endeavours!" he said. "We either grab power or lose everything."

CHAPTER ELEVEN

The rain was hammering down, the wind was howling and on the high ground above Llanduduch Jon watched as huge seas battered the coastline around the bay. It was unpleasant weather, even for February, but as soon as Jon had completed his duties, he had decided it was worth the cold and the wet to get away from the castle, and he arrived at the priest's cottage at midday.

After stabling his long-suffering horse in the priest's small barn, he fed her some hay and made his way across the boggy ground to the cottage. Jon stood with fingers numbed in the small porch, shielded from the wind, and slowly removed his drenched cloak. The noise of the wind was so loud that he was not surprised the priest had not heard his arrival. He gave the cloak a shake and knocked loudly.

After a moment, he opened the door and peered in. The warmth drew him, and he quickly entered and closed the door carefully behind him. In the shadowy room, the fire had burnt low, and the priest was asleep, slouched in his favourite chair. Only one candle was alight, and Jon used it to light another. He had visited this house innumerable times, and had gradually become familiar with its layout, and where the priest kept things. He went to the log stack near the wide fireplace, and built up the fire, and was surprised the priest had not been woken by the noise.

He walked over to him, and gently shook his arm, noticing as he did that there was an empty jug of wine by the side of his chair. "Father Williams!" he called out loudly, and gave him another shake.

The priest's eyes shot open, stared at him for a moment, then

IN THE ASHES OF A DREAM

closed as he rubbed his forehead, and groaned. Gradually, he sat up in his chair. "Get me some water, Jon," he muttered.

By the time Jon returned with a mug of water, the priest was sitting upright. "Well done, my son." He drank the whole mug, and carefully handed it back. "I'm pleased to see you. I hadn't expected you to brave this terrible weather." He stood up and stretched. "I haven't seen anyone for two days. I don't blame them, it's not the weather to be out in." He noticed Jon's cloak on the floor near the door. "Bring over that sorry looking wet garment and hang it there," he pointed to a metal frame near the fire, "and take your boots off, and your stockings as well, and pull up that stool."

After a short while, Jon was gradually warming up as he roasted in front of the blaze with his hands cradling a cup of mulled wine. In the last few months Father Williams had occasionally allowed Jon to share his wine. "I understand you serve behind your Lord at the table, and that you are allowed to drink wine, so this will help you to get a more refined taste."

Father Williams made himself comfortable. "What is the situation with Lord Gwriad?"

"He continues to improve, Father. He's started to take an interest in things, and I had to tell him, in great detail, how you defeated the Picts."

The priest smiled, "Not just me, Jon, not just me."

"Lord Gwriad was amazed when I told him how Lady Angharad had prepared the castle for a possible attack. She had not mentioned it to him."

"How's his memory?"

"Still not good, Father. It's possible that Lady Angharad has told him, and he just forgot. Lord Dafydd is often having to remind him of the raid on the Saxons. He has no memory of punching people, and as far as I know, he has stopped doing so."

"Is the Wise Woman still attending him?"

"Yes, Father. She doesn't give him strong drugs anymore, although he still demands them, and she only visits when the Lady Angharad sends for her."

"Good. Very good." Father Williams sipped his wine, deep in thought. "Is the Lord drinking much?"

"No, Father. Lady Angharad has insisted that he only has two cups of wine at night. After I've poured the second one, Lady Angharad sends me on an errand. When Lord Gwriad demands more wine, she tells him he is not allowed more until he recovers. To prove he has recovered, she insists he has to be able to ride his new horse, which he can't do at the moment."

"Oh?"

"It's his balance, Father. He sometimes staggers when he walks, and he can't move fast or climb up on his horse."

"But, he does seem to be getting better?"

"Yes, Father, he has started sharing jokes with people. When he first returned home he seemed to be in a world of his own."

"How does he treat you?" Father Williams raised his hand. "You are not being disloyal, Jon. I'm your priest, you can tell me everything."

Jon cleared his throat. "Well, Father, he sometimes thinks I'm older than I am." He took a deep breath, finished his wine and stared into the empty cup. "He tells me of his experiences with women, and keeps wanting to know of mine." He looked embarrassed. "He sometimes thinks I'm married. Other times he wants to know about my girlfriends."

"Ah," Father Williams nodded sagely. "In time, you'll meet the right young woman." He stood up and walked unsteadily towards his collection of books. Jon remained sitting, deep in thought. Father Williams selected a book, and made his way back to the fire. "What else do you have to tell me?"

Jon sat upright. "It's… well it's… Megan has been given a job in the kitchen." The whole story came tumbling out: Megan, the cook, had liked the way her namesake had settled in and helped on the day the Picts were expected to attack. Just after the Christ Mass, the cook had persuaded Lady Angharad to allow her to take the girl on a trial, and train her to become the next cook. "Everybody in the castle knows that I like her," John said, "and Megan can't understand why I keep away from her." He gave a long sigh.

"Life is never easy, Jon." Father Williams opened his book.

"Nobody is without some sort of difficulty," his tone indicated that the subject was closed.

Before he left in the mid-afternoon, Jon brought in more logs for the fire, and did some light duties around the cottage. In doing so, he noticed that the place was not as tidy as usual, the priest's robe was stained and he looked unwashed. This surprised him, as the priest was usually scrupulously clean, and was very exact as to where things were kept. He glanced into his sleeping quarters and saw the bedding was in disarray, and there was a pile of empty wine containers in his pantry.

"When will you come again?" Father William asked as Jon dressed for his departure. In the firelight, his cheeks seemed very flushed, and he remained seated, when normally he would have walked to the door to wave goodbye.

"Today is Tuesday, so shall I come again on Thursday?"

"Thursday, yes. Did I give you that book?"

"No, Father. It's best I don't take it in this weather, it might get damp."

"Yes." The priest seemed distracted. "I would like you to get a message to the Wise Woman. Tell her I would like her to visit me."

"Yes, Father. Is there anything I can do before I leave?"

The priest sat up in his chair. "No. Um, yes. Go down to the village, and tell Mrs. Reece I would like her to come up as soon as the storm passes."

As Jon staggered down the hill, he considered everything he had noticed, and when he arrived at Mrs. Reece's hovel, he told her the message and added that the priest seemed unwell. Mrs. Reece was a large, middle-aged woman whose husband had been killed by the Picts, and who had become the priest's occasional housekeeper.

"Oh dear," she said. "I've not been up for a while. I've been ill, you know. Is he feeding himself?"

"I don't think so."

"Right, I'll get up there as soon as the weather improves. I can't make that hill in this weather, you know. I've not been the same since they killed my Roy."

Jon murmured his thanks, and climbed back up the hill to the cottage. He crept round to the one shuttered window, and peered through a crack where he could see the priest asleep in his chair. He collected the horse, which would have preferred to remain in the barn, and began the long storm-battering journey down the side of the hill, and finally along the path beside the river.

The light was fading, and he knew he would not arrive back before darkness. However, he still rode the horse at a walking pace, unwilling to risk an accident, letting the horse find its path as it slowly meandered through mud and deep pools. On his left, the river was thundering, enlivened by the recent non-stop rain, and threatening to overflow its banks. In some parts the path was well away from the river, but occasionally he was uncomfortably close. He peered ahead and contemplated what an unpleasant day it had been.

He worried if the priest might be ill, or just drinking too much. In the spring and summer, it seemed an ideal existence living on the hillside overlooking the village and the bay, but in winter it was cold and lonely. Then, he thought about Lord Gwriad: was he really getting better, or was he as well as he would ever be? Finally, he returned to his constant concern: what to do about Megan?

He had never had a girlfriend, never even kissed a girl, and after the admonition of the priest, he had tried to measure up to his Lord's expectations of how a squire should behave. Except that, apart from the advice of Lady Angharad, he had no real idea what was expected of him. Penn had instructed him in the use of weapons and Lord Dafydd had shown him basic rules of managing a horse in battle; Father Williams had taught him how to read and write and added some history lessons, and Lady Angharad had shown him how to behave around the castle and at mealtimes. She had talked to him about the family history and how life had changed since the time Lord Dafydd and Lord Gwriad served the King of Wales. But nobody had prepared him for the important issues of growing up.

Without the instruction of a father or a brother, and with Lord Gwriad unable to take him to other castles or the homes of landowners to meet other squires, he was without anyone who could give him the advice he so desperately wanted. He was the

IN THE ASHES OF A DREAM

first to admit that his life had improved beyond his wildest dreams, but with his new status came an uncertainty as to exactly what his role was, and he was very aware that he seemed to be missing out on the most important aspect of life that his body had begun to crave.

How did a squire act with girls? How did one meet the right girls? He had listened to Davis and Owen boasting about their experiences with some of the daughters of hill farmers. "They're wild girls," Davis said, his eyes rolling in his head. "They let you do anything!" Jon knew that sounded exciting, but he had no idea what it meant, and he wasn't going to reveal that he knew less than they did. It had to be something to do with kissing. He had seen girls peeing in the bushes and knew they were different, but his lack of knowledge terrified him.

He was so absorbed in his thoughts, that it wasn't until the horse suddenly stopped that he became aware of the two ragged figures that were blocking the path. Jon saw in an instant that he was in trouble. The larger man had a club and the other was waving a knife. "Get off the horse, boy, an' ye won't get hurt."

It was dusk, and the flooded river was raging close to the trail on his left and on the other side was dense forest. He reached for his sword, with his right hand, and pulled back on the horse's bit, at the same time kicking with his boots. The horse reared up, its front hooves pawing at the air, forcing the two men back. It was an action he had practised under the direction of Lord Dafydd, who had, in recent weeks, taught him some useful tips when fighting from a horse. "Remember," he had said, "once an enemy has hold of your horse's bridle, your best weapon has been lost and you are vulnerable."

"We'll do ye no harm, boy. We just want ye horse," the man with the knife said, in a whining voice, as he tried to approach on the side above the river. As he spoke the large man rushed forward on the left. They had chosen a narrow part of the path, where Jon would have difficulty turning the horse, but where it was also difficult for them to approach.

Jon repeated his action, and the horse kicked out with its front hooves, just as the big man lashed out with his club, and the knife man reached up for the bridle. The club smashed down against Jon's shoulder, forcing him to drop the sword, just as the horse's hoof knocked the large man back into the trees.

The smaller man let out a cry of success as he grabbed the bridle with his left hand, and slashed at Jon's leg with his knife. At the same moment, Jon veered the horse to the right, causing the man to lose his balance on the muddy path and be bumped by the powerful rump of the horse. The knife sank into Jon's thigh, but instantly the man dropped the weapon as he fought to control the terrified animal. Jon screamed in pain and, grabbing his small dagger with his left hand, lashed out, cutting the man across the face. In that instant, he saw the man let go of the bridle, and screaming with terror, fall back over the bank and into the roaring torrent below. He was immediately sucked under the tempestuous water.

The panicked horse leapt forward, and it was more by luck than skill that Jon did not fall off. As the animal raced away, he glimpsed the large man flaying his arms as he tried to fight his way out of the undergrowth. The horse somehow avoided falling and breaking its legs, and slowly he managed to get control of the animal and saw the welcoming lights of the castle. His shoulder throbbed and his leg was oozing blood, and as he reached the main gate he was unable to speak.

"Who's there?" Rhodri called out from the parapet. He could see in the twilight it was Jon, but he hadn't noticed his condition. "Say who you are boy, or I won't open..." Jon collapsed in the saddle and slowly slipped off the horse. "Oh, Hell! Hywel! Hywel! Help me open the gate!" Rhodri could not guess what had happened, but he was certain he was going to be blamed.

• • •

WHEN JON AWOKE, HE FOUND himself in the home of the local Wise Woman, who had a small house at the edge of the village and nearest to the castle. Derryth had lived in the village all her life, and having worked with her mother, Afanen, a renowned healer, had inherited her title of 'Wise Woman' when her mother died. Derryth had never married, although it was rumoured that she had many lovers, and as she was approaching middle age, there were some who worried as to who would become the next healer when she passed on.

Derryth had helped her mother treat Lord Gomer's ailments, and when her mother died, had continued to treat the aging Lord, and his nephews, Gwriad and Dafydd. She was widely respected, and when she said that Jon would need constant attention for a few days, it was quickly agreed that the unconscious youth should be moved to her house.

Her home was well constructed and consisted of a main room, with a large fireplace against one wall, a single window near the oak door, and a curtained off sleeping area. Along one wall she had a large cupboard that contained food items, and a remarkable collection of knives, scissors, bowls cutting boards and a heavy pestle and mortar. She had a large sturdy table capable of taking the weight of a body, two chairs, plenty of shelves, and a storage area in the roof. From the beams hung a host of herbs, plants, and seaweeds, and she had glass containers, which contained minerals, nuts, and dried insects.

When people called, they were in awe of her, for not only did she possess things that nobody else owned, but she also had unusual good looks. Her cool, penetrating blue eyes revealed an alert intelligence, and she quickly destroyed the made-up stories of girls with unwanted pregnancies, and men who were suffering from embarrassing sexual diseases. She possessed a phenomenal memory, and could not only recall the roots and herbs to cure a variety of afflictions, but could also remember her patients' family histories and when she had last treated them. As the midwife, she had helped in the births of many of the village's inhabitants, where few lived past the age of fifty.

In contrast to most, Derryth lived an unstressed life, free from the worry of hunger or the constant need to feed a family. She spent her days collecting, observing and playing her harp, happy in her own company, and knowing she had innumerable friends when she needed companionship. She would accept payment for her treatments in flour, hams and root crops from farmers, in fish from the people of Llanduduch, in cloth from weavers and in game birds and venison cuts from those who lived outside the law. The only time she would accept money was from Lords or landowners.

Unlike the typical Wise Woman, she did not own a cat, which she considered was a way some healers convinced people that magic was involved. For her, there was no magic in healing, and she always reassured her patients that it was the power of Nature that healed them. Likewise she did not emphasize religion, and let those who believed in God believe that the Christian God had saved them, or if they worshipped pagan Gods to attribute their recovery to the God of the river, the moon, or whatever else they wanted to believe in. She always avoided talk of the devil, and was grateful that for many years Father Williams had stressed the Christian belief in goodness and the wonder of Heaven, rather than Hell and damnation, and the dangers of witchcraft.

However, she did own a dog. Emyr was a large, longhaired hound who worshipped Derryth, but could sense when anyone was likely to be a problem. A deep, volcanic growl was all that was needed to remind people, especially men, that Derryth was not alone.

Jon lay in a semi-awake state for some while. At times he was aware of movement around him, the cluttering of utensils and the occasional sound of people talking softly. He slowly began to focus on the room. He had been here before, and he felt comforted when he knew where he was.

Soon, he was sitting up in his makeshift bed, and eagerly accepting the potions and broths that Derryth brought to him. She soon quelled his embarrassment over the waste bucket, and within two days he was sitting in a chair, his arm in a sling, and his well-stitched leg strapped in a light cloth.

"You will soon be well enough to return to the castle," she said, "but you will not be well enough to take part in any physical activities for a while."

It was the reference to something physical that triggered Jon's memory. "The priest is unwell," he said, his voice cracking with emotion. "When I left him, he wanted me to ask you to call. He's not well."

IN THE ASHES OF A DREAM

"I'll call immediately, if I can borrow your horse?"

"Of course!" Jon protested. He was not experienced enough to know that she was merely being polite. She was always given the use of a horse whenever she was attending someone in the area. "You must take a guard with you, there's a murderous outlaw in the area."

"Not anymore," she smiled. "The soldiers and some men from the village caught him. They hanged him, yesterday." She looked down at Jon. "I'm leaving Emyr with you. Nobody will trouble you while I'm away."

After she left, he sat and contemplated the room, while Emyr slept in front of the fire. He realized that Derryth was knowledgeable in a host of subjects that he had never even thought about. He had no idea how glass was made, or which herbs should be used for different illnesses or how she knew when there would be a full moon.

She had talked to him about Lord Gwriad's condition, and how rest and many hours of sleep were necessary if he were to recover. "You mean he might not?" Jon had queried.

"Your Lord is his own worst enemy," she had answered. "But with the combined bullying of his wife and his brother, he has a chance. The front part of his brain was damaged, but all parts of the body, given time, will recover. The body seems to want to mend itself."

Jon had been fascinated by this thought, and had asked her if it was ever too late to learn things. "I have noticed," she said, "that young people can learn things faster than older people. Children can learn other languages quicker than I can. You're at the time of your life when you are at your best. Think of the changes in you since you first arrived at the castle." She had chuckled, "When I'd first seen you at Gwbert, you were a skinny, little waif. I would never have guessed you would become a squire." Derryth had playfully ruffled his hair. "You're not a bad looking young man. If I were a few years younger I could have been quite keen on you."

He grinned to himself as he remembered, and absent-mindedly rubbed Emyr's shaggy head. The dog whimpered to go out, and Jon edged out of his chair, and hopped towards the door, unwilling to rest his damaged leg on the floor. He watched as the dog bounded off towards the village. "Off to find his girlfriend," he muttered enviously. Then, it came to him: he could ask Derryth about girls. She was happy to talk about anything, and as a midwife, he was convinced that she would know about these things. He limped back to the chair, and sat staring at the fire; he couldn't wait for her return.

. . .

IN LONDON, THE BELLS WERE ringing and the people were out on the streets celebrating the near completion of Westminster Abbey. For more than a century this site had been a holy place, and King Edward had established his name in history, and in the sight of God, by enlarging the building to be the largest in Britain.

"Your Majesty, God will smile on you for this magnificent offering," the Bishop of Westminster bowed, having already calculated the enormous monetary benefit that this building would bring to the Church. He was a man who lived in luxury and loved power but presented to the outside world a person who lived a life of the poverty and humility.

Edward in contrast, preferred to live a simple life, and cared little for the value of the gold and silver objects that adorned the church, seeing them only in terms of their beauty as a tribute to God. Although other royalty throughout Europe might seek the pomp and ceremony that came with kingship, Edward took it for granted and avoided it whenever possible. He took no enjoyment in visiting his Lords' castles and fortified homes, and avoided travelling throughout the country, preferring to stay in London in the quiet of large churches and be left alone to pray to God for personal guidance.

He considered his regular Court meetings to be an unavoidable nuisance that came with being King, and he made them as short as possible. Those who wanted to impress Edward or seek his agreement had to tread carefully and present their case briefly and to the point. If he had chosen to be, he could have been an outstanding ruler, as he possessed great intelligence and understanding; but as he aged, he intensified his dislike for ambitious people and those who wanted to impress him.

"Bishop, clear the church. I want to have time by myself."

"Of course, your Majesty," the Bishop paused. "When would you want me to arrange your meeting with the ambassadors from the Pope?" The Bishop held his breath; this was supposed to be a great occasion and a grand tribute to him as the Bishop who had achieved the completion of this mighty building in spite of the opposition of the Lords, many of whom had been forced to pay for its huge cost. Despite the Bishop's careful planning of the services, possessions and feasts, the King had abstained from most of them. It was vital, therefore, that his arrangements concerning the Pope's ambassadors were not cancelled.

"What meeting?" Edward snarled, "I've already welcomed them. What more is there to do?" It had been a long day, and he had been forced to sit and suffer the presentation of a seemingly unending line of men, all wearing rich clothing and basking in their own importance. He had particularly disliked the Pope's unctuous representatives who appeared to lack even a modicum of spirituality.

The Bishop knew he was likely to fail if he tried to persuade the King at this moment. Over the past few months, he had come to read the signs when dealing with the aging monarch, and he quickly changed his approach. "You're quite right, your Majesty, now is not a good time. I will arrange a short meeting for tomorrow."

Edward breathed out noisily. "What's it about?"

"The Pope wishes to convey his full support for your decision to appoint Duke William of Normandy as your successor, and the Pope has sent his ambassadors to bring you his blessings in writing, and he wishes to receive your confirmation of your decision on a papal document."

"Arrange it for tomorrow, Lord Bishop," Edward nodded his dismissal, and made his way up the steps to the high alter. Behind him the priests and the church guards quickly and silently cleared the cavernous building. He sank to his knees, and the tensions of the day began to fade. However, before he began his prayers, his active mind focused briefly on the ambitious Harold Godwinson and his cursed family. Edward gazed up at the high alter and admitted to himself that a lack of children was a mixed blessing.

• • •

Jon had his talk with Derryth, and as he had suspected she was not in the least awkward or embarrassed. In fact, she seemed to enjoy explaining the anatomical differences between men and women, and how a man should behave. She was frequently laughing as she told him stories of her early life and tales she'd heard from her patients. "The one thing you will come to realize, Jon, is that there is no great difference between bodies." She laughed. "Young Megan's body is no different to that of a Lord's daughter, just not so clean maybe."

She looked at him thoughtfully. "Father Williams was doing his job when he tried to prevent you causing a baby without knowing why or how. If Megan had had a child, would you have stayed with her? Or would you have refused to acknowledge that you were the father?"

Jon looked shocked, and his face went red. "I wouldn't have left her!" he protested.

"Even if Lord Gwriad and Lady Angharad dismissed you from the castle?"

"They wouldn't do that."

"Why not? They'd given you a remarkable chance in life, and you would have let them down."

Jon frowned. "So, what should I do now that she is working in the kitchen? I can't ignore her."

"Of course not. Does the Lady Angharad speak to Penn the way she speaks to you? Does she ignore him?" Jon shook his head. "Well then, don't be a silly!" She called to Emyr, and opened the door. "You must remember you have some status in the castle, you're a squire. You've even been blooded in action. What a hero! First, a monster boar and now two murderers!" She closed the door and he could hear her laughing as she walked up to the castle. He hobbled to the door and wondered why she was going there. He doubted it was to check on Lord Gwriad, for she normally had a request from Lady Angharad. Perhaps, she was going to report on him?

He began to exercise his leg and his bruised arm, and as he noticed their increased flexibility, he began to realize what a wonderful opportunity the ambush had created for him. His concern over the priest had proved ill founded, as Derryth had explained: "He's an old man, he was lonely, he wasn't eating and he was drinking too much. Now that the weather's improved, and Mrs. Reece is calling on him every day, he should be fine."

Jon felt he could return to the castle, knowing more about women than the other young men, and confident he could be friendly towards Megan but still keep a distance. But most of all he felt that getting to know Derryth was an exciting development. For the first time in his life he had a friend with whom he could talk about anything, and with whom he could genuinely laugh.

Up at the castle, Derryth was shown towards the small room known as Lord Dafydd's Room. It was here that he sought the solitude he often needed. He had a large table that was littered with books, scrolls, and reports, some written on leather and some on vellum. He corresponded with abbots and priors in England and Wales, and with merchants from all parts of Europe. Sometimes he would not get a reply for a year, but he was content, as he ended up with information that he would otherwise have been unaware of.

It was mid-afternoon, and he was in the process of writing to a scholar in London, enquiring about the latest news of Earl Harold Godwinson. Dafydd was sure that the people of Wales had not heard the last of this ambitious Saxon, especially if he became the next King of England.

A servant knocked, entered and announced that the Wise Woman wished to speak to him.

"Show her in," Dafydd replied, quickly getting to his feet and placing a stool near his table. He assumed she wished to talk to him about Gwriad, who had shown some promising signs of recovery in recent days. He thought Derryth to be a very likeable woman, in fact she was the only woman he thought about, other than his wife. He was not a lascivious man, and had never been tempted by female servants, although some would willingly have shared his bed if he had ever shown any sign of noticing them. However, he was attracted to intelligent people, and until recently, that had been restricted to Father Williams.

Dafydd had the reputation of being a calm, unemotional man whose intelligence and learning was second to none in the area, and although he avoided hunting and physical sports, it was reported that on the battlefield he fought without fear in defence of his brother. People respected him, even though few knew him well, and it was generally agreed that he was the planner and Gwriad was the man of action.

He was a good husband and father, though he never spent much time as either, and unlike his brother, his name was never mentioned in the ale houses when men joked about the sexual reputations of other people.

"Ah, Derryth, come in, come in." He indicated the stool, conscious of the fact that he was appearing awkward, and sat down facing her.

"Thank you, my Lord." She flashed him a smile, revealing her fine teeth; she knew when men found her attractive.

"What can I do for you?" He was always aware how clean she was, and how she exuded a slight hint of lavender. He cleared his throat, "You've heard how Lord Gwriad has made some real improvements in recent days? He's got his balance back, and his memory is greatly improved." He gave a small laugh. "Even his face is getting back to normal."

"Indeed, my Lord. But that is not why I'm here. I will visit Lord Gwriad, with your permission, next week, as I think that by then he might have made further improvements." She leaned slightly forward on her stool, revealing her ample cleavage. No, I've come to talk to you about Jon."

"Is there a problem?" Dafydd reluctantly drew his eyes away from her body. "I heard he was mending well?"

"He is, my Lord. It's nothing to do with his health." She took a moment to collect her thoughts. "Jon told me that Father Williams had been unwell, and I visited him, it's nothing serious and I have made arrangements for his care."

IN THE ASHES OF A DREAM

"Thank you, Derryth. I must pay him a visit."

"While I was with him, I told him about Jon's narrow escape from death, and we began to talk about him. Father Williams told me something that you may already know my Lord, but I felt it was my duty to pass this on to you, in case you were unaware of it." She paused and looked unblinking into Dafydd's eyes. "It would appear Jon is related to you."

During an intense conversation, following Dafydd's shocked reaction, Derryth revealed that the previous Lord Gomer ap Griffith, Gwriad's and Dafydd's uncle, had enjoyed a mistress, named Ceri. After a while she became pregnant, and Gomer, believing himself to be past the fertile age of creating children, accused her of sleeping with other men, either in the castle or in the village of Aberteifi. Gomer was a man with a sensitive ego, who was quick to take offence, and could imagine the local men enjoying calling him a cuckold. Furthermore, it was the time when he had just adopted Gwriad and Dafydd, following the death of their father, Gomer's brother, at the Battle of Rhyd-y-Groes. Gomer was keen to present himself to his nephews as an upright man, and Ceri was an embarrassment.

In a fit of pique, he threatened to banish her. She pleaded her innocence, and as she was soon to have a child, he had a discussion with a dissolute fisherman named Dai from Gwbert, who had been a useful soldier on occasions. Dai agreed to take on the woman for a small amount of money, and Father Williams married him and Ceri. The agreement pleased Gomer, for Gwbert was a wretched place that few people from the castle ever visited. After Jon was born, Ceri was forced to endure regular beatings whenever Dai was drunk, and as soon as the child could walk, she disappeared.

"What a remarkable coincidence," Dafydd pondered, Derryth's attractions no longer on his mind. "So, that's why the old woman sent Jon up to the castle." He stood up. "Thank you, Derryth, thank you very much. This explains, perhaps, how Jon has fitted in so well and taken to learning so quickly." He opened the door, unaware of Derryth's curtsy, and rushed to tell the others about the news.

Derryth grinned, "Definitely a man of the mind rather than the body," she mused. Yet, she sometimes wondered what she would do if Lord Dafydd ever made advances to her. There was no doubt, he was an attractive man.

Angharad was delighted when she was told, for she had already come to think of Jon as a surrogate son, and now he really was part of the family. Teifryn also said she was delighted, but Dafydd noticed some reserve in her manner. When Gwriad joined them he seemed somewhat bemused. "So, my squire is actually of my blood line?" Slowly, a big smile enveloped his face. "This is something to celebrate!" And in the old Gwriad manner, which they all remembered, he ordered wine for everyone and drank, copiously, to his newfound nephew. The others agreed that he was recovered.

Back in their room, Dafydd played with his daughter, as his wife stared out of the open window. After a while, he posed the question. "What's the matter, my love?"

Teifryn did not answer immediately. She was a woman who loved her husband and avoided arguments. She had always been a quiet manipulator, getting her way in all the minor things that affected her as a wife and a mother, and in her dealings with Angharad. She was strict with the servants, but always fair, and kept a clear separation between herself and those who served her. She did not have the confidence of Angharad, who could demolish anyone who did not do their job, but was happy to joke with them at a later time.

"This news of Jon changes things," she said quietly.

"In what way?"

"Oh, Dafydd! You are such a good man; it never occurs to you that not everyone sees the world as you do. Up until this news, our daughter would have inherited the castle and the title, and everything that comes with it. Now, Jon will inherit as the only male successor. Our daughter will be pushed aside, and when Jon marries and has children, she will become a nobody."

"Don't say such things!" Dafydd was truly upset. "We, the four of us, are equals in this castle, and when, eventually, Jon inherits, he will be guided by those who remain. Believe me, my love, we have not lost anything in discovering that we have another relative, we have gained."

"Jon is what? Coming up seventeen? Think then, when he's ready for marriage, our daughter will still be enjoying dolls. His wife, whoever she is, may not like this young child who claims equal rights, and will like her less as she approaches marriageable age. If Jon is taken into this family, I want you to draw up an agreement that will ensure that our daughter's future is guaranteed."

Dafydd looked at her as though seeing a new person. His wife, who had always been so loving and grateful to be part of this family, was suddenly revealing a side of herself he had no experience of: the protective mother. He wondered if he was wanting as a father, or whether she was worrying about nothing. "I'll think about it," he said and, to his relief, Teifryn smiled.

CHAPTER TWELVE

In London, the summer heat had made the city unbearable. The stench of sewage, the smell of dead animals and rotting food, always unpleasant in the streets of the big city, became a stinking, infectious, rat-ridden problem in the hotter months. Those who could, sought refuge in the country, where more and more Lords and men of substance owned second homes. Even the River Thames, once noted for its salmon and its clear water, had become victim to the city's open sewers that emptied into it.

"Let's get the business done, and get away from this foul place," Lord Leofwine growled from behind the linen cloth he held over his mouth and nose. He tucked it in the sleeve of his jerkin as he dismounted, and handed the reins of his destrier to a servant. With a final sniff, he walked quickly towards the doors of the palace.

"I've known worse," Harold said. He had been waiting for Leofwine, and had been deep in thought. "This could be important." He followed his younger brother into the cool corridors of the stone-built palace, and handed his sword to a waiting servant.

A smiling courtier, whose livery indicated he was a man of some importance in the palace, approached them. He bowed, "Please come this way, my Lords. The King will not keep you waiting for long."

Leofwine gave Harold a knowing look. They both knew that the King enjoyed keeping them waiting unless he wanted to get to his prayers.

They were escorted to a small room, which, although not a library, contained a number of heavy leather-bound books. In the centre was a large, oblong, highly polished table on which was a collection of scrolls, some quills, and a jug with fine glass goblets.

IN THE ASHES OF A DREAM

A collection of carved chairs was scattered around, as though a meeting had just finished. A wide window looked out on a parade ground.

Leofwine casually examined some of the scrolls, and studied one in particular. "This palimpsest is interesting," he said, deliberately using a word that he suspected Harold did not know. It pleased him to be able to show his superior education. "It's from the Vatican. A bishop suggests, on behalf of the Pope, that our blessed King invite Duke William to visit London, where Edward can make a public declaration of his wish that William is to be his successor."

Harold swore under his breath. "The Church should keep its interfering nose out of my business." He walked up to the jug, and grunted his disapproval. "Water! What else would you expect from our God-loving King." He poured two glasses and handed one to Leofwine, who took a moment to admire the glass.

"So, it's you Edward wants to speak to?" Leofwine continued to investigate the contents of the scrolls.

"Not just me. He wants to talk to us as a family. Gyrth is up North trying to sort out Tostig's latest mess, which is why you and I are here."

Leofwine opened one of the imposing leather books, and slowly turned the pages, admiring the bright ornamentation and the fine workmanship, while Harold paced about the room like a caged wild cat.

A small door at the end of the room opened, and a priest, with a large beak-like nose, entered carrying quills, scrolls and ink. He bowed to the two Lords. "My Lords, the King has been delayed, but asks that you make yourselves comfortable." His eyes widened when he saw the collection of scrolls scattered around. He carefully placed his writing materials on the table and quickly collected the abandoned letters and reports. The brothers watched him without comment as he bowed his way out of the room.

"Someone's going to get flayed," Leofwine observed with a sardonic smile.

"He'll probably lose his conjugal rights," Harold jested.

"He's a priest."

"Exactly." Harold's views on the behaviour and devoutness of the clergy were well known, although Leofwine was more tolerant.

They waited for another hour, at which point Harold strode across the room and opened the small door. Outside, a guard stood to attention. "Get someone of importance immediately!" Harold returned to the window, and noticed a flurry of activity outside. "Now what?" he grumbled. "I won't wait much longer."

The main doors opened, and a servant entered the room carrying a tray of refreshments, and behind her came a worried courtier, who bowed ostentatiously. "My Lords, the King sends his apologies, but he has become unwell. He is unable to see you today, and hopes to be well enough to see you in a few days' time." He began to bow his way out.

"Wait!" Harold roared. "Did you know the King was unwell when we arrived?"

"Um, yes, my Lord. The King was taken ill during a meeting with some envoys from Italy. I apologize for the inconveniences you have suffered."

"And the meeting was in this room?"

"Yes, my Lord." The courtier looked puzzled.

"What exactly is wrong with the King?"

The courtier hesitated.

"I'm Harold Godwinson, Earl of Wessex!" Harold roared, thumping his large fist on the table. "I'm the most powerful man in England after the King. Answer my questions or I'll throw you out of this room in pieces!"

The courtier went a sickly colour of grey. He stared up at the huge man in front of him and was so terrified he could hardly speak. "My Lord, the King collapsed in a meeting in this room. He had to be carried out and upstairs to his quarters. Doctors, bishops and his personal priest were sent for. My Lord, there was considerable upset." He had begun to gabble.

"The bishops and his personal priest were called for because he might die?" Leofwine asked quietly.

The courtier turned to him, relief flooding his face. "It was thought so, my Lord. But he has recovered, and when I left his room he was sitting up and sipping watered wine."

IN THE ASHES OF A DREAM

"Has this happened before?" Leofwine's voice had a calming influence.

"Yes, my Lord. The King is often ill, but this is the first time he has become unconscious. He had a long day yesterday, with the consecration of Westminster Abbey, and this is thought to be the cause of his collapse."

"What's your name?" Harold walked back to the window.

The courtier took a deep breath. "Oswine, my Lord."

"You can go." Harold waited until the door was closed. "Do you think our sickly King will follow the advice of the Pope?"

"No, he won't risk the chance of open opposition. Nor, I think, would Duke William risk his life; timing is everything. Also, it would appear Edward's not likely to be around for much longer." Leofwine inspected his manicured fingers. "There again, I have known invalids like him to take years to die."

"It's time for me to take some action. My reputation around the country has dimmed since my victory over the Welsh, and their recent revenge on my home has become a source of humour in the Court. I must regain the support of the people, and ensure that when Edward dies, I am the natural successor." He raised his hand, as Leofwine was about to object.

"I want you to use your friendship with members of the Witanagemot, to make the point that the Saxon culture will die if William is made King. Emphasize the importance of our heritage over the wishes of our enfeebled Edward. Remind them, his choice of William is based on a personal dislike of me, and the Witanagemot must be made to see the dangers of a Norman King." He frowned, and paced up and down in front of the window.

"Next, I want you to contact Gyrth and tell him to chase Tostig out of Northumberland. He's had his chance, and I don't want him being a problem at the time of the King's death. Lastly, I want you to make a trusted friend of one of the King's doctors, whatever it costs, and ensure that we get prior knowledge when Edward is on his death bed."

Leofwine made an obsequious gesture. "And what, dear brother, will you be doing while I'm arranging for you to be King?"

"I'm going back to Wessex, and Mercia, and I'm going to raise an army to attack the Welsh, most of whom have, almost certainly, gone back to their farms." He gave a bellowing laugh. "People love to hear their side has done well in a war, especially against the Welsh, and I will be their champion once again! I will even let it be known that the King has requested I punish the Welsh for their attack on Hereford."

He pummelled Leofwine on his back, threw open the door, and in a burst of good humour bellowed for his sword and his horse. "It's time for action!" he called back to his favourite brother. "It's time."

. . .

GWRIAD MADE A REMARKABLE RECOVERY once he had regained his balance. His face healed, the terrible bruising faded, and although he would never again be a handsome man, his broken nose gave him a roguish, heroic appearance. He spent hours hunting, visiting distant villages and farms on his estate, and engaging in sword play with Jon, who had become his shadow. With all this activity, he began to lose the weight he had gained as an invalid, and he drank less, and felt fitter than he had done for a long time.

"Gwriad is looking well," Teifryn observed, as she sat weaving with Angharad.

"Oh, yes!" Angharad said with feeling, raising her eyebrows in a provocative way. "He's certainly feeling better."

Teifryn giggled. She was still uncertain if Angharad and Gwriad were really having the remarkable sex life that she hinted at. They had no children, and it would seem that none of his previous lovers had become pregnant, and if Angharad had had previous lovers, as she boasted of, she also had never had a child. Teifryn had spent some time thinking about this, and had eventually come to suspect that Gwriad was unable to create a child, and Angharad was the loyal wife, taking half the responsibility.

"Are you intending to have a second child?" Angharad asked.

"I don't think so. I mean, I found the birth difficult," she seemed agitated, "and Dafydd is very considerate about the time of the month. We both agree that our lovely daughter is enough." She made a point of concentrating on her wheel. What she was unwilling to reveal was that Dafydd had rarely made love to her in recent times. He remained kind and considerate, but seemed tired at night and went to sleep almost immediately. He no longer enjoyed watching her undress, and it was only when she made a determined advance did he react. It was as though he deliberately avoided having sex with her, and it seemed that this had begun about the time when Jon had been injured.

"Jon is becoming a good squire," Angharad said, changing the subject. "Gwriad is finding him a great support and a real friend. It was such a joy to discover that he is part of this family."

"Yes, indeed," Teifryn said. She kept silent for a while, and then had to ask. "When Jon becomes of age, will he be eligible to inherit this castle?"

Angharad stopped work, and took a long, hard look at her friend. "Is that what's worrying you?" Teifryn looked confused and did not answer. "I've noticed you're cool when Jon is about, and you no longer talk to him."

"I do!" Teifryn protested.

"No, you don't, Teifryn, your face and your body actions are an open book."

"Oh." This had not occurred to her. "I'm sorry, I don't know why I'm behaving like this. It's just I worry about Tegwen. What will happen to her when we're gone."

"There's a silly you are!" Angharad moved her stool close to her friend and put an arm around her. "First, she will be beautiful, like her mother, and tall like her father, and she will have all the young Lords in the area sniffing around like dogs on heat. Then, she'll get married and move into some warm, comfortable mansion unlike this cold, stony castle. It's Jon you'll have to feel sorry for!"

Teifryn wiped an eye. "Why?"

"Because unless he volunteers for a holy war in Europe, he'll be stuck as Gwriad's squire while we all get old and cantankerous and make life miserable for him. I wouldn't mind betting that Father Williams has forbidden him to have sex with the local girls. Which could explain why Megan is so miserable."

"You always make me laugh," Teifryn dabbed her other eye. "I hadn't thought about it like that." Teifryn wanted to ask Angharad whether it was normal for men to lose interest in sex, but she had always been modest and easily embarrassed, and she could not force herself to speak about it. "Shall we go for a walk?"

As they walked across the courtyard, Angharad glanced at the woman she knew so well, and wondered if the concern about Jon was really what worried her, or was there something else? Perhaps she had an illness, or maybe it was Dafydd? He was certainly more distracted since the time that Jon had been attacked by the outlaws. She thought about it for a moment, and remembered that the Wise Woman had looked after Jon. Although she had great admiration for Derryth's abilities, she had made it her duty to always be in the room when Derryth came to treat Gwriad. Angharad recognized her as a possible challenge: an attractive woman who exuded energy and good humour and turned men's heads. She determined to be more watchful; in a small castle it was difficult to hide anything for long.

• • •

SOME DAYS LATER AFTER DERRYTH'S visit, Dafydd was making his way along the river path on his way to see Father Williams. It was a warm dry day, and the forest on his left was dark and cool; he stopped his horse at a small crossing, where a tiny stream flowed into the river. He would have been intrigued to know that this was the place where his brother's horse had almost trampled Jon to death, prior to Jon becoming the hero of the boar hunt.

The drought of the past weeks had reduced the stream to the tiniest of trickles, and he dismounted and let his horse drink out of a small pool. He decided to relieve himself and, being of a sensitive nature, walked a few paces into the forest. When he returned, Derryth was standing in front of his horse, gently rubbing its muzzle and whispering in its ear.

"Are you going to visit Father Williams, my Lord?" she asked, without turning to face him.

"Ah, Derryth," he said, not knowing what to say, and ignoring her lack of formality. "Yes, I'm going to visit Father Williams." He felt awkward. "He's been ill."

"Yes, I told you."

IN THE ASHES OF A DREAM

"Of course." He walked towards Derryth, who smiled at him, and even an arm's width away smelt of lavender. She dropped her arm from the horse, and stood still, both arms hanging loosely, her legs apart, and her lips slightly open. He could hear his heart thumping, and knew he could not resist the temptation to kiss her. As their lips met, he felt instantly aroused.

The horse was still champing at the grass around the stream when they emerged from the forest. Derryth was laughing and holding his hand, but when he moved into the sunlight he felt awkward.

"That was fun," Derryth said. "You're quite a man. Your wife is very lucky."

The mention of his wife made him feel guilty. "We must not do that again," he said solemnly, trying to regain his authority. "I don't want you to mention this to anyone."

"As though I would," she leaned against him and touched his nose. "I'm not a loose woman. I'm not wanting money. I just find you a very sexy man, and I enjoyed that!"

"Oh, yes," he felt himself gulping for air. "So did I. But Teifryn would be very upset if she knew, and I never want to make her unhappy."

"Do you make love to her a lot?"

"I used to," he took a deep breath, "but not recently."

"Is that your fault or hers?"

Dafydd did not answer. He looked about, seeing nothing. "I... I think, no, I know it's my fault."

"So, why don't we meet occasionally, and in the between times, you will be a real husband to her. If I discover you are failing to be a regular lover, I will refuse to meet you."

Dafydd stared at her. This was not the way people spoke to him. He was a Lord, and a married Lord. She smiled at him, and he knew she was not an ordinary person.

"When shall we meet next?" his voice sounded like a rough whisper.

"When the time is right," she kissed him on the lips and walked back towards Aberteifi. "Remember," she said looking back, "keep Teifryn happy."

175

Dafydd stood like a statue for a long time, reviewing everything that had happened. Slowly, he mounted his obedient horse and walked it towards Llanduduch. "Perhaps, I should go to Confession?" He shook his head at the thought. There were various reasons he did not want Father Williams to know.

• • •

"I think it's time for me to meet with General Sir Maelgwn ap Owen, and with Prince Anarwd ap Tewdwr," Gwriad said, using their full names for the benefit of Jon, who was still absorbing the names of Welsh leaders. They were standing on the southern wall of the castle, overlooking the river. "I feel certain that once Earl Harold Godwinson has sorted out his problems in London, he will launch raids, or even a big attack on us, just to show he controls the borders."

"Suppose Earl Harold attacked Brycheiniog, would we be able to beat him back?" Jon asked.

Gwriad nodded. "Good question, Jon." He had previously told his squire that he need not preface everything he said with 'my Lord', unless it was important or they were in company, and it pleased him that the youth was so keen to learn after having such a poor start in life. His fighting skills were improving and Gwriad felt confident that Jon could protect his back in a battle. He pointed to the east, "There's a chance, an unlikely event, that the Saxons could invade into Deheubarth and devastate this area. However, Brycheiniog, through which they would have to pass, is not highly populated and offers little in the way of rich villages, and neither does it have suitable roads for an army to make use of. The Saxons would have to travel along narrow, windy paths, over high mountain passes and across many streams and rivers, and all the time they would be vulnerable to ambush."

Jon nodded, unconsciously imitating his Lord. "So, what might they do instead?"

"The best time for Harold to invade is from now and until the weather breaks, but it depends if he can raise the soldiers, and if Saxon politics allow him to. The harvests are nearly in, and his soldiers could live off our farms and countryside. The question is, where would he attack? I know Prince Anarwd keeps a number of spies in England, which is another reason for me to meet him."

They were joined by Dafydd, who had a certain swagger in his walk. "We're discussing my proposed visit to General Maelgwn, Lord Edwin and Prince Anarwd," Gwriad said. "I want to know the latest news from England, and how prepared we are if the Saxons attack us before the summer's over." He raised one eyebrow and Dafydd gave him a rascally smile. Jon did not know what to make of their behaviour and pretended not to notice.

"I've been keeping in touch with merchants in London, and I hear that King Edward is unwell." Dafydd liked to remind his brother that he did more than lounge about the castle.

"If the information is accurate, that should keep Harold close to London, but I would like to hear what our border friends have to say."

"When were you thinking of going?" Dafydd asked. He gazed out over the valley, seeming to admire the river where some older men were fishing in their round coracles, but his mind was elsewhere.

"As soon as I can get it arranged. The harvest has been good so far, and our people should be able to pay their rents, which will enable us to hire some soldiers, you would agree?" As Dafydd was responsible for the family accounts, Gwriad always took it for granted that his brother would know everything about their wealth or lack of it.

"Yes," Dafydd said, returning to the conversation, "you can raise a small army of paid soldiers. I agree you can't expect local men to join you unless they have the hope of pillage; also experienced soldiers would be less of a problem as this is a formal visit. Will you travel to Caerdydd, or travel on to Prince Anarwd's castle in Gwent?"

"I haven't decided. I thought you should have some say in the decision?"

Dafydd looked alarmed. "This is your trip. I'm not going."

"Of course you're going. You're the one who's the diplomat. I couldn't go without you. Also, Angharad would want Teifryn with her."

"Teifryn can't go; she has Tegwen to look after."

"Alys looks after Tegwen. We'll only be gone two weeks. Tegwen can stay here with Alys. There's no problem. We'll have fun." He placed his hand on Dafydd's shoulder. "Nothing like a change of air. You know what I mean?" He winked.

Dafydd felt outmanoeuvred, and was aware that his concern for the well-being of his daughter was not the reason for his lack of enthusiasm. "I'll talk it over with Teifryn."

"She already knows, and both women are looking forward to getting away."

"Why am I the last to know?" Dafydd complained.

"You weren't around." Gwriad looked sad. "You just weren't to be found."

"I was visiting Father Williams!" Dafydd began to feel uneasy.

"Of course you were," Gwriad said in a solicitous tone. "The path to Llanduduch is lovely at this time of the year, and you never know what you might see." He let the words sink in. "Anyway, I think you'll agree that it's a good time to go on a visit."

Dafydd took the hint. "Alright, I agree. It might be the right time to get away for a while." He stalked off, leaving Gwriad looking pleased with himself, and Jon wondering what he'd missed.

• • •

THE NEW MANOR HOUSE FOR Earl Harold was some way from completion, but huge advances had been made and Lidmann was inspecting the recently built defences. The house and supporting buildings were enclosed within an imposing stockade and around the encampment was a deep trench, which had already begun to fill with water from a local stream. At all four corners and around the main gates were raised guard posts that gave clear views over the local flat country. The gates were constructed of heavy oak, with metal bars that could be placed in position to strengthen them in times of attack, and there was a single wooden bridge across the trench.

"Along the inside of this back wall, I want you to build a short-term barracks, where visiting soldiers can stay for a few nights," he said to the builder who was in overall charge. "Construct another kitchen, and another jakes."

"Yes, my Lord." The man could barely conceal his happiness. This had been a well-paid project and he had begun to wonder what might replace it after its completion. "When should I start?"

"Immediately. The Earl wants it completed within two weeks. Employ more men if necessary. The Earl's servants and soldiers will arrive soon, and I don't want your workers having any contact with them, they have a job to do. Your men will continue to provide their own meals, they are not to hang around the kitchen."

"Yes, my Lord." He disliked the officious Lidmann, but had to admit that his organization and planning was meticulous. "Shall I continue to manage the payments to the workers and the suppliers?"

Lidmann moved closer to the foreman and gave him a cool look. "I'm aware you've made some profits from this trusted position."

The foreman paled and could not resist clearing his throat. "My Lord?"

"If you become greedy, you will lose your job and I will have you publicly thrashed." He paused. "Do you understand?"

"Yes, my Lord." He bowed his way out of the immediate area, and disappeared behind the main building. In one sense he was pleased to have further work, but the knowledge that Lidmann had been aware of his petty thieving was deeply worrying, and took away his former confidence. "Curse him," he muttered. He had always got away with it in the past because Lords never counted the small payments, leaving that to the foreman. As long as the job was done well and on time Lords never noticed the difference between the number of actual workers and the number he claimed were on site.

As the foreman plodded over the bridge, Lidmann smiled. Better to keep the foreman he knew than hire a new and unknown person. He was certain that this man would not dare to repeat his crime, and the other men seemed to like him.

Harold arrived ten days later to find his house fully staffed, and a permanent guard of thirty experienced soldiers. He had brought Elditha Swannuck with him, a tall, alluring beauty who was his long-time mistress and handfasted wife. He was proud of her and made no attempt to cover up their relationship. She had survived his political marriages and took no interest in Court intrigues. Her sexual appetites matched his, and she loved hunting, feasting and fine living. She was a strong, passionate woman who, and as far as he could discover, had never flirted with another man, even when they were separated for long periods of time.

As Elditha and her coterie of servants were settling in, Harold did an inspection of the new buildings with Lidmann close at hand. At the back of the compound a large, basic barracks was almost completed as was the overflow kitchen and the second jakes. "You seem to have achieved a remarkable feat: the buildings are ahead of schedule!" he jested. He was striding about at a pace that had Lidmann almost running.

He stopped to watch the construction of the soldiers' kitchen and focused on a large man who was giving orders. "Who's that?"

"The foreman, my Lord. He built your house and supervised the defences. He has a good way with the men."

"But you keep an eye on him?"

"Yes, my Lord."

Harold marched back towards the mansion. "When all the work is completed, send him to me." Before Lidmann could agree, he put a fatherly arm across the younger man's shoulders. "You will have heard that Lord Oswine died recently?" Lidmann nodded. "He has land next to my northern borders. Although old, he was a useful man," he stopped as though a thought had come to him. "You come from a noble family that always supported my father. You have proved yourself, and I need a reliable supporter in this area." He looked down at Lidmann who, although not a short man, lacked the height and solidity of Harold. "I want you to become Lord in his place. This takes effect once the building here is complete."

Lidmann was stunned. His most optimistic hope had been to be raised to a minor role in government, or be given some lucrative administrative post, but not in his wildest dreams had he expected to be raised to a landowner with a title. His mother would be delighted. "Thank you, my Lord. That is most generous."

IN THE ASHES OF A DREAM

"Yes, I agree," Harold smiled indulgently. "Tonight, we will share supper together, and I will tell you what this promotion involves." He laughed, and Lidmann suspected that his generosity came with a price. "Meanwhile," he continued, "appoint one of the guards to sergeant, and if he proves useful, give him overall charge of the soldiers who will guard my palace from now on." He thought of the improvements he would make once he was King of England. This mansion would become his western palace, where he would escape the burdens of kingship, and where he would entertain foreign dignitaries in luxury when he took them on hunting trips. He smiled to himself, and mused on how he would show off to them the desirable Edith.

The supper that evening was, as in the past, an awkward time for Lidmann. The Earl liked to eat prodigious amounts, drink more wine than any two men, and tell highly detailed stories of his sexual experiences. To add to Lidmann's discomfort was the presence of Edith Swannuck, who he had suspected might be a prostitute the first time they had met, and who had a way of revealing her breasts whenever she leaned forward to add more food to her plate. In the area of sexual experiences, Lidmann's contribution was limited, and he left the Earl's new hall feeling they had little in common, and suspecting the Earl felt the same. Edith had spent her time eating and smiling at Harold, and occasionally indulging in improper behaviour, as though Lidmann was not present. When Lidmann was finally able to excuse himself from the table, his head was thumping, his belly was painfully overextended, and he felt physically and emotionally sick.

His suspicions regarding the price that went with his elevation had proved founded. Before he had finished his first cup of wine Harold revealed his expectations. "We'll get the business over, and then we can enjoy the evening," he said. "You will be known as Lord Lidmann," he paused to reflect on the name. "Your title comes with a manor house, and three villages, and will provide enough income to keep you in comfort. You'll be expected to provide your own armour and weapons," he gave Lidmann's slim body a perfunctory glance. "I take it you can manage a sword?"

"Yes, my Lord." He briefly reflected on his meagre experience.

Weapons had never interested him, and he had always avoided violence if possible. He had owned a horse since early childhood, was well educated and enjoyed planning and organizing. Lidmann was happiest when he was in charge, and his eye for detail made him both a valuable ally, and a dangerous foe. He was honest and hardworking but was awkward with women and moderate in his eating and his consumption of alcohol. He had never met anyone like Edith.

Harold leaned over to refill Lidmann's cup, "Drink up, Lord Lidmann!" he joked, and waited impatiently for the young man to empty his cup. The Earl enjoyed excessive feasting, and his close friends were large men of similar appetites. He glanced at Lidmann, who was regarding the wine with some apprehension, and realized the young man would never become a joyful drinking partner. "To good health and success!" he roared, raising his mug and taking a large gulp, and refilling Edith's mug. Lidmann reluctantly sipped his wine; it was going to be a difficult evening.

"Lord Oswine's lands are the closest to my palace, and you will be responsible for my land's security and management when I'm away. Especially in the next few weeks, when I intend to teach the Welsh that they can't attack my property and get away with it."

"You're going to invade Wales, my Lord?" Lidmann asked, trying not to sound amazed. It was the first he had heard of this. Now he understood the recent addition of the short-term barracks.

"Yes," Harold looked pleased with himself. "My spies tell me the Welsh army that destroyed my home and attacked Shrewsbury, has been disbanded and the men have returned to their farms. The army of Prince Anarwd is reduced, and now is an ideal time to punish them."

Lidmann nodded. "So, while you are away, you want me to be in charge of the running of your palace, as well as my new manor?"

"Yes," Harold growled. "Do you have a problem with that?"

"Not at all, my Lord. I simply wanted to understand my roles."

"I imagine you will appoint a reeve, and he will run your estate." Harold finished his wine, refilled Edith's mug and attempted to refill Lidmann's. "Come on, drink up or I'll die of thirst!"

Lidmann removed his cup. "Perhaps in a moment, my Lord."

IN THE ASHES OF A DREAM

He pretended to drink but was already past his normal limit. "How big an army will you assemble, my Lord?" he asked, trying desperately to remove Harold's attention from his wine drinking inability.

"About four hundred experienced soldiers. Enough to destroy an army of farmers." He laughed and finished his wine. "I intend to cut a swath through the south of Wales and punish the so-called General Gwriad, who I understand was behind the recent invasion." He refilled his cup and was about to refill Lidmann's when the younger man interrupted him.

"How many cavalry men will you have, my Lord? I understand the Welsh destroyed our Saxon army that tried to ambush them, mainly with the use of cavalry."

Harold frowned and cut himself a large leg of goose, and kissed Edith, and after groping her, turned back to Lidmann. "They were lucky. I understand the Welsh invading force was in disarray. If our forces could have ambushed their foot soldiers, there would have been a different result." He finished his cup and immediately refilled it; his mind was focused on the Saxon failure as he devoured the meat.

Lidmann realized he had a way of encouraging Harold to drink. "So, will you take a large cavalry force with you?"

"There'll be no need," Harold said forcefully, his red eyes trying to focus on Lidmann. "The officers will be mounted as will the scouts, but our main force will be Saxon shield-bearers, the best soldiers in the world!" He finished his cup, and waved it at Lidmann, who immediately filled it up and made a pretence of refilling his own full cup.

"We're short of horses, but so are the Welsh…" Harold lost his train of thought. He drank the whole cup in one draft, and threw it to the floor. "We're short of horses." He sank back in his chair. His eyes closed. "Horses," he mumbled and his arms dropped to the floor.

"You may go, Lord Lidmann," Edith said with an enticing smile. She pretended to tend to Harold and revealed her large breasts. Lidmann stared entranced, and then suddenly feeling nauseous, he rushed out of the room.

Lidmann signalled to the servant who was standing outside the door. "Get others and take his lordship to his room." He staggered out to the courtyard and took deep gulps of air. For a brief moment, he thought his head was clearing, and then his stomach betrayed him, and he heaved up against the side of the house, vaguely aware of soldiers watching him. "Take me to my room," he ordered. Then remembering he was a Lord, he yelled, "Hurry! Or I'll have you flogged. I'm Lord Lidmann now! I'm…" At which point he collapsed.

CHAPTER THIRTEEN

It was not an easy task arranging the visit to Prince Anarwd. A messenger was sent to inform the Prince of the proposed visit, and to ensure he was not on manoeuvres. Owen was given the responsibility, but before he had left the area of Deheubarth his horse tripped in a rabbit hole and broke a leg. The youth was thrown to the ground and lay trapped under the flaying horse from which he was eventually rescued and found to have a number of broken ribs. A message was sent back to the castle, and arrangements were made to bring him home in a cart, and to send Davis, his friend, as the new messenger.

When Davis arrived at Prince Anarwd's palace, three days later, he was told that the Prince was at his campaign headquarters in Gwent, and it took another two days to give the message. The Prince decided that the sea port of Caerdydd was the most suitable place to meet, as he wanted to combine the visit with the chance to congratulate his cousin, Prince Rhodri ap Williams, who had been conducting a successful campaign against French and Saxon merchant shipping.

At the beginning of his return to Aberteifi, Davis found himself in a narrow lane with high hedges on both sides and surrounded by a large flock of sheep. He yelled and tried to force his horse through. The shepherd, unaware that the young troublemaker was on official business, knocked him off his horse with a powerful blow of his crook. The horse reared up and injured some of the sheep. The shepherd was so incensed he drew his knife and would have killed the injured Davis if he had not screamed: "I'm Prince Anarwd's messenger!" Eventually, the shepherd's wife had looked after him and treated his injured shoulder and the gashes on his face. He left as soon as he was able to ride his horse, but his round trip had taken more than two weeks by the time Davis returned with the long-awaited message.

"What did you do Davis? Did you walk it?" Gwriad thundered, not interested in his explanation, and ignoring Davis' obvious injuries. The summer was almost over, and Gwriad's plans for an extended visit to Prince Anarwd were in the balance.

Davis looked crestfallen as he handed over the leather bag with the message. He had thought he would have been welcomed as a hero. "Well done, Davis," Angharad gave him an encouraging smile. "Go to the kitchen and ask one of the Megans to feed you. Tell them I said you deserved a large plateful."

"Thank you, m'Lady." Davis bowed, handed his horse to a stable boy, and rushed off before he could be held responsible for any bad news the message might contain.

Later, at supper, the family discussed the proposed visit. "Anarwd will be pleased to see us," Gwriad said, "and promises some good hunting, and visits to local Roman sites. He says that Prince Rhodri ap Williams would like to show us his latest vessel, and if the weather's fine he'll take us out on a short voyage."

"I don't think I'll risk that," Teifryn said apologetically, "I used to get sea sick just travelling from Ynys Mon to Caernarfon."

"I was never much good on the sea either," Angharad agreed. "Perhaps we'll leave it to the men."

"Would I be able to come with you my Lord?" Jon said from behind Gwriad's chair. "I've only ever been on the sea in a small row boat from Gwbert."

"Where I go, Jon, you go," Gwriad held out his cup for a refill. "As my squire, you will always be by my side." He raised an eyebrow at Angharad, and puckered his lips. "Unless, of course, my dear wife is next to me," he laughed. Jon lowered his head and stepped back; he was getting used to his Lord's humour.

Two days later, they left for Caerdydd in Morgannwg at first light. The weather was dry and warm, and besides the family, Gwriad had appointed a guard of six soldiers, including Davis, who now considered himself an experienced traveller. They took a supply wagon so their horses were unencumbered, and an older

IN THE ASHES OF A DREAM

man named Alan, from Aberteifi, was selected as the driver. He had once been part of Gwriad's Central Army, and liked to boast about his experience. "I like riding the wagon and cooking the food," Alan said proudly. "Lord Gomer always chose me."

"I remember his cooking," Gwriad murmured in Teifryn's ear. "I hope it's improved." He made a mime of clutching his stomach and almost falling off his saddle. She laughed, it was the first time she had been really happy for a long time, and much as she loved Tegwen, it was a pleasure to leave her in the safe hands of Alys.

"Indeed," Dafydd agreed, bringing his horse to her other side. "He's not very original. Salted pork and onions used to be his favourite."

Angharad joined in: "It's why the villagers call him 'Alan the Onion'."

They rode at a leisurely pace through broad valleys with wide, shallow rivers that flowed from high hills and occasional lofty crags. In a cloudless sky they saw red kites and soaring eagles and heard the plaintive cry of migrating geese as their arrowhead formations flew overhead. At times, they passed through gloomy forests, coming unexpectedly on cleared areas where small, isolated hamlets had established meagre fields for crops and the rearing of animals.

The peasants watched them suspiciously as they passed through, and Jon was aware of his fine clothes in comparison with their rough, dirty garments. Some of the men carried scythes and pitchforks, and their grim faces offered no sign of welcome. Jon suspected that the wagon and its contents might not have been safe without their six well-armed soldiers bringing up the rear.

"What a hard life they must have," Jon observed.

"No harder than the life you led growing up in Gwbert," Dafydd said. He turned to Gwriad, "I wonder which Lord controls this area?"

"I doubt if these people acknowledge any Lord," he answered. "We're in that wild area where the borders of Deheubarth, Brycheiniog and Morgannwg meet. Nobody knows where the actual boundaries are, it's whether any Lord feels it's worthwhile to claim land that produces so little."

At the end of the afternoon, they began to think of finding a suitable place to camp, and Jon, who had found the leisurely pace frustrating, offered to ride on to check the countryside ahead.

"Alright," Gwriad agreed, "but take Lleu with you. He's had a lot of experience, and in this area it's wise to travel in pairs."

Jon nodded, but would have preferred to do the scouting by himself. He had nothing against Lleu, other than he was a much older person, and Jon had looked forward to having sole responsibility for the task. He was unaware that Gwriad's real motive had been that of a protective father towards an adopted son.

They followed a winding path alongside a clear stream, much reduced by the summer drought. On the right a dense pine forest revealed no sign of human habitation, and very soon, they had lost sight of the small party behind them. In spite of Jon's protests, Lleu insisted on keeping the horses to a trot. "After all, the Lords don't want to have to travel too far before they camp, do they?" he pointed out. "So, there's no point in risking the horses, and there's no rush, as we need to keep our eyes open for a campsite, isn't it?"

Shortly after, they came to a bend in the stream where a hard-packed sandy area promised safe parking for the wagon, and for the erection of the tent for the women. The men would sleep around the campfire, and to one side there was an area of brown grass where they would be able to secure the horses. Lleu agreed to ride back to report their success, while Jon inspected the area around their proposed campsite.

He walked his horse down to the stream to allow it to drink, and spent the time sitting on a rock and enjoying the peace and the beauty of the place. He reviewed his past good fortune, made more evident by the tattered folk he had seen in the impoverished hamlets, and he wondered what Caerdydd might be like. He had no experience of anything larger than Aberteifi, and when he thought about it, he had very little experience of anything.

He watched as a bird, which Lleu had called a dipper, flew low over the water and dived below the surface, coming up with a small fish. The lulling sound of the stream made him sleepy, and he knelt down and splashed his face before drinking the cool water. The horse had moved over to the parched grass, browsing contentedly and Jon realized he was enjoying himself. This was the first time he had camped, and the prospect of sitting around a large fire with the others and sleeping outside was exciting.

He suddenly remembered that Lleu had said something about collecting fuel for the fire, and he jumped up and began a frantic search for fallen wood. He had accumulated a large pile by the time that Lleu and the party arrived. Everyone was in good humour, and the fire was soon alight, the tent erected and the horses safely secured. From the comments of the others Jon understood that this was a rare event for them as well, and they were enjoying it as much as he was.

Alan the Onion was soon preparing food; the soldiers began a game of skimming stones, the women disappeared into the forest to relieve themselves, and Jon poured wine for the brothers. Eventually, after the meal was over and cleared away, everyone settled down to amusing themselves. Gwriad dozed contently in front of the fire with a cup of wine, the soldiers played dice and drank beer, the women interacted with the horses and Jon was trying to fish for trout, when he was joined by Dafydd.

"Getting away from one's normal life is pleasant, isn't it?" he said, remembering as he spoke of his original reluctance.

Jon agreed. "How long will it take to get to Caerdydd from here, my Lord?"

"About another two to three days. It's a long time since I went there." He cleared his throat. "You don't have to call me 'my Lord' when we're alone. Also, remember you're a member of the family now." He slowly sat down near Jon. "Any luck? I haven't seen any fish."

"No, although Lleu tells me he's caught lots of fish from this stream."

Dafydd glanced over at Lleu, who was telling a funny story to the soldiers. "I wouldn't believe everything Lleu tells you, Jon. He has a reputation as a bit of a clown. I doubt he's ever been this way in his life."

"Oh," Jon frowned. "I suppose I stand out as someone who doesn't know much?"

"Not necessarily, you must remember all these men here know how you originally came from Gwbert. It's probably got around that you're a cousin to Gwriad and myself. Their jokes are to cover up for their jealousy. They're not bad men, but they see you suddenly raised up socially, when they believe they know more about life than you do."

"Will I meet other squires in Caerdydd?"

"Almost certainly. You must remember that they will be the sons of wealthy landowners or nobles and will have had a lifetime of being addressed as 'My Lord'. They will be used to giving orders to slaves, servants and soldiers. You must conduct yourself in a similar way if you are to enjoy your stay. Remember, they will know nothing of your early life unless one of the soldiers tells them, which is unlikely. This will be a time when you will be tested. Don't let yourself down," he punched Jon in the arm in a good-natured way, "or us."

. . .

HAROLD WAS LEADING AN ARMY of almost five hundred men when he crossed the River Seven at a shallow ford that enabled his wagons and horses to cross easily and allowed the men to cool their legs in the shallow water. They advanced close to the Welsh border, opposite an area known as Brycheiniog. It was a deserted part of Wales with high sombre mountains, and little-used paths that intersected the broad valleys. They made camp before darkness fell, and he sent out mounted scouts to investigate the area, while his army, which was mostly experienced foot soldiers, settled down around their fires.

He had recruited a number of officers, who had served with him in previous campaigns. All of them were committed to Harold becoming the next King, and understood the need to inflict a defeat on the Welsh as a way of raising Harold's status throughout the country. A solid victory for Harold would also benefit their military careers.

It was a warm evening, and the officers stood in a semi-circle in Harold's huge tent, facing a rough map of Wales drawn on a stretched skin that was fixed to a wooden frame. They had eaten

IN THE ASHES OF A DREAM

well and consumed many cups of wine, to celebrate the start of their campaign, and also the success of their carefully planned march that had linked-up with soldiers from other areas. The eight men were in good humour, and only slowly quietened down as Harold rose to address them.

He raised his cup. "To the defeat of the Welsh!" They drank and cheered and stamped their feet. This was what campaigning was all about.

"We're here," Harold said pointing to the map, "and I intend to march over to here," he said pointing to the southwest coast of Wales. There were audible gasps, and some officers stepped forward to check the map. Harold ignored the reaction. "Here," he said pointing to the area of Aberteifi, "is where the two brothers responsible for the attack on Hereford and on my palace live, and I intend to defeat them and ravage the area, so that they will fear us for years to come!"

There was a mixed response. One officer who had drunk too much gave a loud cheer, and slowly became aware of the muted response of the others. "You want us to fight our way across the whole of Wales?" an officer asked in disbelief.

"That's the plan," Harold said. He noticed the lack of enthusiasm. "That's why we've camped at this point. Tomorrow, we leave a few soldiers here to guard the wagons for our return. From here we travel light. Each man takes his own rations and we'll live off the land. It's a straight line to Gwriad's Castle, and we'll be there before anyone knows we're coming. They've disbanded their army, and the fighting men have returned to their farms. At a fast march, we should be there in four days. We'll attack at dawn of the fifth day." His eyes blazed with excitement.

There was a short silence as each officer digested the information and wondered if he were brave enough to disagree. "My Lord, I would respectfully point out that your plan has some dangers," said a muscular, red-bearded man named Hildering. He owned land along the Severn Estuary, and was known as a fearless fighter. "We are within a few hours march of the Welsh reserve army to the north of here, from which, we believe, the attack on

Shrewsbury was originally launched. General Maelgwn is in charge of the area, and my spies tell me he is not to be underestimated."

Harold looked black, "I know about General Maelgwn."

"If we adopt your plan, Lord Harold, we will never leave Wales alive. Maelgwn will soon hear about us, and while we're marching, he will have riders overtaking us and warning Lord Gwriad and every potential Welsh fighter. If we survive a battle in the west, our return will be made impossible by Welsh ambushes, and General Maelgwn's forces will have time to prepare for our last battle." Hildering had a strong, resonant voice that commanded respect, and the others nodded in agreement.

Harold fumed. "I have made it clear that I need a great victory over the Welsh, the news of which will resound throughout England, and will make me the obvious next King when Edward dies." He glared at the assembled officers, as if daring them to contradict him again.

"We agree with you," said Waelfwulf, "which is why we're all here. It's not the reason for the invasion of Wales that is in doubt, it's your plan of how and where to achieve that victory that we are in disagreement with." Waelfwulf was a tall, slim man with long drooping moustaches, whose reputation was as an administrator. Although a survivor of a number of small battles, his courage outweighed his ability with weapons. He enjoyed debating and had a clear, organized mind. "I suggest we have alternatives."

"Which are?" Harold had a respect for Waelfwulf, which differed from his approach to the other officers who all were proven fighters. They were like him: they were good company on campaigns and fearless in battle, men he could depend on, and who celebrated victory with drunken feasting. But Waelfwulf always saw beyond each battle and would sooner have made treaties with the Welsh than engage in yet another of the unending raids and skirmishes. He would have been surprised to know how similar he was to his Welsh adversary, Lord Dafydd.

"We have a number of options," Waelfwulf said as he moved towards the map. Harold sat down, adopted a relaxed pose and drank from his cup. "We could move north at first light and seek to surprise General Maelgwn and his army. But even with more men and the element of surprise, it would be a bloody victory, and might not be seen by King Edward or those away from the Welsh border as very noteworthy."

"Exactly," Harold said. "Which is why I want to attack Lords Gwriad and Dafydd. The people know about them."

Another option is to advance south," Waelfwulf continued, "and invade Gwent. As most of you know, Prince Anarwd rules this area, and it is rumoured that he might become the next King of South Wales; he certainly has the support of the local chiefs."

"He also has a trained army," one of the officers added.

"True, which is why it might be best to go south-west into Morgannwg."

"Why is that better than attacking these Welsh bandits?" Harold objected.

"Because it's closer, less than half of the distance to the west coast. It's got a large town, large for Wales, which is an important port for their attacks on our merchant shipping. We would advance through the lower end of Brycheiniog, here," he pointed to the map, "crossing the top corner of Gwent, here, and then down through Morgannwg, and about here," he indicated with his dagger, is Caerdydd." He was perhaps the only man who had a grasp of the Welsh pronunciation, and few had his knowledge of the area, but they could see that it was ideal for a short campaign.

Harold said nothing, and the other men drank their wine silently, and stared at Waelfwulf and the map.

"The advantages are that we are passing through remote country," he continued, "with few villages, and no roads until we get close to Caerdydd. We are never too far from our border, and if we move fast, we could avoid Prince Anarwd's army and by crossing back the way we came we should avoid any major opposition. Remember Wales is a country of villages, and the only real towns they have are around their coast. If we destroy Caerdydd and the men loot it, the news will echo around Wales and around England." He turned to Harold, "And you will be re-established as England's military leader and future King."

The officers applauded as Waelfwulf took his seat. Harold stared silently at the map and realized that his officer had put more thought into this plan than he had. If he was honest with himself, he had to admit that revenge had been a major consideration. "How long do you think the raid will take?"

Waelfwulf stood up and pointed at the map. "If we leave at first light tomorrow, we should cross into Wales about midmorning, and should get to Caerdydd at the beginning of the second day, if we march for part of the night. Two days later we could be back over the border, here." He pointed to a spot above Gwent. "With the size of our army and the experience of the soldiers, we should be successful."

"This could work," Harold agreed, suddenly enthused. He patted Waelfwulf on his back. "Well done." He faced the others. "Get the troops ready for an early start."

There was an excited hubbub as they left the tent, and Harold followed and stood staring at a cloudless sky, absorbed for the moment in the wonder of the night sky. "I will be King," he murmured. "It's written in the stars."

. . .

"Was this the way you came, Davis?" Gwriad asked. He dismounted and stretched. Although they had travelled slowly, it had been a long day in the saddle and he was aching. He noticed the others did not appear as tired as he felt and was aware that he had yet to make a complete recovery.

"No, m'Lord, I followed the coast road." Davis was grateful that Lady Angharad was nearby.

"Why didn't we come on that route?" Gwriad frowned. He was feeling irritable.

"I wasn't asked to m'Lord. I thought perhaps you were wanting to return by that route."

"That's a good idea," Dafydd said enthusiastically. "It will give us the chance to see more of our local area." Davis gave him a grateful nod. "I've enjoyed today," he continued, as he helped Teifryn from her saddle. He lifted her away from the horse and swung her round in a circle.

Teifryn shrieked with laughter, "Dafydd, put me down! You great silly!" The soldiers, who were setting up camp, winked at each other, and Alan the Onion gave Teifryn a wistful glance. It had been a while since he had frolicked with a woman. Jon watched with interest; it would never have occurred to him that a woman might enjoy such behaviour. He noticed that Lady Angharad was laughing, but at the same time she seemed sad.

Gwriad remained silent and looked enviously at his younger brother. It seemed to him the tables had turned, and it was Dafydd now who exuded sexual energy, while he was feeling like an old man. He remembered when, not many days ago, he had come across Dafydd's horse by the side of the river. He had just rounded a small bend and there was the horse, perhaps forty paces away, contentedly cropping the grass, its back to him. His first reaction was to call out, in case Dafydd was injured, but the scene seemed so peaceful, he concluded his brother had merely gone for a pee, and unlike his own public displays, his modest younger brother had always disappeared behind a tree.

With a malicious grin, he quietly dismounted and led his horse back the way he had come and hid it behind some trees. He walked quickly back along the path, intending to walk off with Dafydd's horse, or surprise him as he relieved himself. It was then he heard laughter, which he recognized as the merriment of people enjoying making love, and he crept quietly towards the sound.

He parted some bushes and stared, fascinated to see his prim brother lying on his back, while the Wise Woman was humping him. They were both having a lot of fun, and he wondered when it was that he and Angharad had last been so sexually involved. He backed silently away and, avoiding Dafydd's horse, removed his own mount and returned to the castle. He wanted to tease the brother, but he realized it was none of his business.

As he entered the castle he met Angharad. "Have you seen Dafydd?" she asked casually. "He was supposed to be visiting Father Williams, but the old priest is feeling better, and I have just heard that he's visiting Mwnt to give communion to the handful of people who live there. So Dafydd is wasting his time."

"No," Gwriad continued on his way to the stables. "I haven't seen him." He wondered, as he walked his horse into a stall, when Dafydd and Derryth had begun to have an affair, and if it was likely to cause friction in their tight-knit family. There was no doubt in his mind that the planned visit might provide the necessary time for Dafydd and Teifryn to get back together, and he was glad he had been able to insist that Dafydd come with them. At the same time, he felt somewhat of a hypocrite when he reflected on his own behaviour: in the early years of his marriage to Angharad, he had engaged in a number of casual affairs. They had never lasted long, and he had come to suspect that Angharad had been responsible for the sudden disappearance of these willing women. The fact that she had never mentioned them made him feel something he had rarely felt before: a sense of guilt.

But that was some time ago, and in the final years of King Gruffydd's tempestuous reign, the military responsibilities and his Court duties had lessened his chance for boredom, which had always been the impetus for his sexual dalliances. Throughout their marriage, Angharad had been his great friend and supporter, and he had come to value her strength and her devotion. She had never shown any attraction to another man, and her powerful personality had often left him wondering why she had chosen him for her life partner.

The second night around the campfire was lively and entertaining. Alan the Onion performed some juggling tricks, two of the soldiers played flutes, while the others sang, and it was clear that these accomplishments had been developed during the inevitable periods of inactivity of earlier campaigns. Towards the end of the evening Dafydd told a story about a Roman leader named Caesar, who had invaded England, and how eventually the Roman troops had invaded Ynys Mon, the holy island, and destroyed the power of the Druids.

The soldiers took it in turns to mount guard throughout the night, and the next day Gwriad ordered two of them to scout ahead. "Now we're out of Deheubarth, I want you to keep your eyes open," he said to them. "I'm not expecting any problems, but they're a bit odd in Morgannwg." He looked grim, and the two soldiers exchanged glances; they had distant relatives in Morgannwg. "But not as odd as some of those fellows from Aberteifi!" he roared with laughter and the soldiers joined in. He was unlike other officers, and they liked him for it. "You can leave after the meal."

After a light breakfast, amid some mockery at Jon's expense for failing to provide trout, they prepared to leave. Gwriad gathered everyone together. "Thanks to Davis," Gwriad said, shaking his head in apparent disbelief, "we don't know exactly where we are, or where we're going." Nobody was sure if he was serious or not, and Davis glanced at Angharad. She gave a slight shake of her head, and Davis breathed out. "So, I want you two," he pointed to two soldiers, "to go south, and Lleu and Davis will go east, and see if any of you can find a route that will lead us to Caerdydd within the next week!"

The four riders took off along the trail, and before long, the two soldiers going south found a path through the thinning forest and disappeared. Davis and Lleu rode as fast as their horses could safely travel, leaving the family, the wagon, and the two soldiers far behind.

"That's good," said Lleu as they left the forest, "now we can see where we're going." They had emerged from the shadows of the trees into a bright landscape of bare hills and scrub covered plains, intersected with occasional streams. Further away, high mountains dwarfed the lower hills, and to the north, beyond some high ground a column of black smoke curled up into a cloudless sky.

"Looks like they're burning stubble, maybe?" Davis said.

"I don't know," Lleu screwed up his eyes. "Seems like it's a very big fire, isn't it? I would say it's about a mile or so away. What d'ye think?"

"Yes, that would be about right. Shall we see what it is?" Davis shielded his eyes from the bright sun.

"Alright, as long as we don't take too long, boy, or Lord Gwriad will eat you for supper." With a laugh he turned towards the great plume of smoke. Lleu was older than Davis, but he'd known the boy for years and liked his happy-go-lucky approach to life and his lust for adventure. After all, he recalled, Davis had successfully completed a journey to find Prince Anarwd and returned virtually unharmed; Lleu wasn't sure he could have accomplished that by himself.

Lleu and Davis galloped up the bare hill side and could see below them, on the other side, a thick forest that led sharply down to a broad valley where the lower areas had been cleared for farming. To one side, on a raised mound, were the remains of a large Roman fort, but close by was a small village in which every building was being consumed by fire. Black smoke belched upwards into a windless sky, and the two men stared dumfounded.

"Look: Saxons!" Lleu exclaimed waving his hand at the marching columns that were moving away to the south. "There must be hundreds of 'em."

"The villagers have taken shelter in the old fort," Davis said, pointing to a crowd of people. "It seems like the Saxons can't be bothered with them." They could see the villagers had gathered to one side of the ruins, watching their enemy move south. "Where do you think they're going?" Davis said.

"Probably the same place we are," Lleu rubbed his hand down his unshaven face. "We must get back to Lord Gwriad as soon as we can now. Come on, boy!"

He turned to see Davis waving his arms. "Lleu! Look there, see, there's more Saxons!"

They watched in horrified silence as, a way off, a cohort of Saxons, led by a line of horsemen broke out of the forest and charged across an open space towards the west side of the old fort. Inside the grounds two men could be seen desperately alerting the villagers to the danger and trying to organize them to resist the onslaught.

"Quick, Davis! We can't do anything here. We must warn Lord Gwriad," cried Lleu. They turned their horses and raced back the way they had come.

. . .

THE SAXON ARMY HAD PASSED through Brycheiniog without meeting any opposition, moving like a dark snake across the open landscape. The small hamlets they encountered were ruthlessly destroyed, and scouts were positioned to prevent any survivors escaping. As

IN THE ASHES OF A DREAM

far as Hildering was concerned, their speed of movement would allow them to wreak havoc and be back across the border before the Welsh could organize any meaningful resistance.

By the morning of the second day, as they moved into Morgannwg, they came across their first sizeable village, built beside the ruins of a large Roman fort, and situated in a valley, with buildings on both sides of a small river. "It's called Gelligaer, which means The Fort of the Grove," a short, dark-haired scout reported. "They know we're here." The scout, like a number of others, had been recruited from among the displaced Welsh farmers who roamed the borderlands looking for work. Their usefulness as translators and as knowledgeable scouts was immense, although their own countrymen hated them.

Harold, and some of his officers sat on their horses and looked down on the distant cluster of buildings. To the right of the buildings were the imposing stone ruins of a Roman fort, to which the frantic villagers were rushing. The Saxons were on a high hill less than a mile away from the Welsh, and behind the officers, stretching away down the hill, were their massed formations of foot soldiers hidden from the villagers' view.

"They've seen our horses, and probably know we're Saxons," Harold murmured, but they'll have no idea of our numbers. We could overrun them before they get organized."

"If we attack them, it might slow us down," Waelfwulf said. "The remains of that Roman fort will prove to be a useful rallying point."

"How far have we still to go?" Harold rubbed his beard. He was tensed up and wanted action.

Hildering beckoned to the scout. "How far to Caerdydd?"

"We should get there before midday tomorrow, m'Lord."

Harold glared at the scout. "Not before then?"

"There's some difficult country ahead, m'Lord," the scout scowled. He did not like this overbearing Saxon.

"If we attack this place, it will certainly slow us down," Waelfwulf murmured. "I suggest we keep to the plan."

Harold swore under his breath, he wanted to lead the attack and vent his frustration on the Welsh.

"I have a suggestion, my Lord," said Hildering. "Why don't we by-pass this place with our main army and continue our advance towards Caerdydd. We can leave enough soldiers behind to destroy this meagre opposition. These soldiers could follow on and meet up with us before we attack our main objective."

Harold gave him a grim smile. This was the advice he wanted. "Go on, I'm listening."

"We could pass to the east of this village, in full view of their inhabitants who will all have taken refuge in the old fort. Meanwhile our smaller force moves down to the right, behind that hill," he pointed to a small piece of high ground that would enable the remainder of the Saxon troops to move down to the valley without being seen from the fort. "I suggest that when we march past, their relief will be such that they will be ill-prepared for a surprise attack, especially if the main army sets fire to their village as they leave."

Harold nodded. "Good. Hildering, you and I will lead the attack on the fort. Once it's destroyed, I want our men to catch up with the main force as quickly as possible. Waelfwulf, you will lead that main force, and I want the other officers to maintain a fast march." He laughed, releasing the pent-up energy that had been pulsing through him. "We'll take a hundred men. More than enough to destroy these Welsh peasants." He felt eager for a fight. "Come on Hildering, we need to separate our heroes."

"I hope you're right," Waelfwulf said as Hildering followed Harold. "That fort could be a problem."

As Harold rode down to the waiting troops he felt better than he had for a long time. He was a man of action, and the Welsh deserved to be punished. In his mind he saw only men fighting to demonstrate their bravery and their marshal skills. He did not consider that it was always the women, the children and the elderly that were the inevitable victims.

. . .

"How much do ye want for that scrawny pig of yours?" Huw asked. He was a stocky, loud-mouthed bully, who was happy to be disliked by most of the village; it gave him a feeling of power.

IN THE ASHES OF A DREAM

Since his dominating father had died of stomach pains, Hue had ruled his family with a combination of threats, blows and very occasional compliments. Little by little, he had expanded his farm and built up the largest herd of pigs in the area. This was market day at Gelligaer, when people came to sell, buy, and most importantly to exchange news.

"I'm not selling to you, Huw," Iago said. He was an athletic old man who had fallen on hard times. "You still owe me for the last pig."

"Listen, ye old runt, I'll pay you when you sell me that pig. If ye don't sell that one, then ye won't be paid for the other."

"I hope you rot in Hell!" Iago yelled. He thought it was about time that he knocked Huw down to size. Although an old man, he was fitter than men half his age. He advanced with his fists clenched, and Huw drew his knife, threatening, "I'll use this if I have to." It was at that moment that people started shouting, and running about, seemingly without purpose. Then, they heard the words: "The Saxons have come!" and the church bell began to toll its warning.

"Bloody Hell!" Huw exclaimed when he saw the riders on the top of the nearby hill. "Saxons!" He replaced his knife and rushed towards his horse intending to gallop back to his farm and get his family and release his herd of pigs into the forest.

"Don't run off, you coward!" Iago cried, grasping his arm. "We need every able man if we are to drive them off."

Huw pushed the older man away with such force he fell to the ground. "Y'old fart! Stay if you like. I'm not wasting my life saving has-beens like you." He clambered awkwardly onto his horse, wishing he hadn't drunk so much at the tavern, and galloped out of the village, ignoring others who waved him to stop. Once beyond the buildings, he turned to the east, and in a few minutes reached his farm.

Iago smiled his thanks as he was helped to his feet by a young woman, who wished him luck and ran into her house to collect her children. "To the fort!" he yelled, running from house to house and urging everyone to drop everything and save themselves. He grasped his sword as he ran, grateful that he had worn it to control the pig if it had been necessary. Normally, he would have left his sword at the farm, and he wondered what weapons the villagers would have to oppose the Saxons. Because of the bell, men rushed in from the fields, the market emptied, and people of all ages fled their houses. Soon the entire population of the village was making its way up to the old fort.

At the beginning of the first century AD, the Roman legions had fought their way into the west of Britain and were strongly opposed by a warlike people who were known at that time as the Silures. Gradually, the Romans occupied what came to be known as Wales and set up a network of forts to keep a grip on the rebellious natives. The fort at Gelligaer had been built at the end of the first century AD and had been garrisoned until the gradual Roman withdrawal from Britain in the fourth century. Almost seven hundred centuries later, the derelict stone structure was mainly unused, except in times of danger.

Originally, it had been a large, square fort with a wide, deep trench and with a set of double gates in the middle of each side of the thick stone walls. Inside these weather-beaten walls had been barracks, storage and administration buildings and even a bathhouse. Over the course of time, the ditch had partially filled up, and most of the interior stonework had been stripped for local building. Much of the outside walls remained standing, but the solid gates were long gone. On a few occasions when a Saxon attack had seemed likely, the local inhabitants had retreated inside its cold and dreary walls and had made stone barricades to stop entry through the gateways. All of these barricades remained except for the eastern gate, which served as the entrance into the walled space. It was a place where the children played and animals were penned, but otherwise the courtyard was seen to have little daily value.

The villagers poured in through the east gate and immediately began to pile up large stones to make a blockade. The children climbed the walls facing north and gave reports on the movement of the Saxons, while the adults laboured to raise the stone barrier.

"We must make sure that each gate has spare rocks to throw down at them!" Iago shouted; he appointed Vernon to be in charge of the west gate and two young farmers to manage the other gates. The three men chose others to help them and rushed off to organize the rock piles.

"If they attack all four gates at once, we could be in trouble," Iago said to the village elders. "Be prepared for anything!" Nobody questioned Iago's right to give orders, as he was the most experienced soldier in the village.

"They're coming! The Saxons are coming!" The children's frightened voices urged the adults to work faster at the gates. Suddenly, an adult yelled, "Oh God! There's hundreds of 'em, but they seem to be passing us!"

The villagers, as an undisciplined mob, rushed over to the east gate and watched in awed silence as the large army moved past on the other side of the valley. The majority of the Saxon soldiers marched past in tight order, but a wail went up from the Welsh as the last formation peeled off to burn their village; almost as if it was an afterthought, an added insult. It did not seem natural that they did not attack the fort.

"This is a trick!" yelled Iago. He was an experienced fighter, and in his earlier days had fought against the Saxons in the great battle of Rhyd-y-Groes. After that decisive battle he had served in the Southern Army for seven years during the reign of Gruffydd ap Llewelyn, and now in his later age he had been helping his son-in-law on his farm.

"How'd ye mean, Iago?" Vernon the black smith called back from the other side of the crowd. He was a friend of Iago and respected his fighting experience.

"We must watch the west gate!" Iago said, as his large friend joined him. "This could be a diversion. Just look at the effect the destruction of their homes has had on them." They turned to look at the villagers who were entirely focused on their burning houses. All their years of work, their memories of many generations, all going up in flames while they huddled behind these stone ruins. The church bell had stopped tolling.

The two men ran towards the west gate, where nobody was watching, and were aware of the distance between the walls.

"Don't be surprised at them," Vernon panted, "if your home was burning in the village you'd be looking east as well."

"I rarely come inside this place," Iago gasped, "I forgot how big it is."

As they approached the stone-blocked gate, they saw the distant forest come to life. Where a moment before the ancient trees had stood in shadowy tranquillity, a sudden wave of armoured horsemen burst out of the dark woods and was racing for the fort.

"Saxons!" Vernon yelled. "Saxons at the west gate! Everybody! The Saxons are coming!"

Instantly, the villagers awoke to the danger and raced to the western barricade, urging their children to stay back and guard the other gates; they knew they were going to be fighting for their lives and did not want their children in the melee. A few peasants had swords, some had spears, a small group of older men had bows and arrows, but the majority carried only knives, wooden pitchforks and clubs. None of them had armour, and they knew, as there was no escape, they would all have to fight to survive.

Meanwhile, the main Saxon force advanced towards Caerdydd, burning Huw's farm and capturing many of his pigs. His daughters and his wife fled into the forest, while Huw frantically dug up his hidden gold, and tried to escape on his maltreated horse; he decided that his family could look after themselves, and that he would be safer if he rode to Caerdydd and pretended to be a hero. Unfortunately for him, he was intercepted by some Saxon scouts, who showed little interest in his offer of gold, especially as they intended to take it anyway. He was knocked off his horse, and knelt, sobbing in front of the fierce bearded soldiers, begging for mercy. They laughed as they slowly cut him to pieces, shouting the Saxon for coward, and he realized as he died, that he had made a series of very bad decisions.

CHAPTER FOURTEEN

Three days before, Prince Anarwd had received reports of a large Saxon build-up near the southern borders of Brycheiniog. He had previously been on manoeuvres in Gwent with a local force of nearly 200 men, mostly foot soldiers, and had been preparing to make his way to Caerdydd to meet with the Lords Gwriad and Dafydd. Long experience of Saxon incursions made the Prince fear the worst and he sent an urgent message to General Maelgwn to bring his cavalry from northern Brycheiniog into Morgannwg.

On receiving the news, General Maelgwn had moved quickly, and by the second day his cavalry units had advanced rapidly through the central hills, using little known paths, and reaching the border of Morgannwg in the early evening. The warm weather and windless nights had made travelling a pleasure, and his men were optimistic as they prepared themselves for a possible battle within the next day. They were travelling light, and avoided fires, so that their position would not be noticed in the dark.

The cavalrymen were among the elite fighters in Wales, having trained together throughout the spring and early summer. They had taken part in the raids on Shrewsbury and on Harold's home, and many had been well rewarded. Unlike most of the Welsh fighters, these cavalrymen had learned the value of discipline and coordinated action in their battles with the fearsome Saxons. They were also well-armed and would be fighting on experienced horses.

There had been no sign of the reported large Saxon army, and Maelgwn had begun to sense that he and his men had received false news. Perhaps the Saxons did not intend to invade, but merely cause confusion and disruption among the limited Welsh fighting units. "We may have guessed wrongly," he said to his officers. "For all we know they may have deliberately caused us to move south, while they attack elsewhere." He stopped speaking as a scout galloped into the camp, his horse frothing at the mouth. Without dismounting, he rode up close to the general, who had taught all his scouts that important messages should not wait on respectful behaviour.

"There's an army of Saxons, mostly foot soldiers advancing this way, they could be aiming for Caerdydd," the scout blurted out. His blouse was wet with sweat, and he breathed heavily.

"How far away?" Maelgwn demanded. This was the news he had hoped for.

"I would say less than an hour from here, M'Lord." The man regained his composure. "They're marching fast and showing no attempt to hide their numbers. There looks to be three hundred of them, maybe more."

"So, they're hoping to achieve a surprise attack on Caerdydd?" he mused. "Are they using the Roman road?"

"Yes, m'Lord."

"Well done, soldier. What's your name?"

"Edwin, m'Lord."

He nodded. "When this is over, you'll get promoted, Edwin. Now rest yourself, we'll be in action before dawn." Maelgwn turned to his officers. "If they marched all night on that road the Saxons could reach the town by morning. Send out more scouts – the Saxons should be easy to find now that they've reached the Roman Road. Send other scouts to find and alert Prince Anarwd's army."

• • •

As he watched from the high ground, Harold was delighted with the way the plan was working out. His aim had been to prevent the fort being used as a strong defensive position, as he knew from experience that such structures could enable the defenders to withstand a superior force, delaying its progress, and causing unforeseen death and injury to the attackers. The villagers were gathered around the eastern gate, with their attention fixed on the destruction of their homes and the gradual withdrawal of the Saxon formations. Women were weeping, children were screaming and the men were making brave threats at the departing warriors. At that moment, they were just a crowd of miserable people, and if he acted quickly, Harold knew he could break through the west side and, once in the fort, he and his soldiers would ensure they remained that way.

He carefully positioned his men in a triple line hidden among the trees and sat tensed on his horse with Hildering and the other officers by his side. Slowly, he controlled his breathing as he prepared himself for the charge over about 200 paces of rocky terrain. He knew that when he and his few riders reached the fort ahead of the foot soldiers, they must dismount quickly and clamber over the broken barricade at the gate to prevent the defenders from manning the makeshift wall. With their armour and weapons, his few Saxons would be more than enough to hold back the poorly equipped Welsh.

"Are you ready?" he looked over at Hildering.

"Ready," Hildering grunted. Like Harold he seemed very taught.

Harold drew his sword, and rode slowly ahead of the others, instantly breaking into a gallop. He led the charge without the usual battle cries or the threatening rasp of the trumpets. As he avoided the jagged rocks that were strewn around he was only aware of the sound of the thundering hooves and the pounding in his chest.

He was at the mid-way mark when he saw armed men appearing along the top of the barricade, and knew they were in for a fight. He found himself smiling, and realized he was looking forward to the battle; it was another chance to prove he was a superior human being. When he was a few feet from the barricade an arrow hit the horse next to him. It collapsed immediately, as though struck by lightning and tossed the rider forward onto the rocky ground, where he lay unmoving. Harold vaulted off his horse and, with his sword in his right hand, began to clamber up the broken wall of stone.

Above him, a line of peasants began to throw down small boulders, and within moments he knew that there was no longer any point in the officers attempting to overcome the defenders before the shield-bearing soldiers arrived. "Fall back!" he yelled, and the officers did so willingly, glad to escape certain injury and without a loss of reputation. "Forward!" he yelled to his soldiers, urging them up the wall. "Up and over!"

A heavy stone narrowly missed him and he stepped back with his horse out of range of the deadly missiles as the Saxons locked shields and began to advance up the rock barricade. A hail of heavy stones crashed down on them, as the villagers used every weapon they had to force them back.

The few local archers were older men, not given to haste, and they took careful aim to avoid wasting the few arrows they had; this resulted in an unexpected toll on the Saxons, who had felt relatively safe in their armour. As some of the shield-bearing Saxons reached the top of the stone pile, they were forced backwards by spears and poles, causing them to fall back onto the line behind them. The shield line wavered under the constant barrage and it finally fractured, with the soldiers falling in disarray. Some Saxons reached the point where they could raise their shields over the stone emplacement but were then vulnerable to the swords and knives of the frantic Welsh who, having nothing to lose, lashed out furiously and effectively at their well-armoured opponents.

Harold watched in blind fury as the shield wall broke, and the soldiers fell back to the accompaniment of a roar of derision from the defenders. It was clear that the well armoured men with their superior weapons and experience would eventually break through, but the delay was unexpected.

"Marshall the men," Harold yelled to his officers, "keep the pressure up." He ran to Hildering. "Take twenty men and break in at an undefended gate." An arrow passed close by, and he wished he'd used more men to start with; an attack on all four gates at once would have finished it. Hildering quickly gathered a group and led them toward the south gateway.

At the west gate, the peasants continued to put up a spirited defence, and the broken stones prevented the advancing Saxons from maintaining their shield wall, allowing gaps to form, which the Welsh exploited from their higher position. Harold knew that

IN THE ASHES OF A DREAM

once the soldiers were able to force their way over the rim of the barricade, the battle would be over, and the Welsh also were well aware of this and fought with manic bravery.

As Hildering's twenty soldiers departed to his right, Harold quickly lost patience. This small fight was taking up too much time, and an unexpected number of Saxons had been killed or injured. "I should be on my way to Caerdydd, not pissing about with these peasants." He knew if it were not for the loss of face he would withdraw his troops from this pointless diversion and make a fast march to catch up with Waelfwulf.

"Come with me!" he yelled at two soldiers at the back of the cohort. He led the way to the left of the fort, moving as quickly as he could over the broken ground. When he reached the north gate, he paused to catch his breath. "If we move fast, we may catch the Welsh unprepared," he gasped. "Make no sound." He dropped down into the shallow ditch and glanced up at the mound of broken stones. He drew his sword, and as he moved forward a child began to scream a warning.

• • •

It was midday when the two soldiers who had gone south returned to report their success. The group had stopped by a small stream, as the women had insisted on taking advantage of the cool water. "We can all do with a wash," Teifryn had said pointedly, "some more than others."

"What news?" Gwriad demanded as the soldiers pulled to a halt. The men were hot, their smocks were soaked in sweat, and their steaming horses moved quickly towards the water as soon as the men dismounted.

"We've found the path that leads to the main road to Caerdydd, m'Lord," The soldier smiled proudly. "It was not difficult, m'Lord."

"Well done, Roy," Gwriad clapped him on the shoulder, "and you too, Merydyth. Davis won't have to do a week of cleaning the jakes now!" he roared with laughter. It was a good day, and he had not felt so relaxed for a long time.

"Horsemen approaching!" Alan the Onion shouted; he had

moved into the forest in search of edible fungi and was ahead of the others.

Jon and the soldiers waited with their hands on their swords as Davis and Lleu galloped up to them. "Saxons!" Davis yelled. "A Saxon army!" The men tumbled off their horses, and quickly reported what they had seen.

"How many were attacking the fort?" Gwriad demanded.

"About a hundred, m'Lord," Lleu answered. "Mostly foot soldiers."

"And the rest?"

"It were a big army, m'Lord. Some hundreds, I reckon." Davis nodded his agreement.

"It looks like they mean to attack Caerdydd," Dafydd said thoughtfully. "It could be Earl Harold wanting his revenge, and perhaps hoping to re-establish his reputation before The Confessor dies."

"No matter who or why," Gwriad snapped. "What are we going to do about them?"

"There's only one thing we can do," Dafydd said gently. "We must make for Caerdydd as quickly as we can and warn them. Although I imagine they already know."

Gwriad looked furious. "How far away is this village that's being attacked?"

"About three miles, m'Lord," Davis glanced anxiously at Lleu, "maybe a bit less?"

"Right!" Gwriad said forcefully. "Dafydd, you, Jon and I will ride to the village and see what the situation is. Davis and Lleu, you'll show us the way, and you two," he pointed at two soldiers, "will come with us. Roy and Merydyth, you will guard the women and the wagon, you know the way ahead." He pointed at Alan the Onion, "Drive the wagon as fast as you are able and find the western approach to Caerdydd."

"What do you think you're doing?" Angharad said incredulously. "Are you intending to leave us in hostile country so the seven of you can attack a Saxon army?" Her eyes flashed, and she strode up to him like a rooster starting a fight.

"We can't just run away!" he thundered. "I need to see what

we're against. We'll soon meet up with Prince Anarwd and his army, and who knows where General Maelgwn might be. If we are to survive, we must take every opportunity to defeat them."

"In case you've forgotten, Gwriad, you're no longer in charge of this part of Wales!" Angharad shouted.

"I'm a senior officer. It's my duty to help Prince Anarwd!" He roared, waving his fists in the air.

"So, you just want to leave Teifryn and me to be raped and murdered by marauding Saxons, while you go off and try and be a hero?" she shouted back, pointing her finger in his face. Angharad and Gwriad were famous for their lively arguments, but for those who had not witnessed them before, it was always a shock.

"Well, say something Dafydd," Teifryn said. "Do you think this is a good idea?" She agreed with Angharad but wanted to be sure Dafydd felt the same way. He had just begun to notice her again, and she did not want to upset the new warmth in their relationship.

Dafydd frowned; he hated being involved in Gwriad's decisions. "The main Saxon army appears to be advancing south and to the east of here. If you go south-west until you meet the sea, you should be well away from them. Also, you don't have to go to Caerdydd, just alert the first people you come across." He took in a deep breath. "I agree with Gwriad, we can't just do nothing. What we can do is assess the situation. But rest assured we're not going to fight an army." Dafydd always sounded so logical, and although neither Angharad nor Gwriad looked entirely satisfied, Teifryn gave him a big smile and the soldiers looked visibly relieved.

"So, alright. But you promise me you won't do anything stupid?" Angharad muttered, her face close to Gwriad's, reminding him, as she liked to do whenever they had a disagreement, that she was the taller.

"I'm not in the habit of doing stupid things," Gwriad said evasively.

"Give me your word!" she persisted.

"Alright! I give you my word!" He turned to Dafydd, "We should hurry." He gestured at the others: "Quickly now!" and in a short time the seven horses galloped off, led by Davis and Lleu.

"Let's get out of here," Angharad ordered. "The bloody Saxons could be anywhere." It was so unlike her to swear that Teifryn quickly mounted her horse and followed the two soldiers, while Angharad urged Alan to turn the wagon and follow as quickly as he was able. She rode up alongside Teifryn. "I still think it's bloody stupid."

. . .

HAROLD RACED UP THE ROCKS of the north gate with the two soldiers close behind and was able to reach the top before the children's screams brought adults to the southern gate. Vernon was the first to challenge Harold, and although both men were of similar height and strength, Saxon armour was the deciding factor. Vernon was wielding the big sword he had crafted in his smithy and wore a leather jerkin he had inherited from his father; he wore no helmet. In contrast, Harold wore a gambeson, a thickly padded coat, with a chainmail vest and a chainmail coif that protected his head and shoulders. He wore a close-fitting helmet with metal cheek pads, and carried a heavy sword, and on a belt around his waist hung a sharp two-edged hand axe. He had left his shield with his horse, to enable him to use the two-handed grip on his sword.

It was a deliberate decision for Vernon to take on the largest Saxon, for he saw himself as a protector of his community and had always felt lucky to have been born with both strength and good health. He rushed forward and delivered a powerful blow at the Saxon giant, knowing that this man had to be killed if there was to be a chance of fighting off the other invaders. Harold blocked the sword and proceeded with cold precision to force the blacksmith backwards with fast, double-handed strokes. Vernon quickly realized that he was opposed by someone who was trained in fighting; while the blacksmith relied only on his brute strength, the Saxon showed he was equally strong and possessed a skill that was deadly.

The end was sudden: Vernon broke through Harold's defence and felt a moment of elation, but his sword was deflected by the Saxon's metal helmet, and at that moment Harold's two-handed

IN THE ASHES OF A DREAM

sword bit deeply into the blacksmith neck and shoulder, and he died instantly. His death caused dismay among the other adults who had rushed to help defend the gate, and they were quickly overwhelmed by Hildering's men, who burst through the south gate behind them. It was only a matter of time before the main body of defenders at the west gate was overrun and, in spite of a heroic counterattack by Iago, defeat was inevitable and resulted in a massacre in which every adult and child was slaughtered.

"How many did we lose?" Harold demanded. He was sitting on stone inside the fort and slowly stretching his neck. Although he had survived the blacksmith's last blow, his head ached and the rush of adrenalin he had felt when he killed the peasant had been replaced with pain and a sense of despondency.

"Too many," Hildering replied gloomily. Although he had suggested this attack plan as a way of appeasing the obvious frustration of Harold, he had not really been in favour of any deviation from the original plan. The battle had taken much longer than expected, and he had been surprised at the fury of the defence by mere peasants. Many Saxons had died, and many more had been injured. They would not be ready to march until they had had time to recover. "We'll have to wait here until morning," he said. "The men are exhausted, and the wounded need attention. They're not in fighting form."

Harold knew Hildering was right, and he detected the hint of blame, but had it not been for his throbbing head he would have opposed the advice. "What do you suggest?" he asked. There was a dangerous tone in his voice.

Hildering had served with Harold for many years, and was familiar with his quixotic moods, and with his terrible pride. He opened a flask, which a soldier had brought to him from his horse. "Our plan is based on a rapid advance, the destruction of Caerdydd and a fast retreat. We must keep to that plan to avoid disaster." He drank from his flask and offered it. "I suggest we stay here and wait for Waelfwulf on his retreat. He should be able to attack Caerdydd soon after first light tomorrow, and should be back here at about this time. Our being here serves a purpose;

we're defending his rear and can provide food and sentry duty for his men."

Harold sniffed loudly and reluctantly took a swig but brightened up when he found it was wine. "You're right," he drank deeply, "we couldn't get there in time for the attack, but I worry whether Waelfwulf has enough soldiers."

"If he catches the Welsh town unprepared, and there is every chance he will, his more than 300 experienced soldiers will defeat any opposition. They should be able to destroy much of the town and be marching back before the Welsh can organize their forces."

The wine dulled Harold's aching neck, and he adopted a more thoughtful manner. "We were unlucky here. If we could have surged over the barricade before they were able to defend it, there would have been no opposition. It shows how stone structures change a battle." He finished the wine without any apology. "It was only a matter of minutes, and we would have dominated the fight," he rubbed his neck. "I should be leading the whole army into Caerdydd, not festering here." He got to his feet and staggered off to find out the exact losses and to pass on the changed orders.

After a few minutes of thought, Hildering called over to an officer who had just returned from a scouting mission and had missed the action. "Egbert, I have a job for you."

The officer approached and gave a casual bow. He was tall and arrogant with bright eyes and a cruel mouth. "My Lord?"

"We're going to be stuck here until Waelfwulf returns. I want you to make good use of the time by killing local Welsh peasants. I want them to remember us and fear our return. Leave now with as many horsemen as you need, and report back to me tomorrow morning."

"That will be a pleasure," Egbert smiled; he rarely laughed.

"See if we still have a Welsh scout with us, and if so take him with you."

"Who knows?" Egbert smoothed his thick beard. "I might find some willing Welsh women!" He gave a humourless guffaw as he strode away.

CHAPTER FIFTEEN

The return journey took Davis and Lleu longer than they had anticipated as their horses were tired, and the two excited men almost lost their way in the forest. Eventually they reached the bare hillside and were able to point out the dense smoke that billowed up from the other side of the hill. "The village is still burning!" Davis yelled. "That's where we saw the Saxon army going that way!"

He waved his arm to the south.

They reined in their horses on the brow of the hill, where they had a clear view of the fort. Below them the battle had come to an end, and it was clear that the Saxons had butchered the villagers who had opposed them, including the children. The wide space inside the fort was dotted with bodies. Some were lonely little figures, and others had died in small groups, with a dense cluster of corpses near the west gate. They had been left where they died.

The Saxons soldiers had abandoned the fort, and the bodies of at least twenty of their dead had been arranged in a line in front of the south gate. Soldiers were collecting wood for cremation piles, others were being treated for their wounds and food was being prepared.

"They put up a good fight," Dafydd said. "They were just peasants against battle-hardened soldiers. They must have had a good leader to cause that much damage."

"We're too late," Gwriad said. His voice was thick with emotion. "If we could have got here earlier…."

"There would have been nothing the seven of us could do," Dafydd said quietly. "We must get back and find the women and hurry down to Caerdydd. We now have something to report."

"They're not getting ready to go," Jon observed. "They've killed everyone and destroyed the village. Why would they stay?"

"I imagine they're waiting for the main army to return," Dafydd said. "They've lost a few of their men, but they're still a dangerous force to be reckoned with. They could provide a welcome reserve for their retreating warriors." As he spoke a group of horsemen galloped off past the smoking village, travelling south.

• • •

"I'm sorry, Lady Angharad, I don't know how it happened." Alan the Onion was close to tears as he looked at the damaged wagon. One of the front wheels had come off its axle, and the wagon had crashed down on one side, forcing the horse to the ground, where it lay in the harness whinnying pitifully. Everyone dismounted and stared at the frightened creature.

Angharad yelled at the two soldiers to get the horse released from the harness, and with Alan's help they finally managed it. But when they lifted the shafts from the animal, it was unable to get back on its feet, but lurched about and then fell back on the ground.

"It's broken a leg," Roy said. "We'll have to put it down." He spoke in such a matter-of-fact manner that Teifryn let out a small cry and kneeled down by the horse's head. "There must be something we can do?" she wept. "There must be something!"

Angharad knelt down beside her and put her arm around Teifryn's shoulder. "There's nothing we can do, love." She helped her to her feet and led her away. "There, there. A horse cannot survive with a broken leg." She nodded at the soldiers as she led her friend a short way down the path.

"It was my fault," she murmured in Teifryn's ear, "if I hadn't been urging Alan to drive so fast, this would never have happened."

"No, Angharad, it's not your fault," Teifryn protested. "Alan should know the condition of his wagon." They hugged each other and took deep breaths. "We'd better get back, the light is fading."

When they returned, the horse had been dispatched and the three men had moved its corpse into the forest; there was blood on the path, the only reminder of the horse. The men were busy collecting the spilled equipment and unloading the remaining stuff that remained in the open wagon. "We're unloading the wagon, m'Lady, so we can raise it up an' get the wheel back on," Alan explained. "Luckily the wheel isn't damaged, and we can use one of the soldier's horses, and he can travel with me."

"Well done, Alan," Angharad said quietly. It was as though the rush was over, and they would just have to face a new situation.

"Couldn't we leave the wagon, and keep moving?" Teifryn suggested.

"Our husbands would think we'd been very wasteful," Angharad laughed. "If we hadn't been here, this is what the men would have done. I don't want to have us blamed for this mini-disaster."

"If we hadn't been with them in the first place, the wagon would not have lost its wheel," Teifryn pointed out.

"Whatever," Angharad said dismissively. She walked over to her horse that was grazing at the side of the path and, pulling up a handful of grass, began to groom the sweating beast. It was something she always found relaxing.

When the men finally secured the wheel and reloaded the wagon, the sun had set, and in the distance a wolf began to howl. The group moved off with Merydyth in the front, then the two women, followed by the wagon with Alan and Roy bringing up the rear. "We'll travel at walking speed throughout the night," Angharad said.

"Perhaps we should stop and camp?" Teifryn suggested.

"Normally we would," she agreed, "but with the chance of Saxons being around, I would prefer to push on. They're more likely to be behind us, rather than in front."

"You're probably right." Teifryn always found it easier to agree than to oppose her strong-willed friend. She acknowledged that their husbands should never have left them, but if she had been left to make the decision as to whether to camp in a strange place or travel along a dark road, she was uncertain what she would have chosen.

They travelled slowly along the dim path that was illuminated by a clear, moonlit sky. An owl hooted, and there were frequent animal noises in the forest. After a while, the path began to climb and they gradually left the trees and entered an area of bare hills and small streams. They crested a small rise and in front of them the path was easier to see, stretching like a white snake twisting across the shadowy valley. There were no lights anywhere, and there was an empty, solitary feeling about the place. They stopped, and it was pleasant not to hear the constant creaking of the wagon.

"Over there!" Merydyth suddenly called out, his voice shattering the silence. "Horsemen!"

They all jolted awake and saw, galloping towards them less than half a mile away, a large group of soldiers. "Are they Saxons?" Angharad's voice was tense.

"I think they're Saxons!" Roy yelled. He was standing up in the wagon. "See their beards, and their helmets. They're Saxons!" He sounded frightened.

"Ride, m'Lady," Alan shouted. "You can't do anything here. We'll try and delay them. Go! Go!"

"He's right!" Angharad shouted. Teifryn gave a gasp, began to tremble, and did not react when Angharad yelled at her to move. She stared ahead, her eyes wide with terror and her lower lip shaking. "Teifryn!" Angharad screamed but was unable to break into the nightmare that had overwhelmed her friend. She grabbed Teifryn's bridle, turned the horse and gave it a slap. The animal galloped off with Angharad riding close behind. Teifryn remained in a daze, making high, unintelligible noises, and staring unseeing at what was before her. Somehow, her natural riding ability enabled her to remain in her saddle, as the horse galloped down the gentle slope towards the forest.

Merydyth turned his horse and took off after them, leaving Roy and Alan to fight their own battle. "We'll kill those bastards!" Alan shouted bravely. They smiled encouragingly at each other and drawing their weapons, took up positions by one side of the wagon. The soldier had a sword and a shield, and Alan had a spear and a long knife.

"All we can do is see how many we can kill," Alan said. "Remember, we fight for each other." Roy nodded and took a deep breath.

In moments the Saxons arrived in a thunder of yelling and

the clashing of metal. They encircled the two Welshmen and the wagon, keeping two spears length away. The leader yelled something and took off after the women with half the horsemen following.

Those that remained continued to walk slowly around the wagon, calling comments to each other. On a signal they stopped, and Alan heard the sound of them climbing onto the wagon behind him. "Watch the front!" he screamed, turning quickly and thrusting his spear at a large Saxon who had climbed up on the wagon, and had his sword raised. The spear entered the man's stomach below his mail shirt, and he tumbled to the floor, screaming. Alan was unable to quickly withdraw his spear and drew his long knife to face another warrior who had climbed onto the wagon. As he prepared to fight the Saxon, one of the horsemen threw a hand axe that impaled itself in the middle of his back, and he died instantly.

Roy knew he had no chance, and realizing that Alan was dead, he rushed at the nearest of the warriors and lashed out with his sword cutting deeply into the rider's leg. As Roy turned frantically to face another rider he was knocked down by the iron hooves of a horse, and immediately killed by the spears of the angry Saxons.

In the forest, Angharad led the way with Teifryn and the soldier following close behind. They re-entered the wooded area on a different path, and as they glanced back they realized that although they had made the best of their escape, the Saxons were gaining on them. "Go separate ways!" Merydyth yelled. "We've got more chance!" Angharad knew that what he meant was he would have more chance, for it was certain the Saxons were more intent on catching them, rather than a lone soldier. As she thought this, Merydyth veered off to the right along a small trail, leaving her and Teifryn to continue along the main path with the Saxons gradually closing behind them. With a determined yell, Angharad turned left down a little used path, urging her horse to keep up its pace, and trying to ensure Teifryn was following.

After a short distance she cried in pain as the end of a leafy branch clipped her face, and Angharad knew they were courting danger by travelling so fast along such a path at night. She glanced back and saw that Teifryn was still not reacting to her situation, and it was only luck that kept her in the saddle. "Teifryn!" she yelled. "Wake up!" At that moment, her horse turned a tight bend to the left, and she had to turn back to control her balance. As she did so, Teifryn gave a hideous scream as she was flung to the right and was catapulted out of her saddle and fell hard. She lay motionless at the side of the path, like a discarded doll, as her horse galloped away into the darkness.

Angharad yanked back on the reins, causing her horse to rear up and try to unseat her. For a few hectic moments she wrestled to gain control of the animal, which wanted to keep up with the other horse, and finally forced it to a stop. She had travelled further than she had expected and was hidden by the bend. As she hurried back to her friend, she could hear the increasing sounds of the Saxon horses and the cries of the soldiers.

The Saxons raced up, coming to an abrupt halt next to the body of Teifryn, who lay face down on the ground. The leader jumped from his horse, and with a triumphant roar stood over the unconscious woman. He reached down and turned her over, pausing for a moment as he saw her fragile beauty in the moonlight. He gave a bellow of delight and, while the other horseman roared their approval, he began to rip off her clothes.

Angharad had always carried a sword whenever she left the castle, although she could not remember when she had last pulled it from its scabbard. She was in a blind fury when she raced back and saw what was about to happen; she drew her blade and was on top of the group before they understood that they were being attacked. The leader stood up and turned quickly to face her, a surprized look on his handsome face. She yanked on her reins, causing her mount to rear up, and leaned to one side as her sword sliced him across the face. He fell back screaming, and the other horsemen who had relaxed their guard to watch the anticipated rape, were shocked by the unexpected turn of events. Her horse reared up again, forcing the other riders to move back, and she rapidly dismounted and raced over to Teifryn.

In the twilight, her friend looked strangely at peace: her pale face was relaxed and her long blond hair was spread around her shapely neck and shoulders. "Forgive me, Teifryn!" Angharad cried

IN THE ASHES OF A DREAM

and stabbed her sword deep into her friend's heart. Without a pause, she turned to face the mass of Saxon horsemen and she raised her sword, determined to fight until they killed her. She would not be taken alive.

The officer was staggering about holding his face and crying in a high-pitched voice and his wild actions prevented an immediate attack by the other soldiers. One man, a red-bearded giant, jumped from his horse and pushing past the blinded officer and lunged at Angharad with a short sword. She parried the blow, and with the extra length of her weapon forced him back to his obvious surprise. The Saxons let out a roar, and instead of joining the attack, were content to enjoy the last moments of this feisty Welsh woman. Angharad moved back as the soldier rushed at her, his eyes gleaming in the fading light. He was determined to end this before he was made to look foolish, but her sword kept him away.

It was at that moment that everything changed. The horsemen at the back began screaming a warning, and immediately there was a mass of horsemen fighting each other in the restricted space of the pathways. Amid the yelling, screaming and the clashing of weapons Angharad fought with all the energy she had left. She heard the yelling of Welsh orders above the chaos that had suddenly erupted, and she knew that rescue could be at hand.

Her adversary seemed unaware of the changing situation behind him, and rushed at her, desperate to finish a fight that was in danger of making him a mockery with his friends. Again, Angharad diverted the blade and was able to change her sword's direction and cut deep into the soldier's unprotected shoulder. She stepped quickly back in order to give herself some space to deliver the deathblow, when she tripped over Teifryn's body, and fell backwards. The soldier roared in agony, and with crazed pain and the disgrace of being bested by a woman, he lunged at her and delivered a sweeping blow that cut across her throat. It was the last thing she remembered before she collapsed into dense bushes.

The soldier was bleeding profusely and was fast losing his ability to stand. He stared at the dim spot where Angharad had disappeared and, as he tried to move towards it, was killed by a Welsh spear. The chaotic fighting between Welsh cavalry and the Saxon horsemen, which was rapidly becoming more difficult as darkness finally descended, suddenly ended as the outnumbered Saxons fled, hotly pursued by the Welsh cavalry.

After a short while, when the Welsh were convinced that the Saxon remnants would not be returning, the riders returned with burning torches. They dismounted and checked the bodies, the Saxons were stripped, their weapons distributed around the group, and their bodies thrown into the forest. The few Welsh corpses were strapped on spare horses, or across the front of the saddles ridden by their friends.

"There was a woman who was fighting against them when we arrived!" an officer yelled. "Find her body, there is a chance she may still be alive."

The area was searched, and before long they came across the blood-soaked body of Angharad. The officer held his torch above her and stared while they moved the light over her body. "Her clothes tell me she was a woman of nobility." He knelt beside her and examined her face and neck. "Bring more light!" He placed his head near her face. "She still breathes. Emrys! Come here."

An older man knelt down on the other side of Angharad, and carefully examined her. He went back to his horse and returned with water and clean rags and spent a long time carefully tending her wound and bandaging her neck. He listened to her soft breathing and felt her pulse. "She must be a strong woman to have survived such a wound. Another finger width deeper and she would have bled to death."

The officer nodded thoughtfully. "The Saxons were attacking a wagon when we first encountered them. We could transport her in that, if it's still there." He called to two junior officers. "Take half the men and return to the wagon and if it can be used, send two men back with it as fast as you can. Get the rest of the men to bury the Welsh bodies and put stones on the graves. Strip the Saxons and leave them there and meet back at the camp." He turned to Emrys. "You're the healer, what would you suggest can be done with this woman?"

IN THE ASHES OF A DREAM

Emrys stood up and eased his back. "She can't travel far in this condition." He was a man of few words. "The wagon is her only chance. There's a farm fairly near here unless the Saxons have destroyed it. They might be persuaded to take her in."

The officer had examined Angharad's hands and noticed her rings. "She's a woman of wealth; they'll be pleased to help her, I'm sure," he said ironically. He walked over to Teifryn's body, and stared, sadly, at the death wound in her chest. "Bury this woman while we're waiting; she also is a woman of rank. I'll take charge of any jewellery or other items that could identify her to her people." He moved around giving orders and making encouraging comments. What puzzled him was why these two women had died alone.

By the time they had buried the unknown woman and found stones to protect the corpse from wild animals, the wagon returned and a space was made for Angharad in the well of the primitive transportation. "Stay with her, Emrys," the officer said. He allocated a guard of ten men to protect the wagon and led the rest back the way they had come. It had been a successful patrol, and he wanted to get back to camp. The reports of Saxon attacks on local farms and cottages had proved correct, and he was keen to report the outcome of their encounters.

Later, in the early hours of the morning, Emrys found the farm he had remembered and which the Saxons had not discovered. The occupants of the farm were rudely awakened and after some fearful discussions, the farmer finally agreed to unbar the door and take in the unconscious Angharad.

"She's a woman of some standing," Emrys said, as the soldiers carefully carried the wounded Angharad into the dim room. "God will reward you," he placed a heavy emphasis on God, as he noticed a cross over the lintel. "We will return in a few weeks, once the Saxons are no longer on Welsh territory."

The farmer and his wife nodded anxiously. They had not missed the emphasis on the return of these Welsh soldiers and they prayed for their own safety that the woman would survive. "We will do our best for her," the wife gave Emrys a slight bow.

"Our family are all Christians," the farmer said indicating a cluster of children. "She will not lack for our best care."

Emrys grunted his approval. He had no time for Christians, but if it meant they believed their God was keeping watch on their behaviour, so much the better. "We beat the Saxon raiders tonight, you should be safe."

The farmer and his wife exchanged surprised looks, they had not heard of any Saxon attacks.

Emrys went out to the yard where his men waited and climbed slowly onto his horse; it had been a long day, he was feeling his age and he wanted to get back to camp. "You can keep the wagon!" he yelled as he rode away.

A big smile creased the farmer's face. "God has blessed us," he said passionately, "God has blessed us!" His wife and daughters were already examining the woman, while the sons built up the fire and lit torches.

"Let us pray she survives," his wife said quietly. "I think she is a woman of importance."

. . .

"They've travelled further than I expected," Dafydd said. His voice was tense and sharp. They had galloped back along the path that they thought the women had taken, but with the dry weather the ground had become hard and the wagon tracks were difficult to follow. For a moment, they sat on their sweating mounts on the edge of the forest, overlooking a moonlit landscape of bare hills and shallow valleys, and gradually calmed their hectic breathing.

"They must have driven the wagon at great speed," Jon observed. "Good old Alan, he was always a good wagon driver." He sensed the restrained anger of the two men towards his flippant comment and bit his lip. Behind them the four soldiers sat quietly, aware of the tension.

"We haven't passed them; they must be ahead with the wagon." Gwriad spurred his horse into a canter. "Keep your eyes peeled, they might have pulled off the path!"

As they came over a small hill they saw clear evidence of a bloody fight. In the cold moonlight, they were faced with the aftermath: dead bodies, stripped of their armour, lying around in heaps, and to one side were recently dug shallow graves with an assortment of stones on top.

"They're Saxons!" Dafydd shouted as he raced around the corpses. He jumped off his horse and ordered the soldiers to exhume each grave. Gwriad walked slowly from each open grave to the next like a man in a trance. After a difficult hour, they identified the bodies of Alan and Roy. The rest were strangers.

"The women are not here, thank God." Dafydd said. "Either they escaped from this fight, and may be ahead of us, or they retreated to the woods behind us?"

"What about the wagon? Would they have travelled in the wagon?" Gwriad sounded deeply confused, like a man who is unsure if he is living a nightmare or struggling with a terrible reality. "If they had been captured here, the Saxons would eventually have killed them and left their bodies. There is a hope they have escaped."

"Merydyth must be with them," Jon added.

There was a silence as the others thought about this. Jon knew it was not his place to comment, and he watched as Dafydd slowly walked around trying to sort out the logic of what might have happened. After a long pause, he spoke: "There are signs of many horsemen approaching on this side, and a mass of hoof prints going around in a circle that might have been around the wagon. There is evidence of a large group splitting off and travelling back over there." He paused. "Here is the wagon track which seems to move back this way!"

"Well?" Gwriad said, exhibiting some frustration with his brother's slow, pedantic analysis.

"I think they were attacked here, and the women may have escaped back towards the forest. I think that the Saxons were attacked by a superior force, which would explain the numerous bodies.

"Are you certain?" Gwriad asked aggressively. He lived in a world of black and white, and though he yearned to be riding in pursuit of his lost wife, he needed to have an assurance that he was right.

"I'm not a scout, but I think I'm right."

"Come on, then," Gwriad snapped. He felt as tense as a bowstring.

Without further discussion they followed the route the many horses had taken, which was close to the original path. Dafydd abruptly stopped as they approached the forest. "They went this way!" he called out, leaning over the side of his horse. They all checked the ground and could see where numerous horses had left the main trail.

They entered the forest, and the churned-up earth was easy to follow, even in the dim light. After a short gallop they almost missed the evidence of the horse trail, and the riders came to a brief halt.

"It looks like they were being followed," Gwriad said. His anxiety causing him to state the obvious.

"Yes," Dafydd agreed, breathing hard. "They're good riders. They should be able to outrun them."

"Can you tell how long ago it was?" Jon asked, keen to be included.

"No," Dafydd snapped. "We must see if we can catch them."

The two men nodded to each other and urged their horses down the path to the left, leaving Jon and the four soldiers to follow. Gwriad was leading, his mind set on catching up with the Saxons before they reached the women, and he was strangely unprepared for the awful sight that unexpectedly appeared before him. He brought his horse to a sudden stop and sat bolt upright in his saddle. Dafydd pulled up beside him, and letting out a strangled cry, jumped from his horse and raced towards the grave that was set to one side of a mass of Saxon corpses.

"Whose grave is it?" Gwriad dismounted and watched as Dafydd carefully removed the stones and swept away the newly-moved earth. He dismounted and knelt by his brother and helped to dig down with his bare hands. Behind them Jon and the four soldiers sat immobile on their horses, staring in the dim light at their two Lords as they scrabbled with the earth.

Suddenly, Dafydd let out a wail that caused everyone to screw up their faces. "Oh no!" he screamed. "Please God, not Teifryn! Not my Teifryn."

Gwriad placed his grubby hand around his brother's shoulders as they stared at the pale face of Teifryn. It seemed impossible that she was dead, and they both sobbed with misery. But, in the back of his mind, Gwriad was grateful it was not Angharad. Yet, a small voice reminded him that the Saxons might have her, and her fate might be worse than her death. He stood up slowly and walked back to his horse, where he stood with his head against its hot neck. He tried to control his emotions.

In contrast, Dafydd had given himself up to uncontrolled sobbing, as he lay prostrate by Teifryn's partly uncovered grave, his cheek against hers. As he wept, he raged against the unfairness of life, the stupidity of killing and the horror of war. He swore revenge on the Saxons and pleaded with his dead wife to forgive him, as he lay by her side consumed with guilt.

Jon and the soldiers were uncertain what to do. "Ride on," Jon said. "Wait for us further down the path." The men moved off without comment, their eyes drawn to the dead woman.

Jon backed his horse away from the tragic scene and silently watched the two men he most respected coming to terms with the brutal death. Tears raced down his cheeks as he stared at Teifryn's partly revealed body. He slowly dismounted and holding his horse's bridle waited for his Lords to eventually recover, as recover they must. His tears continued to flow as he silently mourned both women: Teifryn, who had not always been friendly towards him, but whom he considered the most beautiful woman he had known, and the tragic disappearance of Angharad, who had been a mother to him, the first woman ever to believe in him. He gradually came to realize that the excitement he had sought was not noble and glorious as he had imagined, but fraught with danger, barbarism and loss.

After a while, when the two bereaved men showed no immediate signs of recovering from their loss, Jon decided he must take charge of the situation. He quietly walked his horse away from the area, and then increased his speed until he came upon the four soldiers, who were sitting on their mounts with drawn swords.

"What do we do now?" Davis asked anxiously.

"That's for the Lords to decide, but I imagine we'll aim for Caerdydd, and I'm certain we will have to dig up Lady Teifryn's body and take it with us."

"So, what do ye think happened to Lady Angharad and Merydyth then?" Lleu asked with a meaningful sniff.

No one answered, and Lleu sniffed again and shook the reins as they moved slowly back to the Lords. In the darkness, there was a brooding quality in the forest, and the men kept their swords drawn. Jon felt he was out of his depth but was determined to do the right thing. He dismounted next to Gwriad and placed his arm around his Lord who still stood with his face against the horse.

"You're right, Jon," he muttered, although Jon had said nothing. He walked back to the grave and knelt down by Dafydd, and gradually separated him from Teifryn. "It's time to move on, Dafydd. We will have more time to grieve when we reach Caerdydd."

Dafydd got to his feet, his body trembling as though with a fever. He seemed incapable of making any decision, and Gwriad led him to his horse, while Jon and the soldiers dug out the body with their hands. Then, Gwriad picked up Teifryn and, with Dafydd following like a sleepwalker, he placed her body over Dafydd's horse. He took his brother's arm and helped him into his saddle, then without a word he mounted his horse, nodded to Jon, and led the way slowly out of the forest, heading south.

• • •

IN THE DARK, EARLY HOURS of the morning, General Maelgwn's scouts made contact with those of Prince Anarwd, and both armies met outside Caerdydd. After a brief meeting, the two generals agreed to position their men on both sides of the main road at a strategic place a mile out of town. A strong cavalry unit was positioned to the east of the ambush area, ready to reinforce from the front or to attack the Saxon rear if the ambush went well.

Meanwhile, the Saxon army led by Waelfwulf was advancing quickly down the road with the intention of attacking Caerdydd at first light. The men were in good spirits and were looking forward to the action and, although he had strong misgivings at taking sole responsibility for the attack, Waelfwulf knew he had no alternative.

After an hour of marching, he had reluctantly accepted the fact that Earl Harold and General Hildering would not be joining him, and that the attack on the fort had been, as he had expected, more difficult than Harold had anticipated. Eventually, a scout had arrived to confirm this, with a message from Harold urging him to destroy the town as quickly as possible and guaranteeing him and his army sustenance and rest on their return to Gelligaer.

His main comfort was that the town would not be expecting a Saxon attack, and that as long as his officers could control the men, the destruction of the town should be easy to accomplish, and his speedy return could be achieved without too much loss of Saxon life. He was riding with a phalanx of junior officers at the head of his army when two scouts approached at breakneck speed.

"M'Lord," the senior soldier gasped, "The Welsh have a large army of soldiers and cavalry blocking the approach to Caerdydd."

Waelfwulf blanched. This was not how it was supposed to be. Although he could not contemplate the idea of fighting an entrenched enemy, he still wished to maintain his reputation as a brave man, if not an experienced leader.

"How far away are they?"

"About three miles, m'Lord."

"Can you guess at their numbers?"

The two scouts had a brief exchange. "At least as many as we have, m'Lord, and that doesn't include their cavalry."

"And they've dug in at either side of the main road, m'Lord," the second scout added.

Waelfwulf made no response, but stared ahead, deep in thought. He was aware of the junior officers sitting silently on their horses waiting for his decision, and he knew that if he said they must advance and try to outflank the enemy, they would agree enthusiastically. They were young men who gloried in any chance to prove their valour and did not share the reality of the situation as he did. If he advanced, no matter how he tried to outwit the Welsh, he was certain to lose. They had the choice of battleground and, unlike him, they had reserves and apparently a strong cavalry element. This attack on Caerdydd could only have worked with total surprize as his strongest weapon. Without this the odds were stacked against him, and he was not going to lead his men into certain defeat.

He turned to the two scouts. "Ride immediately to Gelligaer! Tell Earl Harold I am returning with the army immediately and in full strength. Tell him the Welsh have a strong force defending Caerdydd, and that they might decide to follow once they realize we are no longer advancing. Ride fast!"

He turned to the junior officers, some of whom looked mutinous, and gave the order for the men to take a quick rest while remaining in their columns and to be prepared for a fast march back to Gelligaer within the hour.

. . .

IT WAS SUNRISE, AND HAROLD was relaxing with Hildering, drinking his first cup of wine and discussing their unexpected losses at the hands of mere peasants. Everything changed when the exhausted scouts staggered over to their fire and passed on Waelfwulf's message: Harold became almost apoplectic with rage and threatened the lives of the two men, even though they had ridden hard to alert him. He screamed at the sky, at his junior officers and at Hildering. Didn't they understand? It was vital that his plan to gain a major victory over the Welsh was achieved. He cursed Waelfwulf for his lack of courage and his weak inability to lead and swore to dismember him when he arrived. During this rant, the two scouts wisely disappeared.

"It would have been a monumental disaster if he had knowingly led our army into an ambush," Hildering protested. "My Lord, news of a defeat would have ruined your reputation in England."

"The plan was to destroy Caerdydd!" Harold roared, waving his fist in the air.

"My Lord," Hildering said calmly, "you have destroyed Gelligaer."

"Ha!" Harold spat contemptuously. "No one's heard of Gelligaer!"

"My Lord, few people in England, and none in London, know

IN THE ASHES OF A DREAM

anything about Wales, except that it's our enemy. To announce that we have destroyed a major town deep inside Wales would sound like a victory for the common people, and for the Court. Gelligaer must go down as a major victory."

Harold drank deeply from his cup and frowned dangerously, moving his head from side to side as if looking for an enemy. As he calmed down he could not avoid recognizing that he was responsible for the change of plan, and that if he were leading the army, as he should have been, he might have been forced to make the same decision as Waelfwulf.

"My advice, my Lord, is that preparations are made for a speedy return to the border as soon as the main army arrives. That way we can regroup on English soil and prepare for our victory messages to be sent to London and elsewhere!" Hildering was careful not to use the word retreat. "This could still be turned into a military success."

"You might be right," Harold muttered. He stared out at the fort and wondered what in Hell's name had possessed him to change the plan. Hildering was right, it was still possible to turn this disaster into the appearance of a victory. He would not condemn Waelfwulf. "We could form up here and prepare to fight the Welsh if they advanced on the tails of our army?" he mused.

"We could, my Lord," Hildering said thoughtfully, "but we would be in a bad position if they refused to close battle with us. We have few supplies, and if they merely surrounded us in those hills and made constant forays against us, we would be losing men as they continued to increase theirs. We might face a major defeat."

"Yes, yes. I know you're right." He stared up at a hill where a body of Saxon horsemen was slowly making its way down towards the camp. "This raid started so well," Harold grumbled and poured himself more wine.

"The gods be cursed!" Hildering suddenly yelled, jumping to his feet and rushing towards the horsemen who were leading a horse carrying a disabled officer with a rough, blood-soaked bandage across his eyes. "Egbert!" he cried. "How bad is it, my friend?"

By way of answer, Egbert collapsed in his saddle and Hildering was just able to break his fall. The bandage fell away, and the fearsome wound was confirmation that Egbert, if he regained consciousness, would never see again.

"How did this happen?" Harold demanded.

The men looked awkward. "We were taken by surprise, my Lord."

"Did you kill the man responsible?" Hildering murmured as he gently poured water on the officer's face.

Again, there was a pause as the soldiers waited for each other to answer.

"Well?" Harold bellowed.

"It wasn't a man, m'Lord," one of the older men answered. "It was a woman. She was defending her friend." He cleared his throat. "She was a powerful woman and fought like one possessed."

It was then that he noticed a number of the horsemen had injuries. "What's happening?" Harold yelled. "The peasants are fighting like trained soldiers! Even their women!"

"This was not a peasant woman, m'Lord, it was a noble woman, and her friend was too." He dismounted and helped Hildering carry the unconscious body into a covered place. As he moved off with the blinded Egbert, he decided it would be wise not to mention their retreat in the face of superior Welsh numbers, nor their considerable losses.

"Dismiss," Harold grunted. His dream of a quick victory and a hero's welcome on his return to London had evaporated, and he felt a great longing to be back in England, where he would pretend this had never happened.

CHAPTER SIXTEEN

In Aberteifi, the January of 1066 was memorable for its suffering. It was a harsh winter that had begun with snow in November, and had continued with only small breaks until, at the start of the New Year, the ferocity of the storms reached a new intensity. A blizzard had dumped huge amounts of snow that effectively prevented any travel, forcing the peasants to remain imprisoned with their families and their livestock in their small, poorly-heated houses. Those who had not stored enough food began to starve and those without adequate stocks of wood had to rely on their animals and each other for warmth.

The castle, which in past years had provided emergency help to the old and the sick, had become almost moribund, and the fun and gaiety that had marked every previous Christmas and New Year had not been forthcoming. As a result, the local people had been forced to create whatever limited entertainments they were able to arrange, made more difficult by the weather. It was not lost on most of them that their taxes had not been collected, but this welcome relief was secondary to the lack of structure that they all missed. In the small community, the guidance had always come from the top, and the continuation and thriving of the local traditions had always relied heavily on the Lord and his wife to provide the cohesion that bound them together. Without the benign power of the Lord and the enforcement of the law, local tyrants were able to bully and steal at whim, making a bad situation worse.

In the castle, the big kitchen was a popular place for the soldiers and those not serving in the Great Hall. They clustered around the big fire and only moved when the two Megans were preparing food. The basic rules of the castle were still being observed, with Penn insisting on the soldiers keeping guard and helping with the snow clearance. Megan controlled the distribution of food and the provision of fuel and water, and Jon had taken the place of the two Ladies in the running of the castle. He was severe with the servants, insisting on every task being done correctly or they would be dismissed. It was after the first dismissal that they took him seriously, and although the two Lords did not appear to notice, the castle was clean, heated and the meals were served on time.

When the weather improved, and travel was again possible, but still difficult, Jon made a journey to Llanduduch to see Father Williams. He felt he was escaping from a deep melancholy that enveloped the castle, and which he was unable to change, and as his horse plodded through the deep snow, he worried how the old priest had fared during the blizzard and the long freeze, and hoped he was still alive.

Although the weather conditions had been equally as bad as at Aberteifi, the villagers at Llanduduch had fared better. Unlike the bigger village, they had always been a tight community, never relying on the Lord to help them, and constantly guided by their resident priest. Even so, it was a surprise to Jon when his horse finally reached the church and found a path had been dug from Father Williams's house to the church and the village, and that smoke was belching out of the chimney.

The door opened before he reached it, and the rotund priest bellowed out a welcome, reminding Jon never to underestimate his aged friend. "Welcome, my son! It's so good to see you. The last few days have been extremely boring."

After Jon had stabled his horse, he entered the warm house, leaving his snow-clad boots at the door. He was immediately handed a glass of mulled wine and, as soon as he had settled on a stool by the side of the fire, he poured out his worries to his concerned friend.

"Since we returned from Caerdydd the two Lords have taken no interest in anything to do with the castle or the local people," Jon said. "Lord Gwriad is always drunk by the end of the day, and sometimes by midday, and Lord Dafydd stays in his room all the time reading and writing, but rarely saying anything. The evening meal is a nightmare: there are just the two of them, and they never speak, the serving girl, who is terrified in case she does something that Lord Gwriad will find fault with, and me. I serve the wine, which Lord Dafydd rarely drinks, and which Lord Gwriad continues to consume until he is unconscious. Then, I call the guards and they carry him up to his room. Lord Dafydd often leaves before his brother is completely drunk, and this can cause Lord Gwriad to yell and scream. It is an ongoing Hell."

"What does Lord Gwriad yell?" Father Williams asked as he refilled their cups.

"He yells things like 'it's both our faults' and 'I miss Angharad as much as you miss Teifryn' and sometimes he throws things and yells, 'I'd give anything to make it right'."

"What does Lord Dafydd do?"

"Nothing. He rarely answers, and sometimes he starts to cry."

"Does Lord Dafydd ever mention the fact that he had to bury his wife in Caerdydd?

"Lord Gwriad does. He thinks they should have found ice and brought her body back by boat. But on one occasion, Lord Dafydd said it would not have been possible, and Lord Gwriad looked as though he would hit him, but he was too drunk, and fell on the floor. At other times, Lord Gwriad rants on about not finding Angharad's body, and how he should still be in that area searching for her."

The old priest sipped his wine thoughtfully. "They can't continue like this. Everyone is suffering, not just them. I have had sad reports of life in Aberteifi, and the castle and this area cannot continue to be ungoverned. I will visit them when the snow has gone."

"The one good thing is that the Saxons have not tried to attack us again," Jon said. "After their retreat, with General Maelgwn nipping at their heels, I thought they would return in force."

Father Williams gazed at Jon, and marvelled at his progress since he had first met him. He had become a tall, strong young man with a good brain. Even his mode of expression had improved such that he could hold his own in political and even philosophical discussion. "I understand from my fellow priests in Caerdydd that Earl Harold wanted a quick but notable victory to support his claim to the throne."

"It will be bad for Wales if he becomes the next Saxon King," Jon stared into the fire. "I was shocked by the way they treated the villagers in Gelligaer. They slaughtered everyone, even the women and the children." The picture of the abandoned fort with all the corpses scattered around the ground was still vivid in his mind.

"That is what I was teaching you. The battles and conquests of the Romans and the Greeks seem noble and exciting, but all war involves killing and unspeakable suffering. There is no way you can understand that unless you have experienced war first-hand. You have had your first brush with the violence, and I expect it will not be your last." The priest sipped his wine. "I sought a reputation for bravery and courage in battle, fighting the enemies of God, and suddenly I was appalled by the killing, which never stopped. One victory merely led to a pause and soon we were fighting the same battles. It was then I became a priest."

This was the most Father Williams had ever disclosed about his younger life and Jon realized he was trying to warn him of what might happen. "Fighting never worried Lord Gwriad until he injured himself, and even on our journey to Caerdydd he was wanting to attack the Saxons."

"Which is why his wife and his brother's are both dead," the priest replied sadly. He stared unseeing into the glowing fire. "Both men are consumed with guilt, and they can't forgive themselves, or even each other.

. . .

KING EDWARD, KNOWN AS THE Confessor, died on January 4th, 1066, after months of illness. His final public event was the consecration of his beloved Westminster Cathedral a week before, on December 28th. It was at that time, the largest building in England, and can be said to be Edward's main achievement. However, the combination of the length of the ceremony, and the unavoidable cold of the unrelenting weather, destroyed the last of

IN THE ASHES OF A DREAM

his failing strength, and he took to his bed the next day, never to recover.

Earl Harold with his brother Lord Leofwine had remained in London since Harold's return from his Welsh incursion. London had been impressed with the accounts of the remarkable victory that he had achieved over the Welsh, but as there had been no victory parade, and no displays of captured Welsh Lords and soldiers, the incident was soon forgotten.

"I have spoken to most of the Witan," Leofwine said. He had a satisfied air that never failed to encourage Harold. "I have made the obvious point that if they fail to support you, they will lose their last chance to continue the Saxon dynasty, and they will be allowing a Norman bastard to become our King."

"And?" Harold could hardly contain himself.

"They have agreed to ignore the support that Edward had previously given to William, and will say that he had a change of mind on his deathbed. When do you wish to be crowned as the next King?"

"Tomorrow!" Harold could hardly contain himself. "Tomorrow, of course!"

"I will arrange for that to happen at the new Cathedral at Westminster. There may be some opposition from the Bishop and other clerics who have promised Rome that they will support William, but I think we can apply pressure." He looked very pleased with himself. "I will expect a bountiful reward, dear brother."

"Yes, yes." Harold could hardly restrain his excitement. "The troops that I gathered for the Welsh campaign are mostly camped in and around my new palace, and I sent orders yesterday for their officers to march them towards London."

"Before you knew if the Witan would support you?"

"It was necessary. I was prepared to occupy London and raise the people to my flag, and I needed troops for that. In the meantime, I want you to send immediately for your forces from the south and east of London to maintain order. They can be here by tomorrow, and Gyrth has promised to be here by tonight with his contingents from Essex and Cambridge. Now, we can plan for my coronation tomorrow. The presence of all these soldiers will add a powerful message to the people."

"It'll be a rush, and lacking the normal pomp and ceremony," Leofwine grinned. "But I have arranged, at your expense of course, to give free bread and beer to the peasants of London so they will cheer your journey to the Cathedral, the route for which will be lined with our troops." He chuckled. "At your expense, of course." He knew how parsimonious his brother was, and it always pleased him when he could force his elder brother to be generous.

Harold was striding up and down the room, his mind focused on the one thing: he would be King! "Who cares how much it costs. As King, I will have the English treasury pay for everything, and if it runs dry, I will increase the taxes!"

Leofwine gazed thoughtfully into his cup. They were in a finely decorated room in the royal palace, and he wondered how those who had supported the saintly, innocent Edward would adjust to a new King who was as different as rough wine to holy water. "Gyrth is arriving soon and is another keen supporter, and although he's a fervent admirer of Norman architecture and loves the new cathedral, he is one of the most vigorous haters of Normans that I know. God help William if he ever tries to invade us."

Harold stopped pacing. "What do you think Tostig is up to?"

"Since you supported his expulsion from his earldom in Northumbria, he has sought refuge with the King Hardrada of Norway, as you know, and is almost certainly trying to get his revenge on you. I have no definite news, but rumour has it that he is urging King Harald Hardrada to invade, possibly landing on the Isle of Wight or on the East Coast."

"When you hear even the possibility of a planned invasion, let me know. Until then we will forget him. He's been a pain in the arse since he was a kid. Did you know he tried to get Gyrth to oppose me?"

"It shows he's not very bright. Ambitious but not very bright. When you think what a disaster he was as the Earl of Northumbria!" Leofwine shook his head in disgust. "Where else has an Earl faced an uprising from his people? And this is the man who fancies himself as the King of England! God save us from witless people, even if they are related to us!"

"I should have had him executed last year," Harold said, "but he's my brother." He shrugged his broad shoulders. "I knew when I supported his expulsion that he would be a problem in the future."

Leofwine stood up and stretched. "I'm off to make some final arrangements." He looked at Harold who had returned to pacing around the room. "If I were you, I would quickly enjoy your mistress, Edith Swannuck. You may not wish to be so open in your relationship with her once you're king."

Harold scowled. He hated to be told he had to do things, even when he knew he must.

. . .

AN UNEXPECTED THAW AT THE end of January made travel easier, and Father Williams informed the two Lords that he would be arriving for a short visit and asked for a wagon to transport him to Aberteifi. He arrived in time for the midday meal, and Jon met him at the gates wearing a new gown and carrying a fine dagger hanging from a belt with a silver buckle. He had a new air of authority about him and Father Williams noted how the soldiers were relatively alert, and how the courtyard was not the filthy mess that he had expected it to be.

"I'm pleased to see you, Father," Jon said as he helped the priest from the wagon. He bowed and Father Williams made the sign of the cross over his head and took a deep breath before moving forward. "Blessings on you, my son. You're looking well. Are things better since I last saw you?"

"Some slight improvement, Father, which I think is because of your expected visit."

Jon escorted the priest up the steps, where a soldier opened the heavy door to the main hall. Inside a roaring fire had taken the chill off the air, and Lord Gwriad was sitting a short distance from the heat, petting a large hound. He seemed lost in his own thoughts.

"My Lord, Father Williams has arrived!" Jon called across the hall.

"Ah! Father Williams!" Gwriad sprang to his feet and appeared unsteady for a moment. "Welcome. It's been a long time. Come and sit down. Make yourself comfortable." He spoke quickly and with a false sounding joviality, like a man who was unused to trying to be cheerful.

"I'll fetch Lord Dafydd," Jon said. He bowed and left the hall, leaving a fearful servant to bring in a tray with a wine jug and cups, and some bread and cheese.

In his small work room Dafydd was asleep, sitting in front of his desk with his head resting on his arms on top of the scroll he had been reading. Jon stood in the door and took note of the drab clothes and the dull white skin of the man who had previously been so smart and clean. Dafydd had always had an energetic, enthusiastic approach to life, but had over a few months become a shadow of his former self. "My Lord Dafydd!" he raised his voice. "My Lord, Father Williams is here."

Dafydd woke up with a start and was for a moment disorientated. "What? Oh God!" he rubbed his eyes. "Fetch me a bowl of water," he said carefully rubbing his neck, "and soap and a towel." He continued to sit in his chair working the stiffness out of his neck and shoulders. When Jon returned, he removed his leather vest and his discoloured tunic. "Tell them I'll be down in a moment."

When Jon returned to the hall, Lord Gwriad was describing, in detail, the events that had led to the presumed murder of Angharad. He was speaking rapidly, and Father Williams was sitting next to him staring into the fire and listening as though to a confession in church.

"Lord Dafydd will be down shortly," Jon announced. The priest continued to stare into the flames, and Gwriad just waved a hand. The heat had forced them to move their chairs back, and Jon placed in front of them the small table on which the servant had left the tray. He refilled their cups and cut some of the bread. The men took no notice, and he quietly withdrew to stand by the door.

Soon, Dafydd appeared and, as he passed, Jon could smell soap. For the first time for many weeks the grieving man had made an effort, and he seemed to have a hint of his former vitality. Jon followed him to the fire and placed a chair for him. Dafydd

IN THE ASHES OF A DREAM

refused a cup of wine and slowly nibbled at a piece of bread while he waited for Gwriad to finish speaking.

"I'm pleased to see you, Dafydd," Father Williams said.

"And I'm delighted to see you, Father Williams." He spoke with such enthusiasm that Gwriad turned to look carefully at him.

"I hope my coming today will be a turning point in your grief," the old priest said.

There was a brief silence, and then Dafydd spoke. "We need your help, Father." Gwriad nodded and finished his wine.

"You will both agree that you can't continue to behave as you have done since your return?" the priest said softly.

Gwriad nodded his head furiously and made a half-hearted attempt to reach for the wine jug and thought better of it. Dafydd blew out his lips and looked as though he might cry. "Indeed," he muttered.

"I don't have to tell you how much the leadership of both of you is missed both in the villages and in the surrounding area. The castle has continued to function well because of Jon, but your rents and taxes have not been collected, nor have your church tithes been met. In the villages, the law that we have taken for granted is being abused, especially in Aberteifi, where theft and assault is happening. If the Picts had launched a second attack from the sea, we would have been ill prepared and unable to launch a unified defence." He looked hard at both men; Gwriad nodded and pursed his lips and Dafydd cleared his throat.

"It is normal to grieve, but your wives would not want you to drink yourself to death," Father Williams stared at Gwriad, "or cut yourself off from the rest of the world," and he made eye contact with Dafydd. "You still have things to achieve in your lives, and God would not want you to waste your opportunities." While neither brother was religious, they both silently agreed with the priest's assertions.

"So, let me welcome you back to the real world!" Father Williams raised his cup and waved it at Jon, who promptly refilled their cups, and Dafydd agreed to drink a cup. "To life, to happiness and to personal achievement," he said.

They all drank and began to eat silently, each reflecting on what had been said. After a short pause, the priest sat back and wiped his mouth. "I have some news that will interest you both: King Edward died on January 4th and Earl Harold was crowned King two days later on January 6th.

Gwriad gasped. "That bastard who murdered our wives is now King of England?"

"That is so."

Dafydd shot to his feet and stood trembling with his back to the fire. "Is God blind? Is evil rewarded?" He stared wide-eyed at the priest.

"I predict he will not enjoy his kingship for long. The friar who brought me the news carried reports from senior clergy in London. They tell me Harold faces opposition from the Church, from Duke William of Normandy who was promised the English throne, and from the Scots who are invading northern England."

"Perhaps now would be a good time for the Welsh to invade England, and catch him off-balance?" Gwriad let out a bellow, an echo of his former enthusiasm.

Father Williams said nothing, and Dafydd moved away from the fire and poured himself more wine. "We are incapable of organizing such an invasion," he said staring into the distance, "but I do think that we must plan a revenge that is possible. We have suffered, and I'm convinced we will never rest, and never be able to live fruitful lives until we have achieved our revenge on this Saxon monster! From this day on, we will begin to plan a means to destroy him. It will not be easy, but we are driven men, and by the summer we will be ready. I promise you." He downed his wine and bowing to the priest, marched out of the hall.

It was so strange to hear Dafydd talking in this way that the priest, who had known him most of his life, gaped in muted surprise. Gwriad let out a cheer and leaned over to shake the priest's hands. "That's what we needed," he said enthusiastically. "We needed something else to think about, and you have given it to us." He refilled his cup and was intending to fill the priest's.

"No more, my son, I have a journey to make."

"Stay here. You don't have to go today."

"If I leave now, I will be home before dark, and at my age that is a consideration." He took Gwriad's hand. "Start as you mean to go on. Take back your authority in this area, increase your guards to enforce the law, bring new life to this castle, and prepare carefully for whatever you decide to do. Dafydd is right, you need a project."

As he walked to the wagon, Father Williams held on to Jon's arm. "You heard what I said?" Jon nodded. "They might never agree on a plan, but that is not as important as the need to aim for something. Do your best to keep them going: suggest visits to the farthest villages, and regular hunts for Lord Gwriad, and ask Lord Dafydd what plans he has for the better administration of your lands. If both men are kept busy, and if you can encourage Lord Gwriad to drink less, we might see some big improvements by the summer."

"Perhaps I can call on you each week to report how things are going?"

"I expected you to, my son. Remember, one day this will all be your responsibility." He waved his arm around the courtyard. "Come to see me in three days' time, on Friday, and tell me what they're thinking." He climbed awkwardly onto the wagon, and sat next to Davis, who was trying to impress Jon with his skills as a driver. "Travel slowly, my son," the priest said breathlessly to him.

Davis smiled, but by mistake slapped the horse's rump, causing it to rush for the gates. Father Williams fell backwards, and nearly catapulted off the wagon as Davis yanked on the reins and brought the confused horse to a halt. The elderly priest took a deep breath, "Slowly, my son. Slowly!"

"Sorry. Um, my mistake, Father Williams." He looked anxiously at Jon. "Sorry, m'Lord."

"You call me Jon," he said testily. "I'm in charge of the castle, but I'm not a Lord."

• • •

THE FIRST FEW MONTHS OF his reign was a busy time for King Harold who, in spite of his earlier experiences around the Court, was almost overwhelmed by the number of meetings he had to attend, foreign dignitaries he had to meet and negotiate with, and the legal matters he had to decide on. If it had not been for the guidance of his two brothers, it was likely he would have deserted London and taken refuge in hunting and enjoying his mistress in the comfortable palace that the recently-made Lord Lidmann continued to supervise.

"What you're attempting to achieve is the necessary reorganization of your powers as a new king," Leofwine made it sound as if he were talking to a student. "The pious Edward was negligent in his duties and was lucky to have survived on the throne, mainly thanks to the power of the Church. You are preparing for your future and, tedious as these meetings might be, you are solidifying your claim to be King, and ensuring that you have identified your friends before The Bastard hits back, as he almost certainly will."

"I know all this," Harold growled. He hated to be lectured at, especially by his brother who considered himself the brightest of the family.

"Did you see the comet last night?" Gyrth warmed himself by a hot fire. "Those who support you say this is God's confirmation of your right to be King. There are others who say it is a warning of grim times to come."

"It's just a celestial phenomenon that has nothing to do with us!" Harold exploded. "Around the country, every half-wit will be claiming it has something to do with him. What lunacy!"

Gyrth laughed. "Such events can always be used to our benefit if we act wisely."

"Meaning?"

"I have paid for rabble rousers to fan out across the city to proclaim that this is a clear sign that God loves you and will protect you as the King of England, and that you will be the greatest Saxon ruler of all time."

Harold stared at his brother. "Is this helpful?"

"Of course, when anything like this happens, your enemies will want to use it. You can't allow them to broadcast their lies unopposed," Gyrth looked for support from Leofwine. "We must always be prepared to spread our version of anything that the mob might be interested in."

"He's right," Leofwine agreed. "Now that you're King you must

IN THE ASHES OF A DREAM

use your supporters to keep you informed as to what your enemies may be plotting." He stretched his legs towards the fire. "Have you thought as to how you will raise money to pay for the army you will need to oppose William?"

"Yes. Yes, I have," Harold said slowly. He looked pleased with himself. "The Bishop is making a huge amount of income from pilgrims who are flocking to see the new Cathedral, and I intend to get him to give me half of what he earns on that particular money-earner."

"How will you do that?" Gyrth asked.

"I will demand to see his accounts, and then I will decide how much I intend to get him to part with."

"He won't show you his accounts, and he won't agree to pay you anything. He's protected by Church Law, and by the Pope."

"Ha!" Harold laughed. "The Pope is backing William, so I have no concern for what that fat prelate thinks. Also, the Bishop of London is here, within my grasp. I will gently remind him that I could take all of his income from the Cathedral, especially as the saintly Edward diverted huge amounts of the country's wealth to building it in the first place. He'll be grateful to be allowed to keep half, and when I mention that he will be making a patriotic gesture, I know he will be delighted to give me the money!"

Leofwine nodded, "Good, the sooner the better." He winked at Gyrth. "I understand you have decided to remove the beautiful Elditha, known by many as Edith the Fair, from your Court?"

"Also known as Edith Swan Neck," Gyrth cut in, "and most say she is the most beautiful woman in London."

Harold glared at Leofwine. "It was your idea." He cracked the knuckles in his powerful hands, which he did when annoyed. "Elditha has children and believes they're mine. I realized I will eventually have to wed another political wife, and I'm preparing for that event. By setting Elditha up in a Sussex estate, I can visit her when I wish, and keep her away from prying eyes."

"I can understand why you are loath to get rid of her," Gyrth said. "I assume you will keep her children under wraps?"

"I will recognize one of her brood, only if I am unable to produce another boy." Harold walked to the window and looked out on the ordered palace grounds below. "I have come this far and I will not allow some Norman bastard to destroy the Saxon bloodline. With your help, our family will hold the power in this country for generations to come."

. . .

BY SPRINGTIME, HUGE CHANGES HAD come about in Aberteifi, Llanduduch and throughout the Teifi valley. Following Father Williams' advice, Gwriad doubled his fulltime soldiers, and once he was happy with their training, he marched them down to the nearby village of Aberteifi, where they arrested all the known criminals, including the four brothers and the father of the dreaded Morgan family. Dafydd then conducted a legal trial in the centre of the village, and with the villains under guard, the villagers felt able to bring their complaints to the Lords. After hearing accusations including murder, robbery and rape, the Morgan family was found guilty. The father and his two eldest sons were hanged outside the castle walls, and the younger two were reduced to slaves, and sold to a minor Lord in Gwent.

Gwriad had all minor delinquents publicly thrashed, with a warning of being reduced to slavery if they came to his attention again. After this show of strength and decisiveness the atmosphere in the village returned to its former relaxed and balanced ways.

"It's nice when you show your strength, isn't it?" said Derryth, but as she was in Dafydd's arms at the time, he was not sure to what she referred.

Dafydd reminded his brother of Angharad's former promise to provide a fishing boat for Llanduduch, and although Angharad had kept her promise, the importance of the village to the safety of Aberteifi, coupled with the increase in taxes, convinced Gwriad of the wisdom of providing for another larger boat that would enable more sea fishing to be done and result in a peaceful and industrious village. "After all," Dafydd said, "Father Williams will not live for many more years, and who knows if the Church will replace him. He has been responsible for the good behaviour of the villagers, as well as leading their defence against the pirates.

IN THE ASHES OF A DREAM

Before he dies, we need to have some local order and prosperity established."

Tegwen sorely missed her mother and her aunt, and it was Dafydd who suggested that the Wise Woman should be asked to help, and work with Alys, her nurse, to provide all the mothering the child needed. This proposal had worked well, as Derryth and Alys had always been friends, and Alys had felt reluctant to take on the total responsibility for the child in the male-dominated castle. It was only a matter of time before Dafydd and Derryth renewed their passion for each other, but in such a way that Gwriad felt no threat to his position, nor did he refer to it. It was as though, with the passing of Angharad, he had lost his interest in women.

Jon continued to run the Castle and, with Dafydd's encouragement, reorganized and increased the stables to accommodate more horses. This enabled Gwriad to tour the outer villages with a strong guard, which impressed the peasants and accounted for a faster collection of taxes. Now that Father William was no longer so mobile, and without the moral judgment of Angharad and Teifryn, Jon had gradually relaxed his monastic attitudes and had formed an enjoyable but secretive relationship with the younger Megan, who had gradually established herself as force to be reckoned with in the kitchen.

In early June, Jon was summoned to a meeting with the Lords. It was in the morning of a hot, windless day, and Jon was pleased to have an excuse for being in the cool hall. It had been so hot for the past few days that the fire had remained unlit and cold meals had been welcome. "You called for me, my Lords?" Jon bowed, and took a seat at the table around which the brothers sat.

"You were present when Father Williams last visited this castle at the end of January," Dafydd said, "and I am sure you wondered what, if anything, we were going to do about getting our revenge?"

Jon gratefully accepted a cup of wine from Lord Gwriad. "It's something I've wondered about," Jon said. He felt unsure as to what was expected of him and took a deep gulp of his wine.

"Lord Dafydd and I have decided what we will do," Gwriad said, "and it will affect you, Jon, so listen carefully." He sat back in his chair and waved a hand for Dafydd to take over.

Dafydd sipped his wine and stared into Jon's eyes. "What we are going to tell you must not leave this room. You understand?"

"I understand," Jon said carefully.

"Not even to your lover," Dafydd said calmly, as though man-to-man.

Jon felt his face go crimson. He had no idea the Lords knew of his secret amour. "Of course not, my Lord," he said, trying to make it sound quite normal that he would not tell his mistress anything of importance.

"We're going to leave you in charge of this castle while we travel to London for a while," Dafydd held up his hand to stop Jon asking the obvious questions. "We have a few things to tie up, but we intend to leave at the end of July. We do not know exactly how long we'll be away, but we hope to be back by Christmas. You will have the final say in all decisions involving this castle and the running of the local villages, and you will seek help from Father Williams if you need guidance. Penn will be in charge of the soldiers but has been told that he answers to you. We will only take two guards, and they may return before we do. As a way of keeping the soldiers busy here, Penn will lead them on constant patrols around Ceredigion, leaving only a handful to guard the castle."

He handed Jon a piece of vellum, on which was a written list. "Read this carefully and learn it by heart. It is a list of all the important men in this part of Wales, I want you to visit them, introduce yourself and explain the situation. Some are landowners, some are Churchmen and others are long-time friends of our family. You will have a store of letters of introduction, in which you are described as the son of Lord Gwriad ap Griffith," he paused to allow that to sink in.

Jon turned to Gwriad open-mouthed. "Oh. Thank you, my Lord." He kneeled down in front of Gwriad. "Thank you, my Lord, I won't disappoint you."

Gwriad stood up and raised Jon to his feet, suddenly aware that his newly acquired son was taller than he was. "You've never disappointed me, Jon, and now you're a man I'm proud to name you as my son. From now on you may refer to me as Father. I intend

IN THE ASHES OF A DREAM

to gather the soldiers and the servants together and announce that from hence forth they call you Lord."

The weeks that followed were a time of positive activity with only the occasional hiccup. The crops were growing well and farmers were willing, if not happy, to pay their taxes. Llanduduch, having received its second large row boat, boasted record high catches. This was marred by a villager who, in a drunken brawl, killed another fisherman. Jon was detailed by Dafydd to conduct the investigation and to administer justice. "This will be good training for you," Gwriad observed. "Dafydd and I will see if you are tough enough."

Jon consulted Father Williams, who agreed to sit with him at the trial, and simply by being there gave a sense of gravity to the situation. Jon was convinced he would have to find the man guilty and order his hanging, but the old priest said he should listen carefully to the evidence. Jon took the hint, and in mid July, sat behind a carved table on the village green. The priest sat on his right and took careful notes of what was revealed during the two hours of the trial.

Davis, the murdered man, was known to be a bully who beat his wife and forced his children to work long hours. He had been seen beating his dog to death and was unpopular in the village. "He won't be missed," his own wife said defiantly, and none of the children were weeping at the loss of their father.

Merydyth, who was accused of his killing, was the popular tillerman of the recently acquired boat. He had refused to allow Davis, who was already drunk, to be part of the boat crew on that day, which meant that Davis had no chance to catch fish and earn an income. When Merydyth and his crew returned with a huge catch, Davis attacked him with a knife but, being very drunk, was unable to stab Merydyth before the burly tillerman landed a punch on his jaw. The drunken man fell to the ground, hit his head on a stone and died.

Jon summed up the case and, without reference to Father Williams, declared that Merydyth had acted correctly, that the dead man was guilty of assault and that Merydyth was only defending himself and consequently was a free man. The villagers warmly received the decision, and Jon was the hero of the hour. "You did well," Father Williams said as he laboured up the hill to his cottage. "I doubt if that would have been the result in London, where I understand the judges can be bought, but I was very happy with your decision."

When the end of July arrived, Gwriad assembled all the servants and guards in the courtyard and announced that he and Lord Dafydd would be leaving the next day and confirmed that Jon was in charge. "You know what happened to the Morgan family!" he bellowed, his voice carrying a warning. "Jon is now my son! He will act as Lord Dafydd and I would have acted if any of you commit a crime. He is in charge of the guards and all decisions that have to be made in the running of this castle and the security of this area, until we return." He took in a deep breath. "Don't any of you let me down!"

Jon arranged for Megan, the cook, to provide a small feast that night, where the three men sat closely together and discussed the final arrangements, amid an unusual array of roast poultry, fish and venison augmented by local vegetables. The wine flowed, but it was noticeable that no one drank to excess.

"Well," Dafydd said contentedly, "I think we have covered everything." He belched softly, an unusual act for someone who usually ate little and drank wine only on occasions.

"There is one thing you have not told me," Jon said. He had not had the courage to raise it before, but two cups of wine had given him confidence. Both men looked at him expectantly. "What do you intend to do in London that will enable you to get your revenge?"

There was a long pause, as each brother looked to the other to speak. Eventually, Gwriad cleared his throat and looked directly at Jon. "We intend to kill King Harold."

CHAPTER SEVENTEEN

"How much further? Gwriad complained. "We haven't missed it have we?" They had travelled carefully since they had crossed into England two weeks ago and had kept to quiet roads that gradually took them south to the coastal road that eventually would lead to London. They had moved slowly, attracting little notice, and when they met soldiers or large parties, their fine clothes and the two uniformed soldiers allowed them to ignore those who might have been curious. Dafydd had arranged for them to stay at monasteries with which he had always kept in touch, and although they occasionally had to sleep rough, they were able to rest and clean up at the religious houses.

"Peace unto you, brother," Dafydd intoned, much to the amusement of Davis and Lleu.

Gwriad made a distinctly irreligious comment. His legs ached, he needed a drink and he had enough horse riding for one day.

Dafydd had established the belief that they were both on a pilgrimage to Canterbury and would visit the new cathedral in London. For this purpose they both wore large silver crosses that hung over their robes, and they frequently crossed themselves and dropped their heads whenever conversation with other travellers seemed unavoidable.

"There it is, over there!" Dafydd pointed down to some lonely buildings standing in walled grounds. From their position on a slight rise, they could see that the monastery had an idyllic setting near a small stream with its own mill, and nearer the house a large fishpond. Surrounding the buildings were well-tended fields that had been established within a wooded area. The stone buildings had a mellow glow in the late August afternoon.

"Oh, that looks as though they might be able to spare a glass of wine or two," Gwriad remarked happily. "I shall be glad to part company with my horse for a few hours."

Behind him, Davis gave Lleu a thumbs-up sign. Life was better than either of them could have imagined, and although they found the religious houses to be strange, they enjoyed the generous amounts of plain food, and the spartan comforts of their accommodation. "I don't think I've ever slept in such clean surroundings as these places supply," Lleu said, "and it looks like this one will be good as well."

They were quickly admitted into the courtyard of the monastery, and were given a warm welcome by Abbot James, who was happy to be addressed as Father. "I am pleased to meet you after this long time, Lord Dafydd", the monk spoke in Latin, "and after your terrible losses it is a wise and beneficial thing to come on a pilgrimage." Dafydd had corresponded with him over many years, and both men were interested to meet each other. Gwriad, whose Latin was more limited, was content for the two men to finish their greetings and, after being introduced, he walked outside to inspect the fish pond. On the way, he approached a monk who suddenly stopped.

"I hear you're come from Ceredigion?" He was a short, stocky man and spoke in Welsh. He had been hoeing a large patch of cabbage plants, and his deeply tanned skin was evidence of an outside life.

"You're Welsh?" Gwriad could not keep the surprise out of his voice.

"Indeed. The Church does not exclude the Welsh," he smiled, "or even the Irish. I'm originally from Harlech, but I left my village before the time of King Gruffydd ap Llywelyn. I was saddened by his assassination; he was a great man."

Gwriad nodded. "Do you hear much of what goes on in the outside world?" He felt a warmth towards this friendly monk.

"Well, I knew of you when you were General Gwriad and your brother Dafydd was adviser to King Gruffydd." He seemed to deliberately ignore formality and continued to work while he spoke. "I hear that Wales has fractured since the King's death and

IN THE ASHES OF A DREAM

is once again becoming a loose patchwork of warring princedoms and vulnerable again to Saxon domination."

"That's true for the north, but the south still has some degree of cooperation." Gwriad explained how the previous year, England's present King Harold had launched a quick raid to destroy Caerdydd, but had failed, and had been chased out of Wales.

"My name is Geraint. The monks insist on calling me Brother Geraint, but I don't like titles. I know you're a Lord, but you don't need to be constantly reminded of that, nor do you need my recognition of a power you merely inherited. I'll call you Gwriad, and as the others don't speak Welsh, nobody is going to be outraged."

Gwriad laughed and grasped the monk's grubby hand in a firm handshake. "Geraint, you're like a fresh breeze on a hot day!" And without hesitation, he told the monk about the terrible loss both he and Dafydd had suffered at the hands of Harold.

"So, you've never found her body?" Geraint stopped working. "You can think two ways. Either you can live in a state of misery, your mind racked with terrible possibilities regarding her death, or you can hope that because you did not find the body she may still be alive."

Gwriad's first reaction was to deny such hope, but the monk seemed so serene and informed that he stifled his angry response, and stood silently looking at the earth and fighting the flicker of hope that Geraint's words had engendered. He was surprised when the monk placed his strong arm around him in a firm embrace, and he found himself unable to prevent the flood of tears that rushed down his face. Weeping was unmanly, something Gwriad never did, and he wanted to be angry with himself for exhibiting such weakness.

"I think you had that dammed up, my friend. You will feel better soon." Geraint gave him a final powerful hug, picked up his hoe and began to work slowly down the rows of cabbage, as though Gwriad was no longer there.

Gwriad wiped his eyes, looked quickly about to check that nobody else had witnessed his weakness and walked on towards the pond where he stood for a long time watching the fat carp as they swam just below the water. He gradually realized that Geraint was right: he did feel better and if there was a chance that Angharad was still alive, he would hold on to that idea, even if it was like believing in fairies.

. . .

TO MAINTAIN THEIR PRETENCE OF being pilgrims, they journeyed slowly along the road to Canterbury, where Dafydd was able to find a religious house with an elderly prelate with whom he had communicated for a number of years. Father Luke was delighted to entertain the brothers and share a seemingly endless supply of wine. He turned out to be a font of information concerning Harold and his problems, the threat of a Norman invasion, and the situation in the north. One of the topics he was keen to expand on was the immoral conduct on the part of the King and his mistress, Edith Swannuck, whom he was keeping in luxury in a large estate in Sussex. "She has a huge brood of children, and most people in London believe they're his!" the old man said venomously.

"Is she not his handfast wife?" Dafydd asked innocently.

"She's a whore!" the old man exploded. "God will punish him."

"I understand he might marry again for political reasons?" Gwriad suggested.

"He's still married to the ex-wife of the Welsh King Gruffydd," Father Luke said and refilled the goblets. "She disgraced herself when she was last in Court. I have no idea where she is now."

The two brothers exchanged knowing smiles. "How popular is the new King Harold?" Dafydd asked.

The priest looked about the wood-panelled room, as though looking for spies. He lowered his voice: "He is very unpopular with the Church. He has defied the Pope, heaped taxes on the Bishop of Westminster, and he is constantly breaking the Ten Commandments."

"Ah, yes," Dafydd murmured and looked at the floor. "How do the Lords feel about him?"

"He has two clever brothers who act as his advisers, and they have skilfully prevented him from upsetting the members of the Witan and have also guided him into supporting those Lords who did not thrive under King Edward. His main opposition is up in the north-east, where his brother Tostig proved to be a very unpopular Earl of Northumbria." Father Luke sipped his wine thoughtfully. "There was even a popular uprising against Tostig. King Harold had him banished from the Earldom, but rumour has it that Tostig is seeking the help of King Harald Hardrada of Norway. I imagine it is a great worry to King Harold to have such a brother." It was clear that the priest was delighted with the embarrassment Tostig had caused.

"If we wanted to have a meeting with King Harold, could it be arranged?" Dafydd said. He sipped his wine and appeared to be discussing nothing of importance.

"Meet with the King? Why would pilgrims wish to meet with the King?" The idea seemed to be beyond the understanding of the priest.

"As you may know, Father Luke, my brother and I, at one time, held important positions in the Court of the late King Gruffydd, and we were actively opposed to King Harold when he was an Earl on our borders. We would like to pledge our loyalty to him now that he is the King of England. How do we go about arranging this?"

"Yes, I see." The priest muttered. He had pretended to have more influence than he had, and this was not what he had anticipated when he had agreed to entertain these uncivilized Lords from Wales. "I think the best thing would be for you to leave this with me, and I will see when our King can fit you in. You must understand that he is exceedingly busy."

The meeting had ended abruptly, and both brothers had understood that they were unlikely to arrange a meeting with the King through this bumptious prelate.

They decided to leave Canterbury on a fine day in early September when the harvest was almost complete and the fruit was heavy on the branches. The number of pilgrims they met on the dusty road had gradually reduced, along with the numerous beggars that accompanied them. "I would call them easy weather pilgrims," Dafydd quipped. "Their absence should make our journey to London easier."

"I think we should send our two ferocious soldiers home," Gwriad joked. "We have sheltered under their military might for long enough." He glanced back and looked at Davis and Lleu who were chatting with each other, and totally unaware of their surroundings. "After tonight we'll send them back."

"How will they travel?" Dafydd said. "They don't speak Latin, and their grasp of English is limited. I think their journey would be dangerous. There's no way we could expect them to reach Aberteifi without our help."

"You think we should keep them with us? What happens if we are able to get close enough to Harold to kill him? Their chances of survival would be worth nothing." Gwriad beckoned to the two soldiers. "Come over here, boys. You remember at the beginning we said we might send you back once we got to London?" The two men nodded solemnly, their carefree mood had suddenly changed. "Well, we hadn't thought it out. We're not sure how you would get back to Wales without us to speak for you and obtain safe lodgings."

Lleu's face broke into a broad smile. "We've thought of that, m'Lord."

"You have?" Dafydd's voice betrayed a certain doubt.

"Yes, m'Lord. We'll get back to Wales by boat, won't we?"

Gwriad raised his eyebrows at Dafydd, and they both waited for Lleu to explain.

"There's a regular trade from Dover to Plymouth, we could work our passage." Lleu looked pleased with himself. "Dover is just south of here, m'Lord," he said to Dafydd.

"Thank you, Leu, I did know that," Dafydd said coldly.

"Yes, m'Lord," Lleu dutifully nodded his head. "Then we travel overland to a small port on the west coast of Cornwall, called Padstow, which trades with Caerdydd. One of my cousins works on the boats," he said proudly. "As you will know, m'Lord, the Welsh have always been friends with the Cornwall people."

"Even I knew that!" Gwriad said with a laugh. He patted Lleu on the back, "It's amazing what you boys know. And there was I thinking you only knew about fish and sheep!"

"I never thought about that," Dafydd muttered. "What an idea," he smiled. "Well then, we'll release you here. You think you can journey safely to Dover?"

"It's only a day's travel, m'Lord," Davis said, keen to contribute.

"Right then!" Gwriad handed them some silver coins. "Take these, and you can sell your horses when you get to Dover."

After a short exchange of good wishes, the two soldiers took the south road and the brothers set off on the north road to London. "Who would have thought it?" Gwriad said as he glanced back down the road. "I've spent my life thinking that I was the one who looked after my community, and I find they can do very well by themselves and know more about some things than I do."

"Just remember what happened to the village of Aberteifi when we stopped caring. What Lleu has demonstrated is that an extended family can be very useful for gathering information, but we must never forget that as Lords we protect them and provide the stability for our community." Dafydd pulled on his reins. "I'd never thought of escaping that way," he chuckled, "and me with all my education and connections."

"Escaping? If we manage to kill Harold, I don't think there will be any chance of escaping." Gwriad paused and looked at his brother with a thoughtful stare. "Have you ever thought what will happen to Tegwen if you insist on killing Harold?"

"Of course," Dafydd snapped. "I think of her all the time. But with Alys and the Wise Woman to look after her, she will consider them as mothers, and Jon will be her big brother. She'll be fine. Tegwen hardly knows me, and I am committed to killing the man who murdered her mother." He was aware that he had avoided mentioning Derryth by name and he wondered what would happen between them if he were able to return alive.

They travelled slowly, enjoying the fine late summer, and staying at small monasteries along the way. At each stop they enquired about the latest news of the King, and whether the abbots knew any people of influence who could speak on their behalf. At each religious house the answer was always the same: the monks had no connections with anyone who was associated with the top prelates in London, nor did they have friends in royal circles.

Finally, they reached London where their rich clothes enabled them to pass into the city with only a minimum of inconvenience at the gates, and at checkpoints manned by soldiers who saluted for a small coin. But, the city was unlike anything they were prepared for. They had expected many houses and more people than they had ever seen, but they were unprepared for the stench of the place. The rains had still to come, and the smell of sewage, dead animals and putrid food was overwhelming. The narrow streets were unfriendly, and drunks, robbers and prostitutes mingled with the dense crowd of vendors and shoppers. The local people knew how to navigate their way through the crowds, and avoided certain streets where horses were unwelcome. Strangers were left to fend for themselves.

"Where is the Monastery of Saint Peter?" Dafydd asked a ragged priest, who was standing at a corner with a begging bowl. He dropped a small coin into the bowl, and the priest was keen to give them directions, but it was mid-afternoon when they finally found the place. It was a well-built stone building with a high wall and a strong metal gate. They rang the bell, and after a long wait a tonsured monk approached at a leisurely pace and stared at them as though he was surprised to see them.

"Open up! I am Lord Dafydd. Your abbot knows me." The monk seemed unimpressed and stared at the two Lords in their rich clothes, sitting on their tired horses, and after a silent appraisal, turned away and disappeared through a small door. Dafydd felt it was in some way a criticism of his friend the abbot and shrugged his shoulders at Gwriad. "Father Alexander is a frequent writer, I have known him for a while. I wrote to advise him of our visit."

They were made to wait for what felt like an inordinate time, as flies pestered their horses and small children begged for alms. Eventually the monk returned at his leisurely pace and unlocked the gate. He gave no apology for the long time they had been forced to remain outside, and seemed unaware of their indignation. They walked their horses into the forecourt and dismounted as the monk relocked the gate. "Where are the stables?" Dafydd asked, barely able to contain his anger.

The monk stared directly at him and pointed to the left of the main building, then turned and began to walk away. Gwriad ran forward and grasped his shoulder, and the monk spun round with a look of surprise on his face as Gwriad grabbed him by the neck and shook him. "How dare you treat us like this, you fat slug! I could beat the hell out of you!" he yelled in Welsh. The monk gasped and made some odd noises.

"My Lords! My Lords!" an elderly abbot came running towards them. "Brother Paul is a deaf mute. He meant you no insult." He was a thin, intellectual looking man, who spoke in Latin and had the red nose of someone who enjoyed wine.

Gwriad slowly lowered his hands from the flustered monk. "I didn't realize," he muttered in Welsh. He stepped back, wiping the sweat off his brow and clearing his throat.

Dafydd walked forward and gently patted the monk on the shoulder. The man grunted, gave a relieved smile and retreated behind the abbot.

"You must be Lord Dafydd ap Griffith? I'm sorry for your inconvenience at the gate. We have just celebrated None, our afternoon service, and no one would have heard the bell. Brother Paul is not required to attend all the services, as he hears nothing and cannot contribute," he gave the monk a sympathetic smile. "Without our help he would quickly die in the outside world."

"Please accept our apologies, Father Alexander," Dafydd said as he bowed, "we are unused to a big city, and it has been a hot, uncomfortable journey."

"I shall try to improve your day," the abbot said as he gestured to a party of monks who had appeared in the forecourt. "Brother Adam is my chamberlain," he pointed towards a tall, white haired man. "Brother Adam, make sure these two Lords have everything they need." The monk dipped his head.

"And this is Brother James, our kitchener," he indicated a smiling, rotund monk who clearly enjoyed the food he was in charge of. "Brother James, I want you to arrange for these two Lords to eat with me tonight in my office and send the vintner along when you see him." The monk bowed and backed away. "Those monks are on a short period of personal silence when they will only speak if it is a necessity," the abbot said. "Silence is the only way to find God."

That evening, they ate well and enjoyed some excellent wines. The abbot explained that it was not unusual to have noblemen call at the monastery, and he found it politically beneficial to treat them in the way in which they were accustomed, even if it did appear to contradict his vows of poverty. "I must always consider the long-term benefits to the Church," he said gravely as he emptied his glass goblet.

Gwriad winked at Dafydd, who quickly turned his attention to sipping his wine. "I imagine you are in touch with some of King Harold's advisers?" he said casually.

"Indeed, one would think so, my Lord, but the nobles that support the Church are not the ones who support King Harold, who has proved to be unfriendly towards our Church and in defiance of the Pope."

As with their earlier meetings with minor members of the Church hierarchy, the evening proved unfruitful, and they went to bed feeling well entertained but no further forward with their vague plans of meeting the King. They left the next day just after Vespers had finished, and the abbot seemed delighted with a donation from Dafydd.

"I think we have to make other contacts," Dafydd said. He was not surprised at their slow progress, unlike Gwriad who wanted an immediate meeting with King Harold, and a quick and efficient murder. Dafydd had explained that it would be difficult to arrange a meeting with the King, and even though they were going to present themselves as the most important leaders of the Welsh opposition, they would probably not be seen by him and his advisers in that light.

"Remember, Gwriad, Harold is expecting an invasion by the Normans at any moment. He could be facing an invasion from his brother Tostig; the bishops are opposed to him, and many Lords consider his new taxes to be outrageous. We, and the remote possibility of a Welsh invasion, are low on his list of worries. We must be patient and consider how else we might get close to the King." He gave one of his Dafydd smiles that so annoyed Gwriad: the superior 'I know more about these things than you do' smiles.

"Hell with that!" Gwriad snarled. "How long are we going to

IN THE ASHES OF A DREAM

be wasting our time in this stinking city. If we can't get near this monster, let's go home. I'm not enjoying your religious friends, no matter how generous they appear to be."

Dafydd took a deep breath and contemplated the mass of humanity that pushed past them in the narrow streets. It always amazed him how a man on a horse could command such respect. He wondered what would happen if the poor and the homeless realized that a knife in the back would immediately get them a horse, quality clothes and money. Luckily, their horses and fine clothes continued to give them immunity among the awful squalor of the city dwellers.

"Let's be bold," Dafydd said. "Let's turn up at the palace and try, without any interveners, to see the King. They can only refuse us."

"Or lock us up," Gwriad said. London was having a very negative effect on him.

"True," Dafydd said. "But, we have come here with a very loose plan for killing Harold, and we must try every possibility. I warn you though, we'll probably be kept waiting, or perhaps," he tried to engage Gwriad and failed, "we may be given a future date that we may," he emphasized the word 'may', "be given our 'once-in-a-lifetime' chance of meeting the man who was responsible for the deaths of our wives." He let out a deep breath. "I just want revenge."

"We both want revenge, but now we're here I'm beginning to see what a half-arsed plan we have. If it were easy to kill a King, Harold would have died weeks ago. There must be cart loads of people who want him dead." Gwriad sank into a grim silence and glared threateningly at a woman who was about to pour a bucket of waste out of a second-floor window.

They eventually took lodgings in a well-appointed inn near the royal palace, and, after a good meal and a chance to tidy their clothing, they approached the palace in a more optimistic frame of mind. Near the main gates they stopped near a statue and casually watched as Lords and official-looking men rode up to the palace guards and presented them with documents. Some dismounted and walked up to the soldiers and appeared to argue their case, while other men, equally well-dressed, could be seen passing money. Some men were immediately recognized and allowed entry, but not everyone was allowed through the gates. Dafydd remarked that the sergeant, or some other person with slight authority, must be able to read.

After some hours, they returned to their lodgings where Dafydd unpacked some thick vellum and writing materials. He devised a letter that claimed that they represented a powerful Welsh faction that wanted to sign a peace treaty with King Harold. When he had finished he signed it and placed his seal at the bottom of the writing, and Gwriad did the same. "Well, that looks impressive at first glance," Dafydd said thoughtfully as he rolled the letter and tied it up with red ribbon.

Then, they attached short daggers to the inside of their thick trousers and practiced how they might get them out quickly. After a number of tries, they finally achieved the success they had managed back in their castle. At this point they did a cursory check of each other's costume, as they assumed a guard would do when checking a nobleman.

"I hope this doesn't happen too often," Gwriad quipped, "I could get to like it."

Dafydd turned away in a huff, and quietly removed his dagger; his brother's humour was often annoying.

The next day, they talked their way past the guard at the gate, with the aid of a small bribe, crossed the large courtyard, and waited as stable lads took their horses away. "Now for the next part," Gwriad smiled.

"That was the easy part," his brother cautioned, as they approached a large oak door, with a strong body of guards. Dafydd explained to the sergeant that they were Welsh Lords who had come to present the King with a peace treaty. Their swords were confiscated, as they had expected, but they were alarmed by the strong hands that expertly checked their bodies, even though nothing was found. The sergeant took the scroll and disappeared into a room just inside door. They were made to wait until a tall officer with a full beard appeared. He was holding their scroll and went up close to Dafydd. "What is your name?" he asked in Latin.

IN THE ASHES OF A DREAM

Dafydd held himself erect, and after saying his name pointed to it on the open scroll that the officer was holding.

"You're obviously an educated man," the officer continued in Latin. "Do you speak English?"

"I speak it quite well, "Dafydd replied, feeling an unexpected friendship towards this man. "My brother, Lord Gwriad, has some grasp of your language."

"He doesn't speak Latin?" he queried, noticing Gwriad's lack of reaction.

"No," Dafydd gave him a friendly grin, "he's the military wing of our family."

"Do either of you speak French?"

"I do. But I have not used it for a while. I was King Gruffydd's secretary and diplomat."

The Saxon nodded his head as though confirming something. "I'm pleased to meet you, Lord Dafydd," he said in French. "I'm Lord Aethelstan. Please come this way. If you get an audience with the King, you will converse in French." He led them down a long hall, and up an imposing flight of stairs and into a wide room with many chairs and small tables. A host of well-dressed people was either sitting silently, or standing in tight groups in frantic conversation with each other. There were some outbursts of laughter, but most of the talkers seemed to be deep in worried discussions. At the far end was an impressively carved door where three guards in fine uniforms barred any entry.

"I will leave you both here and will present your letter to his Majesty's Secretary. I'm afraid you are unlikely to see his Majesty for some time," he said apologetically. "I am talking in weeks."

"Weeks?" Dafydd protested. "We only wish to agree a basic peace treaty. Nothing too complicated."

"My Lords, in this room are some of the most important people in the realm. They each have a different and important request of the King. You will have to wait your turn." He shrugged. "You have reached this level in your approach to the King, so tomorrow you will not have to go through the earlier checks, apart from the weapon search." He bowed and made his way back down the stairs.

"What did he say?" Gwriad demanded. "When do we see the King?"

"We have only reached stage one, brother. It could be weeks before we meet the King," he looked dejected. "If ever." He rubbed his face and gave a humourless laugh. "We are such country bumpkins! How did we ever think we could get an immediate audience with this King?"

"That Saxon seemed to like you?" Gwriad said, trying to sound optimistic. "What did he say that was encouraging?"

Dafydd looked surprised. If either of them was going to be aggressive and angry, it was usually his brother, but here he was playing the peacemaker. "He said we'd passed the first stage, and now had a right to return tomorrow, and line up here with these other important people."

They spent a long time walking aimlessly around the room. Some people looked at them expectantly, as though waiting for them to say something. Dafydd would bow and move on, and Gwriad would frown as though his business in that room was too important for idle chatter. Some groups would stop speaking and wait pointedly for them to move on. They looked out of the windows at the Palace grounds, admired the wood panelling and watched the comings and goings as people arrived looking animated and left seeming resigned. Occasionally, the guards at the carved door would be in brief discussion with an elaborately dressed flunky and a name would be called out, and a single man or a group of men would be allowed through the door.

Eventually, when servants appeared and lit tapers, it seemed to be the signal for a mass migration to the stairs. Gwriad put his arm round his brother. "So, no point in waiting today, and we'll come back tomorrow when we'll be better prepared for a long wait," he grinned. "We're committed to this one attempt no matter how long it takes. Eventually it will be worth it. We only want one chance." He looked defiantly around the room at the mixed gathering. "You notice the confident, important ones were standing and making sure they were seen and heard, while the anxious, uncertain ones were sitting silently."

"I wouldn't mind betting that those who were sitting have been waiting a long time and have lost hope," Dafydd said. "We won't let it happen to us."

"We have each other, and when we get bored out of our minds I will let out a great laugh, just to remind people we are still here and are not to be overlooked." Gwriad looked carefully around the room. "I don't recognize anyone, which is a good thing."

"I agree. I didn't expect to see any other Welsh Lords here; they're too busy defending their newly acquired princedoms, together with their self-appointed titles." Dafydd was surprised by his own bitterness and put it down to the stresses of the day. He gave Gwriad a brave smile and indicated that he should lead the way out. At the main door they glimpsed Lord Aethelstan in a side office. He was in urgent discussion with a man in bright military attire. "That's a job I wouldn't like, I think he's in charge of the security of the Palace and the King."

"Thank the Gods he liked you," Gwriad said as they waited for the return of their swords. They walked outside and were aware of a gathering coolness in the air caused by a slight breeze. "Let's hope we can see Harold before Christ Mass!" he joked. "Anyway, if we turn up each day I'm hoping the guards will not be so thorough with their searching. The one that checked me was within a finger's width of touching the handle of the dagger." He glanced roguishly at Dafydd. "I was about to protest that I was very well endowed and would he not interfere with me!" He roared with laughter that caused the guards to glance his way.

Dafydd made no response. They waited silently for their horses as the light began to fade. It was the start of a long wait and he wondered if they could carry out their makeshift plan when they had almost been caught on their first visit. If they had to repeat this for weeks, would he last the course? He glanced at Gwriad who seemed quietly serene and realized that his brother prospered when his life was dangerous and exciting. There were times, not often, when he envied his brother's lack of imagination. "It's the only plan we have, and I'm determined to make it work." He scowled toward the Palace, "We have to kill that bloody bastard."

Gwriad raised his eyebrows; it was not often that his brother swore. He was tempted to make a joke of it but seeing the black look on Dafydd's face he resisted the temptation. "Indeed," he said solemnly. "Yes, indeed."

CHAPTER EIGHTEEN

"My Lord King, I have important news of your brother Lord Tostig," the courtier bowed deeply.

Harold was about to yell at the over-dressed flunky, whose name he could never remember, when the name of his dissident brother caused him to pause. It had been another tedious day of complaining priests, disruptive Earls and bad news from the army. He wanted to move on to the promised feast to welcome some foreign Lords that his brothers had assured him were important. He had not recognized their names and was barely interested as to why they were important, but at least he would enjoy himself drinking these so-called diplomats into obscurity. According to his brothers, every person they arranged for him to meet was someone without whose support he was doomed, and he looked forward to the time when his Kingship was assured, and he could begin to travel the country and enjoy himself.

"Give us your news," Lord Leofwine said abruptly, and Harold realized he had been slow to respond.

"My Lord King, Earl Tostig has appeared with a strong fleet off the south coast and is raiding the Isle of Wight. Your militia have repulsed his attempted invasion but are in need of more soldiers as it is believed he will land elsewhere on the Isle."

Harold sat bolt upright on his throne. "Go on!"

"Reports indicate that his forces have destroyed many homes, and the battle with your troops was costly on both sides. Most of his troops are Norwegian as are his boats." The courtier looked to Lord Leofwine for support.

"It would appear that Tostig intends to use the Isle of Wight as a base for attracting the support from dissidents and he will then try for an attack on London."

"He's a pain in the arse," Harold growled. "Can we move troops there quickly?"

"It will certainly be necessary," Lord Gyrth interjected. "But as you know, we had enough men on the Isle to prevent a major landing up until recently, but then we ran low on funds."

"I know about that!" Harold snarled. He did not need to be reminded that his great idea of forming a standing militia along the south coast and especially on the Isle of Wight in preparation for William's invasion had turned into a fiasco when the men stopped being paid and when their supplies stopped arriving. It was only two weeks ago, following unrest bordering on mutiny, that he had been forced to disband the militia, relying on local men to defend the coast.

"The point I'm making is that it will need a big effort on the part of the local officers to recruit those men again, and we will have to provide money and supplies, whatever the cost. In the meantime, I suggest we order our ships out of Southampton to chase their ships away."

"That easy?" Harold sneered, he wanted to believe his brother, but he was finding that things were never that easy.

"Brother, we're dealing with Tostig. He couldn't organize a nuns' prayer meeting!" Leofwine clapped his hands, and the courtier and other servants left the room. "I suggest we enjoy the feast. We only have to worry if he's still off the south coast in a week's time."

"I agree," said Gyrth. "I think he will resort to being a nuisance off our east coast. That's where we should be preparing the local Lords. But we must find some way of paying our militia."

"Over to you, Leofwine." Harold stood up and stretched. "You're the magician with the money." He yawned. "I would enjoy a good fight; this diplomatic stuff bores me to the core. Gyrth, you take charge of the Southampton side of things. We may need our ships to attack Tostig's ships, but we will also need our fleet to be active if we hear confirmation of William's attempts to invade. I want you, Leofwine, to keep in close contact with Tostig's antics, find some money, even if we have to levy the Church, and warn the Lords along our east coast, just in case."

"We can't afford to keep a large standing army outside of London," Leofwine said thoughtfully. He was standing by an open window and watched as a breeze moved the branches of some small trees. "As long as this wind remains constant, William is unable to launch his invasion fleet, and when he does it's almost certain he will aim for Dover, or the nearest and safest beaches that the wind allows. If we can regarrison the Isle, and with the ships from Southampton, we may not have to worry too much about Tostig."

"I agree," said Gyrth, who often found himself in a supporting role with his highly intelligent brother. "Our reports indicate that the Bastard will try to bring over horses in those flat-based, unmanageable ships of his. We know he has a large army but cramming armoured soldiers on his vessels requires a flat sea, ideal tides and just enough wind to fill his sails, and," he paused for effect, "for the wind to come from the right direction. So far, his God has not smiled on him."

"And after October, the seas become more dangerous, especially for moving an army. The Channel is our best means of defence," Leofwine agreed.

"Good. If we can chase Tostig back to his Norwegian mummy, I will be happy to face the Bastard." Harold walked decisively towards the door, and the other two followed. "Tomorrow, I'm going hunting first thing, and I don't care who has to wait," he raised a hand at Gyrth who appeared to be about to protest. "I can't sit on that bloody throne any more until I've had some exercise!" He looked at them belligerently. "It's time for action, not words!" He paused, and a voracious smile crossed his face, "I think I might hunt in Sussex."

· · ·

LONDON WAS ALIVE WITH RUMOURS, and Dafydd and Gwriad were uncertain which to believe. They had been accepted as regulars in the taproom of their local inn, and welcomed by Cerdic the innkeeper, who recognized their social status. As he said to his wife, "I don't know why they're staying here, but they've paid up front, so I'm happy." By keeping to themselves, and maintaining a regular appearance, they were able to overhear the strident discussions of the drinkers and keep up with the latest rumours. It appeared to be a fact that Tostig, King Harold's troublesome brother, had invaded the Isle of Wight shortly after the King's militia had been stood down. While initially successful, the Norwegian soldiers, who were the majority of Tostig's army, had been forced to retreat back to their boats, and they had taken to attacking ports off the east coast.

"It appears Harold's family are causing him a problem," Gwriad muttered contentedly as he drank his ale. "I wonder how that will affect our plans?"

"I think it's a minor problem at this moment. In fact, I can't understand what this Tostig is trying to achieve," Dafydd said quietly. "My main interest is when Duke William will attack. I understand it has something to do with the wind. Not being a sailor, I have no idea how such things can be an ongoing problem."

They were so absorbed with their conversation that they were unaware of a red-eyed Saxon who had stopped to stare at them. The taproom was full and there was a squash both at the bar, and around the scattered tables where men were calling for the busy maids who plied the ale and who spent much of their time trying to avoid the grasping hands. The man edged nearer; he was unsteady on his feet, and took a swig from his tankard to fortify himself. He took a cautious step forward that brought him close to Gwriad.

"Ye'r bloody Welsh spies!" the man shouted to anyone who wanted to listen. He was a thickset man who was well past his prime and had the blotchy face of a drunkard. He wore a dirty cloak and an old sword, hung from his belt. "Lissen men, we've got Welsh spies wiv us!" He staggered against their table and tried to draw his sword.

Gwriad was on his feet in a second and downed the man with a forceful punch to his face. The man collapsed like a sack of turnips on the grimy floor, with blood pouring out of his broken nose. He seemed unconscious.

"I'm sorry our friend can't take his ale!" Dafydd smiled as he stood up and looked around the hot room. "We'll look after him." Most of the men were unaware of what had happened, and those who had noticed were soon back to their own joking and discussions. People often fought in the inn, and drunks were everywhere.

Like a well-planned action, the brothers each took one arm and marched him out of the inn and dumped him in the nearest alley. It was a warm evening and, after checking to see if anyone had followed them, they made their way to the back of the inn, where a side door into Cerdic's quarters enabled them to reach their upstairs room unobserved.

"Now what?" Gwriad said as he checked the empty corridor.

"We can't stay here," Dafydd said, "by tomorrow that drunk will be telling anyone who will listen about the 'Welsh spies' who are staying here." They checked the corridor and quickly entered their small room. "You pack up, and I'll try to pay what we owe Cerdic."

"Don't be stupid," Gwriad said as he began to hurriedly pack their things. "Some people will have noticed. We were lucky it was so busy or we would have had to fight our way out. The innkeeper will realize there's something strange if we want to leave at this time of night. If you feel guilty, then leave some money on your bed, I doubt if he will ever see it, but," he shrugged, "but if it makes you feel better."

Dafydd rubbed his face as he tried to work out the best way to act. "We'll get our horses and go back to the Monastery of Saint Peter. I think the abbot will be pleased to see us no matter what time we arrive. He tossed a silver coin on the bed and helped Gwriad with their baggage. They quietly approached the dark stables, where a few small coins galvanized the stable lads into action.

"D'ye want me to keep this stall for ye, m'Lord?" a stable lad asked innocently. He had noticed their baggage, and the way they kept looking around.

"Of course," Gwriad said gruffly. He patted the boy on the head, "Make sure you're awake when we return." They mounted their horses and without a backwards glance, walked their horses out into the moonlit yard.

"Who's he kidding?" the boy grinned at his friends. He looked at the money that Dafydd had given him. "I didn't think it'd be long before they vamoosed. I were surprised they stayed 'ere as long as they did, them being gentlemen an' all."

"Perhaps this is for the best," Dafydd said as they trotted their horses down the narrow streets. "With talk of invasion, people begin looking for enemies. Our safest place is with a religious house, even though that useful source of pub information will dry up."

"We still have the daily Palace conversations," Gwriad said. He gave a bellowing laugh, "I have to say I really enjoyed punching that drunk, especially as he did threaten our safety."

Dafydd made no comment. His brother would never change, and he knew he would not have been able to silence the man as efficiently at Gwriad had done.

• • •

HAROLD WAS SITTING GLAZY-EYED ON his increasingly uncomfortable throne, listening to a long and tedious report of the reasons for the poor state of the army, and why the success of the Southampton fleet had been limited to scaring the Norwegian fleet away, and why the Saxons had been unable to capture or sink any of the enemy ships.

"So!" he suddenly exploded. "Do you have any more tales of disaster and despair? Why am I surrounded with half-witted naysayers, who have no more courage than a mouse and make up excuses for their lack of ability?" He stood up on his raised dais and seemed to the assorted courtiers and officers to be enormous, and his temper was quite unnerving. "Because of a lack of decisive action against the enemy. My enemy!" he yelled, wanting everyone to remember that he was talking about his brother Tostig, "he's been allowed to escape and is, even now, raiding our unprotected ports up the east coast."

"My Lord King," Gyrth interrupted. He found that reminding Harold he was King was a useful ploy, in that it implied a need for more control. Harold needed to be reminded that it was his power that caused things to happen and his decisions that changed situations. Getting angry achieved nothing. "My Lord King," he repeated, "reports indicate that apart from some limited plundering of our coastline, our brother Tostig is unlikely to be capable of achieving anything else and will soon flee back to Norway."

"Let us hope the reports are correct," Harold rumbled. He walked down to the big window and stared longingly at the sun-blessed courtyard. He turned to glare at the sea of worried faces. "I want my housecarls to parade outside the Palace in full armour in two days' time. I need to be reminded that I have an army I can rely on, and I want the people of London to be reassured that we can defeat any invasion." He stared hard at the assembled Lords and courtiers. "Make sure it is done, and that all of you are there with your families. This will be a show of unity and strength. You may go."

There was a host of bowing, nodding heads and muttered agreements, as Gyrth ensured their quick exits from the throne room and ordered the guards to wait outside. "That was a good idea, brother. Anything that makes the common man feel he belongs." He poured wine into finely decorated glasses and handed one to Harold. "This is what power is about," he murmured as he held his glass up to the light to admire the colour of the red wine.

"Power is an attraction that draws ambitious men like moths to a flame," Harold muttered as he glowered out of the window at the clusters of nobles who were vigorously debating the situation with each other. "I should know, I was one of those."

They both stood silently watching the crowd when Lord Leofwine strode through the door as though he was being chased. He said nothing as he approached them, and quickly poured himself some wine. "Some bad news. Our beloved Tostig has invaded Yorkshire with a strong army led by King Harald Hardrada of Norway himself. The Norse army is mainly composed of Norwegians, who have attacked Scarborough and burnt it to the ground. Our brothers Morcar Earl of Northumberland and Edwin of Mercia are raising the Fyrd and intend to prevent the invaders from taking York."

"Well?" Harold demanded. "I imagine our brothers will send them running. This is exactly why I gave them those earldoms. They're the guardians of the north and have made a better job than Tostig ever did." He frowned at Leofwine, "Is this the bad news?"

"The bad news is that the Norse army with Tostig's forces are believed to number between 10,000 and as high as 15,000. Our brothers will be hard pushed to raise an army to match their numbers."

Harold slowly finished his wine. "It's good I have already called for the housecarls to be mobilized two days from now. I may have to march up there to aid Morcar and Edwin, but I'm loath to leave London and the south coast undefended." He looked thoughtfully at his two most loyal brothers. "What's your advice?"

"My advice would be to assemble the housecarls, but wait for further news," Gyrth said. "With luck, our brothers may be able to defeat them on home ground. I agree with you, it would be a gamble to leave London and the south coast vulnerable at this time."

Leofwine agreed but looked unhappy. "If we have to march north, then one of us must stay to mobilize the men of London, and the surrounding areas south of here, just in case the wind changes. It can't remain forever in our favour."

"Agreed. Gyrth, I want you to remain here and get the whole city on alert."

"Leofwine, you and I will start immediately to get people appointed to organize supplies and gather weapons. Summon our best officers and get them working. We don't have the horses to create a viable cavalry wing, and anyway our men fight best in the shield wall, so we'll use horses only for scouting and transportation of supplies."

"I have arranged for the news to travel fast," Leofwine said, "and if we don't have to march north, it will enable us to prepare for an invasion that must happen soon or be postponed until next year."

IN THE ASHES OF A DREAM

Harold drank another glass and stood up and stretched. He was looking forward to some action. "Time to don our armour again," he murmured as he walked over to where his sword was propped up by his throne. He drew it carefully out of its scabbard and tried some moves. Yes, he thought to himself, it is time for William and I to settle this once and for all.

• • •

GWRIAD AND DAFYDD CONTINUED WITH their frequent visits to the Palace, and were becoming well-known to the guards who had nicknamed Gwriad as the Welsh Lord Broken Nose. Dafydd had formed a relationship with Lord Aethelstan who, when he was not too busy, would invite Dafydd into his office to discuss politics and philosophy.

"Being a Lord and a landowner puts one into an entirely different world," Dafydd said as he drank Athelstan's wine. "If I had been a Welsh farmer or soldier at this time in London, I would have been singled out for abuse."

Aethelstan raised his glass in a silent toast. "Money is equally important. If you had been a penniless lord, you would have been unable to enter the Palace. Money is power, and power recognizes itself."

"Education also opens doors. I would argue that knowledge is more powerful than money."

Aethelstan slowly shook his head. "I wish that were true, but with respect you have lived your life in a backwater. You have been reading and building up knowledge and for a short time you moved in high circles, but you have yet to experience how international politics is governed more by money than logic and philosophy."

Dafydd glanced out at the main entrance, where there seemed to be an unusual flurry of activity. "Is that commotion anything to do with Tostig's attacks on the eastern coast?" he asked casually.

"I'm afraid so." Aethelstan stood up as a courtier entered with a sheet of velum. He read it carefully and slowly moved to his desk where he picked up a quill and signed the sheet. "Show this to nobody other than Lord Gyrth." The man bowed and quickly left the room. Aethelstan frowned and after a long pause walked back and sat opposite Dafydd. "Unfortunately, I have received some bad news that will almost certainly prevent you from seeing the King for a long time to come."

"Oh?" Dafydd looked askance.

The Saxon stared at him for a moment while he considered what he would say. "Lord Tostig, aided by King Harald Hardrada of Norway, has invaded Northumbria after first destroying the town of Scarborough, a sizeable fishing town. A huge foreign fleet has been reported to have entered the River Humber, and it is thought it will sail up the River Ouse and attack Jorvik."

"Will there be a way of stopping Tostig and his allies?" Dafydd wondered if Harold would feel it necessary to march north.

"The two Earls, Morcar of Northumberland and Edwin of Mercia, are younger brothers of King Harold and will certainly mobilize the Fyrd." He noticed Dafydd's puzzled face. "The Fyrd is a local body of trained soldiers who are required to provide their own weapons and armour and have to train for a number of days each year. This is a country-wide force that are the core of the housecarls in each earldom and are the defenders of the realm."

"So, it is for that reason that the King will cease his diplomatic and political audiences?"

"Indeed. The King will have more serious issues to deal with." He stood up and offered his hand. "I'm sorry your delegation did not succeed in its intentions, but I have enjoyed our discussions. Perhaps when this is all over, you will return? I think King Harold would like to know that a part of his border with Wales will be peaceful." Dafydd stood up as Aethelstan opened his office door. "I strongly urge you to return to Wales, immediately. When war is in the air, people look for spies, scapegoats or just for those with a different accent."

Dafydd realized this was a firm and final dismissal. He bowed, shook Aethelstan's hand and left the room. He looked back to see the Saxon standing at his window, already engrossed in thought, and went up the stairs, avoiding courtiers and soldiers who were rushing down. He found Gwriad asleep in a corner. "Gwriad," he said quietly, "we must leave, immediately."

IN THE ASHES OF A DREAM

. . .

THE ROYAL HOUSECARLS PARADED IN the Palace grounds in all their finery and the people of London had a fine spectacle that encouraged their patriotic fervour. Each soldier wore a chainmail coat, an iron helmet with a large nose guard and most carried an axe on their belt. All held a spear and some carried short swords. Attached to each soldier's back was a long leather shield with a metal rim and distinctive metal bosses. As they marched, their metal-capped boots thundered on the ground and they seemed all-powerful and indestructible to the cheering mob.

It was a proud day for Harold, who reviewed his troops as they marched ten abreast. He was also in full armour, carrying only his great sword and wearing a gold circlet on his round-topped helmet. Harold was known to be a very large man, but in his armour and his ironclad boots he was a giant, and to his soldiers and the people of London, he was everything they looked for in their King.

When the soldiers had marched past, Harold returned to his Palace where his favourite brother was waiting in the throne room to greet him. "That was a damn fine show!" Harold exclaimed enthusiastically. "That will get the Londoners on side."

Leofwine took a deep breath. "The enemy, which includes our brother Tostig, has attacked North Umbria with an army estimated at more than 10,000 men in a huge fleet. After destroying Scarborough, they sailed up the River Humber and entered the River Ouse. When they landed they were intercepted by our brothers, the Northern Earls Morcar and Edwin. They joined battle at the villages of Water Fulford and Fulford Gate, which are close to Jorvik. Our brothers were unprepared for the size of this invasion and although they called out many of their housecarls with the mobilization of the Fyrd, they were unable to raise an army of more than 5,000. After a prolonged battle that lasted most of the day, the Saxon forces were soundly defeated by the Viking invaders, who are now believed to be heading for Jorvik. We are not certain if our brothers survived the battle, but if they did they will, almost certainly, make a stand at Jorvik which has strong walls and is capable of withstanding a siege."

Harold sat unmoving, looking into space. His eyes brightened and he was suddenly alert. "Mobilize the housecarls and set about preparing London for war! I want the men to be ready to march tomorrow." He strode to the door. "Get Lord Gyrth!" he bellowed. "Send out for all my officers to attend me!"

He poured himself and his brother some wine and bent over a table where a map of the east coast was laid out. "I want Gyrth to organize London and keep an eye on the south coast. It's a dangerous risk leaving London at this time, but I must act now, or I could end up having two enemies to fight at once. The wind has kept William in his ports for all these weeks. I just need enough time to defeat Tostig and his Norwegian supporter, and then I can concentrate on the Bastard." He raised his glass. "I want you to come with me to defeat our disloyal brother."

"Of course," Leofwine raised his glass in a silent toast.

"I think we could be in the area in four days with a forced march," Harold traced his finger on the map.

Leofwine considered his response. "That might be possible, but the housecarls will be exhausted when they get there. They will not be able to fight until they have a day's rest," Leofwine said. He realized that Harold judged all soldiers by his own abilities.

"I must get there before the Norwegian King has time to retake command of his troops. Following their victory, there will be pillaging and looting and if we move fast, we will catch Hardrada unawares, and our smaller force will have the advantage."

"I agree, but don't judge your troops by your own unusual abilities. Also, you will travel by horse, whereas they have a long distance to carry their heavy weapons. Give them another day, brother. The enemy won't be expecting you for another week or more, and Tostig won't know you happen to have your housecarls already assembled. Another day will make a great difference to their fighting strength."

Harold scowled. "We shall see," he muttered. "Get the section officers assembled and have the supply officers working all night." He finished his wine and his large face radiated with excitement.

IN THE ASHES OF A DREAM

"We can do this, and then we'll have one less problem. I should have executed Tostig last year!" he roared as he left the room. "But, he won't escape justice this time."

. . .

In the Monastery of St. Peter one service followed another in a time-honoured fashion, and the monks moved about in an often silent, almost trance-like way. Occasionally, the younger monks might laugh or even fool around until an older monk chastised them, but otherwise it seemed to Gwriad that he was stuck in a dream world where nothing happened until a bell was rung. "This will drive me mad if I stay here much longer," he complained as a line of silent monks passed them in the courtyard, seemingly unaware of their presence.

"This is only our first day here!" Dafydd protested.

"But without the input from the Palace and the sociability of the tavern, we are not achieving anything and I wasn't cut out for a monk."

Dafydd considered the indignant face of his brother. "I agree. This is just a bolt hole while we reshape our plan."

"Hah! What plan? Like a couple of gwirionyns we arrived thinking we could easily get close to the monster. We haven't got within shouting range. If we can't attempt an assassination, there is no point in being here."

"Do you remember the name Swannuck? Elditha Swannuck? Who some call Swan Neck?"

"Yes, yes," Gwriad said impatiently. He wished his brother would not turn everything into a lecture. "Harold's mistress."

"The abbot tells me she was often seen at the Palace, but soon after Harold became King he moved her to an estate in Sussex."

"So?"

"Harold has been visiting her on frequent occasions, but the gossip has it that he has recently been denied her company because of the military uncertainty caused by both Tostig and Duke William. I'm thinking that the situation in the north-east might cause him to leave London, and if he is planning to do so, maybe he will arrange a night of pleasure before he leaves."

Gwriad smiled. "He might do; I would if I had a woman like that waiting for me!" His laugh choked in his throat, and a look of anguish replaced the smile. "Hell, what am I saying?" he strode off angrily towards their quarters.

Dafydd chewed on his lower lip and slowly followed across the courtyard as the first drops of rain stained the dusty flagstones. "It's definitely time for us to leave," he said quietly and took a seat near the abbot's office.

An hour later, when he returned to their room, Gwriad was well into his wine and was looking pugnacious. "So, what about Harold's mistress?" he demanded.

"She might be the answer to our problems. Her manor is in the country in Sussex, and as this is a secretive affair, he will have far fewer guards with him and most of them will be stationed outside the residence. If we can gain entry, we should be able to get to him fairly quickly."

Gwriad put down his wine and stared at Dafydd. "But we don't know where she lives."

"I've just been speaking to the abbot. This is a subject on which he is a moral authority. We have had a total misunderstanding of who Elditha Swannuck is. She is not just Harold's bit on the side, they were handfasted in marriage and have been for many years, and certainly long before Harold married Ealdgyth. Elditha is a great landowner in her own right, and has given him six children, the eldest is named Godwin. At the moment she is staying at Godwin Manor, which she owns, hence the name of her first son, but she has manors in Hertfordshire, Berkshire and other counties and owns houses in Canterbury. The abbot has given me the name of the village, and the road to take. If we leave first thing tomorrow, we could be there by early afternoon."

"We don't know if he is going to be there. This could be a waste of our time."

"Do you have a better idea?" Dafydd grinned, "Of course you could stay and become a monk?"

Gwriad swore. "You'd go by yourself?"

"Why not? Teifryn is waiting for me to avenge her death. I won't let her down."

IN THE ASHES OF A DREAM

There was a silence as Gwriad contemplated his brother who seemed to have become a different person in recent weeks. "You know I'll come with you." He finished his wine. "Just the one chance, that's all we need." He yawned, "in the meanwhile I'm going to sleep."

They rose early and, having told the abbot they were going to visit some holy sites and that they would soon be returning, they set off for Sussex. The weather had improved, and the rainstorm of the night before had given way to a cloudless blue sky. "The wind's changed," Gwriad observed as they rode out of London. "I wonder if this will help the Normans?"

Away from the big city, the rural roads were alive with activity. Large wains piled high with hay and straw moved slowly along the dusty lanes pulled by huge cobs and driven by silent men who had no intention of hurrying. Herds of cows and flocks of sheep, controlled by ferocious dogs and limping, bad-tempered churls pushed their way regardless of the inconvenience to travellers.

"It's not like this in Wales," Gwriad quipped. "It gives one a new sense of the agricultural wealth they enjoy, and how poor we are."

"It's all to do with numbers," Dafydd said as he forced his horse through a logjam of confused sheep. "If we had the number of farms, the useable land and the population they have around here, we would be as prosperous. Our problem is that most of our land is poor, and such wealth as we have is more to do with mining and fishing." He shrugged his shoulders, "and we produce good fighting men who, unfortunately, like fighting each other."

Eventually, the road emptied, and they found themselves trotting down a sun-baked track with tall, shadowy trees on each side enabling them to avoid much of the sun's heat. "This is unnaturally quiet," Gwriad remarked as he carefully checked the hedgerows.

As if on cue, three large, grim-faced men in tattered clothes stepped out of the shadows a short way down the road. Two were carrying heavy clubs and the third, who appeared to be the leader, waved a rusty sword. He gave an angry bellow and led a shambling charge towards them.

"Retreat!" Gwriad shouted, pulling hard on his reins and

turning his horse in a fast reverse. "When we have some distance, we'll turn and charge them!" Dafydd grunted his agreement and followed close behind, only just outpacing the desperate outlaws. The leader almost reached Dafydd as his horse gathered speed, and it was only a desperate backwards swing of Dafydd's long sword that caused the ruffian to falter and lose his momentum.

They could hear the yells of frustration as they disappeared around a bend in the road. After a few moments, Gwriad pulled his horse to a halt and waited while Dafydd formed up beside him. The shouting had stopped, and it appeared that the pursuit was over. "Now!" yelled Gwriad and they broke into a gallop, each horse racing to keep up with the other. They turned the bend to find the three outlaws standing in a disorganized group breathing heavily from their unsuccessful sprint. Surprise and hatred crossed their faces as they tried in vain to raise their weapons.

The leader, who was the nearest, was cut down by Gwriad who was upon the luckless ruffian before he could use his battered sword to protect himself. Dafydd's horse rode down one of the club-wielding gang who attempted to unseat him, and the heavy club fell to one side as the man disappeared under the metal hooves, his terrified scream suddenly ending. The remaining outlaw was more successful and was able to knock Gwriad's sword from his grasp with a powerful swing of his heavy club that Gwriad was only able to block. With a cry of pain, Gwriad pulled back on the reins with one hand and, turning the horse, he directed its lethal hooves at the attacker who was preparing for a second blow. The man was unable to avoid the inevitable outcome and fell unconscious to the ground.

"Bloody Hell!" Gwriad sat nursing his damaged wrist and continuing to swear loudly while Dafydd checked the dead and unconscious outlaws. "That shouldn't have happened."

"You did well, brother," Dafydd said gently as he helped him from his saddle. The horse was shaking with terror; its eyes large and fearful and he began to gently rub the animal's neck and muzzle, slowly bringing it to a more passive state. His own horse was also fretful, but as a warhorse it had been trained for such an event and was soon quieted. "Even on horses, a long club can be a dangerous weapon," he remarked. "Well done for taking on two of them!" The jest went unnoticed as Gwriad drank from his flask, lost in his own thoughts.

"I must be getting old, I keep getting hurt," he complained. He staggered over to the unconscious body of the man who had injured him and noticed that although the head was a mask of blood there was still a movement in the chest. The tall man looked skinny and underfed, his thick beard was matted and his skin was caked in grime, as was his rough clothing.

"It might have been better if he had died," Dafydd said. "We can't do anything for him, and even if we could he would be hanged as soon as he was able to stand."

"Are the others dead?"

"Yes." There seemed nothing more to say. He took a shirt from his saddlebag and made a makeshift sling for Gwriad's wrist.

As he tied it, Gwriad suddenly looked up. "We have company," Gwriad muttered. "I think these bodies will be looked after."

Dafydd reached for his sword, but relaxed when he saw a little huddle of women, who were partly hidden behind some bushes, about fifty paces away. Their unwashed faces and tattered clothes indicated that they were related to the would-be robbers.

Without further comment they mounted their horses, and advanced slowly down the road towards the poverty-stricken women. As they passed, they heard sobbing as some of the group mourned their men folk. With autumn fast approaching, their situation would be bleak, and without stopping Dafydd threw a small money purse in their direction, and began to canter down the road. Gwriad remained silent and, as he urged his horse forward, he glanced back to see the women scrabbling for the bag.

It was late afternoon when they finally reached the village of Godwin. It seemed to be more prosperous than many they had passed through, and boasted a large, well-appointed inn called the Red Hen. "It shows how a wealthy landowner affects the local district, especially if there are regular visits by the nobility and their followers. We should find this a comfortable place to stay." Dafydd said, as he dismounted and stretched. "I could do with a hot meal."

Gwriad, who was usually the first to rush to the taproom, remained on his horse; his wrist was throbbing and he was unhappy about the incident. "It's too quiet." He waved to a stable lad and tossed him a coin. "Has the King arrived at Godwin Manor?"

"No, m'Lord. There's been no reports of the King or any of the Court arriving."

"You would always know if the King had arrived?"

"Yes, m'Lord. The Hen is always very busy when the King's followers arrive."

He frowned at Dafydd, "This is a wasted journey." He sounded depressed.

"Not necessarily," Dafydd handed his horse to a stable lad. "We relax tonight and get your wrist properly bandaged. Tomorrow, we'll call on the Lady of Godwin Manor. We are Lords paying a courtesy visit." He seemed in good spirits and stretched his shoulders as he entered the inn.

Gwriad slowly dismounted and made his way wearily towards the front door. "Let's hope the food is good," he yawned. He was losing enthusiasm for their hairbrained scheme, and he wondered how much longer their money would last. "Not long if we give it away to everyone who wants to kill us," he muttered, and kicked open the door.

CHAPTER NINETEEN

In a nunnery in Morgannwg, South Wales, the Prioress was changing the light dressing on the neck of the mysterious woman who had unexpectedly arrived a year before. There was no doubt in her mind that this woman was a Lady of some distinction: her clothes, her jewellery and her behaviour had all indicated this. Over the many months of her recovery she had shown an ability to read and write but seemed to be unable to recollect who she was or why she had such a grievous wound.

"I'm afraid you will never speak again," the Prioress had answered when the Lady had written the question: 'When will I recover?' "God has spared your life, and until you can remember who you are and where you come from, we are happy to have you stay with us."

Gradually, over the months, the wound had healed, to the amazement of the Prioress and her nuns who had never known anyone recover from such a serious wound. In fact, none of them had ever encountered such a savage injury. The original loss of blood had been immense, and for many days her life had seemed to be in the balance, then one day she sat up and began to take liquids by herself and seemed keen to eat the porridge that was thought to be safe for her damaged throat. The next day she had been able to stand, and although very weak, had indicated her need for a bath. The other nuns were amazed at her lack of modesty, but it was soon clear that she was used to being obeyed.

The Prioress, who was known as Ceri, had felt an immediate kinship with the injured woman, as she also was from a noble family that had fallen on hard times. Her mother had placed her in the safety of the Church when she was approaching womanhood, to save her from the dangers that her father's death and the family's sudden poverty had caused. As an attractive young woman, she had become the focus of interest for the dangerous men of a rival family, and her mother had feared for her safety. Ceri had arrived secretly at the convent in the middle of a stormy night and never left the walled grounds until she became a mature woman. From the start she had proved to be a bright and willing young novitiate, who adapted well to the rigours of religious life, and had eagerly embraced the opportunities for learning and art. Her good looks and gentle manner had soon endeared her to the nuns of the convent, and over the years she had taken on various responsibilities, including that of pharmacist and nursing sister. When she was past the age of forty, the elderly Prioress who had run the nunnery since Ceri had first arrived, died unexpectedly, and the nuns, under the direction of the local bishop, held a traditional election for the new abbess, and Ceri had been elected unopposed.

The arrival of the strange Lady had introduced an entirely new phenomenon into the tranquil life of the closed community, and for Ceri the stranger was both a challenge and a welcome companion. It was not unusual for rich women to seek refuge in the nunnery, some for a short while and some for the rest of their lives. However, in most cases the women had been lacking in both education and understanding, and had even lacked the basic skills of life. None had interested the Prioress beyond her concern for both their general welfare and their integration into the religious community. But this woman, whom she had named Elen for want of a better name, was an independent, educated woman who had clearly been an important person in her community, and with whom the abbess had an instant affinity.

"So, Elen, you want to keep this dressing over the scar?"

Elen nodded. In a glass reflection she had seen the terrible damage to her throat and did not want the other nuns to be forever staring at her. She watched Ceri as she quietly tidied up her study, and she wondered for the umpteenth time how she had come to be in this religious house and with such a grievous wound. She had spent hours gazing at her rings and the clothes in which she had arrived and which she no longer wore, but they had failed to trigger her memory. Ceri had suggested that Elen had experienced such an horrific attack that her mind had been shocked into a state of numbness. "Perhaps, when you have had time to allow your mind to recover, you will gradually come to remember who you are."

'I have not forgotten how to read and write,' she had written on her slate. 'Why have I forgotten my former life?'

"There are many things in Heaven and Earth that are beyond our understanding," Ceri said. "When we are ready, God will reveal his wonders."

Elen had soon let it be known that she did not believe in a Christian God and had refused to attend prayers. On occasions, she would sit at the back of the chapel and enjoy the singing but had no interest in listening to readings from the Bible. As she had become stronger, she had revealed a talent for organization and management, and because of her suggestions, there had been improvements in the infirmary and in the lavatorium where the nuns washed themselves in cold water.

The Prioress was convinced that Elen would eventually accept the Christian message and had explained to her that although some wealthy women brought riches to the convent, those with nothing were accepted in return for honest labour and an acceptance of the monastic rule, a chapter of which was read each day in the chapter house. Over the months, as she became more familiar with her environment, Elen became more of a positive influence in the nunnery. She introduced some new approaches to healing and made friends with those nuns who were less popular because they were often disorganized and forgetful, and were, therefore, frequently in trouble for breaking minor rules.

Elen had agreed to wear the simple habit of the nuns and for appearance sake wore the plain, silver cross around her neck. Wherever she went she carried her slate and her chalk, and with the addition of her expressive face and a range of hand signals she was able to hold an understandable conversation with the nuns during the periods when they were allowed to speak.

At harvest time she had applied for permission to work in the fields, and although Ceri had tried to explain that her skills were more suited within the nunnery and that field work was for the less educated, Elen had persisted with such passion that the Prioress had agreed. Her appearance in the fields had increased her reputation for humility, as everyone recognized that she had once been a Lady.

Working in the fields satisfied Elen's increasing need for a physical outlet, and her mind was frequently focused on the sexual desires of her body. Her memory refused to identify her former lover or lovers, but she was certain she had experienced at least one such man, but no matter how much she tried to focus on her past loves, she could never bring a memory to life.

Sometimes, she would sit in the cloister's shade and experiment with different ideas. She would imagine tall men, short men, fat men and any other format, seeing if such a combination would create a person she recognized. Other times she would focus on the large country houses as described by Ceri but nothing helped to stimulate her memory. It was then that she decided that she might like to become a Prioress and be able to devote her life to creating and maintaining a thriving community.

When she approached Ceri for her opinion, the older woman had smiled sadly. "Elen, you can only run a nunnery if you are a devout Christian, and so far you have shown no interest in the Bible or in prayer. You have often told me you don't believe in God, and until you do there can never be any thought of you being trained as a Prioress. Also," she had smiled sadly, "you have to be a nun for at least ten years, be older than 40 and finally, there will be no position for a Prioress in this nunnery until after my death."

Elen had hurriedly bowed her way out of the Prioress's office, her face flushed and her eyes full of tears of embarrassment. She could not believe she had been so thoughtless.

· · ·

IT WAS A COOL MORNING when they approached Godwin Manor, which was set in a large estate with farm houses, barns, tended fields and fenced animals. They had to pass a manned gate that allowed them entry onto a long, straight, tree-lined path that led

IN THE ASHES OF A DREAM

to the impressive home of Elditha Swannuck. A deep trench and a substantial wall surrounded the rambling building with its extensive gardens and lawns; guards patrolled both inside and outside the walls. A single gate allowed entry, and two alert soldiers in smart uniforms manned this.

"This should be interesting," Gwriad remarked as they approached the gate. "Imagine the security if the King were here."

Dafydd explained the purpose of their visit, and after waiting for some time they were allowed to enter after leaving their horses and swords outside the gate. They followed a colourfully-dressed flunky into the house, where they were shown into a homely, wood-panelled room with leaded glass windows and where a bright fire was burning in a cavernous grate. There were woven carpets on the floor, tapestries on the walls and an array of carved chairs and tables. Jugs of flowers gave the air a subtle perfume, and an old hound greeted them and quickly returned to its place in front of the fire. It was a room decorated by a woman who loved comfort and good living.

A servant took their cloaks and hats, and they were shown to chairs on one side of the fire and offered wine. They had just moved their chairs away from the heat of the fire when Elditha Swannuck entered. They stood up and bowed, but neither failed to notice that she was an extremely beautiful woman with a long white neck. She sat down and waved them to their chairs. Two silent guards had followed her in and stood watchfully by the door, their hands on the hilts of their swords.

For an interlude just long enough to cause Gwriad some unease, she stared at them. "Gentlemen, I understand that you have been wanting to see King Harold Godwinson, and had hoped to find him in residence at my house?" She spoke with authority and a certain condescension.

"Yes, my Lady," Dafydd smiled, "we have travelled from the Welsh coast to bring a peace treaty to the King on behalf of all of the Lords of the South and West of Wales." He looked at her unblinking eyes, "I am Lord Dafydd ap Griffith and this is my brother Lord Gwriad ap Griffith."

"But why have you come here?"

"Because we have waited for many days at the Palace in London, hoping for the chance of a short interview with the King, but he has been too busy to see us. It was mentioned that his Majesty might be travelling down to this house, and we decided to make a final effort to present our peace treaty to him before he becomes focused on the problems in Northumbria and the imminent threat of a Norman invasion."

Lady Swannuck did not respond but continued to give each of them a thoughtful stare. She reached for her cup of wine and as she sipped her eyes examined their clothes and their appearance.

Gwriad raised his cup, "Your good health, my Lady."

"Indeed, and yours." She sipped her wine. "I am not unaware of who you are," she glanced towards the guards, who stood to attention. "I know you were both important advisers to King Gruffydd ap Llywelyn." She turned towards Dafydd, "You were his Secretary and Chief Adviser," she stared coldly at Gwriad, "and you were the General of the Central Army." She glared at them, "I know that you were both involved in the attack on my husband's palace near Chester, and that my husband would consider you an enemy." Gwriad shuffled awkwardly, but Dafydd maintained a dignified pose and reached for his wine.

"That is correct, my Lady," Dafydd said in measured terms. "The Welsh have never considered the Saxons to be allies. Your husband, the Earl of Wessex, was responsible for the invasion of North Wales, the destruction of our King's Palace and the defeat of our army, but as you will know, our King's death that followed was at the hands of a rival family in North Wales," he sipped his wine. "It was also your husband who attempted to destroy Caerdydd shortly before he became King." He nodded his head. "We have been enemies for generations and it has not benefitted either country. My brother and I would like to discuss a treaty, which would allow Wales to live in peace, and would enable King Harold to feel secure on his western boundary, while he concentrates his energies on family and Norman threats." Dafydd gave another small bow of his head as he finished his speech. Gwriad tried to keep a straight face as he marvelled at his brother's duplicity.

She regarded Dafydd under her long lashes. "I will pass on your message to my husband," her manner was polite but icy. "I can assure you that he will be unable to meet you at this uncertain time, and I would strongly advise you to hurry back to Wales while you are still able. All foreigners are going to be in danger, no matter how friendly their intentions may appear to be." Her slight stress on the end of her speech left them in no doubt that their attempt at diplomacy had utterly failed.

Lady Swannuck stood up and swept towards the door, without further interaction. "See these men out," she ordered the guards, and disappeared. As they moved towards the door, the guards stood to one side, and followed them out. A servant handed them their cloaks and hats, and they were ushered unceremoniously out of the main door. The two soldiers followed them down to the gate where a number of mounted guards were assembled. They were handed their swords and their horses in silence and were marshalled briskly down to the main entry. As they passed through the gate, it was firmly closed behind them.

"I thought we might be in for a fight as we reached the gate," Gwriad glanced back at the stern faces.

"I think we've been warned. Any further attempt to see the King could prove fatal." Dafydd urged his horse into a trot. "I thought I might be able to win her over, but I had sadly underestimated the Lady."

"Now what?" Gwriad muttered. "I'm ready for home."

"We've no alternative," Dafydd agreed, his previous enthusiasm had faded. "We'll stay one more night at the Monastery of St. Peter and make our way home via the religious houses." He rubbed his eyes. "It seemed such a good idea when we started out."

Gwriad gave a hollow laugh: "Especially as we had no other."

• • •

"We've made good progress," Lord Leofwine surveyed the thousands of Saxon soldiers who marched along the broad valley below the hill that he and the other officers had chosen as their vantage point. It had amazed him how their army had marched all day and part of the night, with only occasional rests, for four days. They all carried heavy shields on their backs and either spears or swords or hand axes. He had felt tired and travelled on a horse, unlike these men who had marched through rough land, across streams and rivers and over hills and into deep valleys. He shook his head in wonder as he watched the light fade behind the distant hills. "We should make contact with the enemy early tomorrow." He looked anxiously at his brother, who sat proudly on his destrier, perhaps the largest warhorse in England.

"There are no troops anywhere as good as our housecarls and many of our thegns have answered the call," King Harold spoke proudly, as if reading his mind. "If our scouts are correct, the invaders will not be expecting us so soon."

"I agree. If I was Tostig, I would imagine you would still be in London trying to muster your housecarls." He paused, delaying the inevitable. He hated giving bad news to his emotional brother.

Harold looked at him curiously. "So, what's the latest news?"

Leofwine took a deep breath. "Our brothers Morcar and Edwin retreated to Jorvik as we expected, but instead of preparing for a siege, they have opened the gates to King Hardrada, and agreed a treaty with him."

"What?" Harold's face became a mask of fury. "Why would they do that?" His former calm and confident attitude was suddenly replaced with a dangerous anger.

"It seems they did not expect us to arrive for a week or two, and the size of the Norwegian army was such that they feared they could not defend the city against an all-out siege." It was not the action that he or Harold would have taken, and he was constantly aware of the weaknesses of many of their large family. He cleared his throat. "They were afraid that if they opposed the Norwegians, then the city would be torched, and the citizens massacred. It appears they opened the gates on a promise that the invading soldiers would not be allowed to loot the city. Our brothers also agreed that the remnants of their Saxon army would disarm, and that hostages and food would be supplied."

Harold swore in a seeming unending volley of oaths, but when eventually he had run out of the murderous things he would do to his younger brothers, Leofwine continued. "The good news is that the Norwegian army has not occupied the city, other than to leave a few soldiers at some key points. The King and Tostig and the bulk of their army have returned to their huge fleet near Riccall to reorganize and arrange for the army to rest after the battle, and to prepare for a march on London in a few days' time."

They are still unaware of our advance?"

"The scouts are convinced the invaders are totally unaware that there is another army close by. After their bloody victory, and the collapse of any opposition, they are confident that time is on their side."

"We will advance on Jorvik this evening and check on the situation with our feeble brothers and prepare to attack the enemy soon after first light." Harold smiled, his moods changing like April weather, "Perhaps Morcar and Edwin have done us a favour. It would have been difficult if we had been forced to attack the walls of Jorvik."

Shortly after dark, Leofwine led a party of officers and soldiers dressed as peasants into the city, where the few Norwegians were overwhelmed, the gates were secured and the Saxon army was deployed to prevent any person from leaving. The two disgraced Earls were lambasted by their elder brother, which was an experience they had suffered many times in their younger days, and the bulk of the tired army was allowed to rest and prepare for the promised battle in the morning.

"Have you sent them the supplies and the hostages?" Harold demanded.

Morcar, the Earl of Northumbria, shook his head. He was a surly, unhappy man, who suffered from stomach problems and had always envied and disliked his elder brother. "We were sending them tomorrow. That was the agreement," he muttered.

"Are those the supply wagons that are parked below?" Leofwine was staring from the meeting hall down at the congested square. Dozens of oxen carts and horse drawn wagons were lined in rows while soldiers kept guard.

"Yes, your timing was perfect," Edwin, Earl of Mercia, made it sound like a joke. He had always been an optimistic man, with a likeable personality, but as a Lord he had never managed to convey the authority that was a necessity for a noble: he had been unable to take a ruthless stand against those who challenged him, and had frequently relied on his older brothers to rescue him. When Harold had appointed Edwin as an Earl, it was in the hope that he would eventually grow into the job, and by appointing Morcar at the same time Harold had calculated that the two would be able to control the North by relying on each other.

"Where are the hostages?" Harold growled.

"We have them locked up." Morcar grimaced, clutched his stomach and reached for a cup of wine.

"They are the sons of important Jorvik families," Edwin explained. He seemed uncomfortable. "They weren't happy, and their families are threatening an insurrection."

"Well of course they weren't happy!" Harold thundered. "Hostages are never happy!" He turned away and poured himself more wine. "Tomorrow, we will send to King Hardrada and our disloyal brother the wagons and the hostages, and then we will destroy the invaders!"

• • •

AT FIRST LIGHT, THE SUPPLY wagons left the city and made for an area near the Derwent River, where the bulk of the invading army was resting. It was low, flat country that flooded in winter but was a wide suitable camping ground in summer. It was bordered by low hills and provided easy access to water, and firewood. Hidden in the covered wagons were heavily-armed Saxons, and the hostages who marched under what appeared to be a heavy guard were wearing swords and axes under their cloaks. As they approached the large encampment, Harold's housecarls were advancing from two directions and were undetected until they suddenly raced down the nearby hills, catching the Norwegians completely off-guard.

Following the bloody battle at Fulford, many of the Norwegian soldiers had been allowed to leave their heavy armour with their huge fleet anchored an hour away in the River Ouse, and until waves of screaming Saxons burst into their extended camp, there had been a sense of well-being and the satisfaction of victory. It had not been officially calculated how many of their 10,000-plus army had been killed or injured in the fierce Fulford fighting, but it had been unexpectedly high, and King Hardrada had sent many of the injured to the boats to seek rest and treatment and ordered those who had not been involved in the fighting to come ashore. At the time of the early morning attack the sentries were coming to the end of their watch, and many were half-asleep.

The initial attack succeeded in causing chaos among the edges of the camp, but soon the Norwegians were able to reorganize and formed a powerful shield wall, which blunted the Saxon advance and forced them to retreat. Both sides then advanced their shield walls, while the Jorvik hostages and those Saxons hidden in the wagons attacked the feeding and organizational tents in the camp. As the battle developed, the lack of heavy armour among many in the Norwegian shield wall became a major weakness in their formation, allowing the Saxons to force breaches in the wall, and exploit these to their advantage.

A shield wall consists of many lines of armoured men whose shields are locked together yet allow those behind to use their spears against the enemy. It is almost unbreakable. Once it starts to advance it is usually unstoppable. However, it relies on the strength of the men in the front line, and the skill of the spearmen behind, and once the opposition's spears can find weaknesses in the armour, the line begins to falter. As men fall, others take their place, but this has to be accomplished without allowing the breach to be widened. In the Norwegian ranks, men without heavy armour moved into important parts of a faltering line, and a sudden collapse was threatened.

When the Saxon forces appeared to be demolishing the Norwegian wall and it seemed only moments away from a slaughter, and when the bodies of the dead and injured had become a major problem to both sides, the invading forces were unexpectedly reinforced by the those who had earlier returned to their ships. This large influx of fresh soldiers could have been catastrophic for the Saxons, but luckily for them, the majority of these men were either injured soldiers from the previous battle, or were sailors who had manned the ships. The first were determined but not fully able to fight, while the sailors were brave but wore no armour and carried only the weapons that others had discarded. Although not the best of fighting men, they were fresh and, therefore, were more than a match for the Saxon housecarls who had marched for four days and had been locked in a deadly shield wall for more than an hour.

Harold was easily recognized as he was taller than most and fought with a fearless aggression that encouraged his housecarls and caused terror in the enemy ranks. He had felt confident that his men were gaining the upper hand, and that his shield wall was holding, when he was aware of a change in the battle. The enemy's wall had become miraculously stronger, and the Saxons around him were starting to give ground. "Hold!" he yelled, "Hold!" Yet, he could not stop the gradual slipping and staggering that was infecting the whole line. The corpses of Saxons and Norwegians became entangled with the legs of hundreds of his army as they were slowly pushed back. His men were losing their balance and were being cut down when their shields were lowered, and it was clear that the fighting was moving to a new phase.

At this critical juncture in the battle, Harold gave the order for Leofwine to commit the reserves. This was a chosen group of experienced soldiers under the command of his most trusted brother. They had been ordered to be ready but not to become involved until their King gave the command. These heavily armoured soldiers, who were eager to fight, burst into the exhausted ranks, reversing the momentum of their shield wall and causing the final collapse of the invaders' army. The Norwegians knew that as long as they could bind their shields together and keep the unity of the line they were safe, but once a major breach was caused then a massacre was inevitable. Men died or were injured, and many were trampled underfoot as the Norwegian shield wall was abruptly forced backwards, and soon the fighters were standing on the bodies of friends and enemies in a tight, restricted area that had become a literal blood bath. When the Norwegian collapse finally happened, the Saxons swept into the breach and uncontrolled butchery occurred. Soon, the central conflict ended with only a remnant of the proud Norwegians able to fight their way back to their ships in some military order.

IN THE ASHES OF A DREAM

"They're defeated, utterly defeated!" Harold yelled and those nearest cheered. "Let the survivors limp home. The victory is ours! We have killed King Hardrada and the traitor Earl Tostig!" The good news spread fast but did not lessen the final bloodletting as the Saxons wreaked their revenge on isolated enemy soldiers and the injured that lay in great numbers around the battlefield. For some, this was the time to steal from the hundreds of dead and dying, but for others it was a time to celebrate and search for their friends.

What Harold did not reveal was that the remnant of the Norwegian army was retreating as a small but determined force, still capable of killing more Saxons; soldiers that he knew he could not afford to lose. "Without their leaders they have no purpose! Let them escape in their ships. We have won a great victory!" he yelled at Leofwine. His rock of a brother had sustained a minor injury to his sword arm as he had led the reserves to prop up the right wing of the Saxon shield wall. He had continued to direct the rest of the Saxons reserves as they broke through the enemy formation. "You did well, brother. That was a perfectly timed action and turned the battle into a total victory for us."

Leofwine nodded his head. He had achieved his aim and was satisfied. As Harold gave personal congratulations to his officers and men, Leofwine arranged for their injured soldiers to be conveyed back to Jorvik in the so-called supply wagons that had been an important element of their surprise attack.

Harold left the battlefield in good spirits, and returned to Jorvik, where the news of the victory had already reached the townsfolk. The walls were lined with cheering people, who only a day before had faced the prospect of being under the iron rule of the Norwegians whom they called Vikings. Many of the surviving officers rode or marched with him, as did his personal housecarls, most of whom were exhausted, yet determined to enjoy the hero worship that they felt they deserved.

In the central square, Harold spoke briefly, and praised the courage and determination of his army to wild cheering, and once the celebrations were well under way, Harold and Leofwine left for the quiet of their rich quarters, which their brothers had previously allocated to them, albeit under pressure.

When servants removed the King's armour, it slipped off like an outer skin, heavy and sweat-impregnated. He washed his face, donned a clean tunic and on a whim placed his circlet of gold, his favourite crown, on his head. It was a symbolic gesture, even though he did not intend to make another public speech. At last he felt like a King: he had defended his right to rule and the Saxons were with him. Action was what he craved, and victory was what he expected, although his abortive raid on Caerdydd still wrangled with him. In the main room, Leofwine had poured wine for both of them and Harold drank deeply, feeling an unusual weariness come over him. He sank into a chair and reflected on his aches and stiffness. "I must be getting old," he murmured.

"You've seen 44 years, brother," Leofwine laughed. He was still wearing most of his armour, as the desire for a drink had overcome other needs. "You have a right to feel tired. I know I do, and I'm two years younger."

They drank their wine in silence, each reflecting on different moments of the day. "What happened to Morcar and Edwin? I didn't see them on the battlefield, or their soldiers." Harold slowly relieved the stiffness in his neck.

Leofwine shrugged his powerful shoulders, and gently rubbed his bruised arm. "They didn't arrive. A good job we didn't depend on them."

There was an immediate tension in the room. "Sergeant!" Harold jumped to his feet and began to pace the room, as a soldier of his personal guard hurried through the door. "Find the Earls Morcar and Edwin and bring them to me now! Take a full patrol with you and bring them under arrest if necessary!"

"Couldn't it wait until tomorrow?" Leofwine yawned. "They won't be going anywhere."

Harold drained his wine and continued to move abruptly around the room. He did not reply. Before long, there was the sound of marching feet, and both brothers were man-handled into the room by soldiers with drawn swords. The two Earls looked terrified.

"Leave us!" Harold's face was a mask of fury and the soldiers withdrew quickly. "On your knees!" Morcar looked as if he would refuse, and Harold, who was a much bigger man, grabbed his neck and forced him down. Edwin fell to his knees immediately and stared at the floor.

"Are you my brothers? Are you members of the Godwinson family?" he roared. "Today, I had to kill one traitor in my family! Am I forced to execute two more for treachery?"

"Brother, it was…" Edwin began.

"I'm your King! You're no longer brothers of mine!" He was so consumed with anger that it seemed he might assault them. "Neither of you left this city while Leofwine and I fought for our lives in order to save you two worms from Norwegian rule. You didn't even send your much-needed soldiers!"

"On our honour, we could do nothing else!" Morcar protested. "We'd given our word, with our hands on the Bible, that we would no longer oppose King Hardrada, and would use our troops only to maintain order within the city."

"I sent you direct orders this morning as to what your roles would be in the battle!" Harold roared. "You did not say then that you would refuse to leave the city. It seems you would have been better off if I, your King and brother, had lost the battle, then my enemies would have rewarded you. But Leofwine and I have utterly defeated them, and you will no longer be Earls. I have yet to decide whether to have you publicly hanged as traitors!"

"We could do nothing else!" Edwin wailed. "We did what we thought best for the people of Jorvik. When we agreed a truce, we had no hope that you would arrive here so soon." His voice choked. "I'm not a traitor, I had given my sworn oath on the Bible. I prayed for your victory! Truly, I did."

Harold stood before the two cringing men barely able to control his desire to beat them to a pulp. "Get out," he turned away from them, shaking with anger, "before I kill you with my bare hands!" He flung open the door, "Take these men away and lock them up," he ordered, "and keep them under heavy guard."

When the room emptied Leofwine refilled their cups. He said

nothing, waiting for the fury to leave Harold's face. After a long silence, he raised his cup. "To victory and a long reign."

Harold slowly refocused. "To victory." He was gradually realizing how tired he was.

"Let them stew in a jail for a night," Leofwine finished his wine. "Tomorrow, you will be able to judge them with a clear mind."

"Perhaps I should leave them in jail for the rest of their miserable lives," Harold grumbled. He refilled his cup and unfolded his huge body into a chair. He drank deeply, closed his eyes and was soon unaware that he had dropped his half empty cup.

Leofwine smiled, he drank another cup and gradually fell into a deep sleep. In a jail below the building the two former Earls were wide-awake.

. . .

LOMBARD STREET WAS THE RECOGNIZED area of London for those who wanted to borrow money or use a rudimentary banking system that enabled merchants to avoid travelling with too much gold and silver. Like most of the thoroughfares in the overcrowded city it was a narrow, evil smelling street, but with one important difference: armed guards stood outside the heavily-fortified buildings, and each reinforced door bore the name of the particular business.

"Is this the place?" Gwriad muttered. He was still unused to this type of density of housing, and the idea that the whole street was concerned with one type of transaction seemed bizarre.

"Where's the house of Isaac Goldman?" Dafydd demanded of a guard trying to keep the Welsh accent out of his speech.

The guard pointed further down the lane. "The big house, with the steps outside, m'Lord."

Gwriad acknowledged the man, but Dafydd stared ahead as they rode slowly down the dim and humid street. "We're Lords, Gwriad," he hissed. "Do not show any sign of friendship, they will see it as weakness and in the present time all foreigners are enemies."

"Let's get this over with." He hated his younger brother treating him like a halfwit, but as he looked at the faces of the guards, he knew his brother was right. It might only take one of these bored soldiers to yell "Welsh spies!" and they would soon be overwhelmed. It was only their horses, their clothes and their Lordly disdain that kept them safe. Gwriad frowned at a guard that stared at him, and the man quickly looked away.

They stopped outside a big building with steps; a rare feature in this street of unattractive houses. Two guards with dark complexions came to hold their horses as they dismounted, and Dafydd did the speaking. "Is Isaac Goldman at home?"

"Who shall I say it is, m'Lord?"

"Lord Wirt and Lord Modig," Dafydd said tersely, taking a perverse satisfaction in using the names of two of the Saxon Lords who had died in the attack on King Gruffydd's palace.

They were shown into a large room with metal bars on the windows. The immediate impression of a jail was softened by a collection of comfortable chairs around a small unlit fireplace with a single long table on which were a collection of quills, inks, sealing wax and a thick candle with a pleasant aroma, and a delicate weighing machine. In one wall was a small barred window behind which they could see the face of an elderly bearded man, who regarded them with some suspicion.

"My Lords, what can I do for you?" The man had an obvious foreign accent, and it was of interest to the brothers that he appeared safe enough in the city to hire his own guards, perhaps members of his family.

"I was given your name as a man who would treat us fairly if we wanted to sell our gold jewellery."

"Indeed, my Lords, and who was this gentleman?" There was a slight emphasis on the last word.

"Lord Aethelstan," Dafydd said with a sharpness in his tone.

"And how, my Lord, do you know Lord Aethelstan?"

"I have come to know him over a number of weeks during my business at the Palace."

"Ah," the man nodded thoughtfully. "Show me what you want to sell."

Dafydd was annoyed with the man's brusqueness but decided to ignore it. He nodded to Gwriad who removed a bag from inside his jerkin and placed the contents into a recess in the wooden shelf that stretched both sides of the iron grill. Isaac carefully studied the assortment of gold rings and a gold necklace.

"Family items," he murmured.

"They belonged to our wives," Gwriad voice betrayed him.

Isaac studied Gwriad and after a moment scooped up the items, unlocked a door and entered into the room. "I am satisfied that these are genuine, and I am prepared to do business with you, my Lords." He sat down at the table, and carefully weighed the gold items. "Do you want silver or gold coins?"

"Mostly silver, some gold," Dafydd said. It was what they had agreed.

"Please wait here," he old man said, taking the gold with him. They heard the turning of the lock after he went through the door.

"A trusting fellow," Gwriad quipped.

"Those guards outside indicate that he must live in constant danger." Dafydd examined the weighing machine. "What a fine instrument."

After a short wait, they heard the lock click back and Isaac entered with two small bags, which he emptied on the table and counted gold and silver coins into piles with a practiced skill.

"Are we agreed, my Lords?"

Both brothers nodded, and Gwriad stood up and offered Isaac his hand. "We thank you for being honest."

Isaac stood up. "Thank you, my Lord, but I cannot shake the hand of a Christian."

Dafydd looked outraged, but Gwriad laughed. "You can still shake my hand because we're not Christians."

Isaac seemed confused. "I know you're Welsh, my Lord, but is not Wales a Christian country?"

The fact that they had not convinced Isaac that they were Saxon lords was not lost on Dafydd who wondered if the old man had sent out for help when he was out of the room.

No such worry seemed to concern Gwriad. "We were raised by an uncle who had no time for religion, and if we have any leanings, it would be to the early pagan beliefs of the Druids." He laughed, "Like you we have to take care for our safety." He held out his

IN THE ASHES OF A DREAM

hand. "So, there is no reason why we cannot shake hands on this deal, and part friends."

Isaac looked hard at Gwriad. "You know I'm a Jew?"

Dafydd nodded, but Gwriad merely shrugged. "I don't mind if you're a Turk, you and I meet in your house as friends."

Isaac appeared quite bewildered, and as though in a trance slowly extended his hand which Gwriad grasped in a firm handshake.

"Will you report our visit?" Dafydd asked, not offering his hand.

"No. Why should I, my Lord? We are all suspects in an alien society." He indicated that they should sit, and he rang a small bell and sat opposite them. A young woman with long, black hair entered and exchanged a brief conversation with Isaac in a language the brothers did not recognize.

Once he had decided to accept them, Isaac proved to be an interesting host, and enquired as to the reason for them being in London at such an uncertain time. Dafydd kept up their original pretext of a peace treaty and explained how they had spent a fruitless time waiting to see the King. "It was how I came to make friends with Lord Aethelstan," Dafydd said.

Isaac made no comment as he nodded to the girl to set down a tray of exquisite glasses and a flask of wine. After she left, he handed each man a glass of red wine that had a rich bouquet the brothers had never experienced. "You are the first people outside my race that I have ever drank wine with." His austere face gradually changed into a warm smile. "May you be successful in whatever you wish to achieve." They all raised their glasses and reflected on the quality of the wine.

"We have wasted our time and our money trying to arrange an interview with the King, and finally we travelled to the home of Lady Elditha Swannuck in Sussex, in the hope that the King might visit her before he travelled northward," Gwriad added. "But now, with your help, we will leave London and go back to our lands on the Welsh coast."

"You may not have heard, my Lords, but King Harold has won a great victory in a battle near Jorvik, killing his rebellious brother Tostig and the Norwegian King. I understand that only a small fraction of the Viking forces escaped, and that most of their fleet was set alight before they sailed home."

Dafydd's jaw dropped, "When did this happen?"

"Three days ago, on the 25th of September."

"You are well informed, Sir," Gwriad smiled in open admiration. "Do others in this big city know?"

"I doubt it, my Lord, but it will be common news in a day or two. I mention this, because when the King returns he might be more willing to talk peace with you, and this might be a reason for you to delay your return to Wales."

They finished their wine, accepted the money and with respectful bows on both sides, left Isaac's house in a thoughtful mood.

"What do you think, brother?" Gwriad muttered after they had left Lombard Street. "Is it worth waiting for the bastard to return, in the faint hope he'll see us, or should we turn for home? I don't know about you, but I'm mightily sick of this place, with the exception of Isaac."

Dafydd was still meditating on the fact that if it had not been for Gwriad's open-handed approach to Isaac, their visit would have remained a strictly business affair with a mutual distrust on both sides. "I wonder how long Harold will remain up north?" He pursed his lips. "How about staying for a short while longer and see how things develop?"

Gwriad exhaled loudly. "Oh, all right. But only as long as you don't go giving our limited money away to people who don't like us, and only as long as we leave before we have to part with any more of the family possessions." He scowled, "Not that we have anything left, anyway."

"We'll return to the Monastery of Saint Peter. The abbot will be happy to see our money, especially as we know something he doesn't." Dafydd tried to put a positive note in his voice. He was equally concerned with their precarious situation, yet still unwilling to give up when there was a gleam of hope.

CHAPTER TWENTY

It was later the next day, on the 29th of September, that word reached London that Duke William of Normandy had landed his army near a small village called Pevensey on the south coast in Sussex on the 28th. The long wait was over.

"What does this mean?" Gwriad asked, looking both ways in case anyone was listening. They were drinking ale outside a quiet, run-down tavern on the south bank of the Thames. Inside, a few locals were in an excited state and making brave threats about what they would do to foreigners. It was not a good time to be accused of being a Welsh spy.

"Well, Harold won't hear of this invasion for about another three days," Dafydd meticulously cleaned his nails with his dagger. He did not share his brother's excitement. "It will be at least another week before he can march his army back to London. In the meantime, I imagine William will be wanting to defend his landing area and get as many of his troops over before the weather changes. He won't know that Tostig and the Norwegians have been defeated, nor will he know that Harold is not in London."

"Do you think the Normans will attack London?"

"I doubt it. If I were William I would be trying to consolidate my forces. You need a lot of troops to attack a big city, and this city is not his next problem, Harold's army is, and until the big battle is over, the capture of the city will not be his priority."

Gwriad nodded and kept silent. He had always thought he was the military mind in the family, but sometimes he had to agree with Dafydd, and on those rare occasions, he suspected his brother's reading of history gave him a broader view of strategy.

"What I suggest is that we stay at the Monastery and see what develops. It's possible that William might beat him in battle, in which case he will have done us a favour."

"So why are we waiting? Let's go home," Gwriad finished his ale and looked despondently into the empty mug. "We can always hear the good news when we're back at Aberteifi."

"We came here to kill Harold. We have spent a lot of money and had some difficult times. I want to wait to see what happens." Dafydd looked defiantly at his brother. "It occurred to me that if Harold wins, he would almost certainly seek the warm arms of his mistress Elditha Swannuck. We know the place, and after a battle, things will be disorganized. I feel certain we could find our way into the manor."

Gwriad stared in amazement. "Does it occur to you that the area might be very dangerous, no matter who wins?" He stood up with the intention of fetching them some more ale. "Just being in that area will cast doubt on any reason we choose to give. Not many pilgrims will be travelling those roads unless they want a fast passage to their maker."

He was about to expand on his joke about pilgrims when a party of five armed men trotted up, dismounted and, having quickly tethered their horses to a rail, marched silently into the tavern. The last one, a tall ruffian with a thick red beard, was waiting to enter and glanced in their direction. He came to an abrupt halt and gave them a long curious look. His hostile gaze took in their hair, their short beards and their travel-worn clothing. Dafydd casually replaced his dagger and pretended to take a relaxed posture on the bench. Gwriad, having glanced at him, nodded his head and drank from his empty mug. The man continued to glower at them, but as one of his party was holding the door for him, he followed them in, looking highly discontented.

Dafydd was immediately on his feet. "Let's go! They'll be back."

"He could tell we weren't Saxons, and it worried him," Gwriad agreed and led the way to their own horses. As Dafydd was mounting, Gwriad directed his mount over to where the men's five horses were loosely tethered. He jumped down, untied each one, and then sprang back into his saddle. The horses seemed unsure of their freedom and just stood shaking their heads until

IN THE ASHES OF A DREAM

he reached over and slapped their rumps, yelling at the top of his voice.

At that moment the tavern door burst open and the five soldiers surged out carrying their mugs of ale. The excitement on their faces as they looked forward to a drawn out and violent interrogation, changed to outrage when they saw their horses being stolen and the strangers escaping. They dropped their mugs, pausing only to arm themselves, and raced across the uneven yard, but by the time they reached the road their horses were galloping off into the distance, and the two strangers were beyond capture.

"Keep chasing their horses!" Gwriad yelled as he urged his stallion into a gallop and they quickly increased the distance between themselves and the angry, yelling Saxons. Eventually, the loose horses scattered, and the brothers slowed their animals to a walk. "That was too close for comfort. If they had decided to come straight out of the tavern instead of getting their drinks first, we would have been fighting for our lives. We don't look like Saxons!" Gwriad protested. "It didn't matter when pilgrims were everywhere, but now that everyone knows that the Normans have landed, they're in a state of panic and want to hang a few foreigners. Many don't know that Harold has won a victory up north, most don't know he's not still in London!"

"So, what are you suggesting?"

"We can't stay here any longer. We must leave first thing tomorrow."

Dafydd frowned and said nothing; he still wanted to confront Harold. However, his attitude altered when their ringing of the bell at the locked gate of the monastery was not answered. After a long wait, Father Alexander the Abbott and brother Paul, the deaf-mute monk, came to the gate. The abbot did not welcome them: "My Lords, before I let you in I must insist that this will be the last night you stay here."

"What's wrong?" Dafydd asked. He had a sinking feeling.

"There is nothing wrong, my Lord. But, this is not an inn. We offer people like yourselves the opportunity to stay a short while when they are involved with religious activities. I think you must agree that your religious research and your visits to the holy shrines are over." He turned away and indicated to the deaf-mute brother to open the gate.

"Well, that decides it." Gwriad was checking his weapons and had begun to test the sharpness of his sword. He looked around their bare cell. "This place was useful, but our time in London is over. You do agree?"

"Yes, I agree," Dafydd said despondently; he felt like a punctured bladder, all his energy had faded. "But what is the safest route? This is a confused time, and people act as though every stranger is an enemy."

"Do we have a choice? We have to go back the way we came. The religious houses provide the safest accommodation, and we know what to expect at each stop."

"If they'll take us in," Dafydd said slowly. "I don't believe the abbot's reason for getting rid of us. He's too fond of the money we've been providing. I think the religious houses may have been ordered to close their doors to anyone who could be a problem to the next King, whoever that may be. The Church is hoping that William will become King, the Pope has made that very clear, and the bishops do not want their religious houses being seen to support the wrong side."

Gwriad gave a hollow laugh. "Well, that puts us in a fine pickle. We'll have to trust to the doubtful safety of the inns."

"We could go back a different way."

"Oh yes, of course, we could sprout wings and fly!"

"We could travel by water."

Gwriad was about to make another sarcastic comment, when he realized what his brother had in mind. "You mean the way Davis and Lleu travelled from Dover?"

"Indeed. Can you think of another way?"

"Well, I don't know, it sounded like a good idea in the summer, but now the nights are closing in and the bad weather is about to start, I wonder if sea travel is safe? Also, with the invasion under way, will merchant ships dare to travel south-west from Dover?"

Dafydd nodded. "Good points, but we should find out for ourselves. The alternative sounds worse. If we leave first light tomorrow, we should be in Dover before the end of the day. If there are no ships going west or the weather is bad, we'll have to think of another way."

"And don't forget that there's an invasion just down the coast."

"Alright! You choose, then," Dafydd was slowly losing his usual calm composure.

After a pause, Gwriad stood up and patted his brother on his back. "No, you're right, let's go to Dover, and see if we can bribe a captain to take us west. We have nothing to lose."

• • •

AFTER HER FLEETING THOUGHTS OF being a Prioress had been so abruptly terminated, Elen lost her enthusiasm for becoming a nun. For a brief moment she had considered working towards the leadership of the closed community and had been willing, to that end, to pretend that she had gained religious convictions. But when there seemed to be no chance of achieving this, she became depressed. No longer did she think how lucky she was to be alive, but her mind focused on the repetitive boredom of the life she was now forced to lead. Although she could not remember a better life, she became very discontented with her present situation.

She no longer accepted the monastic rules as being sensible and necessary, but began to rebel against their guiding instructions, seeing them as petty and the punishments as vindictive. She would deliberately avoid the chapel gatherings to which she was expected to attend, and would mislay her slate and chalk, thereby reducing communication with senior nuns. She did only those tasks that she considered useful and refused to accept punishment from the cohort of elderly nuns who expected to be obeyed.

The Prioress asked her three most senior nuns to her office to discuss the unusual problem that Sister Elen had become. It was not unusual to have girls from poor or dysfunctional homes having a problem settling in, and punishments from caning to hard labour were normal in the early months to teach them how to behave. Often women who had been rejected by wealthy suitors, or rich women who wanted a safe life away from violent men, would be slow to realize that they had embraced a very different life to the one they had been used to. Most of them adjusted with only minor punishments on the way; some left before a year was up, and a few came to embrace the monastic life with an enthusiasm that marked them out for future responsibility.

"You will have to punish her, Holy Mother," said Sister Megan, the cellarer. "She sends silly messages to the younger nuns during silent periods."

Sister Neta, the sacrist agreed: "She has become a nuisance, Holy Mother. She pretends not to understand what we say and is causing upset among the younger nuns."

"And especially among the older sisters," Sister Joan said solemnly. As Almoner, she was always highly regarded, although whether she was serious in her comment about Elen was unclear, as it was known that she had formed a warm friendship with her.

The Prioress stared down at her hands. She was well aware of the recent change in Elen and the reason for it, and had reluctantly come to realize that this unusual woman was unsuited to the rigid life of the nunnery. It was clear that Elen needed a challenge that was not spiritual, but Ceri wondered how Elen would manage if she was released into the outside world. "What do you suggest?"

"She must be severely punished!" the cellarer erupted, her spittle spraying on the floor. "Sister Elen has been allowed far too much freedom. The young nuns notice these things."

"I think she should be made to take her meals by herself, and for a few days she should be given only bread and water," the sacrist pronounced in her deep voice.

"I think she is going through a crisis," the almoner said, studiously avoiding the outraged looks of the other two older nuns. "I think she has suffered more than we can imagine. It is bad enough to lose one's ability to speak and to be horribly mutilated, but to lose one's memory must be devastating. There is the loss of one's former life: not knowing if you have loved ones; not having any recall of bonds you may have created or achievements you may have perfected. I think she does not need punishing, but rather she should be given some chance to be responsible for something. She is clearly a bright woman, who has probably been in a position of power and authority, and though she might not remember the details, her instincts are to oppose the restrictions and petty rules that our nunnery lives by."

"Petty rules!" the sacrist protested. 'We are living together in religious harmony...."

The almoner smiled, "Religious harmony? Then why do we need punishments?"

"We live in religious harmony!" the sacrist thundered. "God demands high standards of us in our behaviour and our worship. We only get a clear understanding of what it means to be a Christian woman as we get older. Sister Elen has a lot to learn if she is to stay here, and she must be punished to force her to conform."

"Sisters," the Prioress said gently, her voice barely audible. "I thank you for your different views and advice, and I will now think on what you have said, and with God's help I will make a decision."

After the senior nuns had left, the Prioress knelt down on a cushion before an image of the Virgin Mary and Child and prayed for guidance. She would often kneel for long periods intending to pray but frequently finding herself in a state of meditation from which she would emerge feeling refreshed and ready to take on the constantly changing issues involved in the running of the priory. Her fingers had no sooner started to move along her rosary, when there was a soft, but insistent, tapping on her door. Sister Rhiannon, the only nun allowed to enter her office when she was at prayer, stood silently by the open door.

"Yes?"

"Holy Mother, the Bishop is here."

The Prioress continued in a position of prayer, while her mind raced. What was the Bishop doing here? He rarely visited her lonely priory, and only after some arrangements had been made for him to see the records of the income and expenditure, and the nuns had had time to prepare for his inspection. It was a time when recently-approved nuns would be given the blessing of the Church, and the Bishop would conduct a ceremony where they were officially married to Christ and could wear a ring to indicate their status. But all of this involved planning and enormous preparation, and none of this had happened. She stood up and led the way to the courtyard, where the Bishop, two monks and a handful of soldiers were sitting on restless horses. The sweating animals indicated the Bishop had been in a hurry, for the weather was cool and damp.

The Bishop held out his left hand with its thick gold ring with a large ruby. The Prioress kissed the ring and stepped back. "Welcome, Lord Bishop."

"You seem in good health, Ceri," his informality was based on gender inequality rather than friendship. He dismounted and indicated that the monks should do the same, as nuns led the horses off to be watered at a stone trough. The soldiers were ordered to stay on their horses.

"We don't want them chasing the nuns!" he joked as he followed Ceri towards her office. He was a tall man, past middle age with greying hair and a recent increase in weight. When Ceri had first met him, he had been thin and birdlike, but over the years had become ponderous and was showing the effects of constant good living. His large hooked nose was contoured with red veins, as were his cheeks, but his bright, alert eyes missed nothing.

Ceri had indicated for Sister Rhiannon to bring wine, and it was already waiting when the Prioress led the way into her office. "Wine, Lord Bishop?"

"Of course," he gave her an appraising look as he sank into a chair. "I imagine you're wondering why I'm here, Ceri?" He finished the glass and held it out to be refilled.

"Indeed, Lord Bishop." She leaned over and refilled his glass, keeping as far away from him as possible.

He sniffed. "I was passing, on my way to Caerdydd, and I remembered you had some new candidates." He smirked, "I thought I would see how the novices are settling in."

"As you would expect, Lord Bishop, the nuns are at Sext None, followed by their midday meal." Ceri had to force herself to be polite, as the Bishop was all-powerful. He could send her away to a large convent outside the area, reduce her to an entry nun and even have her freedom restricted. Her mind went back to her early days in the priory when other young nuns had revealed the inspection he performed with most young women. He had a reputation as a groper, who would insist on them removing their clothes purportedly so he could ensure that they did not have any rashes or other problems. He claimed it was his duty to closely examine their naked bodies in order to make them ready for Christ. Those young women who came from poor families were subjected to a further outrage: he would say that he had to investigate whether they were virgins; some confessed that they were not, but that did not prevent him subjecting them to a protracted investigation, when they were aware of him breathing heavily and suddenly losing interest.

Ceri had been warned of his practices, and when her time came, she pretended to be a virgin, although she had experienced a vigorous sexual life with a local landowner, who would have been considered to be below the expectations of her father. After his sudden death, and in a paroxysm of fear, bereavement and a mother's knowledge of the promiscuity of her daughter, Ceri had been placed in the care of the Priory where she had made a life for herself. Her strong personality had cooled the Bishop's ardour, and ever since he had held her in some awe.

"I noticed there was a novice who was not at the service?" he said in a vaguely disinterested manner.

"Yes, that is Sister Elen who is no longer able to speak. She is the one I wrote to you about."

"I don't remember. What is her reason for being here?"

"She remembers nothing of her earlier life. She has no idea how she was so grievously injured, nor where she lived or what her real name is. But, she is obviously a woman of distinction, who wore quality clothes and possessed expensive rings."

"Where are the rings?"

Ceri took a deep breath. "They are in my safe keeping."

The Bishop held out his glass for a refill. "Good," he murmured, although his expression conveyed displeasure. "I think it is time I got to know her, to ensure that she is a suitable novice." He leered at Ceri. "I will use this office. Send her to me."

Ceri left her office, almost overwhelmed with anger. She knew that nothing more than gross humiliation would happen to Elen and that she would soon recover from the embarrassment, but as a true Christian the Prioress was appalled at the lack of moral leadership that was being exemplified by the corrupt Bishop.

She found Sister Elen in the library and explained that the Bishop wanted to meet her. "I must warn you…" she placed her hand to her mouth, unable to continue. Sister Ellen stood up and placed her arm protectively around the Prioress, who had always treated her well. She steered the older woman to a seat, and sat opposite her, waiting for her to continue.

After a moment, the Prioress regained her composure. "I'm sorry to say that our Bishop is a perverted human being. He will subject you to an embarrassing inspection of your body." She took a deep breath. "He has ultimate power. He can exclude you from this priory and he can demote me as Prioress if he sees fit. Every young or good-looking woman in this priory has had to suffer his unwanted attentions." She looked into Sister Elen's unwavering eyes. "I wanted to prepare you and explain why I can't stop him." She stood up, "Follow me."

When Sister Elen entered the Prioress's office, the Bishop was pacing about like a caged animal. He held out his left hand for her to kiss his ring, but instead of obeying, she stared at him with such anger that he pretended she had obeyed. "As your Bishop, I have to examine you to make sure that you are worthy to become a nun." He turned away, and waved his hand as though giving seeds to birds. "Take off your clothes."

When he turned back, Sister Elen was standing facing him, fully clothed.

"I said take off your clothes! I am your Bishop. You will obey me!

The Bishop was not entirely clear as to what had happened next. He remembered he had just given his ultimatum when the nun had hit him. Her blow had knocked his head with such power that he had fallen to the ground, and as he lay there she had raised his tunic, and having laughed derisively, in a way that he still bitterly recalled, had kicked him hard in his groin. As he lay groaning in pain, she had stamped on his ample belly and spat in his face.

The Prioress had witnessed Sister Elen storming out of

her office, and on entering had found the Bishop exposed and groaning on the floor. As he slowly recovered, his anger and outrage increased. He threatened to have Sister Elen publicly whipped and ejected from the priory. "By attacking me, she has attacked the Holy Mother Church. I will have the soldiers take her away in chains!"

After a second glass of wine, he began to regain his equilibrium but remained adamant that Sister Elen would be banished from the priory. It had not escaped him that the soldiers had witnessed the nun's angry exit from the office, and the tenderness around his left eye left him in no doubt that he had a visible bruise. "I will not have that woman make a laughing stock of me," he muttered. But he knew that would be the case and he deeply regretted his weakness in delaying his journey. "I will check the finances another time," he said as he checked the Prioress's inscrutable face before marching out to his horse. The two monks stared at his face in alarm and the soldiers sniggered.

When Sister Elen did not reappear by Vespers, the Prioress ordered a full search of the buildings and the surrounding land, but she was not to be found. In her cell were her habit and her silver cross, but her own clothes, that had not been worn since her arrival when the bloodstains had been removed, were missing. The next day a man who farmed close by did recall seeing a woman walking along the road going south. "First, I sees some churchmen and soldiers. Going towards Caerdydd they were, an' they be in a right hurry, isn't it?" He carefully scratched his matted hair. "Then, this woman appears, as if she'd been hiding or something. Strange, she didn't look the sort to be walking by herself."

The Prioress discussed the situation with her Almoner. "We both know why the Bishop was here, and I have to admit to a certain satisfaction that he has been punished for his sins. I fear we have lost Sister Elen, who may have a greater ability to survive in the outside world than I had suspected."

"Her departure will satisfy the Bishop, and perhaps we will all benefit from her brief stay among us, and by her spectacular departure. I will miss her," the Almoner smiled, "as I'm sure you will."

IT WAS LATE AFTERNOON ON October 6th, when King Harold led his tired men into London, where they were given a hero's welcome by the populous who had heard about their great victory at Stamford Bridge. It was a celebration mixed with relief that their army had returned to protect them from the Normans.

"It took us four days to reach Jorvik, and the next day we defeated Tostig and the Norwegians," Leofwine gave Gyrth a tired smile. "It took us five days to return, and I never want to do such a forced march again. Our brother sets such an example that the housecarls are proud to march with him. No matter what he expects of them, they're determined to deliver."

"I'm more than glad to see you both," Gyrth said, "and I'm really delighted you were able to return before the Normans attacked London." He refilled their mugs. "I couldn't believe our bad luck when the wind changed in William's favour. In another week or so the late autumn weather would have forced him to abandon the invasion," Gyrth shook his head. "He risked everything putting his trust in those flat-bottomed troop ships, but his gamble seems to have paid off, damn him."

"He wouldn't have attacked London," Leofwine rubbed his eyes. "I'm certain he's putting all his efforts into increasing his numbers and bringing over more horses. Unlike us, he puts a big emphasis on cavalry."

"True, and he also uses more archers than we do. I sometimes wonder if putting the majority of our emphasis on heavily armoured foot soldiers is a wise move when we are fighting armies that use more variety."

"It worked well at Stamford Bridge."

"It worked because the enemy had the same military approach. There is no doubt that our housecarls are the best trained and the toughest soldiers in this part of the world and, as long as they hold firm, their wall of iron is almost undefeatable. But I fear that massed archers, when they deliver a constant rain of arrows, can find the undefended parts of any soldier's body, and once men begin to fall they weaken the shield wall and destroy

IN THE ASHES OF A DREAM

the confidence of their friends and officers." Gyrth paused as he realized that this was not what his brother wished to hear. "On the brighter side, I'm confident that our shield wall with its bristling spears will withstand any cavalry attack."

"There I agree with you."

"Where are our brothers Morcar and Edwin? They weren't killed, were they?"

"You mean at Stamford Bridge?" Leofwine gave an empty laugh. "Not likely, as they both refused to leave Jorvik on the day of the battle." He finished his wine and held out his mug for a refill. "When we arrived, they had already signed a peace treaty with the Norwegians in return for the city's safety. Harold ordered them to follow him into battle with the remnants of their army, but they refused as they had sworn on the Bible not to attack the Norwegians. Of course, they didn't tell Harold that before the battle."

"What did Harold do?"

"He took away their earldoms and locked them up. It was all he could do not to kill them with his own hands."

"Are they still locked up?"

"No. He relented and gave them back their earldoms. It was not all brotherly love; however, he needed some stability in the area. When he had the news of William's invasion, Harold led the march back and our two brothers, having assembled their soldiers, promised to follow. I understand they turned back after a few hours of marching."

"This time he will surely hang them!" Gyrth exclaimed. "How could they do this?"

"You and I know that they've always envied the three us, as did Tostig. Morcar and Edwin are motivated by greed and self-preservation. They did not expect Harold to beat the Norwegians, and they're convinced he will lose to the Normans. If Harold defeats William he will finally have eliminated all opposition to his kingship, and our treacherous brothers will have to flee for their lives."

Having paused in the doorway, Harold walked defiantly into the room. "There must be no doubt that I will defeat William!

Whoever you speak to make them believe that we are going to win. Our soldiers are understandably tired but, in a few days, they will be ready to fight." He accepted a mug of wine and began to pace the room. "How's the muster going?"

"The reports are not encouraging," Gyrth said, refusing to be quelled by Harold's glare. "The majority of the Londoners of fighting age are refusing to leave the city. They think they will be safer behind the walls than taking on cavalry. Their hope is that you will keep your army here and will not leave the city until William has wasted his army in a protracted siege."

"Treasonous bastards! I'm their King, they must support me!" Harold raged. He had entered the room in a confident state, having completed the arduous return march before William could possibly have expected him, and he had arrived in the room ready to discuss tactics with his two most valued officers. He had not expected further bad news. "Don't they understand that every day we allow William to remain on the south coast is another day for him to reinforce his army?"

"I have summoned the Fyrd, and we are expecting housecarls from the north-east and from the west, but they'll not be here for at least another week."

"We can't wait that long," Harold's impatience was fast turning to anger. "Every day is a bonus to William; he continues to increase his numbers and his soldiers are having time to recover from their seasickness. Reports tell me he is expanding his foraging expeditions and has let it be known that he will spare those Saxons who don't oppose him. He cannot be allowed to choose his own battlefield."

Leofwine yawned. "We need time to recover, and the men need time. I understand your reasons for a quick response, brother, but you have to balance the fighting ability of our men and the need for fresh soldiers, with your understandable desire to drive William back into the sea at the earliest time."

"If I can attack him in the next few days, he'll not be expecting me! Battles are won by doing the unexpected. Surprise and tactics are as important as numbers."

Leofwine stood up and stretched. "I agree, but you must

remember we lost many men at Stamford Bridge. We need more soldiers, no matter how long it takes." He pulled open the door and left before Harold could reply.

"He's exhausted, you should be too," Gyrth marvelled as Harold roamed about the room. He had always admired the strength and energy of his eldest brother, and although he did not always agree with him, he was content to be his constant supporter.

"We have to plan. I had hoped to discuss our attack on the Normans."

"There's no way your army will be ready to fight for at least a week, and I agree with Leofwine, you need fresh soldiers. We have plenty of time to discuss what is possible."

"I want you to get all the officers for the London guard to meet with me tomorrow and arrange for the leaders of all the guilds to meet with me in two days' time," he went through a list of requirements for his housecarls relating to provisions, weapons and transport, pausing occasionally only to drink his wine.

Gyrth nodded in agreement, he could see it was pointless to argue. He understood that Harold was driven by a fevered brain and had still to calm down after the unrelenting physical demands of the past two weeks. He wondered if there had ever been a King like Harold: a man for whom nothing was impossible and who expected utter loyalty at all times. You either admired him or hated him; even his brothers had been forced to take sides. "You're the last Saxon King," he observed in an attempt to divert Harold's focus on planning. "When this is all over, you'll have to marry some other King's daughter and one that the Church approves of."

"To Hell with the Church! I'm handfasted to Swannuck, and our son Godwin will be the next King after me." He sat down heavily and hastily refilled his cup, splashing wine over the table.

"The Church does not recognize your marriage."

"Damn the Church! When I have beaten William, the Pope will listen to me or I'll make every rich bishop a pauper." He began to laugh. "That's not a bad idea. It would pay for my army." He slurred the last word, slipped down in his chair and was instantly asleep.

Gyrth removed his mug of wine, covered him with a rug and

as he quietly left the room, muttered: "Thank God, he's human after all."

• • •

The sea had changed and was no longer a flat blue expanse of gently undulating water, but a tormented expanse of grey, white-capped waves that were anything but inviting. The calm sea that had favoured William was a past memory.

"We might have difficulty persuading any captain to leave port in this weather," Dafydd remarked as he gazed out at the sea off the coast of Dover.

"That's alright with me," Gwriad said with feeling. "There's no way you could persuade me to go out in this weather; I'd rather fight the whole of the Norman army."

"If we stay here much longer, you may have to."

They had arrived at the port of Dover on the 10th of October, as word spread that King Harold had beaten the Norwegians two weeks before. By the 12th they had news that the King and his army had reached London six days ago, and the rumour was that he was preparing the city for a long siege.

For two days Dafydd had insisted on checking the few boats that remained in the harbour, only to discover that none of their captains was intending to sail along the coast and past the Norman beachhead. "Them controls the sea in that part of the coast," one captain had explained, as though they were children who understood nothing. "It be too dangerous with all them's boats. I ain't risking mine."

Dafydd had tried to explain that it might be better to risk sailing through the Norman fleet, as their ships were slow-moving troop-transports, rather than wait for the Norman soldiers to march into the port and capture all the ships that were anchored there. "After all, it's only a few hours march from the Hastings area where they have set up camp." But the captains were adamant, saying they would prefer to move up north than encounter the Norman ships. None of them said they were concerned about the weather.

"Alright. That's it. I don't want to spend another day waiting for a miracle to happen. I don't know what bright idea you have next, Dafydd, but you can count me out. I'm going to make my way back to Wales, and the security of our castle. I've had enough of seeking revenge and trying to be who I'm not. Nobody likes us here, and it's a long time since I looked and acted like a Lord. My clothes are worn, I feel like a pauper and probably look like a cutthroat. We have only the silver coins left, and I don't intend to starve."

"Good for you, brother, that must be the longest speech you're made for a long time, and I agree with everything you said." Dafydd gave a tired smile and leaned over the table at which they were sitting, and patted Gwriad on the shoulder. "Let's start for home as soon as we've eaten."

They were sitting in a dockside tavern, where the sailors from many countries packed the low-ceilinged room, and where having an accent went unnoticed. A blousy woman, who had left her youth behind many years ago, served them their food, and ensured that her ample breasts were clearly visible. "D'ye want anything else?" she said provocatively.

"No, thanks, darling, I'm giving it up for Lent," Gwriad winked, and as neither of them knew when Lent was, the joke passed off without offence.

Dafydd frowned at his plate. He always found his brother's sexual humour distasteful.

"How far north do you think we have to go to avoid the Normans?" Gwriad chewed earnestly on the gristly contents of the pie they had been served.

"I don't know," Dafydd sounded depressed, "your guess is as good as mine. But I don't think they will move far from the coast. I think the Normans will wait for Harold to attack them, and if he doesn't they'll eventually have to advance on London. Now that we know Harold has reached London, the big question is will he attack or will he stay behind the walls of the city? We don't know if William has news of Harold's unbelievable march from the North, but it is unlikely that he is expecting an attack in the next week. That means that we should have time to ride west as long as we avoid Norman scouts and those sent out to pillage and steal supplies."

They finished their beer in silence as they both considered their journey back to Wales. Gwriad looked cautiously around the room and noticed there was a sudden intensity in the conversation. "What are they saying, Dafydd?"

Dafydd focused on the group of excited men nearest to them. "They say King Harold and his army are on their way to attack the Normans!"

"That's hard to believe," Gwriad muttered. "If the reports we've heard are true, Harold's just marched down from the North. His army must be exhausted. It's only a few days since he reached London." He noticed there were arguments breaking out among the tavern's regulars, men who were military experts after a few beers. "Let's go. This is no longer our concern."

As they rode out of the town, they encountered small groups of people who were leading animals and walking beside overloaded wagons carrying their meagre possessions. Some of the men brandished weapons but were clearly uncertain what they should do with them. "Stay and fight!" one woman yelled at them as they rode past.

"The Normans will be defeated!" Gwriad yelled back. "Don't you worry."

When they reached the country road that headed west, they stopped and checked around. There was nobody behind them and the countryside seemed strangely empty of people. "Everyone's scared," Dafydd said. "Their futures depend on a battle that they have no way of influencing. I'm glad we don't live near here."

"Either way, the result of this battle will eventually affect us," Gwriad's sullen face slowly broke into a huge grin. "But not for a long time! Not for a long time, brother. Let's get out of here." He urged his horse into a canter and began to bellow a children's song about going home.

It was when they came to a crossroads that they once again encountered refugees. There were hundreds of them, filling the road for as far as the eye could see, and all travelling in the direction of London. Gwriad approached a family who was slowly driving a horse and cart; the husband and wife were in the front, with an assortment of young children and an elderly woman in the back.

"What news?"

"The Normans are coming!" the man said, his eyes wide with fear. "We're going to London until King Harold defeats them."

"Have you seen King Harold's army?"

"No. He's defending London." The man spoke as if to a simpleton. "That's why we're going there." He rode on shaking his head.

"Who to believe?" Dafydd murmured. "Let's keep going west."

They forced their way through the unwilling squash of people and, once through, continued along an empty road with dense forests on both sides. It had begun to rain by the time they reached a large village called Tonbridge, which boasted a wooden church and a stone bridge that passed over a shallow river connecting the two halves. It was unnaturally quiet, and they were aware of people spying on them from behind shuttered windows. There was a single horse tied up outside the only tavern, and when they dismounted no stable boys appeared.

"Let's hope they have some food," Gwriad rubbed his empty stomach and led the way through the door and into a gloomy room lit by a single candle burning at a simple bar. A stocky middle-aged woman was leaning over the counter and talking in hushed tones to a younger man. Both looked up anxiously as Gwriad stepped into the room.

"We're closed," she said in the firm voice of an experienced barmaid.

"We have money," Dafydd said, "we just need some food and a drink, and we're not fussy." He gave her one of his endearing smiles.

She glared up at him. "I said we're closed." She softened when she saw the disappointment in his face. "Don't you know what's happening? We could have either the Norman scum raiding us, or a Saxon army demanding supplies as they pass through. I'm leaving. My son here has been warning me. We're going west."

"If I give you silver, can we help ourselves to any food we can find, and pour our own ale? If you expect this place to be pillaged soon, it will all go anyway."

"Alright," the youth said, his hand on the knife at his waist, "but you keep your hands off me mother!"

Gwriad held out his hands. "We're not robbers or rapists. Our clothes are travel worn, but we're good people."

"Oh, help yourself, there's food in there," the woman pointed to a small pantry, she sounded close to tears. Dafydd handed her some silver coins which she grabbed and left the room, followed by her son who gave them a worried frown as he closed the door behind him. They heard the sound of a bolt being pulled across.

"Let's grab what we can and get out of here. They know something we don't." Dafydd raced into the larder while Gwriad poured two mugs of ale, which they drank quickly, and exited with a dark brown loaf, a cheese and the remains of a pork pie. They loaded their food into their panniers after breaking off a hunk of cheese each. "I'm glad our horses are still here," Dafydd said meaningfully as he mounted. Gwriad nodded and, checking the road for any sign of life, moved quickly away.

They cantered down to the bridge, constantly looking behind. There was no sign of life and the landscape was wet and depressing. It came as a shock to them when, having crossed the river, they were instantly surrounded by Saxon horsemen who carried both swords and spears.

CHAPTER TWENTY-ONE

Despite Leofwine's protests and the pleading of Gyrth, who wanted to wait for further reinforcements, Harold insisted on marching out of the city with his much-reduced housecarls at the earliest opportunity. He arrived at Caldbec Hill after a two-day march in drizzling rain on the evening of October 12th, only a week after reaching London. Caldbec Hill was an obvious choice as it was a large hill that had never been ploughed, had firm natural undergrowth and a steep side facing south and overlooking the area occupied by the Normans. It was about an hour's march from the invaders' camp.

"With luck, they won't know we've arrived," Harold said confidently as his army began to form up around the rim of the hill. Slowly, the heavily armoured soldiers took up their positions in the shield wall for which they were famous: three lines of powerful men, with their solid shields, their metal and cow leather armour and their sharp, iron weapons. All around the hilltop the yelling and swearing of the sergeants competed with the crashing of metal as the best positions were selected. It was a more difficult hill to defend than had first been appreciated: the top was uneven with small clumps of trees, broken stone areas and a narrow gulley that presented problems for both sides. The sergeants and the officers could only concentrate on their immediate areas, and had no overall picture as to how the army was forming up.

"Hell! We don't have enough men to defend this hill!" Leofwine suddenly yelled. "We need more men!" He stared aghast at the back sides of the hill, which had only a thin line of defenders, and the reserves, on the brow of the hill, were minimal. "I told you to wait for the local Fyrd to assemble!" He glared at his brother. "We have no choice, we'll have to move our position."

"Enough! Send the scouts and local officers to me. Now!" Moving his position was something Harold was unwilling to discuss. He was aware that he should have waited in London for more men to trickle in, but each day enabled William to rest his troops and receive reinforcements. But the biggest advantage of arriving here so soon after returning from the North was the element of surprise, which was worth hundreds of soldiers. Now, he would have to re-establish his army on a new hill, and his fear was that he would be discovered before he achieved it.

"There's a hill near here called Senlac. It's the right size for our army, and it's only about an hour's march away." The youngest of the three brothers, Gyrth could always be counted on for the most optimistic assessment. He was also a realist, and decided not to remind Harold that the word had gone out for latecomers to muster at Caldbec Hill. If they wanted to fight, those who had answered the muster could easily follow the wide muddy trail that over 5,000 men created when they marched.

"Good." Harold patted him on the back and concentrated on keeping his own breathing under control. He was aware that the odds were stacked against them and that he was responsible, but he was their King and he would save the Saxon nation no matter what the personal cost.

"The scouts do not report any unusual movements in the camp, so we might just get established on Senlac before they discover us." Leofwine knew, they all knew, that the Normans had hundreds of cavalry and archers, and their army certainly outnumbered the tired Saxons. Their only hope for achieving a victory was to get their shield wall into position on a hilltop. Once there, their solid combination of shields and spears could hold out against the cavalry and their long shields would block most of the deadly arrows. But, if the Saxon army were caught marching on low ground, their hastily-constructed shield walls would be decimated by the Norman armoured cavalry, and by their arrows dropping like rain from different angles.

Harold adopted an unemotional pose, and his officers would

IN THE ASHES OF A DREAM

never have guessed that the move to another hill was anything other than a ploy to confuse the enemy. "We move at first light and I want you to conduct a fast march to Senlac Hill. Keep the men quiet as we move into position and tell the sergeants that they are to give their orders in low voices until it is clear that the enemy is aware of us. When that happens, I want them to bellow their orders, and for the men to beat their shields, as though we were double our number. Remember, Senlac Hill is closer to their camp than Caldbec Hill, and the enemy has more chance of discovering our advance."

The officers posted sentries, maintained a constant stream of scouts and ordered the men to sleep with their weapons. The supply wagons had gradually formed up at the bottom of the hill, and preparations were made for the army to be fed and watered before their march to Senlac Hill in the early morning. During the night, Harold drank wine with his top officers, slept for a short time, and was one of the first to walk down to the supply wagons, fully armed and ready for battle.

He would have left his horse with the wagons and marched at the front of his army, if Leofwine had not persuaded him to stay on his horse until they reached Senlac Hill. "On a horse, more men can see you. We will be with you on our horses and our squires will carry our flags. Our presence at the front of the army gives soldiers something to believe in, for most of them will be fearful, and they need to be reminded why they are risking their lives."

Harold nodded. He was never afraid and had to remind himself that other men did not approach a battle as he did. For him it was exciting; a chance to demonstrate his huge strength and test his skills against those who dared to oppose him. At times he had generated such hatred for an enemy that his anger had turned him into a killing machine spreading panic in the opposing ranks. He could not remember a time when he had ever felt fear and was unaware that he was a legend with his housecarls, who respected a King who towered over them, and never gave in.

· · ·

IT WAS NOT UNTIL DARKNESS was beginning to fall that Elen's

slowly fading anger gave way to a cool assessment of her situation. For months she had lived in a place of rigid discipline and order, where regular meals, sleeping and waking were taken for granted, and where personal decisions were reduced to bodily requirements and what to volunteer for. For the first time she could remember, she was having to consider where she might sleep and how she might eat.

After leaving the priory, she had walked down a long, rutted road where evidence of farming had been limited and with dense forests following immediately after each cleared area. She had drunk out of the small streams she had passed and eaten a few late berries, but had met nobody on the road, and seen no sign of life in the occasional distant hovels set far from the road. Occasionally, she had heard a dog bark and she had wondered if there were wolves in the area.

The thought had set her thinking about what things came easily to her memory and how her personal recollections had been obliterated. She stopped by a pile of wooden poles that someone had stacked by the side of the road, and carefully selected one that she could use as a walking stick and as a weapon. With the stick clasped firmly in her hand she felt more confident that she could deal with unexpected threats.

There were still some glimmers of daylight when she turned a corner and came upon a small hamlet with people sitting outside their meagre buildings, enjoying a lively social gathering in the twilight. A small fire flickered in the centre of the hamlet, adding to the friendly atmosphere. One man was playing a drum, another a flute and a woman with long grey hair was playing a harp; everyone appeared to be singing, and children were dancing and laughing.

As Elen came closer, someone touched the drummer and pointed towards her. The music stopped, and everyone watched her approach with curious but not hostile expressions.

The drummer stood up, "Welcome to our gathering!"

She nodded her head and smiled, but as she moved forward she suddenly felt weary and staggered slightly, dropping her stick.

IN THE ASHES OF A DREAM

A young woman rushed forwards and guided her to a long bench on which other women were seated. "Are you alright?" she asked.

Elen sat down and smiled gratefully at everyone. She realized that she had to explain quickly why she was not speaking. She opened her mouth, pointed at her tongue and shook her head slowly. Everyone gathered around and the drummer, who appeared to be the headman, squatted down in front of her. "You can't speak?" His bright eyes noticed her worn but quality clothes and the ring on her finger. "What has happened to you?"

She carefully undid the scarf around her neck, revealing the wide, ugly scar. A gasp went up from the group and many of the young girls cried out, while some of the boys crept nearer for a better look. "Who did this to you?" the woman with the long grey hair asked. She stepped forward and took Elen's hand in her own. "Get her water and bread."

After she had eased her hunger and thirst, she was able with lip reading and mime, to convey some brief details of what had happened. When she indicated that she could write she was told that nobody in the village could either read or write. So, she resorted to drawing in the dust, and was able to show that she had been looked after by nuns and, after some attempts, that she had lost all memory of her former days. She failed to get them to understand her name, and when they began to suggest a name, she indicated that they should name her. The drummer stood up, and having everyone's attention said: "We will call her Angwen!" Everyone cheered and Elen was pleased to accept the name as it meant 'very handsome'.

It was soon clear to Angwen, as she now saw herself, that she had been lucky to come across this friendly, closely connected group of people, and that her unexpected arrival was the most exciting thing that had happened to them for a long time. The peasants soon agreed that she should spend the night with them, and the harpist, named Bethan, invited her to her home which was slightly larger and better built than many of the other houses. As they walked towards it, Angwen learned the young woman who had rushed to help her, proved to be Bethan's daughter Gwenllian; she blushed when her mother revealed that she was betrothed to a lad in a nearby hamlet. "There are no big villages around here," she explained, "because the forest is difficult to clear, and the soil is poor. People live simply; we're lucky to have a blacksmith."

Bethan's home was a single large room with a small fire in the centre, and two curtained areas along one wall. She placed her harp in a corner alongside a large spinning wheel, and against a part of another wall was an upright weaving loom. "That's how I make money." She paused, "My husband was a skilled weaver, but he was killed fighting the Saxons."

Angwen opened her eyes in horror and indicated the hamlet. For some reason she had a clear memory of Saxons and how they were responsible for bad things.

"No," Bethan said reassuringly, "they've not raided here, but they did come close a year ago, when they were heading for Caerdydd," she gave a short laugh, "but our Welsh soldiers chased them back over the border!" She kindled a fire then lit a candle and brought two stools near for Angwen and for herself. As there were no other stools, her daughter was content to sit on the bare floor. The fire gave off a comfortable warmth as the heat of the day was gone and the evening coolness reminded everyone how winter was approaching.

"My husband was killed about two years ago after he joined Prince Anarwd ap Tewdwr's army when they invaded England." She gazed into the fire. "We all wanted to get our revenge on the Saxon demon called Harold Godwinson who defeated our King." She looked down at her hands. "My husband was a good man and I miss him. Were you married?"

Angwen looked down at the gold ring that she had received from the Church and realized her own rings had remained with the Prioress. But the thought of the rings did not help her to remember how she came by them or what they signified, and she shrugged her shoulders and shook her head. She looked around and, pointing at the harp, she touched the area of her heart.

"Yes, it's lovely. It was my mother's, and when I die my daughter will have it. She already plays well." The girl smiled happily. "The spinning wheel is another wonderful gift from my mother," Bethan said, "and she encouraged me to marry a weaver."

IN THE ASHES OF A DREAM

"My father was a handsome man," Gwenllian said. She giggled, "When I get married and move away, I think my mother has her eyes set on another man, who might come to live here."

"For shame on you, girl!" Bethan said, but it was clear she was not annoyed.

Later, Gwenllian served up mugs of cow milk, "Fresh from the cow tonight," she said. "My mother shares a cow with the man who plays the drum," she waved a finger at her mother, "and that's not all she shares!" She hooted with laughter.

"It's time you left home, my girl," Bethan protested, but Angwen could tell it was a longstanding joke, and no offence was meant. She wondered if she had ever had children, and if all families were like this one.

When the candle began to burn down, Gwenllian put more wood on the fire while Bethan fetched a blanket and a straw-filled paillasse for Angwen to sleep on and placed it on the other side of the room, near the loom. Within moments of lying down, the exertions of the day overcame any worries Angwen might have had, and she slept like a child.

• • •

"THAT WASN'T A GOOD IDEA," Dafydd muttered as they rode surrounded by Saxon horsemen through the tidy village of Hawkhurst. Ahead, a line of supply wagons lumbered along the narrow lanes and in front of the wagons a long line of heavily armed soldiers was marching up a hill at a pace that had to be seen to be believed. They were all moving south to muster at Caldbec Hill, and the brothers had become the unwilling supporters of the man they had wished to murder.

"What else could we have done? We were outnumbered. It was either die then, or agree to fight in a battle which we may just manage to survive," Gwriad growled angrily. The grim expression on his face matched those of their companions, who were preparing themselves for a battle they knew would be bloody. "They didn't want to know we were Welsh diplomats, they just wanted to know if we were fighting for them or against them. Our

Welsh accents made us highly suspect. If I hadn't volunteered, we could be dead by now."

Dafydd glanced around at the riders, and had to reluctantly agree that they were a fearsome bunch "But you didn't have to offer our services!"

"Of course I did! Didn't you realize they just wanted an excuse to kill us and take our horses?" He stopped when he realized he was speaking loudly in Welsh and that the nearest horseman was showing some hostility towards them.

"He always gets excited before a battle," Dafydd explained in Saxon, he winked, and the horseman spat on the ground and moved away. He turned back to Gwriad. "If you'd kept quiet, I'm sure I could have persuaded them we were messengers for the King but, because of you, we've agreed to help guard their supply wagons. This is an absurd situation."

"Just be thankful that the Saxon army prefers to fight as a shield wall and we're merely guarding the supplies. We could have found ourselves in their cavalry section if they'd had one."

Eventually, they reached a valley with a large hill on their right. "Wait here," an officer ordered. "This is Caldbec Hill. You can all dismount." He trotted up the long, gentle incline of the hill, following the path of the soldiers, while the rest of the riders checked their animals and refreshed themselves with whatever they had in their saddle packs. The wagon drivers watered their horses and relaxed, the camp followers and cooks prepared to feed the army and the tension seemed to lessen. After checking what the others did, Dafydd drank from his water flask and ate an apple picked on his journey. Gwriad stretched and slowly consumed a large sausage, washing it down with the remains of the ale he had poured into his flask at the last tavern.

"I reckon the housecarls will decide their positions on the hill and then rest up," Gwriad said and belched loudly. "I wouldn't want to march for days with one of those shields on my shoulders, they must weigh as much as a small sheep." He glanced up at the cloudy sky. "There won't be any fighting until tomorrow. So, it looks as though we could have an uncomfortable night."

"Then what?" Dafydd looked around. Apart from some of the

IN THE ASHES OF A DREAM

cooks and wagon drivers, everyone was wearing some form of armour, and many looked curiously at their clothes and swords and assumed they must be part of the King's Court or agents for the King.

"Once the fighting starts, we'll mount up, draw our swords and pretend to guard the camp and patrol the perimeter. When these other horsemen are occupied, we'll look for a chance to escape, and…" He was prevented from further discussion when the mounted officer returned down the hill at a breakneck speed. "Mount up! Mount up! Get the wagons moving. Continue along this path!" he yelled, pointing frantically. "Hurry!" He raced off to another part of the camp repeating the same message.

"It looks like they've come to the wrong hill," Dafydd observed. "Someone's in deep trouble." He ran his tongue over his teeth, savouring the taste of the apple, "I wonder if that's good for us or not?"

It was darkness when they reached another, smaller, hill that the officer called Senlac. "The army will arrive at dawn. They are resting tonight," he announced. "We will patrol the area, and arrest anyone we find. Kill them if necessary. We hope to surprise the Normans, so keep well away from their patrols, and only engage them if you think they have discovered us."

The camp was established, no fires were allowed and guards were posted. Gwriad was chosen to be part of a patrol of five riders. "They're splitting us up," he whispered dramatically. "Perhaps they don't trust us?"

While he was gone, Dafydd walked around the silent camp. Men were sitting in small groups talking quietly, or trying to doze on the damp earth. The wagon drivers and cooks were envied as they could sleep in their wagons among the camp supplies, but Dafydd knew they would be hard pressed to feed the thousands of housecarls when they arrived at first light. When Gwriad returned, another patrol went out, and Dafydd was pleased to discover he had not been chosen. They hunched together in the cold damp darkness, with their horses close by, and talked in a way they had not been able to do since beginning their fruitless attempt to get revenge.

"If we die tomorrow, we have nothing to regret," Dafydd said. "What we have tried to do was, in its way, noble. We're simple Welsh Lords who have very little understanding of how the more advanced world works. We have learnt some important lessons, but it's time for us to leave England, where we don't belong, and return to the people who know us and like us."

"Who would have thought that we would be present at a battle that could change the very country we have come to hate. By this time tomorrow, Harold will either become the most powerful man in our immediate world or he'll be dead, and we will, I hope, be witnesses to his death." Gwriad took a deep breath. "I have to admit, I regret leaving Angharad as I did. It's possible that even if we had stayed with our wives the Saxons would have overwhelmed us," his voice wavered, "but at least I would have died with her." He began to sob quietly. "At least we would have died together and I would not be forever tormented by not knowing where her body is."

Dafydd embraced his brother in a tight hug. "I also suffer the regret of leaving my wife, but at least I was able to see her body, and know that someone respected her in her death." He released his grip and stared into his brother's face, which he could barely see. "We will survive tomorrow and return to our home. I promise you."

The housecarls began to arrive long before dawn and small torches were lit to enable the food and ale distribution to begin, after which the soldiers marched up the hill and began to form their shield wall. Gwriad and Dafydd were ordered to join a large group of scouts who patrolled the area until daylight. They paused near the top of the hill, with the army forming up above them and surveyed the landscape as the light intensified. They could clearly see the distant grey blue of the sea on which many small boats, mere specks, could be seen moving slowly towards a dense forest of thin masts. In front was a vast encampment of tiny tents with flags flapping in the rising breeze. From the Norman camp to Senlac Hill the ground rose gradually until at the base of the hill it became a steeper incline to the top. The officer in charge stared at the distant salt flats that slowly gave way to thick forests of oak

IN THE ASHES OF A DREAM

and elm. He searched the terrain with a professional eye for any movement or unnatural activity. "Look carefully," he ordered, "it's our job to give our army notice of any advance by the enemy." It was still early and an unwilling sun was gradually breaking through a cloudy sky. Gwriad was conscious of his stomach rumbling, and hoped they would soon return to the camp for some breakfast, while Dafydd sat on his horse in a trance, and occasionally would sit up with a jerk as though he had been dozing.

"There!" the officer yelled, pointing frantically at an area to their right. They all stared and were amazed as, in the distance, a large body of horsemen almost magically appeared, moving carefully through the forest with the occasional beam of light reflecting off the silver hue of their armour. "Norman cavalry!" he glanced back to where a hundred paces above them the shield wall was gradually forming, but was nowhere near ready to withstand an attack. "Follow me!" he manoeuvred his horse up to the line of Saxon soldiers and followed their perimeter until he came to a break in the wall. Beyond the gap, officers were directing operations and sergeants were bellowing orders as soldiers marched forward from an uncoordinated mass and formed up as ordered.

The officer turned to a junior officer and ordered him to return with the riders back to the camp and alert everyone that the Normans were advancing. As they began the descent, they could see King Harold and his personal guard arrive and take up a position on the brow of the hill well back from the assembling shield wall. They watched as the junior officer raced towards them to give the vital, but unwanted, news.

"I feel sorry for the front line if the Norman cavalry attacks in the next hour," Gwriad muttered as they descended the hill and witnessed hundreds of soldiers still marching up from the camp.

• • •

ON HEARING THE BAD NEWS, Harold marched over to the centre of the shield wall, where it was now three men deep, and saw for himself the steady advance of the cavalry. "Send out all my scouts and discover if this is just a cavalry advance, or whether their archers and foot soldiers are on the march in those forests."

Officers began to identify considerable movement on the salt flats, but the forest prevented them from gaining a full picture of the enemy's movements.

"Mount up!" the officer commanding the scouts raced down the line of yawning men who had only just dismounted. "Everyone on their horse!" When they were assembled he gave a short, hurried speech. "We have to find out if the rest of the Norman army is close, or whether it is just their cavalry that's approaching. You must not seek to engage the enemy. They have hundreds of armoured cavalry and we have very few. Your horses are valuable, and your job is to bring back information that will help us win this battle. Remember, no heroes!"

He sent half of the riders to the left and led those on the right. "Break into small groups when you reach the forest. Come back as soon as you have something to report." He galloped off, setting a clear example to the others. In the sudden panic, Dafydd and Gwriad found there were only two other Saxons with them, and not ones that they remembered from their meeting on the bridge.

"This might be our only chance to escape," Dafydd whispered. Gwriad nodded. They followed the other two horsemen into the forest where all four immediately slowed their horses to walking pace. The Saxons were dismissive of the two Welsh riders who wished to fight with them, and when they began to weave through the trees, it was easy for the brothers to fall back, and eventually separate themselves from the two scouts. They were just about to break away when, from just ahead, they heard the sounds of fighting and the screaming of injured men.

"Quick!" Gwriad turned sharply to the right and rode his horse as fast as he could through the trees, followed by Dafydd, who was constantly checking behind them. After a short while, they came across a heap of fallen trees that had been felled a long time ago. Gwriad stopped and dismounted, and led his horse behind the curtain of broken branches. "We're safer here than risking being ambushed by the Normans."

Dafydd had no better plan and agreed, tending to leave such decisions to his brother. They tethered their horses and drew their swords as they scanned the forest, trying to imagine what they would do if they were discovered by a strong contingent of the well-armoured Norman cavalry. It was a long time before the silence of the forest was gradually replaced by the noise of a distant battle. They could imagine the Norman cavalry charging up the hill, forcing their horses into the solid wall of Saxon shields attempting to break the structure of their defence. They agreed that the risk of encountering stray patrols was lessened as each side concentrated their forces.

"Let's move west. I have no wish to be here when this battle is settled." Gwriad climbed onto his horse and waited for Dafydd to cautiously check in each direction. A watery sun occasionally revealed itself in a threatening grey sky, allowing them to roughly identify the south-east, and they moved in the opposite direction. Around them was a mature forest that allowed them to walk their horses without the danger of low branches, but the maze of thick roots made it impossible to hurry. At times, a startled deer would make them reach for their swords, but they saw no human beings. Eventually, they came to a little used path that seemed to be heading towards the west, and were able to travel faster.

They gradually became aware that the sound of battle had been replaced with a cacophony of birdcalls, and they cantered along enjoying the freedom of their escape both from the Saxons and the confines of the forest. At times, they came to open fields, and cautiously passed through small communities where the inhabitants stared at them from behind sheds and fences. They could sense the tension and the fear, as the peasants tried to imagine what a Norman invasion might mean for them. One old man was sitting on a stool outside a hovel and had clearly been unable to move quickly when the rest of the hamlet had fled. He waved a hand in hopeful friendship, and gave them a toothless grin. "Be the Normans coming, m'Lords?" he asked in a quavering voice.

Dafydd stopped his horse and forced a smile. "The King has a big army. He'll drive them into the sea."

"The Normans won't come 'ere then?" Relief flooded his gnarled face.

"You'll be fine," he glanced uncomfortably at Gwriad. "Take care of yourself, old man." He moved off quickly, and Gwriad followed, and glancing back as they came to a bend they could see the old man waving his arms and shouting, "The Normans ain't coming!" at the top of his voice.

"What could I say to him?" he looked apologetically at Gwriad. "Run for the woods?"

• • •

THE POWERFUL NORMAN CAVALRY ATTACKED without the support of the rest of their army in the hope of exploiting the weaknesses in the Saxon defences, which were clearly incomplete. As they charged up the hill they felt confident that they would not meet a hail of arrows, nor a cavalry that could challenge them. The Saxons were known for their shield wall, and the major component of their army was the well-trained housecarls. If the cavalry could overwhelm even one segment of the Saxon shield wall, then it would inflict a major weakness on Harold's army, one that might prove fatal.

Harold watched as the enemy ignored the area where the soldiers were well prepared and threw themselves against a part where only the frontline was in position. Leading the charge, Harold raced for the embattled section with a wave of soldiers behind, all of them aware of the seriousness of the situation. With his great height, his men recognized him and fought with renewed confidence. The Norman cavalry used their powerful horses like battering rams, determined to break the wall of shields, and in one small area they were able to force the Saxons back. As soon as this retreat began, the unfortunate soldiers in the front started to slip and entangle themselves with each other, and were unable to respond effectively to the murderous onslaught of the well-armoured Normans, who used the frenzy of their terrified horses to force a breach.

At that moment Harold arrived with a strong force of his personal guard, an elite group of tall, powerful fighters who were chosen for their fanatical faith in Harold's leadership, and their utter belief in their own invincibility. They surged into the breach roaring their battle cries, which reached a crescendo as Harold single-handedly decimated the front riders who were attempting to get past the broken elements of the shield wall that had been forced aside. In moments, the tide of the battle changed as the front line of the charging cavalry was suddenly engulfed in a wave of foot soldiers that attacked from both sides, hacking them off their horses and causing those that followed to become embroiled in a seething mass of riderless animals. The charge stalled and in the chaos the riders lost their supremacy and their initiative, making them vulnerable to the spears and axes of the Saxons. Those horsemen who were entangled in the melee and unable to escape were quickly dispatched, and the survivors who fled back down the hill were conscious that their pride had caused an error in judgment. Back at camp, the exhausted survivors were greeted, not as heroes but as fools and idiots by an incensed Duke William who ordered them to lead the next cavalry attack to regain their reputations, and almost certainly die in the process.

Harold's army had won back the essential time it needed to reinforce the shield wall and prepare for an assault by the main army which began soon after, with a withering storm of arrows. The housecarls sheltered behind their shields, but so intense was the attack that a small number were killed and many more received injuries. When the Norman archers had established the range, the foot soldiers marched into position, and began to ascend the hill. The archers continued a constant wave of death from the skies until the cavalry began their attack on a number of key points. They raced quickly between the wedges of their spear-carrying soldiers that rushed up to reinforce the attack once their cavalry was engaged.

On the insistence of his brothers and chief officers, Harold reluctantly agreed to move back to a safe distance. "You serve no purpose, brother, if you are killed before we win this battle," Lord Leofwine joked. But Gyrth, who failed to see the humour, said: "If you're killed by an unlucky arrow, the men will lose hope and the Royal Saxon bloodline will end."

"For the moment then," Harold grudgingly consented, "but once the close fighting begins and the arrows stop, I will take my place as their fighting King."

The expected massive attack was repelled after considerable losses on both sides, and William ordered a temporary withdrawal to enable his men to regroup. However, some of his foot soldiers at the front of the battle mistook the falling back as a sign that the fighting was over and they turned and ran down the hill, fearing the other Normans would leave them to die. The obvious panic was seen by some of Harold's men as a sign that the Norman army had given up and, despite the orders of their sergeants, they broke ranks and chased the fleeing enemy.

It was soon evident to them that they had made a bad mistake when the Norman cavalry turned and charged back, forcing them to form a small shield wall and begin a difficult retreat back up the hill. A number died in the counterattack; if the rest of William's army had not been engaged in a structured withdrawal, the Saxons would have been massacred. The officers on both sides raged at their men who had misunderstood or disobeyed their commands.

Throughout the day the Normans, who had superior forces, failed to break the seemingly invincible shield wall, and William had an emergency conference with his senior officers. It was getting late, and he knew he had to win by dusk, or his men would be at a grave disadvantage. A young officer, who had been part of the charge that attacked the Saxon infantry when they broke ranks to chase the fleeing Norman foot soldiers, spoke up. "My Lord, can I suggest that we launch an attack with our soldiers and suddenly, at an agreed moment, retreat. It's possible the Saxons will chase us again, and if we wait until they are committed, our cavalry could destroy them." Duke William knew that most battles are won by strategy and deception and, after further discussions, agreed, and the plan was put into action.

Harold was beginning to feel confident of victory. His housecarls had proved to be indomitable, and if the Normans were unable to beat them by the time darkness came, then he felt he could destroy them. His two brothers who had survived some fearsome fighting shared his optimism, and were not surprised when the Normans launched a massed attack, seemingly their final attempt at defeating the Saxon army. It was preceded by a heavy rain of arrows and followed up a frantic attack by foot soldiers, who had in some cases climbed up the hill many times that day. But when they reached the top of the hill their attack appeared to be half-hearted, as though they no longer had any enthusiasm for winning the battle.

"They know they can't beat us," Leofwine chortled as the Norman soldiers began to pull back after only a brief exchange with the Saxon wall of armour. Suddenly, they were not just retreating but were running away, and Harold stared in disbelief. "This is a trick!" he roared, "Make sure the men don't break ranks!"

But the housecarls did break ranks. After fierce fighting throughout the day, when they had been made to stand and take wave after wave of cavalry charges and vicious attacks by well-armoured soldiers, their enemy appeared clearly beaten and was retreating in confusion. The cavalry had retreated and were nowhere to be seen, the archers had ceased to fire while hundreds of Norman foot soldiers were racing back down the hill towards the safety of the forested area at the bottom. With a bloodcurdling roar the front line burst forward and chased after their enemy. Some of the Saxons paused to hurl their spears at the backs of the retreating Normans, killing many and confirming in their minds that their enemy was finished. Many in the housecarls who had previously obeyed their officers, were convinced they were witnessing clear evidence of a shattered enemy. With a roar, they too now broke ranks, keen to take part in the slaughter of the hated Normans who had killed or injured many of their friends. Revenge was going to be sweet.

Harold and his officers ran along the lines of the remaining housecarls urging them to remain in position and, in spite of a certain reluctance, no further troops left the security of the hill. "Where's their cavalry?" Harold wailed. "They wouldn't sacrifice their soldiers for nothing. They've succeeded in doing what they've been unable to do all day, and our shield wall is fatally weakened!"

Below, the Normans, having reached the trees, turned defiantly to fight the screaming mass of Saxons who raced towards them. Harold and his brothers stared in horror as the Norman soldiers transformed into an organized wall of shields reinforced by hundreds of fresh infantry that poured out of the forest. It was a reversal of what had happened all day, and Harold's worst fears were confirmed as trumpets sounded and powerful columns of cavalry surged onto the battlefield from both sides, trapping the amazed Saxons and racing through them like men scything wheat. Many Saxons who were still descending the hill, turned and tried to run back up to the safety of their army, but the cavalry cut them down or ran them through with their spears. From above the Saxon army was forced to watch the slaughter, unable to help and realizing that they would soon suffer the result of their friends' fatal mistake.

"Draw back, reform the wall!" Harold bellowed. His cry was taken up by the sergeants, few of whom had left their posts, and a frantic reformation of the shield wall took place, with those at the front facing down the hill and at the carnage below, while those on the sides and back withdrew to form a tighter wall.

"Prepare for arrows!" Leofwine shouted, and almost immediately the sky was black with them, approaching like a cloud of hornets. The men defended themselves from the arrows as best they could, cowering beneath their shields until the first formations of cavalry attacked, followed by waves of reenergized infantry, forcing the Saxons to panic as they desperately reformed their wall.

Gyrth was the first of the brothers to fall, killed by a cavalry lance as he tried to replace a soldier at the front line. As the battle moved into its final stages, with heavy losses on both sides, the Saxons were forced to steadily shrink their circle as the Normans threw in their reserves in a last-ditch attempt to overwhelm the seemingly indomitable housecarls. Harold continued to fight like a monster, his mighty sword threatening death to any who opposed him.

The end came suddenly. Leofwine became isolated when the Saxons on both sides of him were killed and, although he fought bravely, in spite of many injuries, he was eventually downed by an iron ball wielded by a Norman Lord on a huge destrier. His death preceded an unexpected pause in the battle, as the Normans appeared to withdraw. But this was only to allow the archers to come back into the battle. Wave upon wave of arrows forced the surviving Saxons to take shelter, and caused the death of Harold as he sought to encourage his men. With his death the Saxon resistance slowly crumbled, and many fled down the hill towards the camp, only to find it had already been captured. There was a blood lust in the air and individual fights continued into the evening, when a meagre few of Harold's once indomitable army was able to escape.

"Show me King Harold's body," William demanded. It had been a long day, but his victory had energized him, and he had a clear plan of how he wanted things to unfold.

"It will be easier to identify him tomorrow, my Lord," an officer suggested.

"You will find him now. I must know that he's dead. I'm not having his supporters pretending he escaped. That could cause an unending series of uprisings. We must act quickly, before the news of the battle becomes known. There can't be too many giants in expensive armour!"

"My Lord, the hilltop is covered in hundreds of dead bodies," another officer protested. "It will be easier at first light."

"Organize a search now!" William demanded, his eyes blazed and all in his tent knew he would be obeyed.

Some hours later, William walked into a small church. Outside the rain hammered on the roof, and inside a cluster of torches flickered in the drafts, illuminating the naked body of a tall man who had died from an arrow through his face. The facial features were badly mangled as the corpse appeared to have been trampled by horse hooves, but on his skin a number of unusual tattoos would make for a positive identification. But someone had to vouch for them as being Harold's. Someone who knew him intimately.

"Pierre," William said, "I believe you've met Harold's mistress?"

"Indeed, my Lord. She's a very beautiful woman," the courtier bowed.

"Forget her looks. She lives close by in a well-guarded manor. I want you to take a strong detachment of cavalry and bring her here tonight. If anyone can identify this corpse, she can." William marched out of the church and began giving further orders to the officers around him. They knew he would take a day to calm down, and they resigned themselves to a long night.

Pierre arrived at Elditha Swannuck's guarded manor in the early hours of the next day. His men had knocked down the doors of a number of houses in their quest to find Godwin Manor, and had little time for the few guards who tried to protect her, leaving none alive.

"Fetch your Lady," Pierre demanded of a trembling woman who met them in response to their knocking. He pushed her aside as he marched into the house. "Tell her to get dressed and prepare for a journey to meet Duke William. Hurry!"

The terrified woman fled up the stairs and gave the message to her mistress who had hastily dressed when she had first heard her guards trying to defend the manor. She donned a thick cape and came slowly down the stairs to meet the Norman Lord who waited impatiently in her hallway. She retained her composure despite the realization that Harold must be dead, and the Saxons had lost the battle. She remembered the Norman courtier from a brief meeting at a Court function. Elditha had not liked him then, and in the circumstances liked him less.

They departed in pouring rain, and as she glanced back she saw that her manor was on fire with flames lighting up the darkness. "Was that necessary?" she asked calmly, trying to remain in control.

"Orders," was all that the Norman courtier would say.

Eventually, having become lost a number of times, they arrived at the small church, and waited in the aisle for William to arrive. When he strode through the door, Elditha faced him and did not curtsey. Before he could speak she pointed at Pierre. "Was it necessary for this oaf to burn down my house?" She spoke with a clear voice that showed no trace of fear.

William paused and considered her. "Your time as a rich woman is over. You were the handfasted wife of King Harold, and will no longer be in a position of power. If you do as I ask, I will allow you to live. Refuse my request and you will be executed." He turned away and walked down to where the corpse was laid out. "Is this your husband, King Harold?"

She walked slowly towards where William stood and gazed

down at her late husband's naked body. On occasions they had enjoyed some good moments, but there had been many times when she had hated him for his preoccupation with kingship. It had been the most important focus in his life, and it had been a rare occasion when he had considered her or her family. "Yes," she said quietly, "that is my late husband, King Harold Godwinson."

"You recognize him in spite of the fact that his face is destroyed?"

"Of course. He has fathered five of my children. I know his body, his tattoos and his immense size. That is King Harold."

"Turn away," William ordered. "Now describe his tattoos and where they are."

She spent a while slowly listing the marks and designs on the dead man's body. A nearby scribe was making notes and preparing a document. Eventually, William was satisfied. "Alright, you may go after you sign the statement confirming Harold is dead. I never want to see you again." She did not move. "Well?"

"My Lord, it is still dark and the roads are dangerous. Will you give me a guard to escort me back to my village?"

William stared at her, startled that she should request anything of him. "Pierre, you know where she lives. Take an escort and see her safely to her village." He paused and frowned at the courtier. "You will ensure, on your life, that she arrives safely."

The courtier bowed and strode off. Elditha signed the document, and gave a slight curtsey to the man who had killed her husband. It was the last time the two would ever meet.

CHAPTER TWENTY-TWO

As the day advanced the thin rain slowly gave way to a torrential downpour, changing the rutted paths into rivers of mud and drenching those that were unlucky enough to have to travel. After many hours, the two brothers came to a sizeable village. There was no indication of its name, but with the light fading and a tavern in the centre, they felt they would have to take their chances or risk dying of fever or starvation. Outside the unattractive building a handful of horses were tethered to a rail under a low shelter. A sad looking youth was trying to keep dry, and appeared to be acting as stable boy and guard. He carried a sturdy pole and regarded them with a hostile stare. He was clearly not used to strangers.

"We need to stop here," Gwriad said out of the side of his mouth. "I'm hungry, thirsty and I'm ready to fight my way if I have to."

"What's your name?" Dafydd demanded, staring down at the youth.

"Ord," he said reluctantly.

"Well, Ord, I want you to guard our horses." He dismounted and handed the youth a small silver coin. "Do you have hay?"

The boy nodded enthusiastically, his eyes locked on the coin in his hand. It was more than he received in a week. In fact, his food and a place to sleep was his usual pay.

"Look after our horses, and make sure no one steals our baggage and I will give you another." He strode into the building, closely followed by Gwriad, who winked at the amazed Ord.

Inside, a motley cluster of men was engaged in a lively discussion that stopped abruptly as the brothers entered. They were bunched around a hot fire; one younger man stepped forward and his hand

IN THE ASHES OF A DREAM

went to a knife he displayed on his belt. Gwriad glowered at him and touched his own sword. The man swallowed, licked his lips and dropped his hand as he looked away, his bravado short lived. The rest of the men stared silently like a gathering of weathered statues.

"What can I do for ye, gentlemen?" the man behind the bar asked. His manner was unfriendly, and he kept one hand out of sight.

"We want ale and whatever you have that we can eat," Dafydd said. The man did not move. "We've come a long way today," he paused, "all the way from where the Normans are attacking King Harold's army."

This comment brought an immediate reaction as everyone began to ask questions and the man behind the counter lowered the club he had intended to use. "What be happenin'?" he bellowed, and the rest took a breath as they waited for Dafydd's answer.

"We need ale and food," he said firmly, and placed a coin on the grubby counter. "Then, we're going to warm ourselves by your fire, and not until that is done will we tell you the latest news." Gwriad gave them all a threatening stare and the tavern owner, who reminded Dafydd of an ancient wrestler, quickly poured two mugs of ale, which they both emptied and pushed them back for refills.

"I got some rabbit pie and bread 'n cheese," the man said.

"Good," said Dafydd as he and Gwriad marched towards the fire. The men moved back, giving up their seats on the benches that were closest to the warmth. The brothers removed their wet cloaks, spread them out to dry and sat on either side so they could watch the movements in the dimly lit room. "Where are we?" Dafydd demanded. There was an unusual aggression in his voice, and Gwriad, whose Saxon language was limited, was impressed.

"Midhurst," one of the men quickly answered.

"Where's the nearest port?"

"That be down at Chichester," another man volunteered. The rest nodded in agreement.

"How long will it take to get there?"

"If ye be in haste an' leaves at first light, ye'd be there by midday, I reckons." There was general agreement.

The tavern owner brought two wooden platters, each with a large slab of cold pie, a chunk of bread and a lump of cheese. "So, what's 'appenin', then?" he asked as he handed them the food. His were eyes wide with expectation, and the rest nodded excitedly.

Dafydd took a large bite of the pie, nodded his head in satisfaction, washed it down with ale and renewed his attack on the food. Gwriad was no less enthusiastic, and the small crowd of men was forced to watch them demolish the food, knowing they would get no information until it was finished. Finally, they were getting close to the last of the bread when Gwriad raised his empty mug and indicated he wanted more. The owner scowled, grabbed the mug along with Dafydd's and went to refill them.

It was at that moment that they heard the sound of horsemen. Before the local men could react, Gwriad was at the door, peering out into the darkness. A gusting wind was moving the heavy rain like curtains, but it was clear to see the village road was full of armoured horsemen.

"Normans!" he yelled. In moments the men were piling out of the room by a back entrance, while Dafydd and Gwriad grabbed their cloaks and followed them out, leaving the tavern owner standing irresolutely in the middle of the floor uncertain how to react.

They ran around the back of the building to the makeshift stable and cursed as the other men ahead of them, having mounted their horses, tried to force their way out onto the dark road. Their panic attracted the attention of some of the soldiers, who thought they were being ambushed. The locals, knowing their way in the darkness, galloped off with the Normans in hot pursuit. The brothers untied their horses, mounted and walked them to the back of the tavern. They were about to attempt a cross-country escape, when the drenched figure of Ord appeared. "What'll I do?" he wailed.

Gwriad was about to ride off, but Dafydd grabbed his arm. "Ord, the Normans have come. It means they've won the battle and beaten King Harold. Run to your home and warn them."

IN THE ASHES OF A DREAM

"I ain't got no 'ome," the youth blubbered. "I ain't got nobody in this village."

"We must go!" Gwriad raged.

"Ye won't get far in the dark in this weather," Ord yelled. "Not if ye tries to keep off the road. I could 'elp ye. I knows this area."

"He's right, Gwriad!" Dafydd shouted, trying to be heard above the noise of the wind. He turned to Ord, "Climb up behind me."

Without further discussion, Ord climbed up and directed Dafydd away from the village, across a water-logged field and onto a path that led them up a gradual hill. Soon the ground was firmer, and Dafydd's horse was able to increase its speed. After a while, the rain abated, the wind lessened, and a bright moon slowly emerged through the broken cloud. As they travelled Dafydd was aware of the heat of Ord's body against his back, and realized that every other part of his body was damp and cold. When they reached a level area, Dafydd called a halt. "I must rest my horse," he said emphatically.

Ord eased himself off the horse, and stood trembling in the moonlight. Gwriad was already dismounted and was walking about slapping his hands against his body. Gradually, Dafydd climbed down, feeling thoroughly drained of energy.

"Should us make a fire?" Ord suggested. "Or would that be dangerous?"

Gwriad looked about; there was no sign of life. "I don't think the Normans are worried about us," he patted his horse. "I imagine they just want to secure the main towns and villages." He turned to Dafydd, "Tell him if he can find some dry fuel, we'll try to start a fire." He patted Ord on the shoulder. "Good."

Ord smiled as the older brother moved away; he had not been sure of that one.

"I'm amazed they've made it this far, and so soon. After a major battle, their troops must be exhausted," Dafydd searched for his flint box.

"I think William has the intention of securing this part of England before he moves against London. It's what I would do in his place."

Ord had the innate skills of a country lad, and soon they were warming themselves around a blazing fire, while their horses cropped the sparse grass. "I be list'nen' at the door, and I 'erd ye was goin' to Chichester," Ord said proudly. "I ain't never bin there, but I 'as an uncle what 'as a farm nearby."

"If we take you to your uncle's farm, you'll show us how to reach Chichester?" Dafydd raised his eyebrows. Ord nodded.

Dafydd punched Gwriad playfully in the arm. "See what a bit of kindness does."

Gwriad and Dafydd took turns to keep watch, unwilling to trust their new friend with their horses. But it was hard to sleep when the ground was so cold and uneven. At first light they mounted up and it was only a short time before they could see the sea. "It be down'ill all the way now," Ord said confidently, "an' I'll be leavin' ye." He was not going to complain, but riding behind someone else was not comfortable.

"I reckons ye'll be there for breakfast," Ord said as he pointed down the path towards the sea. Dafydd gave him another silver coin.

"Good luck, Ord." The youth beamed and waved as he disappeared into a small forest.

"Don't look so disapproving," Dafydd trotted off. "We'll have to sell our horses when we get to the port. Then we'll have plenty of money."

They arrived in Chichester before breakfast as Ord had predicted. It was a small town with a number of warehouses, barns and taverns along a ragged waterfront, and situated at the end of a natural inlet, some distance from the main channel that led to the sea. There was a mass of small boats pulled up along the muddy bank, but only one ship anchored off the quiet port. They could see men moving about on the deck and throwing what looked like soil into the water, while others were working on a large sail. They appeared to be getting ready to leave. "Don't worry," Gwriad pointed towards the water, "the tide's out. The captain won't leave for a while, especially as this place is some distance from the sea."

It was usually a busy, friendly atmosphere in a trading port where people were used to foreigners, but when they entered a tavern on the waterfront, they could feel the tension in the air.

IN THE ASHES OF A DREAM

Groups of men huddled together in small groups, each involved in hushed conversations exclusively about the Normans. Dafydd ordered some food and weak beer and listened carefully to the discussions that were taking place.

When the serving girl brought their order, Dafydd asked if she knew who owned the ship in the port. The girl was pleased to help, especially as he gave her a coin. She pointed to a stocky man with a thick black beard, who was dominating a discussion with a small group of well-dressed men. "That's Captain Morgan. He owns the boat. It's called 'Gwynedd', after his dead wife. He sails between here and Caerdydd, and brings Welsh sheep. He'll take anything back, as long as he makes a profit." She smiled, "He doesn't like Saxons very much."

"But you like him?" Gwriad winked at her.

"Oh yes. He's a very generous man." She blushed, curtseyed and retreated into the kitchen.

"He's Welsh!" Dafydd muttered under his breath. "We could be in luck."

They both pretended to concentrate on their food as they listened to the increasingly animated conversation. "I don't care what you say!" Captain Morgan stood up and banged his fist on the table in front of him. "I'm leaving at full tide, with or without a cargo, and I won't be back until I know how the Normans are going to treat us."

"What about our investment in your boat?" one man protested.

"D'ye want to buy it?" the captain shouted. "No, of course ye bleeding don't! Nobody wants to buy a boat at this time and nobody wants to use this boat at this time! D'ye want me to wait until the Normans arrive and steal it? What'll happen to your precious investment then?"

There was a short period of angry mutterings from the well-dressed men, during which the captain glared at them but made no response.

"Well, you just remember that we all own part of that boat," one man said bitterly as he stood up. The rest followed suit. "We'll send you a message just as soon as things settle down, and we'll expect you to deliver a full quota of sheep."

351

The captain took a long drink. "An' ye remember to have a cargo for me to take back, or I'll double the cost of ye sheep." He pointed a muscular, tattooed arm at them, and the angry men stalked out of the tavern. The captain called for another mug of beer. "Bloody leeches," he stuck out his chin. "What do I owe ye, John?"

"Let me pay, Captain Morgan," Dafydd placed one of his last silver coins on the counter. "We'd like you to join us," he said in Welsh.

The seaman looked him up and down, noted the travel stained clothes and the sword hanging from his belt. He raised a suspicious eyebrow, but followed Dafydd to where Gwriad was finishing his meal. "Well?" his tone was unfriendly. He had often been approached by penniless Welsh rogues, the flotsam and jetsam of any port in this part of the country, who thought because he was a Celt that they could get a free passage back to Wales. He could tell that these two were no sailors, although they might pretend to be in order to get on board, and he was uncertain of them, especially the second man, who looked tough and wore a dangerous sword.

"You carry live stock?"

"Yea," Morgan was not impressed with the second man's smile.

"We have two war horses that we want to ship back with us to Caerdydd, and we want to travel with you on the next tide." Gwriad stood up and offered his hand. "You have every right to be suspicious of us, Captain Morgan. I'm Lord Gwriad ap Griffith and this is my brother Lord Dafydd. Perhaps you've heard of us?"

The captain shook his head slowly. "Why should I?"

"You've heard of the great General Cydweli?"

"Yea, maybe." Everyone in South Wales knew his name. He was a national hero after the battle of Rhyd-y-Groes. "So what?"

"We're his sons," Dafydd said looking straight into his eyes. "We served the late King Gruffydd ap Llywelyn. Gwriad was the General of the Central Army."

"Bloody Hell!" Morgan gasped, and he shook their hands vigorously. "M'Dad served with Prince Rhodri ap Williams when he were Admiral of the Southern Fleet." He frowned, "That was when we had a Southern Fleet." He stared vacantly at the floor,

"M'Dad died at sea." After a moment's pause, he stood up and walked towards the door, waved to the serving girl, and led them out into a dull, cloudy day with a slight breeze.

"These ye horses?" he asked as he walked towards them; it was clear that he knew how to handle animals. "Do they travel well?"

"They've never travelled on water."

"No matter. They looks well trained." He pointed towards a wide flat boat close by. It had oarlocks near the front on either side, and the rest of the boat was divided into simple enclosures, each with a covering of sheep muck on the floor area. "We'll take out the dividers, and have a horse on either side, with you two controlling them in the middle."

The operation turned out to be easier than imagined. Other members of the crew rowed over to help, and the two horses were walked onto the flat boat, where they were safely secured. With their owners standing next to them, the two large horses were rowed out to the ship where a winch was used to lift them onto the deck. The captain sent out for hay, extra water and supplies, complained about the "bloody awful state of the deck", and by the time the tide was in, the boat was ready to leave.

"We've bin' lucky," Morgan said quietly, as the crew began to row down the channel. "I feared them Normans might reach 'ere before the tide changed."

He licked a finger and held it up above his head. "Once we gets out of this channel, the wind should be good for us."

"Where are you heading for today?" Dafydd continued to look anxiously at the grass-covered banks on either side. He could imagine Norman archers firing down into their defenceless ship.

"I'm sailing to a small port called Swanage, where we stop the night, and I take on some cargo." He gave a throaty laugh. "Them leeches who own part of this ship never knows what other trading I does." He realized that Dafydd was unimpressed, and cleared his throat. "I stops at a number of small ports and then, if the wind holds I sails round Land's End." He spat into the water. "That's the dangerous bit. I never sails there in the winter."

The voyage was a nightmare for Dafydd who became seasick almost immediately, and felt he would die when the sea turned rough off Land's End. They eventually rounded the tip of Cornwell and reached a small port named Newquay. "We'll stop here for a few days while I does some business, and try to find out the latest news," Captain Morgan grinned. "A chance for you to walk ye horses."

"A chance for me to avoid death," Dafydd murmured. "Do you think we can continue on horse, and never set foot on a boat ever again?"

Gwriad patted him on the back and gave him an encouraging smile. "We've done the worst part, isn't it? We'll soon be in Caerdydd, and then we'll be back on Welsh soil, man. Think of that."

"We don't have enough money to stay in an inn," Dafydd glared at the small port, "barely enough to afford to eat."

But Gwriad explained he had arranged to get money from Morgan by acting as his armed guard during dockside transactions. "Not a very lordly thing to do," he agreed, "but better than starving on board this smelly ship."

A week later they finally reached Caerdydd, and Gwriad gave his word as a Lord and an ex-General that he would send Morgan the money for the voyage as soon as he returned to Aberteifi. "I trust you," Morgan said. "I wouldn't trust ye brother though," he gave a bellowing laugh. "Just look at him!"

Dafydd had lost weight, was deathly pale and with his sunken eyes and a week's growth of reddish hair looked almost inhuman. He stared at Caerdydd with a grim expression, like a prisoner looking at the prospect of freedom, and not convinced it will happen. "Get me off this cursed ship," he growled, "and get those poor horses onto firm ground."

"Oh, of course," Gwriad fought to keep a straight face, "the horses! Of course!" He turned to Morgan, "Good thing he can't see himself," he spluttered, "or he'd do himself in."

After some delays, they left the malodorous boat and gave their horses a chance to recover from the voyage before leaving the big town. They decided to take the inland route rather than risk the possible dangers of the coast road, and as Dafydd put it: "I want to travel slowly, and I have to tell you, I'm not feeling my usual self."

IN THE ASHES OF A DREAM

Gwriad nodded. It was rare for Dafydd to be ill, and as one who had received a number of painful injuries he felt compelled to show some concern. They knew they still had a long journey in front of them, but each decided to use the time to talk through their experiences, and share their realizations. "We've both suffered the loss of the women we loved, and we've failed to get our revenge," Gwriad said, "although it would appear that the Normans have done it for us." He gave his brother an encouraging smile. "Now we have time over the next week or so to plan for the rest of our lives. Who knows, we might find new women?"

Dafydd gave him a dark scowl.

"Well, we're not too old to start again!" he protested. "What about Derryth, the Wise Woman? You can't tell me you haven't thought about her?"

They rode in silence while Dafydd composed himself. "Yes, I've thought about her, and when I do, I get consumed with guilt. I can't imagine finding another Teifryn. I'm convinced I'll become a hermit, who only appears from his room when he runs out of reading material."

"Utter tripe! You'll become a famous Welsh leader who, with my help, will save our country from the Normans. You'll be the planner and I'll be your right-hand man of action. We might even involve Jon, if he hasn't married himself off to some fisher girl."

As the long country roads slowly unfolded they began a lively debate about their private hopes and dreams, the first for years, perhaps the first ever. They both felt like new men, with new lives ahead of them.

. . .

OVER THE WEEKS, ANGWEN BECAME an accepted member of the small hamlet. An old lady had died a few days before she arrived, and it was agreed that Angwen could have the use of the empty hovel. Over a short time, she cleaned it, made some improvements and welcomed anyone who wished to help. She became a regular visitor to Bethan's house where she demonstrated her grasp of spinning, although she had no memory of ever having learned to use a spinning wheel.

Weaving was a totally new craft, which she embraced with an intelligent enthusiasm. For her the loom was a means of creating beauty, and it was such a wonderful occupation in contrast to the life she had experienced at the priory, which she remembered as a loveless, tedious repetition of prayers and services. She realized that it was listening to the singing that had been the one creative element that had enabled her to endure as long as she did. Pretending to be a nun was not for her.

She learned how to make the warp and how to weave back and forth to create the weft. Some days she worked for hours, completely lost in work that soothed and allowed her to be absorbed in a world of her own. Bethan encouraged her, and said that she would provide food and when they sold the weavings, she would pay her for her work. It was a quiet, uneventful existence, and for the first time that she could remember, Angwen was truly happy.

She quickly realized that Bethan was much in love with the drummer, who was also the blacksmith, and that they were only postponing their marriage until Gwenllian left home to get married and live elsewhere. "Garyth is a good man," Bethan said, "he holds the community together. If there's a dispute between neighbours, or if someone has lost an animal, then Garyth sorts it out." Whenever she mentioned him, which was quite often, she would lose track of what she was saying and become wrapped up in her dreams. Her daughter would tease her, and everyone would end up laughing.

One day, when Gwenllian had gone to visit her future husband and the house was quiet except for the hum of the spinning wheel and the click of the loom that Angwen was working on, Bethan began to ask questions. This was a method she had adopted as a way of communicating with her new friend. Sometimes Angwen would draw a shape in the dust, and Bevan would guess the subject she wished to discuss. They had already agreed the subject was children, and Bevan said that Gwenllian was her only child, although she admitted that many women in the area had lost their babies at birth, and in many families the children below five died from illnesses and accidents.

IN THE ASHES OF A DREAM

"Do you remember having children?" she asked. Angwen shook her head.

"When you see children in the hamlet, do you feel anything?" Angwen made a face and shrugged her shoulders. Bevan persisted: "What is the first real memory you have?"

Angwen sat still and forced her mind to recall any fragment. After a moment she drew a building with a cross. Bevan understood she meant the priory, and asked her why she left. She drew a man, then added a small cross and then drew a big cross. "A bishop?" Angwen nodded her head. "Did he throw you out?"

Angwen shook her head, pointed to herself and then added a stick coming out of the front of the stick man. Bevan gave an incredulous cry, "Oh, what did you do?" Angwen formed a fist and swung it at Beven, coming to rest gently on her face. "You hit the bishop?" and she began to laugh, especially when Angwen mimed the bishop dropping to the floor and herself kicking him between the legs, then changing her clothes and running off.

"What a story!" Beven chortled. "Tonight, when we gather, I'll tell your story and you can mime it. It will be the funniest thing ever! Nobody in this hamlet likes the priests. They only come here when they want to make us pay tithes which they say are going to benefit some poor people, but we know they spend it on themselves. Have you ever seen a thin monk?"

When Bevan went to negotiate with a local farmer for more wool, Angwen decided to go for a walk. It was something she did every day, and she was slowly beginning to familiarize herself with the area. When she saw anyone in the distance, she would hide herself until she had established if she knew them. If they were farmers or people who lived elsewhere, she would remain hidden, as it was too much trouble to try to get them to understand that she was unable to speak. Once, on a small road, she had met an elderly farmer driving a cart filled with stinking manure who had accused her of being 'a stuck-up old hen' because she had been unable to answer his greeting. At another time, two farm boys had followed her, making increasingly rude comments in the belief that she was modest or half-witted. When she became annoyed with their behaviour, she picked up a useful stick and set about them with such ferocity that they ran off crying and calling her a witch.

Most of the paths connected small communities to each other and had thick forests on both sides; there were some paths that wound around the edges of rough fields, while others snaked up the sides of high ground, giving way to bare hillsides and ragged sheep. She loved these walks and had no thoughts of being assaulted or threatened; her lack of past memory prevented her from dwelling on the awful possibilities, and left her with memories of when she had bested the Bishop and chased off annoying boys. In her mind she was unencumbered by fear.

She was walking along a path that she had not explored before. It was on the low ground and the forest was dense, having never been subjected to the axe. As she rounded a slight bend she saw two horsemen in the distance, and hid behind a bush sheltered by large oaks. She had rarely seen people ride horses, as these were for important people or soldiers and there were very few of either in this area. Whenever she saw a horse it was pulling a wagon or more likely a cart, and she was fascinated by the huge size of these horses.

As the riders came closer, she could see that they wore clothes quite different to the drab smocks and locally woven tunics of the hamlet. Bevan had told her that the quality of her dress, although now well worn, showed that she had once been a rich woman. Angwen had laughed at the thought for, like everything else in her past, it no longer mattered. She had sometimes wondered about her rings that remained with the priory, but they seemed unimportant in the peaceful, basic life she had embraced.

As the two men came closer, she could see that they wore long swords and carried knives in their belts, and both wore broad hats. She wondered if they were outlaws, but their clothes, although well worn, were clearly of good material, unlike the outlaws she had seen seeking food at the priory. The two men were riding their horses at walking pace and seemed to be in a light-hearted discussion. They were quite unalike to look at: one was tall and noticeably thin and sat high in his saddle, and under his hat a mop of wavy red hair with streaks of grey bounced on his skinny neck; the other was short, black haired and broad-chested, and might have been handsome if it were not for a badly broken nose. He was the one whose voice was rich and powerful, and as they passed her hiding place she heard him laugh as he spoke.

"I wonder if Jon's married that kitchen wench or whether, like me, he's got himself a reputation as the castle rake!" He roared with mirth.

"I never believed half of what you claimed, Gwriad," the tall man said, and casually looked around. "Before I met Teifryn, I used to think your behaviour was normal. Teifryn was as innocent as I was, and she always believed everything that Angharad said. Eventually, she came to believe that you two were inveterate liars. We both did."

"Well, brother, I'm never going to tell you!" the stocky man roared.

As they continued down the path, the tall one looked back, and she heard him say: "Did you see that woman hiding in the bushes back there?"

"No," the other said dismissively.

"There was something unusual about her. She looked as though she'd had her throat cut."

"Most peasant women look as though they've had their throats cut!" the other joked. "I'm not surprised she was hiding, it's probably the first time she's seen a red-haired skeleton on a horse!"

When they were out of sight, Angwen continued on her walk, and wondered who they were. She had quite liked the shorter man with the loud, merry voice.

ABOUT THE AUTHOR
BARRY MATHIAS B.ED M.A.

A writer of historical fiction and short stories. Barry emigrated from England with his wife and two daughters in 1990 and moved to Pender Island in 1995. He taught English at Camosun College in Victoria and later opened a bookstore on Pender Island. He created the unique Southern Gulf Islands Car Stops program, is a keen supporter of community and is involved in theatre and Island transportation initiatives. *In the Ashes of a Dream* is his fifth novel.

OTHER NOVELS

The Ancient Bloodlines Trilogy
Book 1: *Power in the Dark*
Book 2: *Shadow of the Swords*
Book 3: *Keeper of the Grail*

Celtic Dreams of Glory

Website: www.barrymathias.net